PRAISE FOR

"Lyric River is a novel with heart, real heart, and it may break yours. But it will also make you laugh and smile and fall in love with the characters and feel what it means to be alive and human and to live for a while in a real world. Lyric River is full of witty dialogue, touching love stories, and quirky twists like the odd attic boarder who thinks he's God. Lyric River is about things that count—family, friends, the search for love, for joy, and the river, always the river. The writing is finely crafted, drop dead gorgeous throughout. It's a sweet book set against a dark menace, in which life isn't always sweet or fair. But love, good cheer, friends, loyalty and the natural world help compensate for what humans do to one another. Lyric River is subtle, funny, sad, tender, loving, rich in thought and feeling—an altogether wonderful novel that deserves a wide readership."

—Paulette Alden, author of Feeding the Eagles and The Answer to Your Question

"I have spent my entire career reading and writing about the Mountain West, and few have been the times I have so thoroughly enjoyed a book about my home turf. Mac Griffith manages to capture the culture, the lifestyle, the vernacular, the various sometimes frantic and disjointed modi operandi of life at altitude in a way that is simultaneously enlightening, edifying and, most importantly, entertaining. His grasp of the eccentric characters that call the Rocky Mountains home is spot on. Lyric River is perceptive, incisive and flat-out a hoot."

—M. John Fayhee, editor of the Mountain Gazette and author of Up At Altitude: A Celebration of Life in the High Country, A Colorado Winter and A Colorado Mountain Companion.

ALSO BY MAC GRIFFITH

Strong Hills: Tales from the Mountains

LYRIC RIVER

a novel

Mac Griffith

Basalt Books

Copyright

For my parents and for Carly, bookends—
and for Atticus, trailing clouds

And thanks.

This project has taken many years from then to now, so I am certain to forget to thank someone, probably someone to whom I swore eternal gratitude. Thanks for detailed and thoughtful critiques of early versions to Melanie Kercher, Noah Landwehr, Sue Landwehr, Kari Bryan, Philip Mervis, Carolynn Sonda, and the late Paul Sonda. Thanks also to Nancy van Doorninck (and Bill). Joyce and David Roll provided valuable optometric services. Eula and Glenn Boelke tried to improve both the book and my character and succeeded by exactly half. Thanks for critiques and sheer fun to the members of the men's book club of Grand Junction, a gang of rascals, some of whom are also scamps. While it is undeniably, inarguably, indisputably true that John Fayhee tried to kill me on the hike up Peak Two, he also gave me writing jobs and confidence that I could write a little bit. Paulette Alden is the perfect teacher because she lets you think the good ideas are yours. Special thanks for administrative services to Shannon Friel and her faithful staff, Patricia Griffith and Francesco Dorigo.

This book is fiction. Any resemblance to real people is beside the point.

A Note on Geography

Summit County, Colorado is a real place, a high place that sits under the western eave of the Continental Divide. There are a number of small towns, some new, some old, and four ski areas in Summit County. For purposes of this book, I have rearranged its geography, so that those who live in the county, and the many more who have visited it, may be confused, or, more likely, think I am confused. Wanting some hilly streets and Victorian homes, I picked these up (with a large crane) from Breckenridge and set them down ten miles away in Frisco. Still not satisfied, I used some very, very large cranes and picked up the whole town of Frisco and set it down where I wanted it, five miles away, beside the Lower Blue River. In doing so, I inadvertently buried the town of Silverthorne, but never mind—I was satisfied.

A Note on Light

"She gave me the smile that I had never seen and will not see again in this world, and it covered me all over with light."
—Wendell Berry

All the songs are in the river.

PART ONE

Chapter One

God lived upstairs. Ben had tried to rent him the larger basement room, but he chose the cramped attic space with its narrow window that looked out over the length of the valley and the curling river. He was a quiet boarder, given to long and mysterious absences, and Ben and his daughter sometimes forgot he was there. God seemed preoccupied, and Ben and Sarah had their own troubles. When God was home, he rarely left the rocker that faced the narrow window. When he first knocked on Ben's door, looking for a room to rent, looking like no one in this world but Willie Nelson, God introduced himself simply as Hank Miller. This Hank had lived in Ben's attic for three months before casually confessing, over a late-night beer, that he was God. At the time, this divine revelation commanded Ben's full and alarmed attention, but he gradually got used to the idea. Ben was a doubter, but he had no doubt that Hank was no danger to Sarah, that he was a good person. If he wanted to be a good God, this was fine with Ben. The position, after all, seemed open.

Ben Wallace had found his way to this mountain town during a springtime when he could find his way nowhere else. The Blue River carved graceful arcs through this valley, and as the river and the mountains had no separate existence from each other, so, too, with Ben and Sarah. Ben loved his daughter with nothing held back. He was coming to love the Blue and its own cradling mountains in the same way. With this child, at least, with this land, at least, he had in his heart no caution.

The little town of Frisco, in the valley of the Blue, was beginning to take in Ben's small family. Born as a mining town in the Colorado mountains, Frisco hung on after the silver bust with ranching and primitive cabins for summer tourists, hung on until ski lifts came to the mountains. And out of the skiing came wealth, and from the wealth came real estate, golf, mountain biking, kayaking, sailboats on the high lake, fly fishing in the Blue, and tourists from every place, come to gasp in the thin air. And beneath all this wealth, beneath all these mixed blessings, there was yet a small town where locals took their kids to school, struggled to pay their bills, zigged when the tourists zagged, loved each other, and, failing love, hated.

On this March day, a 1996 Sunday, it was sunny and forty-five degrees, a feverishly hot combination after a long winter at nine thousand feet. Ben tuned his skis in the quiet basement of his rented home and happily recalled his luck on his first full day in town, two long Marches ago, a day, unlike this one, pelted by snow.

.....

On that day, Ben had sat with Sarah in The Roaster, on Frisco's small stretch of Main Street. Recently thirty-one, again separated from Karen, Ben drank coffee, read the local paper, and thought, as he turned the pages, that his marriage should be in here somewhere, in some section of the paper headed Passing Strange. Ben did not find this section of the paper, but he did find a small-town editorial, under a picture of a small-town editor, named George Monroe, that argued that every dog owner should scoop up his dog shit and be legally required to deposit said shit on the artsy front stoop of every real estate agency in town, because real estate agents were shit, and shit should be forever joined together. George Monroe, his newspaper picture full of wild hair and beard, looked ready to burst off the page and personally start flinging dog shit at real estate agents.

Ben said to Sarah, "It's a good thing we don't have a dog."

Sarah, then seven, was curled under his arm, reading a book that was too hard for her. She looked up, distracted.

"Why?" she asked.

"Because it says here that in this town you have to pick up your dog shit from the sidewalk and throw it at real estate agents."

2

"Don't say shit, Dad." Sarah returned to her book, frowning in concentration, moving her lips slightly as she read.

Ben had glanced up as a tall woman streaked past the front window of the Roaster. She seemed to be trying to outrun the driving, tumbling snow but stopped abruptly at the door and came inside. She quickly closed the door and, with one hand against the door frame for balance, leaned over and removed odd devices from her running shoes—there was a heavy rubber strap stretched around each shoe and, underneath, crisscrossing wire coils. She wore black fleece pants and a black fleece pullover with a hood. When she stood up, she stood very straight; when she pulled the hood back, her long black hair, flecked with gray, spilled out. She brushed a thick layer of snow from her shoulders. Ben saw, in profile, a strong, hooked nose. She left her odd shoe attachments beside the door and came directly to Ben's table beside the window. She frowned at Ben, but the frown smoothed when she took in Sarah. Without asking, without hesitating, she joined them at their table, even though The Roaster at midmorning was deserted.

"What are those?" Ben asked, motioning to the devices left beside the door.

This woman looked completely at Ben and held him in a gaze that was absolutely impassive. "Yaktrax," she said. "For running in the snow."

"I'm Ben."

The woman did not reply.

Sarah let her book fall to her lap and looked up from under Ben's arm. "I'm Sarah."

"And I am Iris. Read me something from your book."

Sarah was a first grader who understood the difference between a command and a request. She read a paragraph about a grumpy bear, and Iris listened gravely, with elbows on the table and chin in both hands. "A little more," Iris said, and this time the command was a request. Sarah stumbled over a word, but Ben, looking over her shoulder, did not help, and Sarah figured out that the bear was grumpy because its back itched.

"You read well," Iris said. "You're lucky."

Ben watched Sarah, and she seemed fascinated but not intimidated by this strange Iris.

"My daughter can't read," Iris said.

"How old is she?" Sarah asked.

"Twenty-five," Iris said. "She's retarded."

Sarah winced. "Don't say retarded."

For the first time, Iris smiled. She reached over and touched Sarah's blond hair with the barest tip of her finger. "OK," Iris said. "Do you read to your father?"

Sarah returned smile for smile, and Ben knew she was pleased with herself for having won over this woman. Sarah confidently said, "Only stuff that's not too hard for him."

A man in a flannel shirt came over from behind the counter with a toasted bagel, smothered in cream cheese, and a tall glass of orange juice, foaming at the top. He set these on the table in front of Iris and shrugged apologetically. Iris patted his elbow and nodded.

"Good run?" the man asked.

"Good run, Abner."

Abner left, and Ben said, "Ah. That's it. We took your table."

"It's Abner's table, not mine."

"Abner did his best for you. The table was covered with books and a tub of dirty dishes when we came in. We moved them out of the way because it was the best table in the house. I didn't understand that Abner was using all the junk to save your spot. The dumb tourists come to town and mess up your scam."

Iris laced her fingers together under her chin and Ben noticed the strong veins across the back of her hands. Iris could have been forty-five or sixty; strength obscured her age.

Iris looked at Ben, "Maybe you're not as dumb as you look."

Ben grinned, "And maybe you're not as mean as you look."

They talked over coffee, the three of them sitting at the best table in the house, with the spring snow falling outside the big window. In the tradition of mountain towns, they talked first of their favorite games and last of their work. Ben reported on himself that he liked to ski and fly fish and hike in the mountains. During her turn, Sarah chose chocolate ice cream as her favorite recreation. She liked to read. She also liked those same things that her father liked, and she reminded Ben that he had left reading off the list of things he liked. Iris liked to run and garden. She liked to ski but did not ski so much in recent years and she was not sure why. Abner passed by and, on some signal that Ben could not see, he leaned his head close to Iris for a whispered instruction. He came back with one small bowl of chocolate ice cream.

Iris had lived in this valley all her life and her parents and grandparents before her. Her husband was dead, and Ben could tell that she paid a toll for saying these words out loud. Iris did not mention holding any job. She did say that her daughter, the one who could not read, lived in a group home in Denver. Ben and Sarah had been living with Karen, wife and mother, also in Denver, after having lived in Houston. They had lived one wonderful year in Crested Butte, but the airport there was no good for Karen's work at a Houston commercial real estate firm. No, Karen was not with them on this trip. Ben and Sarah wanted to live again in the mountains. Ben glossed over Karen's role in this plan, and Iris, sitting with her strong fingers laced together, listening closely, asked no questions about this.

Ben and Sarah planned to come back to Frisco in June, after school was out, to find a place to rent. Ben would give up his job teaching high school history in Denver. Maybe he could find this same work that he loved in the mountains. If not, he could shovel construction dirt in summer and shovel snow in winter. He knew how to wait tables and tune skis, but, because of Sarah, he could not do this if he had to work at night.

For an instant, Ben wanted to tell Iris about his life with Karen, but he could not because Sarah was there and because he knew he could not make Iris understand. Women often judged Karen harshly, and Ben did not like traveling this tricky path. Karen knew, or once had known, how to make Ben as joyful as he had yet been. Ben had a gift for small happiness, for good cheer, but he had no gift for joy. Karen had a gift for experiencing every emotion, good and bad, at delirium's threshold. Ben could make enough money to squeak by, while Karen could make money in large buckets. Ben could take care of Sarah; Karen was a reckless, sometimes destructive parent. Ben, wary of joy, rejecting a life of quiet desperation, led a life of not-so-quiet good cheer. And he grinned to himself at the thought of trying to explain this to the stranger across the table. Iris must have seen this shadow of a grin because she asked him what was funny; Ben shrugged and smiled and told her it was only a joke on him, and Iris nodded gravely and accepted this evasion.

Iris warned that rent was expensive in the mountains. Ben nodded and forced himself not to look worried.

"Maybe you will move up, then, in June," Iris said.

Ben and Sarah looked at each other. "We will be here," Ben said.

"And will your wife be with you?"

"I don't know," Ben said. "We'll see." Ben felt Sarah's hand find his.

Iris borrowed a piece of paper and a pencil from Abner. She wrote on it Iris Gibbs and an address on High Street and handed it to Ben. "Come to see me when you get to town. I will rent you the house next door to mine. It's an old Victorian, in decent shape. It's small, but it has a good front porch and big trees for Sarah to climb."

Ben looked at the piece of paper. "Should I get your phone number? Or give you mine?"

"Why?"

"I don't know. In case you rent it out before, or your current renter decides to stay."

"There is no current renter, and I won't be renting it to someone else. If you don't show up, I will know that you decided not to move. You don't need to call."

"We will be here," Sarah said, and Ben could hear in her quiet, stubborn voice perfect echo of his own.

"Good," said Iris. To Ben, she said, "Move in. Get a job. Then I will decide about the rent."

"Done," Ben said, "on one condition."

"I don't like being bargained with," warned Iris.

"Well, you will have to learn to like it," Ben said. "The condition is that I buy your breakfast."

Iris smiled. "That's easy." She stood and Ben stood. She had the strong grip that Ben expected. Sarah stood and held out her arms. For the first time, Iris seemed unsure of herself, but she leaned down and accepted a hug. Iris walked straight to the door. She snagged her Yaktrax in one smooth motion and was gone into the snow. Ben stopped at the counter to pay the bill, but Abner was uncooperative. "Iris has already paid."

"But I saw her walk straight out the door."

"Iris never carries money."

"She runs a tab?" asked Ben. Abner nodded. "Well, I want to pay for her breakfast, so don't put that on her tab." Abner shook his head. "Iris wouldn't have it," he said. Ben was confused. "OK, then I need to pay the bill for Sarah and me." Abner shook his head. Ben was beginning to catch on. "Iris wouldn't have it?" Ben asked. Abner nodded. Ben took out a ten and stuffed it in the tip jar. "Does Iris control the tip jar, too?" he asked. Abner weighed solemnly this question and said, "No, that's allowed."

......

It was thus that Ben and Sarah met Iris and moved to the valley of the Blue. Two years after this meeting, tuning his skis in the basement of the home he rented from Iris, Ben began to realize that he had not heard Sarah rattling around in the house above him in some time. It is the curse of parents to be soothed by noise and alarmed by silence. He searched and found that Sarah was not in the house, not necessarily a cause for alarm. Sarah might be at Iris's or simply roaming the neighborhood. There had been no sign of God for the past few days, but Ben climbed the creaky stairs to the attic to be sure that Sarah had not taken over her friend's duties, which consisted mostly of sitting in the rocker and gazing patiently out the narrow window. Ben found himself tempted by the rocker, with the old, gray afghan draped over the back. God knew more yarns than Lincoln, had a weakness for Fat Tire, and highly irregular work habits; those unfamiliar with his station in the universe would think he had the same problems as everyone else. Although God sang badly, even under the influence of Fat Tire, he looked more like Willie Nelson, braids and all, than the original. As Ben descended the stairs in search of his daughter, he wondered again how such resemblance was possible. Ben wished he had a better clue as to how long Sarah had been gone. He walked outside and stood on the front porch, looking up and down High Street.

The spring snow in the small yard was rotten from the warming weather and patchy over the brown grass. The wind blew down from the mountains and melted the snow when the sun was bright and crusted it again when clouds crept through the valley. Cold nights froze the mud in place and in the daytime the rivulets of melting snow brought it back to oozing life.

Ben went back inside and phoned Iris, who told him that Sarah was not with her. Ben asked if Ollie, Iris's Labrador, was at home. Sarah and Ollie often went for walks together. Iris said that Ollie was snoring at her feet. Iris asked if Ben wanted her to start searching the neighborhood.

"Too early for alarm," Ben said. "She's a nine-year-old. Her job is to explore the world. I'll poke around."

"Call me if you need help," said Iris.

Ben put on his hiking boots and a light jacket and went off in search of his daughter. He crossed to the other side of the street to get a better look down the steep, curving hill. He was about to start down the hill when he recalled Sarah's love of climbing trees. He looked up into the trees around his house. There was nothing in the trees, but he saw a shoe, extending just past the attic gable, on the steeply pitched roof. Ben walked to the other side of the house and studied the climbing routes. A wooden apple crate, probably filched from Iris's house, sat under the kitchen window, a small footprint in the muddy ooze beside it. Apple crate to window sill to the shed over the woodpile to the roof, and there you were. Ben followed this route and was disturbed by the precarious lean required to get from window sill to shed. He was even more disturbed that the pitch of the roof demanded hands and knees and was best done while not looking down. Ben crossed the roofline and switched to his butt for a careful descent to where Sarah sat between chimney and gable. She slid over so he could wedge himself beside her in this narrow space. Ben pretended not to notice that Sarah had been crying.

"How'd you find me?" asked Sarah.

"The red tennis shoe. It was sticking out below the gable."

"What's a gable?"

"What you were hiding behind."

"I wasn't hiding. I was thinking."

"I know," Ben said. "It helps to have a place to think."

They sat together in silence and looked out from this high perch at the valley's ruffled hills.

"I haven't been crying," Sarah said, as she wiped her cheek.

"I know."

"Mom called."

"Ah. I was in the basement. I didn't hear the phone ring."

"She hates me," Sarah said.

"What was she mad about?"

"I don't even know. I said something about Iris fixing my hair, and she started yelling about how you should be the one to fix my hair."

"You know," Ben said, "I think that sometimes she doesn't even know she's yelling. If it helps, your mom's OK with me taking care of you, but the idea of another woman helping out bothers her."

Sarah slammed her fist against her knee. "Why don't we just divorce her, Dad?"

"<u>We</u> don't divorce anybody. I know I'm not really qualified, but I'll be the grownup here."

"I know. I know. She just makes me so mad. Besides, we're not really a family."

"I don't know, little one. We're a kind of a family. Granted, your father's a little weird...but, other than that, I think we're pretty much shipshape." Ben could hear himself reverting to his ongoing patter of reflexive jokes, and sometimes he kicked himself for it. But Sarah was used to it, and Ben knew that most of the time it soothed her, just as it soothed him in the face of questions that seemed to have no answer. Ben thought of how the great Lincoln, seeking sanctuary, camouflaged himself in improbable yarns.

Sarah lay back against the roof and stared at the sky. Ben could tell she was beginning to relax. Ben lay back also against the roof. Both of them had to keep their knees bent and their feet pressed firmly against the shingles to keep from sliding down and over the edge. Ben thought that maybe he needed to buy one of those books on how to be a parent. All he knew was that Sarah was good company. If he listened closely enough to Sarah, and there was no one he would rather listen to, she eventually told him how to be the father she needed.

Sarah said, "Forget I said that stuff, Dad. I really do love my mom."

"I know. I love her, too. We have had lots of wonderful times. Sometimes it seems like we still can. I don't know." It came to Ben that he lived on memories, many of them memories of good times with Karen. If he divorced her, or she divorced him, then, by some crazy definition, the good memories would become bad ones and be lost to him. He would not have bet a nickel that this was a rational thought, but it felt like divorce promised a life of bad memories.

"What about Megan?" Sarah asked.

"I was such a fool," Ben said.

"For what?"

"For teaching you to talk. What was I thinking?"

"You like Megan," said Sarah.

"I do." Ben worked not to show it, but he was happy to be reminded of Megan, happy to think about her. He confessed, but only to himself, that lately he did not require reminders of Megan. Ben laughed to himself that he had come to the mountains and met, of all people, a librarian. He laughed at himself for thinking, like a schoolboy, that she was perfect, and then he went on thinking that she was perfect. He told himself that this probably meant something and then told himself that he was probably not deep enough to figure out what. He told himself that he was attracted to the facts of Megan: smart, witty, kind (most of all, kind), independent, athletic, a lover of the mountains. In rare moments of personal honesty, he also acknowledged that he was perhaps influenced by the fact that she was the most beautiful librarian on the planet. In moments of doubt, which were not so rare, he was troubled by the apparent fact that Megan only sprang into being from the time she went away to college. Megan had stories of every part of her life from college forward, but no stories that she would tell of what came before in her life. Having been raised in this valley, she was a person without family. Ben pictured her springing, at age eighteen, fully formed, from some secret place in the mountain. Megan admitted to the presence of a brother, who lived nearby, but still stubbornly denied the existence of any family—yet another thing that Ben found passing strange in his life. Iris, who knew everything, everyone in this valley, would offer nothing except that Megan was wonderful and her brother was the sorriest, meanest piece of shit in the county. Ben was a student of history, a sometimes teacher of history, and he was uneasy without a historical guide to this wonderful Megan.

"Well?" prompted Sarah.

"Well, what?"

"Well...Megan."

"Well, here's the well. The well is that your father has decided that there will be new rules for your life. You are never to think again. You are never to talk again. Change that. You're allowed to say only two words for the rest of your entire life. And those two words are, 'Yes, Father.'"

"Yes, Father," said Sarah. "So what about Megan?" Ben wished he knew. It seemed such a simple thing to leave an old love for a new—people did it all the time.

Ben said, "I'm going to throw you off the roof. And that's another thing. No more climbing on the roof. It scares me. Please, no more roof. Deal?"

Sarah grudgingly said, "Yes, Father."

The two of them lay looking at the endless blue of the sky and the snow-covered hump of Buffalo Mountain, filling one corner of their world. Ben thought of the hidden folds in the vastness of the mountain and thought irresistibly of hiking these secret places with Megan. There was a massive avalanche scar on Buffalo's southern flank, and Ben idly wondered what it must have been like at that moment, years ago, when the snow cracked, like a shot, and carried in its fearsome path a great tangle of boulders, of uprooted trees, and unsuspecting living creatures.

Chapter Two

Monday, late in the day, Sarah was watching TV, and Ben walked across the front yard to ask Iris to babysit. Iris, neighbor, landlord, friend, was in her yard, picking up the dead sticks of winter, hurrying along the season of gardening. Hawk nose, hawk eyes, she measured Ben without blinking. Iris, born to command, grown to ferocity, looked at her fellow creatures and saw scurrying mice. Ben remarked on the weather and tried to divert her with talk of gardening. Iris peered past Ben's small-talk zigzags to the precise coordinates he would occupy when she swooped. Iris had lately made clear that the question of Ben and Sarah, of the life they were to have, was much on her mind. She also made clear that Ben was too damned directionless for her tastes. Iris patrolled the skies above him and sometimes swooped low and flared her warning wings.

Iris said that of course she would babysit. She had an elk stew on, so Ben should not bother to feed Sarah. Iris never hunted, but she had elk because people brought her things, in consideration of a long history of favors rendered, old acquaintance, or tribute to local royalty. Ben did not tell her where he was going, but he knew that she would guess that Megan was his destination. Iris stayed out of this as much as it was possible for her, but she made clear that she favored this idea of Megan. Ben had entertained himself with the idea that, as long as Iris thought he was going to see Megan, she would take care of Sarah every night, and he could spend all his evenings getting drunk in bars until he passed out on the pool table. This seemed a pretty romantic notion, wild and unfettered, until he reminded himself that he did not care much for spending time in bars. It occurred to him that in this business of passing out he would probably drool on the pool table and snore with his mouth open.

There was also the danger that Iris, once she caught on to having been tricked, would break both his legs, just above the kneecap. Ben thought that he could still be a substitute teacher with both legs in a cast, but he could not figure out how he could pursue any of his other fill-in jobs, as bus driver, snow removal specialist, or ski tuner. Also, if he spent every night in bars, he would miss Sarah. And Megan. And even Iris, kneecap specialist.

"How is Sarah?" Iris asked.

"She's good. She had a happy day at school. We've already done her homework. Ask her about her math facts so she can show off." Ben knew that Iris, in comparison to her life with Laurie, her own daughter, was discovering a new and miraculous world in a child who could actually read and do math.

"What about climbing on the roof?" Iris asked. "I hope you punished her for that."

"Severely," Ben said. "I should've told you that she won't be able to sit down for a week."

"If you laid a hand on that child, I'll..."

"Break both of my legs?"

"OK. OK. But that roof is steep. She needs to learn..."

Ben grinned. "I talked with her about it, Iris. Any further punishment, up to and including kneecapping, I leave to you. I'll be back in time to tuck her in."

When he was almost to the truck, Iris pounced, talons in the small of Ben's back. "How are you ever going to raise that child?" Ben, not knowing the answer, ignored her and drove away.

The truck's engine growled as Ben geared down to save his marginal brakes on the steep pitch of High Street. As he shoved the truck into first, his aggravated answer to Iris's question came to him: he would raise Sarah the way he had always raised her. Sometimes Ben and Karen had lived together, sometimes apart, but it was Ben who answered the cry in the night, who knew where the snow boots were, and who knew that Sarah liked to have the peanut butter mixed with the jelly beforehand rather than spread separately on the bread. He thought about turning the truck around to tell Iris this but realized that it would be poor comedic timing, and it wasn't precisely comedy. It just felt like comedy watching the twitchy reactions of women to a single father of a daughter. And, technically, he wasn't even a single father.

Karen, nominal wife, skipped in and out of their lives. She was now more out than in, a consolation and a loss. She had moved back to Houston from Denver two years ago when Ben and Sarah moved to Frisco. Karen rarely came to Frisco, and Ben did not like Houston. Mostly Ben just sent Sarah to Karen during school vacations when this fit the demands of Karen's work. Karen, at least, was not twitchy about Ben rearing Sarah. Karen did not mind as long as both were available to her when the fleeting urge for family struck. Trotting out family for occasions of state was the style of royalty, was the style of many successful men, and it suited Karen—in the same way, life with Sarah, in a ramshackle Victorian in the mountains, with God renting the attic room, suited Ben. Ben suspected, however, that Karen might develop a case of the royal twitches over Sarah if Ben became a raving Jeffersonian and pursued life, liberty and happiness with a beautiful librarian. She might try to take Sarah away—she might succeed.

It was mostly other women, Iris included, who twitched in unpredictable ways when they gave thought to the family of Ben and Sarah. Iris frequently reminded Ben that he and Sarah could not manage without her, and Ben as frequently reminded Iris that she thought this about everybody. Women looked at Sarah and thought, poor baby! Or, from others, how wonderful! Ben cheerfully accepted all manner of help from women who did not extend this same help to single mothers. Women of casual acquaintance looked at Sarah and Ben together and found Ben either keenly attractive, which Ben did not mind, or an enemy of the natural order, which Ben did not mind. He found this part of his life to be much fuss about not much.

As he drove to see Megan, Ben wished that his newfound roles as technical husband and actual adulterer were so simple. Iris would know precisely what he should do: leave Karen for Megan. Iris was always certain, took no counsel from fear, and acted as if apparitions had no substance.

. . ...

The small public library sat under a cluster of cottonwoods beside the Blue River. Fed by the river, the trees were huge. The great, spreading limbs divided and reduced themselves until they were slender twigs, reaching out to a memory of leaves. Megan had turned off the outside lights when she closed her library, and Ben stood, hands in the pockets of his wool pea coat, watching the pattern the dark branches traced against steel, twilight sky. Megan unlocked the door and pulled him inside and her arms went inside the warmth of his jacket and held his back. Her face buried in his neck, she would not look up at him and would not let him go. Ben savored the honeyed hair that pressed flat against his face and swirled over her neck and shoulders. Her back was strong, fragile. She kissed him, finally, opening wide her blue eyes, and he could feel a quick shiver slip across his back.

They sat, then, on the love seat in the library's alcove that looked out over the hurrying river, no longer blue but gone to steel to match the sky. Ben thought that the river must run out of an ocean to move so fast and never run dry. The sky was one ocean and the river liquid thread to another.

Ben and Megan talked about their day. In his unpredictable life as a substitute teacher, Ben had faked teaching social studies. He had lectured about the Dred Scott decision, and an airhead student wanted to know what business it was of the Supreme Court whether a person wore dreadlocks. The class laughed at her, and Ben managed to transform airhead to heroine by pointing out that she had delivered up a perfect memory device for a judicial ruling that black people, with or without dreadlocks, had once been considered property. Another student remarked that slavery was against God, and Ben reminded her that ministers in the South used Saint Paul to defend slavery as God's plan for blacks. In the tangle of argument that followed, a boy remarked angrily that God had no plan. Ben started to say that he could ask God, his upstairs boarder, about the existence of a plan but thought better of it.

16

Megan had spent much of her morning helping an elderly ranch couple research their ancestors online. The couple, vaguely Norwegian, found that the husband had a Sicilian ancestor and went away pleased, thinking of it as a sturdy, sinister knot in an otherwise bland family tree.

Ben leaned and gently touched the tip of Megan's nose with his finger. "If I am very good, for a very long time—say, twenty minutes—will you tell me about your family tree?"

Megan's open face closed. "What has Iris told you?"

"Nothing that I had not already figured out for myself," Ben said.

"And that is?"

"That is that you are wonderful."

Megan's face softened. "Sometimes I used to wish that Iris could be my mother." She laughed softly. "Which is kinda crazy. What would it be like to be a teenager and come home late and have Iris meet you at the door? She would..."

"Break both of your legs?"

"I don't know about that," Megan said dubiously. "Iris is more of a beer bottle to the head type."

"Really? Iris?"

Megan stared at Ben. "OK," Ben said. "I don't mean to sound dumb. I guess I think of her as having a ferocious will. Like Godmother Corleone. But I just tease her until she gets over it. I never thought of her as actually committing violence."

"Ben, Ben...there's so much you don't know. Besides, she apparently adopted you and Sarah on sight. Who would've thought it? Sometimes I'm jealous."

"It's true that there is much I don't know. About Iris. About me. About you."

"Ben, can't you just leave it alone?"

Ben leaned back and looked at the dim recesses above the wooden beams of the high-ceilinged room. He knew that one of the simple reasons he wanted to know was because he was trying to decide between Karen and Megan, between one life and another, with Sarah at pivot's point. He thought he knew, also, that one of the reasons Megan did not want to tell him was that she wanted him to decide based on who she was now. That was fair enough except that it collided with his fixed belief that now was not separable from then. Megan, with her sweet, hard reason, also made clear the stark calculus of decision. He needed in some near future to make a decision about Karen for Ben and Megan to continue, but no decision that he made came with any guarantee signed by Megan Flanagan that Ben and Megan would continue. Again, fair that.

"I will find a way," Ben said.

"A way to what?"

"To leave it alone." He doggedly wished that life could be as simple as he wanted it to be.

Megan took her turn to study the unlit space above them. "And I'll find a way to tell you my life when you have to be told, when we know each better."

"We know each other pretty well," Ben said stubbornly. Ben knew this to be only a piece of the truth, and at that a wishful truth. They had met here, in this lovely library, at the beginning of last summer, when Sarah was spending time with Karen. Ben had not been able to afford to buy books. In the swoop of one lucky day, he found the library, Megan, and God. Ben was delighted to find that the books lived beside the Blue River, and, among the books, beside the song of the river, was Megan, lovely, twenty-eight, and unaccountably single. Not only was Ben too broke to buy books, his prospects for buying groceries were getting a little sketchy. But meeting Megan made him feel charmed, so it seemed only right when God chose the same day to knock on his door, inquiring after rooms to rent in the neighborhood. God paid in cash, and Ben took Megan to dinner. It had been for them a wonderful summer, a glorious fall, and then, when love became too scary, a quick falling away. This falling away happened without recrimination, with the simple recognition that every path before them seemed blocked by some problem of family. Ben found himself surprised and grateful that Megan placed no blame. After all, his family problems bobbed brightly on the surface, an easy target, while hers swam submerged, glimpsed only in shadow. They hibernated in separate lives through the winter, awakening sometimes for a tenuous cup of coffee at the Roaster, and then returning to grogginess. With the first sign of longer days, Ben found his way back to the library; he followed his feet and whatever connection they had to his heart. When his feet took him again to the library, Ben had lied to Megan and told her he was only there for a book. She had smiled at him, a smile with life in it, an awakening perhaps of her own, and told him that he was both a lying dog and a lovesick fool.

Ben smiled at this memory and said, "OK, maybe we don't know each other so well. Maybe it's only you who knows me well. But you can't deny that we're falling in love."

"We are falling in love. And it's wonderful. But I've felt like I was falling in love before. I want to fall forever. And keep on falling a little farther every day. Maybe I can't do that. Maybe you can't do that. You're right that there are things about my past that I don't tell anyone. Have never told anyone. Maybe I never will. So be it. There are things about your past that I don't understand, either. I don't understand why you can't let go of Karen. It always seemed kinda crazy to me, but then one day I noticed that you never complained about it, and I realized you were saying, like me, 'So be it.' We are both, I think, 'So be its.'"

"From the famous lost tribe, the Sobeits," Ben said.

"Talking to you, Ben, can be a bizarre experience. You know that, don't you? But you're right—that's the tribe. And as one member of the tribe to another, I'll break my rule and tell you one serious thing about the brother I don't have. Watch out for him. Tyler's mind is all twisted up. He knows we've been seeing each other, and he's got it in his head that he doesn't approve. If he bothers you, let me know. I'll deal with him."

Ben teased, "Now, you sound like Iris, another version of the Godmother." He teased but also wondered how Megan could promise so serenely to deal with this twisted Tyler. He had remarked this quality of Megan before, without being able to give it a name. Maybe it was simple composure. Maybe librarians took a composure course to set quiet example for rambunctious readers. Whatever it was, it seemed inseparable from Megan's silky skin. Once, in a moment preoccupied by the mysteries of her past, Ben had imagined her finding, in some childhood forest, a knight's suit of armored mail, this one woven of magical silk, delightful to the touch, and capable of intertwining with her very skin. What young girl, alone in a forest, could resist trading nakedness for such silken armor?

"Ben, the last thing I want is to be your Godmother, but there are worse things than having the women in your life take care of you. Don't start getting some dumb pride thing going."

Ben touched Megan on the cheek. "Yes, ma'am. I am warned about the brother you don't have. And if I knew what he looked like, I would avoid him. Now, can we go back to the falling in love part?" He tried to remember the point when he had stopped falling in love with Karen and begun to simply hang on.

"OK. I like that part." Megan held Ben's hand against her cheek and studied his face with mock concern. "There must have been something I once saw in you. Maybe it will come to me later."

"I'm thinking it was my irresistible good looks," Ben said. And behind the patter, beneath the jokes, Ben thought: what of Sarah? of Karen? of Megan? He considered adding Ollie to his list of responsibilities but decided that Iris could continue to be responsible for her dog. It did occur to him that Ollie would be a lot simpler.

Megan said, "Your looks are completely average. This is a ski town, full of gorgeous men."

Ben put a finger to his face. "What about here, this place on my chin? When I was shaving this morning, I noticed this part was getting better looking. This little spot could be the beginning of a miracle; handsome could spread from this spot to my whole face. I think there's hope for me."

"Completely average. Trust me on this. Women know these things. Your nose actually starts out to be distinguished, but then it goes on a little long, if you get my drift. You have nice hands."

Ben sighed. "I'm not getting much credit here."

"Close your eyes." Ben did so.

"That's it," said Megan. "With your eyes closed, I find you totally resistible."

Ben reached and took her hand. She began to rise up to his arms, and he gently pushed her back. "I just want to study your hand." He kneaded the back of her hand with his thumb, traced with a finger the blue veins, and studied her palm. Ben reveled in the simple fact of holding Megan's hand.

"Can you read my palm?" Megan asked.

Ben squinted. "Sure. It says you can't keep a good Sobeit down. And there's this lifeline something or other that says we will love each other."

"We will love each other, but from what distance?"

"That part isn't clear, but there's a bunch of squiggly lines that says Ben will try very hard to get his shit together. And wait, there's a line down here, a bold line, that says Ben is a lot better looking than Megan is giving him credit for and she should be very, very ashamed."

Megan looked closely at Ben's face. She touched the spot on his chin that he thought might have become miraculously more attractive. "I think you might be right," she said.

"About getting better looking?"

Megan sighed, as for a slow pupil. "No, for me, you might be right for me. I don't know. I wish I had some real, live standard to judge you against. I wish I could know. You feel right. You feel like someone I almost knew. For now, that will have to do."

"I'm confused," Ben said.

She reached and brushed with her lips the spot on his chin. "Of course you're confused, my Benjamin Wallace. Have I told you that I like that your name has three syllables? Maybe that is what feels right to me. Maybe, when I was a child, I had already fallen in love with a man with three syllables in his name. Maybe."

"Wallace only has two syllables."

"Shut up, Ben."

Megan got up and turned off the lights. They found a way to make love on the small couch in the reading alcove overlooking the Blue River. The river murmured and gurgled, swelling over submerged boulders, slowing in the deep pools, impatiently moving from one ocean to another.

Chapter Three

On the evening of the same day, late, Ben leaned back in a kitchen chair, feet propped on the worn pine table, and meditated on the nature of God. God, the wanderer, was home; Ben had heard the slight creak of the rocker from the attic room. Ben grappled with the theological question of how long it would be before God came down for a beer. Having spent the evening with Megan, having tucked Sarah in for the night, Ben sat, nursing a cup of coffee and reading the *Mountain Gazette*.

So far as Ben knew, everyone did not let a room to God. He supposed it was theoretically possible that everyone did, given the notion of omnipresence. Ben's God, however, was only sporadically resident at Ben's home, so this cast doubt on the idea of being everywhere at once. Ben was mostly satisfied with God's itinerant ways. It was a break to have a quiet boarder, except for the creaking rocker, and a break to have a boarder who was mostly not home. Ben did wish sometimes that God was more reliable with the rent, but Ben's modest dreams did not envision a flawless God. As much as Ben enjoyed their odd conversations, he had no wish to be always in the presence of God.

Ben found God to be in equal measure kind and irascible. The fact that Ben found Hank to be so sane was one bit of evidence that argued that he actually might be who he said he was. Ben did not know of anyone else who claimed to be God who was not nutty. Ben's first reaction, when Hank came out as God, was alarm, but Hank demanded no special privileges on account of being God beyond the one he already exercised, which was a mooching access to Ben's supply of Fat Tire. Ben was also relieved to find God yawningly indifferent to whether anyone believed in him or not. Ben had once cautiously asked him whether he was looking for converts.

"Converts? What possible difference could it make to me whether someone believes in me or not? I know who I am, more or less. Do I doubt my own existence because others don't believe in me? How dumb is that? I'm God, God damn it." God, it turned out, was seeking neither converts nor publicity. He did not issue a commandment, but he made clear that he preferred that Ben not reveal to anyone else that he was God. Ben was satisfied with this arrangement, since it was ultimately with Iris's consent that he was allowed to make a little extra money by having a boarder. Iris did not take much interest in Hank, but Ben was cheerfully surprised to learn that she liked and approved of him. She explained that he reminded her of the mountain men, mostly rolling stones, she had known as a child. Out of concern for Sarah, Iris had Hank checked out by her friends, Hector Morales, the sheriff, and George Monroe, the newspaper editor. No one turned up anything bad on Hank, or turned up much of anything at all, except for confused tourists who kept thinking they had sighted Willie Nelson taking refreshment in the Moose Jaw. Iris found occasion to have a beer with Hank and reported back to Ben that he probably drank too much (for Iris, this was simultaneously vice and virtue), but that she could find in him no fault.

God wandered, both with his feet and in conversation. When asked where his feet had taken him, his conversation drifted, and he never quite said where he had been. When he was home, he fell into a grandparent role with Sarah and told her wandering, fanciful stories; the topics of these stories could be the life history of the particular junco then at the birdfeeder or the letters that the Phoenicians considered and rejected for inclusion in the alphabet. Sarah reported to Ben that Hank told the same kind of stories that Ben told her, only stranger. Ben looked forward to his own talks with God, which usually occurred over a beer late in the evening after Sarah was in bed. As with Sarah, Ben liked God's stories, liked his fund of knowledge that was borderline omniscient, and liked their mutual ragging.

At some bend in one of these rambling conversations, Ben had come to the view that if Hank wanted to be God it was OK with Ben. If Hank was playing a role, it suited him, perhaps suited them both. If Hank was playing a role, it was one in which he never stepped out of character. One evening, over a beer, Ben grinned and asked, "Why me, Lord? Why knock on my door?"

"Why not you?" replied God.

"Because I'm not a believer."

"You don't believe in God? To whom, then, are you talking?"

Ben made out to scratch his head. "You're about half smart, so I know you're not the village idiot. Besides, this particular village already has me. But that doesn't mean there couldn't be a pond somewhere missing an odd duck."

"Ah, Ben. You've answered your own question. That's why I picked you. Even looking into the very face of God, you're still a smartass."

"I don't know that I'm looking into the face of God. It looks a lot like the face of Willie Nelson."

"Shouldn't that impress you? That I can assume any appearance I want?"

"Well, if you can choose to look like anyone, how about assuming the appearance of Elle MacPherson?"

"I grant you that's one way of getting worshipped. But insufficiently godlike."

"So you reveal yourself to me because I'm a skeptic?"

"Apart from the simple pleasure of your company, that's one reason. To tell you the truth, I've never had much use for believers."

Still cautious, Ben had inquired whether his tenant might require being worshipped.

"No worries there," God said. "It's the damnedest thing that people have this need to worship me." God took a long drink from his beer and touched the cool, brown glass to his forehead. "They have these houses of worship where they preach that I should always be in the thoughts of the faithful. All these people thinking about me—gives me the creeps. Sometimes I think that maybe I should return the favor, but I can't figure out how any of this amounts to a favor, on either side. Should I build a church and worship humanity? Being worshipped is a curse I would wish on no one. Do they think I'm an insecure rock star? If I wanted to be worshipped, I would take your advice and assume the appearance of Elle MacPherson."

Now, alone at the kitchen table, with the creak of God's rocker above him, Ben put down the *Mountain Gazette*. The woodstove beside the wall popped and the glowing logs shuffled downward as they consumed themselves. A curling sliver of wood smoke found the loose seal in the stove door and slipped into the kitchen, carrying with it memory of Megan. Earlier, a strand of Megan's hair had lain across Ben's hand as he held her face, feeling soft cheek through his fingertips and the feather of hair across the back of his hand. Ben and Megan had curled tightly on the too-short love seat of the darkened library, as their breathing slowed to a whisper and the faint hymn of the river again slipped through the high, arched panes of this cathedral room.

God tapped Ben lightly on the shoulder as he made his way to the refrigerator. He retrieved a Fat Tire and sat down across from Ben at the table.

"How do you do that?" Ben asked.

"What?" God leaned back in his chair and swung his cowboy boots up on the table.

"It's not possible to come down those old attic stairs without making them creak. I've tried it. And it's certainly not possible while wearing those absurd cowboy boots. But every time, you manage to sneak up on me. How do you do that?"

"Beats me. Maybe I have godlike powers," God said.

"Maybe you're blowing smoke."

God shrugged. "Maybe you're such a lovesick fool you wouldn't notice if an elephant, on roller skates, playing a slide trombone, came down the stairs."

Ben shrugged. "Point taken."

God said, "Why not just enjoy the moment?"

"Come back?"

God sighed and held the sigh for an extra, dramatic beat. His face, lined and furrowed, was tired, but his eyes were cheerful. "The moment. The fireplace is warm, glowing even. Something tells me that Megan is at home, glowing, stretched out on her couch, a book forgotten on her chest. It's only you, with your Puritan conscience, who feels the glow of the moment and fights it off."

Ben looked over at the warm fireplace and looked up in time to see the bottle cap from the Fat Tire sailing over to the kitchen counter. "That's another thing. All the time I've spent drinking beer with you, or watching you drink my beer, I look up and the bottle cap is spinning through the air. No bottle opener. Do you open it with your teeth or is this some cornball proof of divinity?"

God said, "Cheap parlor trick. Probably beneath my dignity. I could teach you to do it if you were smart enough."

Ben sighed and prolonged his own sigh for the same extra beat. He threw in an eye roll in the direction of heaven for good measure. God ignored him and drank his beer, and the two of them listened to the small, lively sounds of the fire.

Ben said, "You're right. I am happy. It was a happy night. And not just the sex."

"Such a Puritan. Defending yourself when you haven't been accused. I never said anything about sex, just happiness. But since you bring it up, how was it?"

"Happy," Ben said, evading the trap. God smiled appreciatively. Ben added, "But I don't know what my father would say about Megan. Can you answer me that one?" Ben had never forgiven his mother for hurting the father he had worshipped. Both were dead, and he did not know whether his father had forgiven, did not know what had passed between them. He thought that since they had not discussed it with him they had never discussed it with each other. Ben grinned to himself for thinking like a child, but he wanted his father to come back and tell him what to do, tell him whether he was on a path to become his father or his mother.

God said, "Sure, I can tell you what your father would say. Doesn't mean you would listen. You've already decided that he would say you have to stay with Karen, no matter what."

"So what would he say?" Ben had no reason to think that God knew the answer to this question, but it was part of why Ben liked having God around. In the late hours of the night, it was sometimes good to have someone to talk to; absent anyone better, it might as well be God.

God said, "Your father would have said to you that he loves you."

Ben again rolled his eyes. "Bromides? From God, I get bromides? Since when did you become the god of advice columnists?"

"Make fun if you must. And in your case, clearly you must. But sometimes even advice columnists get it right. Who said your father would have wanted you to be like him? Has it ever entered your pea brain that your father was a victim of his sense of duty. He was a sweet, simple man, with a strict code. And a funny guy. But at the end he was mostly laughing to keep from crying. And at the end, he was terribly remote."

Ben was angry at this particular bit of omniscience. God sometimes knew things he was not supposed to know. With all their rambling, late-night talks, Ben was sometimes uncertain of the line between what he might have told God and God's talent for the inspired guess. Or, perhaps God did know everything but failed to do anything about it.

In his anger, Ben said, "My father was never remote from me."

"True for you. You were his only tether. Without you, he would have simply drifted away to some distant corner of space. Good on you, my friend. But that still doesn't mean he would have wished his life on you. He's dead. You don't have to hold the tether anymore."

Ben could no longer meet the eyes of God. He stared stubbornly at the dim glow of the stove. God finished his beer and swung his cowboy boots off the table.

God said, "Bedtime for this Bonzo." Ben did not answer. God stood up, walked around the table, and paused at Ben's shoulder. "Earlier, you asked me why I picked you, and I told you it was for the simple pleasure of your company. True thing. But also true that I have some experience with a life that is remote. I do not wish it on you. Or anyone."

God left the kitchen and climbed the attic stairs, which again did not creak.

Chapter Four

On Easter Sunday, Ben took Sarah fishing. He didn't ask Megan on this trip; he was not sure why but told himself it was to hold Sarah at safe distance from the complications of his life, and he was satisfied there was a piece of the truth in there somewhere. With Sarah, Ben had a family that held him in contented harness. Ritual arguments with Sarah over bedtime reliably resolved into the peace of some absurd, invented story, into soothing words that rounded to proper rest the day. Karen was becoming a visitor in their lives, Megan, a question asked. Neither visitor nor question, Sarah was bedrock, home, the home to hold safe against dangers Ben could feel more than name.

Ben and Sarah drove two hours to the Roaring Fork River in search of lower elevation and warmer water. As always, Sarah fell asleep in the truck. She loved to travel because for her it was a matter of falling asleep and waking at some lovely mountain destination. The snow was gone from the banks of the Roaring Fork and the air warm in the sunshine. Ben pulled on his fishing gear. Sarah wanted to fish and Ben helped her wriggle into her small but still oversized neoprene waders.

"Hurry, Dad."

Sarah could not stop looking at the water. Ben struggled to loosen the laces on a pair of his old hiking boots, boots that served Sarah as wading shoes, big enough to fit over the bulky neoprene.

"Hurry up, Dad," said Sarah sharply.

"Should you be using that tone of voice with your father?"

"Only if he's the slowest person in America."

"Well, there is that." Ben finished with the shoes and rigged her small fly rod.

"Finally," sighed Sarah. She turned to head for the water and stopped. "Dad, lean over." Ben was confused. "Bow your head to me," Sarah commanded. Ben did so. Sarah removed his hat and kissed the top of his head.

Sarah looked like the Michelin Man, with a blond ponytail, as she lumbered down to the water. Ben stationed her in a shallow, quiet riffle below a row of boulders that extended into the river. He stood behind her and pointed to where fish might be holding. The breeze was running hard downstream, and she had trouble casting against it. Ben showed her how to let the fly line stretch out in the tugging water behind her, how to use the resistance of the water to bow the rod, so that she could simply give the rod a sharp upstream sweep without having to back-cast, sailing the fly low over the water, beneath the driving wind. Sarah tried this unorthodox solution; it worked, and she patted Ben's hand.

"You're the best fly fisherman in America," she said.

"As well as the slowest person in America."

"That, too," said Sarah.

Sarah began to cast into the April wind. Her eyes were fixed on the little orange strike indicator as it drifted towards her, bobbing and dipping in the broken water.

Ben returned to the bank and retrieved his fly rod. He found a place to fish the heavier current thirty yards below her. Always when they fished, he kept her upstream so that he could fish out his daughter if she lost her footing and was swept away. Ben waded into the deeper water that pushed hard against his thighs. He crimped on a weight near his fly to sink it in this bigger water. Using the same casting trick he had given Sarah, he sent the line arcing into the smooth, heavy water in the middle of the river. He could feel the lead weight as the current ticked it against the bottom of the cobbled river. He watched the strike indicator with one eye and Sarah with the other. On his third cast, the fluorescent orange indicator stopped in the hurrying current, as though abruptly confused about the directions. Ben lifted the rod tip and could feel the trout shake its head at the bottom of the green, clear water. The indicator changed direction and dived beneath the surface, racing upstream. Ben let the fish run, happy to have it tire itself running upstream, happy with the feel of this first fish of the year. Ben could feel the fish in the light, pulsing rod and in the smooth line running between his finger and the butt of the rod. The line slowed under his finger and the trout turned towards the bank and quieter water. Ten feet from Sarah, it sliced out of the water and shook itself in the air, flinging droplets into sunlight. Startled, Sarah lifted her rod tip to see if she had caught a fish without knowing it. She spun and looked back at her father. She smiled and shook a triumphant fist. Ben applied more pressure now and the tired fish slid down the slippery current towards Ben. In the shadow of Ben's looming presence, it ran briefly again, and then let itself be swept into the hole in the water made by the net. Ben lifted it into the air. Sarah cheered and Ben waded with the fish to Sarah. He wet his hand in the cold water, grabbed the fish around its big belly, and removed the hook. Sarah tucked her rod beneath her elbow, wet her hands, and carefully took the fish from him. She held it to her chest as Ben took her rod. Sarah hugged the fish and traced with her finger its colorful body, silver, rose and green, sparkling in the light. The river ran around and under her and fractured the light in its shifting riffles. The trout struggled and Sarah cried out and hugged it tighter against her chest.

"Enough," said Ben softly.

Sarah petted the fish one last time and then lowered it into the water, carefully facing it upstream. She loosened her grip and the fish, free, let itself rest against her hands as the current pushed it backward. It breathed and rested and then slowly moved back into the stream. Sarah watched until it became once more an invisible part of the river.

A little later Sarah hooked a small fish that jumped and splashed around her as if she were a maypole and then dropped off the hook. Ben cheered, and Sarah used this victory as an excuse to quit fishing. She loved the water but, unlike her father, had more sense than to try to catch and turn loose every single fish in the river. Sarah took off her waders and dug a snack from the truck. She found a sandy place to sit, with a smooth white boulder to lean against. Ben waded in the heavier water and caught fish. He held each one up for Sarah to admire until he found she was asleep in the sunshine.

When she awakened, Sarah fetched the basket of Easter eggs from the truck and hid them among the river rock. She motioned Ben to come in, and he reluctantly obeyed. Sarah allowed him a drink and a snack and then gave him the empty basket and required him to search. He found eleven of the twelve. Sarah could not recall where she had hidden the twelfth. Some of the shells were developing cracks from being hidden among the rocks. Sarah went behind the truck and only peeked a little as Ben hid the eggs. She darted and swooped as she found the easy ones. Ben began to give hints about cold and warm as she searched for the rest. They still had eleven, though now with more cracks. They both loved finding a flash of color in the nooks and crannies of the river rock. The oval river rocks seemed to Ben to be nesting their colorful offspring. It was more plausible that an egg could grow up to be a rock than a chicken although this theory suffered as the eggs showed more cracks.

"Dad, I have a question for you."

"Forty-three."

"Could you wait 'til I ask the question? Forty-three is not the answer."

"OK. Seventeen. If it's not forty-three, it's got to be seventeen."

"Shut up, Dad. Do you think I'm too old for Easter egg hunts?"

"Probably, but that's not the point."

"What's the point?"

"The point is that the Easter egg hunts aren't for you. If you get too old, who will I hunt Easter eggs with? In this, as in all things, it's all about me, kid."

"Beth got a new dress for Easter."

"I'm sorry."

"For what?"

"For Beth. The dress probably had ribbons on it, too. She has to spend the day wearing a dress with ribbons on it, while we hide Easter eggs and fish."

"I'm sorry, too," Sarah said.

"For?"

"Beth. But not that sorry. She's really kind of a witch."

Maybe Sarah really wanted the dress with ribbons. If so, she tucked the conversation away neatly with a joke, using her father's tricks to fool her father. Ben understood that she was too eager to please him but did not know what to do about it. He was no less eager to please her, so maybe you just called it love, called it even. Ben worried that Sarah lied too much, driven by this eagerness to please, but he had no recollection of how much he had lied at that age, so he let it go and hoped for the best. What was a kid to do who felt she had only one parent? Survival demanded that she keep that parent closely watched. Ben remembered watching his father's every movement and mood. As a teenager, Ben regularly turned down a friend who wanted to go fishing when Ben knew his father was overwhelmed with chores on the farm. At some point, the friend unwittingly gave Ben away to his father, who blinked his faded blue eyes, shook his head in wonder, and gently told Ben he could be spared to go fishing. Even then, fishing was Ben's love, but as nothing compared to survival. Late in his shortened life, Ben's father had expressed regret that he had no interest in fishing and had not taken Ben fishing enough. The words literally made no sense to Ben; it had simply never entered Ben's mind that there was more his father could have done.

While Sarah hid the eggs again, Ben sneaked back in the river to fish. He cheated and watched Sarah carefully considering crafty places to hide an egg. She was to him unbearably beautiful: overalls, blond ponytail, graceful movements among the rocks, thoughtfully tilted head. She was perfect physical miniature of her mother. Ben recalled a spring when Sarah was three, and Karen hid Easter eggs for Sarah. Karen filled the backyard with exuberant joy until Sarah could not find some of the eggs and began to whine for help. Karen became irritable and then the phone, her rescuing angel, rang with news of a commercial real estate deal on the Gulf Coast that wanted attention. She was on a plane within the hour, and Ben and Sarah were disappointed. Eventually, together, they searched out the missing eggs. Karen had hidden one of them in a rain gutter six feet off the ground. Ben and Sarah took turns hiding the eggs and gradually their disappointment gave way to relief and then to contentment.

Ben came in again from the river and searched for eggs. Sarah cheered him on and then ate the egg with the most cracks. Ben borrowed Sarah's place in the sand and stretched out with his back against the boulder. The breeze blew down the river without resting and a different, higher breeze blew the white clouds in the opposite direction. The sun warmed his face and the breeze cooled it and the river sang in the background. He told Sarah he was going to rest his eyes and cautioned her not to go near the water. Half asleep, he dreamed of a happy day with Karen as she dozed on a ragged, multi-colored quilt beside another river; in his dream, Ben fished in a cloud of mayflies that arose from the water and drifted past him in the air like sailboats.

Ben awoke to a sharp slap against his arm. He struggled to make sense of the fact that he had just been slapped by the thrashing tail of a water snake that Sarah held with two hands and struggled to control. Ben scrambled to his feet, lurching away from the snake that Sarah kept trying to thrust towards his face. Knowing his fear of snakes, she alternately laughed and grunted with the effort to keep her grip on the snake. Ben got away from her and she lost her hold on the writhing snake. It slithered fast up the hill and Sarah leaped over rocks to stay a step behind it. She dived once and had its tail, but it coiled and jerked itself free and escaped under a pile of rocks.

Sarah came back, rubbing a skinned elbow. Ben sat on his rock, cursing softly and threatening to kill her. She sat beside him, full of glee and merriment, and the two of them slid down to the sand, holding fast to each other.

On the ride back, Sarah was uncharacteristically awake and alert. She pointed out odd rock formations in Glenwood Canyon. Three bighorn sheep grazed on the new green shoots ten feet from the road. Their fur ruffled with the wind from each passing truck, but the sheep calmly ignored the roar of civilization. Ben and Sarah tried to locate, without success, some break in the sheer canyon wall through which the sheep had descended. Ben suggested that the sheep must have parachuted into the canyon to get to the new grass.

"But how will they get back up?" Sarah challenged.

"Jump. Bighorns are major jumpers."

Sarah craned her neck to the top of the canyon wall, hundreds of feet above them. "Why do the trout jump?" she asked.

"I don't know. To escape the hook?"

"But sometimes they jump even when they're not hooked."

"Wouldn't you jump just to see the world above the river?" Ben asked.

"I don't know. It's so beautiful inside the river."

Sarah was quiet then and Ben thought she would sleep.

"Mom wants me to come to Houston for the summer when school is out."

"I know. She told me she would take you to a musical. I forget which one." This was becoming the summer ritual of de facto divorce, holding for each of them the unknowns of dread and delight.

"*Cats*," said Sarah.

"You love musicals. Plus, you get a chance to dress up. Your mom buys you beautiful clothes."

"Why won't she come here?" Sarah asked.

"It's hard for her because we're separated."

"Why won't you go there?"

"Because we're separated. It's hard to explain, but I don't like to leave the mountains."

"I don't either. Who will take care of you while I'm gone?" Sarah asked.

"Since when do I need taking care of?"

Sarah raised a small, blond eyebrow.

"Iris will take care of me," Ben said. "George and Julie will have me to dinner."

"Megan?" Ben thought he could hear in Sarah's question mirrored image of his own confusion. Sarah, a child, was only along for the ride, but it was the ride also of her life; she was shareholder in Ben's confusion.

"Yes, Megan," Ben said." "Maybe Megan."

"I wish I didn't have to go back and forth." Sarah was resigned. She was also candidate for the Sobeits, famous lost tribe.

Chapter Five

On Thursday after Easter, Ben met Megan on the paved bike path that ran around the lake. A dozen kindergarteners alternately clung to her and bounced away in odd directions. Absent a mission, they lost all unit discipline. Ben's job was perimeter patrol, and he was late. Megan gave him a look that was exasperated welcome. She called the children to crisp order and took station at the head of the line. Ben fell in at the rear. Baffled by freedom, the children were now content. They had learned the essential lesson of kindergarten: in school, you behaved as fish. Turn left with the school, right with the school—hover as one, eyes wide, fins quivering imperceptibly. When guided only by their own initiative, they ran with scissors, colored outside the lines, and glued colorful bits of construction paper to the hair of the nearest available classmate. Their chaotic minds craved the classroom liturgy: don't hit; form a reading circle; line up in orderly rows; do not color in the Golden Book.

On this nature walk, Megan led them to a station under the trees. The children formed semicircle around her, sitting in the pine needles, legs crossed, hovering. Megan sat on a stump and talked about squirrel families. Through magical coincidence, she was able to point to a squirrel nest high in a lodgepole pine directly overhead. She produced from her bag a partially chewed pinecone, and the magic was complete.

Ben sat on a log in the background and occupied himself with the magic of Irish eyes, smiling eyes, blue, mixed with a little green from the home country. When Megan looked at him, her eyes grew wider. He allowed himself to dream it would always be so. Karen, in recent years, looked at him with narrow, considering eyes. Megan's cheekbones were dangerously high, and he could feel them, across the forest floor, over the upturned heads of kindergarten children, in each of his fingertips. Megan's face stood perfect proxy for all of her, a face both strong and delicate. Karen was beautiful; Megan was simply lovely. An athlete, Megan had no fat to obscure the precise line of those strong cheekbones. Tall, willowy, she moved with strides that were long and firm, strides that seemed barely reined in from a run. Megan's face was fine and delicate, but her legs were strong, solid, and her calves bunched with muscle when she rose on her toes. When she looked at Ben, she often seemed to be suppressing a smile, and when the smile was not suppressed, it was lovely and warm and inseparable from her eyes.

Ben wondered what to do with such wonder, with the temptation of Irish eyes. He had roamed the library for books and in that roaming had first met Megan. Finding a book, absently flipping pages at the checkout counter, he found Megan looking up at him. They looked at each other a little too long, not long enough. Looking away, they swapped immediacy for anticipation.

"*Huckleberry Finn*?" She raised an eyebrow. "You haven't read it?"

"Many times. I loaned my copy and it leaked away."

"Do you always read books over and over?" Her look inquired, anticipated. Ben looked again at eyes that filled the moment.

"I'm Ben."

"I know."

"You do?"

"From your library card."

"Oh."

"I'm Megan."

"From your nameplate. Megan Flanagan."

She put out her hand, and a deal was sealed, a compact that covered everything but the future's fine print. They were innocent of everything but names, of *Huckleberry Finn* lying between them, the not quite natural sound of their voices, the fact that, knowing names, they were now free to look at each other. Megan's blue-green eyes saw intense brown, and Ben's look reversed the colors, the startling immediacy of contact making moot the past, making mystery of the future. They were innocent, in this moment, of each other's past, though not of their own. A conspiracy of the future lay ahead, but for now this conspiracy was as innocent as Huckleberry's heart.

"You like Huckleberry?" she asked.

"Life is fine on a raft."

They talked in the small, deserted library, the tall cottonwoods outside for a canopy and, for a melody, the ceaseless river. They tried to talk about mountain biking but quickly wove biography into offhand remarks. I have a wife, who sells commercial real estate in Houston, and we are separated, and in Ben's voice, there is a heart of two minds. I have a daughter who lives with me, who almost is me, and there is wonder in this recitation of the heart. I had a boyfriend and we lived together until he bent my hand back until my wrist broke, snapping like a wishbone. Without thinking, she rubs her left wrist, and Ben sees that it is whiter than her arm, still white from the cast. And did he break your heart with your wrist? No, I refuse to call it that, to concede Larry that much. All he did was make up my wavering mind for me. He still looks at me longingly from a distance, but as long as he keeps that distance I guess I can live with it. And yes, I want to be on a raft with Huckleberry, so my life is not a tangle. Ben says aye, yes, I like your eyes, as their eyes and their lives begin to entangle.

The Huckleberry Reading Club was born in that moment. The reading club was their raft, and life was fine. They quickly found that *Huckleberry* was a hard book to read aloud because of the nigger word. They agreed the word could not have been different, because of the time in which it was written, because the book was the story of Huck's journey down the Mississippi to escape the meanings of that word. Had the word been African-American, had it been black, there would have been nothing to escape. But still, it was an ugly word on the quiet page, and uglier spoken aloud. Thinking back to the movie, *Little Big Man*, where the tribe referred to themselves as "the human beings," Ben suggested they substitute human being for nigger, and they delved happily into the exploits of Huckleberry and the human being Jim. Iris saw them reading to each other in the Roaster; Ben noticed her, but she smiled and dashed out. They read in the library after hours and sometimes in the Moose Jaw over a beer. They took drives and parked overlooking the lake. Here Ben first ran into Megan's wall of silence about her family. She had none she would claim. If Ben needed her to have a family, he was welcome to count in some people he already knew about: Iris; Buster, Iris's dead husband, especially Buster; George Monroe at the paper; and Billy Mapp, outsized driver of snowplows. Ben was not welcome to count Tyler, her brother, who had some baffling connection to Larry, breaker of wrists. Ben was accustomed to having strangers walk up to him on the street and tell him their darkest secrets; after all, Hank even confided to Ben his divinity. Ben complacently thought that people saw something in his face that made them eager to tell him everything. Megan had looked at his face, had kissed his face, but she told him nothing, and he was welcome to get used to it. Ben considered this unjust for exactly as long as it took him to recall the secrets about his family that he had yet to tell Megan.

Megan looked out over the lake and said, "At the end, Huckleberry lights out for the territory because he can't stand being civilized. Will he lose his innocence in the territory?"

"Meaning, will he lose his innocence when he grows up and gets a girl?"

"Yes."

"I certainly didn't. To this day, I have a clean mind in a pure body."

"And this is why, when I am reading, you look at my breasts?"

"That's only because I can sense that they are clean. My clean mind craves clean things to focus on. Besides, you always prop the book against your chest."

Megan picked up his hand and placed it against her breast. She closed her eyes and leaned her head back against the car seat. Ben leaned his head against her shoulder, smelling her neck. They reclined, so, along this path, a path strewn with happy meetings, Roaster coffee, a view of the sunset lake, and a hand cradled between Megan's breast and *Huckleberry Finn*.

Megan stroked his hair. "Innocent no more. We're in the territory now, Huckleberry."

"It's better than being civilized. Besides, it feels innocent."

"No, dummy. You're confusing innocence with bliss."

"Yes, ma'am."

Having traveled back to the place of their beginning, Ben now returned to his studies, the study of Megan's eyes as they dazzled the dozen kindergartners seated before her. The children already knew about squirrels, of course. The children and the squirrels shared the space close to the ground. At odd, surprising moments, as they randomly crisscrossed the forest floor, the children and the squirrels met. The children seemed to like it that Megan, a grownup, also understood such moments.

The show and tell over, Megan allowed discipline to relax on the walk back to the library. Ben walked beside her, and now and again, their shoulders touched.

"Good show," Ben said.

"I know."

"I have no idea what you talked about. I just watched your eyes."

"I know."

The path under the tall pines was light and shadow. The children eddied around them, larking about, and a mountain chickadee, gray and white, peeked from a green pine bower. When their shoulders touched, Ben could lean in and smell pine needles and Megan's hair.

"Is he your husband?" asked a little girl of Megan.

"What do you think?" countered Megan.

"He might be."

"Yes, he might."

The little girl might have been Sarah. And Ben thought on this. Can I take Sarah from her mother, even if Karen only fitfully wants to be her mother? When Sarah thinks about her mother she is a jumble of anger and love and sadness. And I am the same jumble. What is it that some people have in them, or don't have in them, to let family go? There must be no tribal petroglyph of family etched on their bones. Karen came to Ben on the run from her crazy mother, her mother who was only fully alive when creating misery in others. Her mother, almost as beautiful as Karen, was even then on a downward spiral, measured by the fact that now each new husband

41

was a little less rich than the last. She held all the husbands in contempt for loving her. She held Ben in contempt because he did not love her. She resented that he was sane, resented that he took Karen out of her orbit. But she never lost confidence. She studied her lacquered nails with satisfaction, idly sharpened them against the brocade of her sofa, and measured Ben across the room. She pointed these nails at Ben and made high-pitched, histrionic conversation about how wonderfully Ben had changed Karen's life, how he had made Karen so very content. Her cat eyes narrowed to daggers, her smile was wide and yawning, and Ben did not know for a long time that she thought him a simple, penniless fool. She stretched, flicked a shining nail in his direction, and her throat hummed with the knowledge that Karen would, in the fullness of time, follow only her.

Huckleberry solved his great moral crisis by deciding he would go to hell before selling Jim down the river to slavery. Ben was ready to take his chances on hell, but who to sell? And with which sale did he also sell himself? Sarah loved her mother because she was her only mother and because children do not list the reasons for love. Ben knew that Karen had turned off a switch with his name on it. She loved him in sporadic emotional gusts, but he was simply no longer part of her plan for herself. It is, he thought, a simple switch; he should be able to find it in the dark, find it in its usual place, and bring light to the family room. He believed, naively, that he was smart and smart people can find a way. He loved Karen, was still dazzled when she threw a switch and made the sun to shine upon him. Sarah—if he could only divine Sarah's heart, he would do whatever she wanted him to do. But in this, she kept hidden her heart and refused to be his teacher. Megan was the indecipherable future. Ben recoiled from the divided hearts of blended families. Pessimism, born of his marriage, reached out and fancied another failed marriage to Megan, and a future of serial love, each love more faded, more jaded that the last. Surely, this was not what Huckleberry had in mind. Sell Megan, who promised hope, who was optimistic in the face of broken bones, who trusted him? Perhaps she trusted him to do the right thing, or more simply, perhaps she just trusted him to try. He was still falling in love with this Megan, but his mind was a jumble on the question of love and the unacceptable idea of loving two women at once.

Ben and Megan had the past summer, the fall, full of fresh delight in each other. Then, with winter's onset, they retreated from each other, each with the prudent reasons of cautious hearts. Ben was stuck on the problem of Sarah, on the minefield of his marriage, on stepping exactly in his father's faded footprints. Megan was stuck, perhaps on unhappy times with men, perhaps also on the ghosts of family past. Two weeks ago, holding each other in Megan's library, Megan reached for a rueful silver lining and held up the thought that at least their doubts about each other were loving ones. The coming of spring was reviving them, melting a little their loving doubts, but their cautious hearts did not yet pass over into abandon.

Chapter Six

Ben found himself being called more often to substitute teach; he hoped this was a good sign for his job prospects with the school district. He liked his other jobs, but teaching gave his restless mind more to rummage about in. In the second week of May, a Thursday, he was teaching, and the office delivered a message to call Iris.

Iris said, "We don't see much of your wife up here, so a heads up. She'll be waiting for you when you get home."

Confused, Ben asked, "Is she at your house?"

"Yours. I saw her go in about an hour ago. Fifteen minutes later, Hank left, in a hurry. Karen walked him out on the porch. From a distance, I would say she's a little steamed. Were you expecting her?"

"It's news to me. Thanks for the call. Have you talked to her?"

"Not me. I've gotten better judgment in my old age. I'm just snooping out the window. Karen has a temper. I have a temper. What she lacks is my practical experience. Believe me, she doesn't want to talk to me when she is angry."

"OK, very wise. Would you do me this favor—pick up Sarah from school and take her to a movie or something? Give me a couple of hours with Karen?"

"Good idea."

There was one more period left in the school day, and all Ben had to do was supervise a study hall. He tried to think of someone he could ask to cover for him, but he was too much a newcomer to be able to ask favors. He was left to pretend to watch students who pretended to study. His attention concentrated by the prospect of seeing Karen, he contemplated the institution of (his own) marriage.

Ben assumed that Karen had found out about his relationship with Megan, probably from something Sarah had said. Ben had never told Sarah what she could talk about with her mother. He should have told Karen, but, from a mix of anger and stubbornness, he had told himself that it was none of her business. He admitted to the possibility that he was just chicken. But they were separated, separated to avoid, for Ben, the constant emotional fireworks that wore on him. They were separated so Ben could live in the mountains, so Karen could pursue her work, and Ben assumed, so she could pursue a more interesting life, in all respects, than Ben provided. He thought they had an unspoken separation agreement to ask no questions of each other. He knew that Karen had reasons to want no questions asked of her. Oh, well. There would be a scene. He had had some practice. Much more than the scene, though, he feared the calling towards love of Karen, a calling that seemed absurd to everyone but him.

In the beginning, for Ben, was not the word, but only Karen's beauty, beauty that tied his tongue and took away his ability to breathe. She noticed him and invited him with a smile, which further reduced his ability to breathe, and took all oxygen from his brain. From this single instance, she developed the idea he was shy and had never let go of this idea to the present day. He was asphyxiating, a medical emergency, and she diagnosed shyness; she was always a master of the daffy conclusion. More accurately, it was love at first sight. With the eventual onset of marital jaundice and fatigue, Ben wondered on this. Separated, he could still take her picture from the drawer and feel again as he did on that first day. Before there were words between them, Karen made perfect match to some template in his brain that he had not even known existed. It was medical mystery, a physiological event beyond the reckoning of the rational. He had seen beautiful women before, had dated enough of them to know that women found something in him to be attracted to. He was prepared to be moved by beautiful women; he was not prepared to have his brain smashed by the mere physical form of a woman. But smashed it was, perhaps permanently, with no word spoken, only an instant vision of perfect love. As the years went by, Ben listened to others describe love, love at first, second, or even hindsight, and he never seemed to hear anything that matched his

45

own experience. But perhaps people used different words to describe something that words could not be fitted to. In the beginning was something else besides the word.

Over time, as the words came between them, Ben realized that it was bad luck that Karen was constantly beautiful and intermittently loony. He never tired, though, of looking at her. In the mornings, with first light and fresh hope, he studied her peaceful face and thought that his life, that day, and all the days, would be as fine and as peaceful as that softly breathing face that he wanted to trace with one light fingertip. Many of these days, however, worked out badly because Ben craved peace and Karen chaos.

For a while, the two of them smugly preached a gospel of opposites, and Ben told himself that this must have been what his brain was calling out for at first sight of Karen. He came home from work one day and Karen was shimmering naked in the tub. He joined her with all his clothes on, and it felt that Karen was freeing captive parts of himself. And she was. For her part, Karen put in a vegetable garden, sweated in the Texas humidity as she moved, humming, from stake to stake, and calmly savored the cornucopia lined up on the kitchen window sill. But two hours later, when Karen, in a rage, threw a red tomato at him, for the very good reason that her chili gave him the hiccups, even Ben began to see that the center might not hold.

They married anyway, reason a pauper to love's riches, and Ben found more surprises in store. To the extent Ben gave it any rational thought, his understanding was limited to the fact that he was "getting married," whatever that meant, to the woman of his dreams. He was not a great respecter of religion or institutions. Sometime, much later, after Sarah was born, when life became real, when the piper dropped by with the bill, it popped into Ben's mind that marriage vows were a promise. It seemed painfully hilarious to him that he had overlooked this small point, a bit like living for twenty-five years and failing to notice the bright, round thing that appeared in the sky every day. But there it was. So, while he cared nothing for religious vows, he did care for his father, and his simple, stubborn father cared for promises, so there it was, and there he was, dumb enough to find the sun's existence a surprise.

Ben's distrust of religion was equaled by his distrust of the little psychological gems brought to him by friends. He, or Karen, or both were codependent. Why not cocoa dependent? There must be a twelve-step program for that. Ben tried to imagine a relationship, a marriage, a family, in which you were not dependent on each other. "You are the sun, the moon and the stars to me, but please remember that I am utterly indifferent to anything you might say, do, or feel. I am not dependent. Neither am I codependent, nor cocoa dependent. Rather, I am the sum of all things stupid." Concerning most things pop psychology, Ben was not a fan. Words like dysfunctional and victimization, rather than striking an emotional chord in his heart, made him feel like taking a shit. He and Karen freely made their choices, as long as you understood that freedom was heavy as a rock, heavy with child, with love, with hurts and joys.

So they met. So they separated and reunited and separated and continued on. Ben came to the clear view that Karen was loony, volatile, self-absorbed, and manipulative. Ben also had some idea of the clear view she had of him, not all of it flattering. But, if Karen was all these things, so what? This was not everything about Karen; about everyone, there was always something more, sometimes something wonderfully more. Ben was the child of reserved parents, so Karen made him feel more loved than he had understood to be possible; if her anger was intensely expressed, no less was her love, and this carried Ben through. And if love was intermittent, like shower and sun, he came to understand that it was no less real.

Ben thought that Karen could not quit the marriage because it felt to her like signing over title as a mother; he could not quit without a permission slip from his father. To become a full member of the tribe of Sobeits, all that was necessary was to understand that complaining was fully as useless as explaining. Before Megan, Ben found that the separations were a relief, a simple way to have a simple life, but he knew that with every separation, with every step towards emotional simplicity, there was a slip for him into the emotional remoteness into which his father had disappeared on his way out of this world.

The bell rang; the students in study hall quit pretending to study; Ben quit pretending to know enough to be a teacher of anything; and he went home to his wife.

He opened the front door and was unsurprised to find Karen angry.

"Who the hell is the guy upstairs?" she demanded.

"God?"

"My ass."

"Is great?"

"You are a piece of work," Karen said. "Raising my daughter in this dump. There's some weirdo thinks he's Willie Nelson living upstairs. You're a hick. A small-town, schoolteacher hick. You think it's OK to live this way because it's a Colorado mountain town. It's still hicks and losers. I must've been out of my mind."

"Good to see you, Karen."

"You asshole," Karen screamed. "Don't talk to me. You think I don't know you're fucking some slut librarian. Phony bastard. Mr. Upright. Mr. High and Mighty."

"Good to see you, Karen." Ben had disappeared into the soothing cocoon he wrapped around himself at these times, a calmness that, not coincidentally, infuriated Karen. It was good to see her. She was beautiful even when you knew she had fashioned beauty into a business tool. She had colored her hair an even more vivid blond. She let her dark eyebrows grow thick, and the contrast seemed striking and oddly natural. She had slimmed her voluptuous body in the interest of her current, competitive real estate phase. Commercial real estate was a world of greed and guile. It was a man's sizzling world of expensive homes and cars and restaurants. Despairing that Ben would ever accomplish squat, Karen put her hair up, put on elegant suits, and sizzled. She sizzled until real estate moguls reached a pawing fever; then, at the ripest moment, she switched on a gale of "how dare you" rage that left them drenched, steaming, and frightened. Having launched these screaming emotions, she then calmly took out a pen and had them sign her version of the deal.

"You bastard. You're not even going to bother denying it, are you?"

"I'm sorry," said Ben.

Karen picked up a knickknack from the coffee table, a small wooden bear, and threw it hard at Ben. He ducked enough that it struck him just above his left eye. The bear glanced off and clattered across the wood floor, spinning to rest on its side in a dusty corner. Ben and Karen stared at each other, tied together in this moment by the bear's straight line through space. They waited for the thing that came next, as Ben's heart slowly pumped blood from his center to smaller and smaller arteries, finally into the capillaries over his eye, now open to the world, and leaking a broad sludge of blood towards his eyebrow.

"Oh, shit," said Karen, exasperated that her bloody intentions had produced a bloody result. She groped a tissue from her purse and blotted at Ben's forehead. Ben was, at bottom, a farm kid, unruffled and unsurprised by the occasional bloody injury, accidental or otherwise. He pushed her carefully away.

"You'll get blood on your suit," he said. Even a farm kid, especially a farm kid, could recognize an expensive suit.

"I don't care about the damned suit," Karen said. She pulled his head down against her chest, letting her pale, barely blue blouse catch the blood that now flowed freely from the primed pump of his heart. She pulled him to the couch and held his head pressed tightly against her, not bearing to look at the wound she had so wanted to create. She stroked his hair and kissed the crown of his head in this loony moment of love.

"I'm sorry," she said. "I'm so sorry."

"Your aim is still good. You know, it's the stupidest thing, but I always think I can duck. In the instant after you pick something up, I always become very calm, certain in the knowledge that I have the reflexes of a jungle cat. I'm damned if I know why I think that. It's just something I always think. Maybe if you would start throwing paper airplanes?"

"Oh, I love you, Ben Wallace."

"Savagely."

"I know, I know. But the only time I feel normal is when I'm with you. At moments like this, when all the craziness is out of my system, I feel normal. I feel like I could just be a shopkeeper and live with you and Sarah. I could. I know I could."

Karen pulled her suit jacket loose from between them and blotted the blood with its lapels.

"Look at you," she said.

"You're going to ruin your clothes."

"Screw the clothes. I made ninety-three thousand dollars on Tuesday."

"And that's a good thing?" Ben asked.

"Here we go again."

"OK. OK."

"Just shut up about my job. I went out into that crappy jungle and made that ninety-three thousand dollars. Some bastard is always trying to cheat you. You wouldn't believe the things men will do. They tell me how beautiful I am, and they think that it will get them a better deal, or that I will think it's the best thing that ever happened to me to give them all the profits and jump in bed with them. Men are just bastards…"

Ben noted that the craziness had not stayed out of her system for long. He listened again to the great, circular argument. Men are bad. Bad people deserve what they get. Women are victims and entitled to fight back with any means at their disposal. You, Ben, are good, but good is not enough; you have to be saintly to restore my faith in men. When you are not saintly, or even good, you are the most evil creature alive because you were my last hope. The argument had not changed in years, and she could carry it forward, talking nonstop, for hours at the time; except, like curved space, the argument went forward only to arrive again at its beginning. Karen was still holding forth, "And I thought you were different, but the truth is you're not. You're just not, and I have to get used to that." Sometimes Ben found something to say to stop it but in recent years mostly not.

This time, Karen stopped herself when she looked back down at the blood on her blouse.

"We have to get you fixed up." She took off her jacket and left Ben holding it to his forehead. She returned with a damp washcloth, bandages, and adhesive tape. Ben wondered how she found these things so efficiently until he recalled that they kept the first aid kit in the cabinet over the sink in every home they had lived in. She cleaned and bandaged tenderly and finished her work by kissing him on the lips.

"My Ben has feet of clay after all. How could you have some cheap affair?"

"Why do you think it's some cheap affair?"

"Because it's me that you love. I'm impossible, but I'm your great love. You can't ever stop loving me."

"Maybe I can."

"No chance, Charlie. I know you all the way through to your dreams."

Ben lay on the sofa and Karen perched beside him on the sofa's edge. She stroked his face and leaned over and kissed his forehead and her hair fell around his face. He thought of all the times that hair had surrounded his face.

"You know my dreams, and I know yours, and they are not the same," said Ben.

"I can't live in these small towns. People think I'm weird."

Ben thought, meanly, yes, because in a small town you can't hide who you are.

Ben said, "I lived in the city with you. But you weren't there, even when you were."

"I used to think you were the smartest man in the world. But it's no good without ambition."

"Everything we say to each other has a 'but' in it."

"I know," Karen said.

"Sarah."

"I know," Karen said.

"Sarah."

Karen said, "I know. I know. But she loves you more than me. Don't I get some credit? You and Sarah are the two people I love the most. I can't give either of you what you want, so I at least give you each other. Doesn't that count for something?"

"It counts. But it's crazy thinking. And it's not nearly enough, not for Sarah."

"Or for you," Karen said.

"Or for me."

Karen swiped at a seeping tear.

"Did you cry?" Ben asked. "Did you cry when you found out I was having an affair?"

"I cried. And the next day," she said fiercely, "I went out and made ninety-three thousand dollars."

"Screw your ninety-three thousand dollars."

"Screw you. I went out and undid the top two buttons on my blouse and screwed Blue Island Holdings, Inc. out of an extra three million dollars. Besides, I owed you that affair."

"I know. I know that."

"I won't be stopped," Karen said. "Not by you or Sarah or anybody. But I can take the two of you with me. Please come with me."

"No."

"You have to. You love me. Sarah loves me. We need each other to be complete. Just love me enough."

Another tear seeped from the corner of Karen's left eye, the one that always cried first. In spite of the drama, the manipulation, Ben knew it was a real tear tied to real moments in their lives. She began taking off her bloody silk blouse. Some of his blood had seeped through to her bra and darkened it as though she were leaking milk. Ben touched that spot with the tip of his finger. He touched the wet tear at Karen's eye. Karen licked a remaining smudge of blood from over his eye and her hair fell around him and turned the room to twilight. Ben kissed her, feeling again a part of the first moment of Karen. But this time Megan was also in his thoughts, Megan and the sound of the Blue River curling like smoke around her library. Sarah was there, and even Iris, his friend. Ben kissed his wife and was drawn up into the kiss and wanted to follow it back to the beginning of love, but there were too many swirling thoughts in this fog of love, too many thoughts for one simple act. Ben could hear Ollie scratching at the door because it was time for Sarah to be home from school, time for her to throw sticks for him. Ben lifted Karen by her shoulders, lifted her up and placed her solidly at the end of the couch. She started to protest but looked at his face, and Ben knew she found there whatever it was that his face looked like in those rare moments when no one, not even Karen, dared find out what came next. Ben went to the door and let Ollie in as Karen sat speechless on the couch, surprise her only company.

Chapter Seven

Having been deposited abruptly on one end of the couch, Karen became thoughtful. She put away attempts at anger, at love, and treated life as if she had spent four thousand straight days in this place, ordinary days on the gently rolling hills of family life. She changed into jeans and a sweatshirt. Ben marveled at the natural confidence of this transition. She knew that this was his vision of family life, and, as one old campaigner to another, she was untroubled that he knew that she knew this and might consider it false. Karen filled so completely the moment's role that there was no room in it for contradiction; she was, at every changing instant, completely genuine.

Ben asked Karen how she found out about Megan. He had thought the answer would be Sarah, but Karen casually reported that she had received at work a long, detailed, and anonymous letter, complete with a touching picture of Ben and Megan kissing under a tree. Ben was baffled and Karen was dismissive except to remark that even Ben, the diplomat, seemed to have made an enemy in this small town.

When Iris dropped Sarah off, she rushed into her mother's arms, but Ben could tell she was unsettled when she first saw Karen. He knew that Sarah did not like surprises. Life worked better for her when she could prepare her feelings in advance. She habitually talked through upcoming events with Ben, describing how she would feel and what she would say until she had it organized in her mind. Ben accused her of being a master of planned spontaneity; this small joke was lost on her, and she continued her planning ways.

Karen pulled Sarah down on the couch and held her in her lap, as Sarah buried her face in her mother's neck. Iris waved at Karen and Ben and tried to back out the door, but Karen beckoned her over with her free hand and reached to shake Iris's hand. She thanked Iris for taking such good care of Sarah and Ben. Iris was wary but polite; she talked about what a joy Sarah was. Ben understood that these two strong women could never be anything but enemies. He was relieved when Iris made a quick exit so they could be alone, well before Iris reached her low threshold for that which spoke to her of social bullshit.

Ben studied the portrait of mother and child entwined on the couch until he felt an intruder on tenderness and felt he could not watch more. He slipped out to the kitchen, put on a pot of coffee, and sat at the table, watching the alpenglow on the still snow-covered hump of Buffalo Mountain. After a long while, Karen called for him to join them. Sarah was sitting up beside her mother on the couch, and her eyes went immediately to the bandage over Ben's eye, which Ben had forgotten. Sarah jumped up to inspect it. Ben quickly made up a mildly entertaining story about being abducted by space aliens from New Mexico who were going to steal his brain but lost interest when they discovered he did not have one. Sarah wasn't buying and furiously demanded to know of Karen what she had thrown. Karen shrugged and pointed to the wooden bear.

"I'm sorry, baby. You know me. I didn't mean…"

Sarah examined the bear minutely for damage, as though looking for evidence of further destruction that she could blame on her mother. This seemed a little beside the point to Ben, but Sarah had her own ways. Sarah put down the bear and walked over and socked her mother hard on the shoulder. Karen did not flinch.

Karen calmly said, "I didn't mean…," but Sarah had run to her room and slammed the door.

Karen said, "Once again, I'm the bitch."

"I'll go talk to her," Ben said.

"Sure, Ben. You go talk to her so you can be the good guy. Once again, you win."

"It's not a competition."

"Everything's a competition, Ben. You're just so pious you don't admit it." Karen sighed and got up from the couch. "I'll talk to her.

I'm going to tell her I only did it to stop you from breaking up our family."

Ben understood this to be a kind of bitter joke, but he did not like the truth in it, for any of them. Parents did not compete for the affection of a child, except for when they did, and then they competed with Disneyland and divorce lawyers and fanged offhand remarks. How can you not fight to protect your child from a stranger, and who could be stranger than someone you once loved?

Ben heard raised voices from the bedroom but no breakage, and he decided to take Ollie for a walk. They circled the block twice. Ollie was momentarily confused by the unaccustomed second lap but unfailingly agreeable. Life was good for Ollie when he got to go for walks and fetch things.

When Ben returned, Karen and Sarah were in the kitchen, working under some flag of truce, probably having to do with the necessity of dinner. Karen pulled a saucepan, one familiar from their days together, from the cupboard; this pan was a crucial building block in the jumble of utensils that Ben had crammed into the cabinet. The remaining pots and pans, deprived of precarious balance, crashed downward, jostling for fresh angles of repose.

"How can you live like this?" Karen asked mildly.

"We live just fine," Sarah said. Her anger was still close to the surface, and Ben granted she had reason in this case. In general, though, it seemed to Ben that daughters specialized in finding fault with their mothers. Ben could ruin Sarah's favorite white sweater by washing it with her favorite red sweater, and Sarah would pat him on the hand and swear that pink was her favorite color.

"Sorry, baby. I wasn't criticizing. Just teasing. Right, Ben?"

"True that," said Ben. "Your mother has made fun of my lousy housekeeping since before you were born. She only teases me because I'm so hopeless."

Sarah said nothing and continued to set the table. She had found a white tablecloth that Ben had forgotten they had. The tablecloth covered the assorted schoolwork that Sarah had embedded in the soft pine of the table. Sitting at the table, Sarah wrote her school assignments on a single sheet of paper. When her concentration was intense, her effort determined, the schoolwork carved itself through the paper and into the wood. Ben had reminded her on a couple of occasions to use a pad under the paper and then had let it pass. He liked reading the table over coffee as the slant of early morning sunlight illumined the traces of his daughter. She wrote math problems. She wrote Sarah Wallace repeatedly, so she could be sure it was still her name. She wrote, "I love Dad." Ben liked tracing her name, these words, with his finger as the morning light lifted them from the wood.

Sarah arranged the blue plates on the white tablecloth. She carefully turned the plates so that any white chip around the edges faced the center of the table, not quite grasping that her mother would see, then, the chips in the plates across from her. Ben sat at the table as the women in this part of his life busied themselves around him.

"The table looks lovely," Karen said.

"It's not like your house, but we like it."

"My house is your house, too," Karen said.

Sarah said nothing.

"The food smells wonderful," Ben said. The three of them ate in the shadow of Sarah's anger. Karen told stories about Ringo, her new kitten. Ringo was afraid of his battery-powered mouse. Ringo needed someone to play with. He had soft gray fur and blue eyes. He sometimes slept at night curled up in Karen's hair. He loved to purr against Karen's neck as she fell asleep. In the telling, Ringo leaped and lunged, and his escapades defied both gravity and reason. The telling of his tales was carried by Karen's husky voice and confident laughter. Karen could cling to the tilting deck of the Titanic, disdaining lifeboats, and launch confidently into a story, a story so long that its rising and falling parts were destined to disappear beneath the rolling waters. Ben admired her fearlessness. There was something in the tale of Ringo, thought Ben, for everyone. A slapstick kitten needed a child to chase it around the house, needed its soft gray coat stroked as it napped on a child's stomach. When this same kitten was tempted to curl up in the tangle of Karen's flowing hair on the pillow, it should only find Ben already there, already purring against Karen's neck. For everyone, thought Ben, there is a promise. And the promises flowed like an unending river, and the dreams went round the room, and all the hard edges wavered and became soft.

Karen believed. She believed vividly in making promises but only faintly in keeping them. Most passionately, she believed that no one should ever be allowed to remind her of a promise unmet. Because a promise was love; and you do not question the power of love. Whenever Karen felt love, she made a promise, love's perfect expression. If you insisted that the promise be kept, you must be some sort of accountant. The promise itself should be enough and it almost was. Promises were stories, and you could feast on a story, at least until you craved bread. Ben and Sarah, stubborn, practical souls, sometimes tried to eat the stories, but this made them a little mad, a madness that bent their lives.

Sarah had softened over the evening. She seemed happy when Karen suggested they take a bath together and wash each other's hair. Afterwards, they brushed each other's hair out. Karen put on music, and she and Sarah danced. They pulled Ben up with them just long enough to make fun of his Caucasian male terpsichorean arrhythmia before pushing him back down again. The two of them commandeered Ben's bed for the night, and he was left to choose between Sarah's small bed and the couch. He chose the couch and found a blanket. He was drowsily reading his favorite Chekhov story, "A Day in the Country," when God appeared beside him, holding two opened beers in one hand. God scooped Ben's feet out of the way, sat down on the end of the couch, and plopped his booted feet silently on the coffee table.

"Did it to me again," Ben said, as he took his beer. "Can't you see I'm reading?"

God swigged his beer and looked at the ceiling. "I'll skip you to the last paragraph, the good part. Chekhov ends with, 'The children fall asleep thinking of the homeless cobbler, and, in the night, Terenty comes to them, makes the sign of the Cross over them, and puts bread under their heads. And no one sees his love. It is seen only by the moon which floats in the sky and peeps caressingly through the holes in the wall of the deserted barn.' That Chekhov was one happy dude when he found that ending."

Ben flipped to the last page of the story, which he had read many times in the old book, and every word was perfectly recalled. "Damn, you're an aggravation."

God was pleased with himself. "What, you thought I was here to bring you comfort?"

Ben said, "Comfort. Wisdom. You got any? Or do I need to get religion for that?"

"Not something I would recommend. As Mr. Gandhi said, 'God has no religion.'"

"Abraham Lincoln…" Ben began.

"There was a man," God said.

"Lincoln said that the only church he would join would be one that had the Golden Rule as its sole creed."

"Both pretty fair rules," said God.

"Both?"

"Lincoln's rule about not joining churches. And the Golden Rule. 'And as ye would that men should do to you, do ye also to them likewise.' It's not crafted in a very lawyerly fashion, because it assumes that everyone wishes to be treated well. Hitler was driven to kill or be killed, thus giving us the Holocaust. The evangelical imperative assumes that everyone, deep down, wants to be evangelized, thus giving us Jehovah's Witnesses. So it's not perfectly golden, but still a beautiful thing. I love also the part about loving your enemies as well as your friends, because any numskull can love his friends—I'm paraphrasing here."

"Ah," Ben said, "but you're paraphrasing Jesus."

"Who was, in turn, paraphrasing the accumulated thinking of millions who had come before him, millions of wise, patient farmers, millions of grandmothers rocking a child. It's not like nobody ever thought of this stuff before Jesus. A good idea does not have to be original—it only has to maintain its loveliness across endless repetitions. The simple phrase, 'I love you,' is endlessly repeated and no less endlessly craved. The Golden Rule, the commandment to love thy neighbor—it's a call to a higher standard. It's so beautiful it sometimes makes me cry."

"I don't know what to do. That makes me cry," Ben said.

"Sarah is first."

"Agreed. But, if I am in her shoes, I do not know what I would want done. I don't know that I would be old enough to know. And she keeps hidden from me what she wants."

"Yes," God said.

"Do you know what she wants, what is good for her?"

"Yes."

"Would you tell me?" Ben asked.

"No."

"Megan, Karen, me. We all have the same problem. We can't figure out how to shape our lives to the symmetry of the Golden Rule."

"Maybe that's because it can't be done," God said.

"Then I need a better rule."

"There isn't one. Except…"

"What?" Ben asked.

"The call to a higher standard. It's one of the few good reasons for having me around."

"We progress from vague to murky. How do I apply some higher standard?" asked Ben.

"God knows."

"And isn't saying."

"Sucks, huh?"

"Why create such a system?" Ben asked.

"Honest Injun? I'm not even sure myself. But it appears, by failing to provide clear instructions, I have left the door open to the possibility of tragic choices. Try not to make one."

"Do my best." Ben took a deep breath that ended in a sigh. "Another beer?"

"Nah. Errands to run. Be back when I'm back."

Ben recalled his conversation with Iris. "That's right. You ran into Karen today. I'm guessing you might not be done with the errands until after Karen leaves?"

"Remarkable woman. Very determined. Reminds me, meant to tell you. It wasn't just the sex."

"Come back."

"It wasn't just the sex that attracted you to her. Granted, she's hot. But also remarkable. She threatened to kick God's sorry ass all the way down High Street. I believe she might have done it if I had not decreed that I should leave."

"Wise move."

"See, you started this conversation by asking for wisdom, and there you are."

God left with his customary eerie silence and Ben went to sleep. In the morning, he got up and phoned Sarah's school that she would not be in that day. Sitting over coffee, he dialed part of Megan's number before deciding to let that call wait for a clearer brain. Standing over the sink, he washed the dishes from the night before. He set the table and fixed bacon and eggs. When the smell of bacon frying was ineffective in rousing Karen and Sarah, he began to sing, loudly, in his best voice, and continued until muffled yells for mercy swam through the door. Over breakfast, Ben announced that Sarah's school was closed for the day, for fumigation, because the principal had gas. Sarah, an easy mark for fart jokes, giggled. Ben began to make suggestions for things Sarah and Karen might like to do that day until Karen caught his eye. She had an appointment in Houston, a plane to catch, and she was gone by ten, with Sarah saying stay, and Ben hiding behind studious neutrality. She was gone, and Sarah veered through the day. She talked excitedly of things she and her mom were going to do in the summer. She went blank and curled up with Ben on the couch. She went to Ben's room and pretended to read among the scent of tangled sheets. She came out and yelled at Ollie to quit pestering her, which hurt his feelings. She then curled up with him on the floor, and he licked her face, happy to be forgiven his trespasses.

Chapter Eight

Karen left on Friday, and the next morning Ben sat at Iris's dining table having coffee. He quickly suppressed his habitual impulse to lean back and put his feet up on the table. Unlike his table, Iris's was elegant, glowing cherry. In the spirit of contradiction, her coffee table was a squat, oak structure, deeply gouged from years of rough use and discolored by rings from beer bottles beyond number. Ben had once ragged on Iris about this, and she was at a loss to explain her theory of interior decoration. She finally pointed out that her husband, Buster, had made the coffee table in his high school shop class. She pondered the dining table and explained that she had wandered into an upscale furniture store, looking unsuccessfully for her friend, Jose Rivera, who drove their delivery truck. On the way out, the cherry table caught her eye. When she got to the door, it popped into her mind that she was rich. She turned around and told the owner to have Jose deliver her the table because she needed to talk to him.

That morning, Iris had once again remembered that she was rich. She hatched with Sarah a plan to go for the weekend to the Brown Palace in Denver. They would pick up Laurie, Iris's daughter, from the group home and make a threesome of it. Ben was unsure because he thought, after Karen's visit, that Sarah might need quiet time at home with him. Iris told Ben that what Sarah really needed was to get away from all family, including her shell-shocked father, and Sarah apparently agreed because she was enthusiastic.

Ben mildly protested that he was not so shell-shocked, and Iris waved him off. "Men are weak-minded on the subject of women. They can't even figure out the difference between love and sex."

Ben smiled. "And you do know the difference?"

"Oh, yes. That's one of the few things I do know."

"Can you teach me?" Ben asked.

"Sorry, not interested."

"No, no, I meant…"

"Gotcha." Iris smiled. "It's my new strategy. I don't get propositioned as much as I used to, so I've started treating the most random remarks as propositions. Guy on the street says good morning, and I apologize and tell him he's not my type—adds to my air of eccentricity. Plus, it's the damnedest thing, but about half the time, some kid half my age will give me a second look. Like, wait, did I miss an opportunity here?" Iris ran a finger across the rich finish of her expensive table. "Love was Buster," she said, "and sex was everybody else."

"Good definition, Iris, but not one that does me much good."

"I guess you would have had to be married to Buster to understand."

"From what I know of Buster, I have never thought of him as my type."

"You're a smartass and Buster was a dumbass. Riding his bike for more beer in the dead of a moonless winter's night, just so he won't get another DUI, and he gets rear-ended by a confused tourist. What a moron."

"Which one?" Ben asked.

"Both. The drunk tourist goes to jail for killing my drunk husband. And I miss him every day. And if you ask which one again I'm going to break your neck. Two drunks collide at the bottom of High Street, and what's that do for me and Laurie?"

"How is Miss Laurie? She's not been up much lately."

"It just confuses her," Iris said. "She keeps expecting her father to walk in and tickle her feet. I think she likes it better when I go to Denver and visit her at the group home. Maybe it helps her to be away from it all, to live with other people who are mentally retarded."

"Sarah doesn't like it when you say retarded."

Iris laughed briefly, gravely. "Make any word you want. Call it glymph if that suits you better. The fact is that Laurie doesn't quite have the alphabet straight; she can read about fifty words on a good day; and she can't add and subtract worth beans. When she talks, sometimes she sounds like a normal young adult, and then the next words sound like she is six."

"Point taken," Ben said. "I kind of like glymph."

Iris said, "Life in Denver doesn't give Laurie so many memories of her father. She's learned to say by rote that her daddy's dead, but it doesn't make much sense to her. I don't know if dead means anything to her, except that your crazy dad isn't tickling your feet anymore. God, that girl loved her father. She used to rush out the door every morning to bring him his paper. I had to watch her like a hawk to make sure she wasn't outside half-naked, prowling up and down the street. She'd come back and spread the paper in front of him as he was having breakfast and watch him read. As long as one of them could read, that was enough for her."

"I'm sorry," said Ben.

"I didn't ask for your fucking sympathy."

"Yes, ma'am."

The two of them drank their coffee and watched Sarah skylarking with Ollie. Ben looked at Iris and thought how lucky he was to have this friend. The thought of all the things he was afraid of at this moment also pressed into his mind.

Ben said, "Answer me this. No bullshit. Have you always been so fearless?"

Iris shrugged and looked away. "Ben, I don't know. I started out wild and too dumb to be scared. Now, four years without Buster, I'm not sure what there's left to be scared of." She looked a warning at Ben. "Take care of Megan. I don't want her hurt."

Ben nodded. He had called Megan early that morning. She was hurt. He did not like talking to her on the phone but did not want to leave Sarah and did not want Megan to find out about Karen's visit from someone else in this small town. Someone had told Karen about Megan, and it occurred to him that could work both ways. He suspected Megan's ex-boyfriend, who apparently watched her longingly from a distance. Megan had pressed Ben, calmly and directly, for every detail of Karen's visit. In describing his actions, his feelings, he had spared her nothing, nor had he spared himself, but he hated trying to squeeze such cacophony through a phone line. He hoped she believed him that he did not sleep with Karen, but she said only that it made no difference. He took this to mean that he was already damned enough, and this seemed fair. He asked to see her, but she would only commit to the possibility that she might be at the Moose Jaw.

. . . ..

On Saturday night, Megan, in this time of trouble, had taken refuge in the bosom of family at their favorite bar. The bar was the Moose Jaw, and it had known how to be a bar for a long time. It was not as big or famous as the Woody Creek Saloon near Aspen, but it served, served beer and good burgers and shots. The sign outside had giant moose antlers but no moose jaw; antlers made a better sign, and jaw a better name. There were onion rings if you didn't have a date and had abandoned all hope of getting one. The Jaw sold a lot of onion rings because of the nature of its clientele and because, like all ski towns, there weren't enough women to go around. Women who migrated to Summit County had to find happiness in a good set of fleece underwear instead of elegant dresses. Avalanche beacons were a fashion accessory. Toes were always cold, and noses always red and cracked from skiing in the cold. For women, the upside was that there were a lot of men, many of whom lived in pretty decent cars and savored the evening warmth of onion rings in the Jaw.

When Ben entered the Jaw, he immediately spotted Megan at the bar with George Monroe and Billy Mapp. They were part of the family she admitted to having, part of the family she said raised her; George was in his fifties, Billy maybe ten years younger. George and Billy waved Ben over and Megan glanced up and back down again. Ben snagged a barstool and pulled it over into their small semicircle at the bar. Billy and Megan were seated, and George, who thought barstools were for sissies, stood at the bar. Billy, a shy man, always sat, hunched low over the bar, and Ben wondered if this was to hide his huge bulk. Billy was a natural wonder; he filled doorways and caused small children to stare, up and up as though at the foot of a mountain. Much of the time Billy seemed to be wishing for a mountain to hide behind. Iris was a longstanding part of this odd family, but she had mostly retired from bar life. Ben was a member of this group although he understood his status to be probationary. He knew George the best because they both were natural talkers. Billy was a kind mystery. Ben sat down and ordered a cup of coffee. Billy smiled and nodded to him, and George asked after Sarah. George inquired about the bandage on Ben's forehead, and Ben told him that Iris beat him up for being late with the rent. Ben was not sure how much George and Billy knew about his recent adventures. Megan stared at her beer and said nothing. Silence, which was bad bar behavior, followed.

George, who seemed to know something, looked at Megan and said, "Horse walks into a bar, orders a beer and a shot. Bartender says, 'Why the long face?'"

"Bad joke, George," Megan said.

"Who's joking? Why the long face?"

"I'm morose."

"What asshole made a beautiful lady like you morose?" George Monroe's question, directed at Megan and Ben, boomed across the bar. Moose Jaw regulars gave heed mostly to their own thoughts, their own conversations. Like securities dealers, of whom, as chance would have it, there was not one in the Moose Jaw, the regulars also idly monitored the blaring ticker tape that broadcast George's half of all his conversations. In response to George's question, Ben raised his hand. Kari, the bartender, approached the four of them, but George waved her off.

"That's not a drink order," George said. "It's a confession. We've identified the asshole."

Kari retreated. Megan nursed her Fat Tire. Ben sipped his coffee.

"What's morose mean?" asked Billy.

"The blues," George said. "It's what I get from wasting my valuable time with illiterate snowplow drivers like your own self."

"Ah," Billy said. "The blues. Been there."

66

Ben noticed that Billy, having learned that Megan had the blues, did not look at her. They were family. Billy was one of the adults in the childhood of which Megan would not speak. Ben saw them occasionally together. They talked in the familiar way of people who took each other for granted, who depended on each other, but they never looked each other in the eye, not even by accident. It was a marvel, which Ben meant to ask Megan about if she decided ever to speak to him again.

"Why can't I be the one to make you morose?" George asked. "I dream of making beautiful women morose."

"Because you're married," said Megan.

The three men greeted this remark with a silence both delicate and perplexed. None quite knew the words to this song.

"I shouldn't have had that last beer," Megan said. "It made me stupid. I know Ben is married. But he's not married in the same way that you are, George, or Billy. Is he? Or am I just stupid?"

"You're no more stupid than the rest of humanity. But you're a lot more morose," said George, for once softly.

"I may be stupid, but I refuse to be morose, at least in public. I'm going to drink a toast to happier days and go home." She tapped her bottle against George's. Billy extended his bottle for a tap, without looking up. Megan pointedly ignored Ben's lifted coffee cup.

"I'll give you a ride," Ben offered.

"Nope. I'll walk." She left, walking too carefully upright.

"I was morose once," George said. "It drove me to drink."

"Did drinking help?" Ben asked.

"Must've. Haven't been morose since."

Billy got off his barstool to go visit with a friend eating dinner against the far wall. The barstool groaned as he shifted his weight. As he passed, he looked Ben in the eye and patted him sympathetically on the shoulder. His face, round and plain, almost smiled, but seemed to hesitate, so that it frugally communicated only the intention of a smile.

George lowered his voice. "Aside from me, Billy Mapp is the smartest guy in the county. You drive into a snow bank at three in the morning, in a whiteout, you hope it's Billy comes along in the snowplow and not that moron, Phil. If Billy can't figure out how to drag you back on the road, then you just leave the car in the snow bank 'til spring. Billy sees a question, he asks a question. The only thing holding him back in life is that no one in this town, except me, is smart enough to give him any answers. It's also a handicap to him that he quit junior high to work on a road crew. I asked him how he got hired at that age. Turns out he was already six-four and two hundred pounds when he was fourteen. Grown some since. He was in here one night and asked me why ice forms on ponds before it does on rivers. I had to fish back to my college chemistry before I could give him a decent answer. He then spent a month pestering me with questions about chemistry. He's the most curious man in the county. I tried to hire him as a reporter, and I could tell he wanted the job, but how's he going to support his family on what I pay? Besides, as big as he is, he'd scare the county commissioners into telling the truth, and then there'd be nothing left for me to investigate. It would be the end of history in Summit County, and I'd have to close the paper."

George Monroe published the local paper, meaning he was the local paper. He wrote. He edited. He told merchants they were full of shit if they did not buy advertisements, and he stopped tourists on the street and dragged them into the same merchant's store and told them they were full of shit if they did not buy the new parkas that Fred had advertised that very morning. George wrote editorials on the new landfill (for), leash laws (against), and the march of real estate development. He wrote an editorial expressing his willingness to rethink his opposition to leash laws if they were applied only to bottom-dwelling, scum-sucking real estate agents. He once wrote an editorial excoriating himself for publishing ads from real estate companies.

George wore a brown beard that bristled straight out and wide. His bristling beard, his booming voice, his truculence, occupied a large space. In simple fact, he was a short, stocky man whose flannel shirt was always un-tucked, whose jeans were always frayed, and whose hiking boots were always immaculately oiled. There were very few simple facts about George, and he worked hard to keep it so. He often spent his evenings in the Moose Jaw arguing strenuously against his own editorials.

"So, my young friend," said George, "I'm guessing you have no idea what you're doing."

"Not a clue," Ben said.

"One more hopelessly confused motherfucker in paradise."

"You're the smart one. Tell me what to do."

"Can't help you," George said. "All guys are hopelessly confused motherfuckers on the subject of love."

"I suspected as much."

"I can tell you that Megan is a fine person."

"Agreed," said Ben.

"I don't know how she turned out so fine. Her family is flat-out whacked. And her ex-boyfriend is a worthless son of a bitch."

"He must be. The question is: who's worse; the worthless son of a bitch or me?"

"That's a question but a dumb one. A better one is why you come to a bar and drink coffee."

"Because all the lively people are in bars," Ben said.

"People in coffee shops aren't lively?"

"You're confusing lively with jittery."

Ben noticed George turn his head slightly to look behind him. George frowned. Following George's gaze, Ben saw that two men, both glaring, had taken station directly behind them.

"Hey, asshole!"

Ben looked at George. "I didn't read the paper today. What did you write to make these guys mad?"

"Sorry," George said, "this is one of those rare occasions where I'm not the asshole du jour." George ignored the men standing behind them and continued to speak directly to Ben. "Don't you remember how earlier you confessed to being an asshole? These two upright citizens agree with you."

"Me? I'm the asshole?"

"You're elected," said George.

Ben swiveled on his barstool to face the two men. He searched their faces and came up empty.

"The piece of work on your right," George said, "is Tyler Flanagan, Megan's older brother. The scumbag to your left is Megan's ex-boyfriend, Larry Porter. Larry is a great skier, who beats up women on the side."

Ben was confused. He tried to make sense of why this unlikely combination stood before him. Larry was unremarkable for Summit County: tall, athletic, a mop of blond hair. He looked like someone who had talked himself into this particular confrontation by spitting violently on his bathroom mirror. Tyler had an ordinary face with features that would have been even were they ever at rest. The muscles in his face clinched and unclenched in rhythmic waves, but the waves on one side did not match the waves on the other. Ben, a connoisseur of waters, thought of a river, running downstream on one side of Tyler's nose, upstream on the other. Stout, ponderous, square-jawed, he could have been a battering ram; except that when Ben looked into his eyes, they fluttered, as if nervous about what they might be asked to see. Ben noticed that Tyler had Megan's blue-green eyes; this was their only physical resemblance, but it made Ben angry.

"Stay out of this, George," said Larry. "Nobody cares that you were a tough guy twenty years ago."

"Get your sorry asses out of here," said George.

"Wait," Ben said. "What do you want with me?"

"We're going to teach you not to lead my sister into sin. You're of the Devil."

"You're Megan's brother? How can that be? What are you doing with the guy who broke her wrist?"

"Larry has come to Jesus. He wanted to marry Megan and remove the stain from their lives. Megan has always been willful and disobedient of God's Word."

Ben looked for some clue in Tyler's face that he might be using this language as a joke. Larry took a step to his right.

"Get off the damn barstool, Ben," whispered George, urgently. "He's about to hit you."

Larry reached into his jacket pocket. His fist emerged clenched and abnormally thick. Ben slipped belatedly off the barstool. He was telling himself that he could duck even a speeding bullet as Larry cocked his right fist beside his ear. The fist stayed there, frozen, as though Larry had turned into a statue of a boxer. Slowly, Larry's torso twisted backward away from Ben. He yelped in pain and the roll of dimes popped out of his fist and clattered to the floor. Billy let go of his wrist.

"Go home," Billy said. "Fighting gives me the morose."

"Makes you morose," George said.

"OK," Billy said.

Larry turned and shoved Billy hard in the chest. Billy took no notice except that he took both of Larry's hands in his. They could have been about to jitterbug except that Larry's hands had disappeared inside Billy's, like the hands of a baby. Billy squeezed and Larry's knees did a graceful dip.

"Go home," Billy said.

"OK, I'll go," Larry said. He glared at Ben. "Goliath won't always be around to protect you."

"I guess not," Ben said. "I just don't get why I need him." He turned to Tyler. "Why can't this be between me and Megan?"

"I love my sister," he snarled.

"So do I."

"I have to take care of my sister. I have to make sure she makes it home to God," Tyler said. His breathing was ragged. "She has been handmaiden to evil." The strange words made no sense to Ben; he could not decide whether they were rote repetition of stale phrases or a report of family anguish, fresh from Megan's life. Larry jerked his hands away from Billy's grip and rubbed them against the pain. Tyler rubbed his eyes, his temples, trying to rub away some other pain. Ben had the odd feeling that Tyler had forgotten him, had slipped into another, more vivid, present moment. Tyler stretched his neck, turned his face to the side, and pushed hard against his cheek with the flat of his hand. For a moment, his eyes rolled, as if he were looking at something over his shoulder, and his mouth stretched wide, showing a cave of yellow teeth. It was, Ben thought, a mouth shaped to fit a scream. Tyler took his hand from his face, his mouth closed, and his eyes came forward again and

71

looked on and through Ben. Tyler shook his head, motioned to Larry, and the two of them left. Ben struggled to find some emotional kinship between Tyler and Megan and was grateful he could not.

"Thanks, Billy," Ben said.

"No problem. I like to watch you and Megan reading to each other. I'll tell you a secret. I've started reading to my wife every night in bed—*Lonesome Dove*, great book. She says it's romantic, and it is. Married twenty years, three kids, and she's hot for me all over again. I didn't tell her I stole the idea from you."

"My God," George said, "romance could start blossoming all over the county. I might have to do a series in the paper." He finished his beer. "I'm out of here."

"It's early," Billy said. "You getting old, George?"

"Old, hell, I'm going home to read a little story to my wife."

Billy went back to sit with his friend, and Ben sat alone at the bar, watching the rippling surface of his coffee and thinking of the strange flow of Tyler's face.

. . . . .

"Pissants," said God.

He and Ben were squeezed into God's attic room. Ben had fetched two bottles of Fat Tire home from the Moose Jaw. Hearing the creak of God's rocker, Ben had climbed the stairs. The room was dark. As always, God faced the narrow window, watching a spray of stars arc over Buffalo Mountain. God had a ragged, gray afghan, knitted by Ben's grandmother, over his shoulders. The afghan was dimmed to a smudge of charcoal in the dark room. God's hair, also gray, unbraided now, fanned over his back. Ben stretched out on the narrow, hard bed and looked at God's back and the window over his shoulder. God looked old.

"Who?" Ben asked.

"Who have we been talking about?"

"Larry and Tyler?"

"Fundamentalists, birdbrain. Fundamentalists of every religious persuasion. Christians, Muslims, Jews, you name it. They're hateful little pissants. I love that word. Pissants. Very descriptive."

"What if Tyler is right?" Ben asked.

God's tone was impatient. "How can a pissant be right about anything?"

Ben was not sure. Maybe Tyler was right that Ben was wrong for Megan, right that she should not be seeing a married man with a divided heart. The imperative of family chose that moment to overtake Ben. This was the imperative that his father lived, at a cost that Ben could always feel as a child. Even his mother must have been driven by the same rule though Ben could never feel the price she paid. It occurred to him that his father did not exist only in Ben's world; that his father must have felt the cost to his mother because there was a cost to everything, and nothing was more emotionally spendy than family. Maybe Tyler, pissant that he was, had a grip on this piece of truth about the pull of family. Family was encoded in genes, in tradition, in religion; it took a terrible effort to destroy a family and, godlike, create another from fresh clay. This was the boldness of creation, to create yourself, to create a family, immediate and extended, related or not, to anchor yourself in your own place within a universe of your own devising. Tyler understood in some way the importance of family, but for him everything was created by God, and Ben found himself groping towards his own creation.

"Exactly," God said. "Your own creation, for better or worse. I may have screwed mine up, but maybe you will do better." Ben was so lost in his own thoughts that he did not know whether he had spoken aloud or to himself. God took a long pull from his beer and held the cool bottle against his cheek.

"What did you screw up?" Ben asked.

"I'm still waiting to see whether religion triumphs or not?"

Ben was confused. "And which side are you rooting for?"

"I am God, and I am without religion. My revelation to you is that I am a contrarian God; in addition, as you well know, to simply being contrary. The task of mankind, which is still in doubt, is to outgrow religion."

"Wait a minute," Ben said. "This is your revelation to me? What about your revelations to others, to the great religious figures?"

"Anybody who spreads God's word has never heard God's word. The only reason I reveal myself to you is because you don't believe in me, and you will never be a prophet to anyone but Sarah, and that will surely end about the time she is thirteen. I can rely on you, my friend, never to gossip about your conversations with God."

"So," Ben said. "You deny revelations to Moses, Jesus, Mohammed?"

"Remarkable people in their own way, but I never had the pleasure. To you, my skeptical friend, I will reveal all you need to know about religion and the Tylers of this world. There is a God. I am sitting before you. God likes Fat Tire. I get lonely on occasion and pay a visit to some kindred spirit like yourself. I am horrified at my own fallibility. Sometimes I simply can't remember what I must have been thinking. When religious figures assert the existence of God, it is only a lucky guess—they know nothing of me, and I know only slightly more. The responsibility of mankind is to dope out a way to conduct their affairs as if there were no God. Theology is simply astrology without that fun star chart. I gave no commandments. I am not the jealous God of the First Commandment. I am not barbaric enough to punish four generations of your offspring if you place another god before me; I would be nothing but grateful if you could find another god to assume responsibility for this mess. There are no chosen people. Who would choose one child over another? I don't play favorites, and I won't support either your football team or your country. I don't give a damn about anyone's sex habits, much less their dietary habits. If there were a message I wanted to communicate to the world, I am smart enough, and I hope kind enough, to think of a better way than having my own son tortured and killed. The idea of moral absolutes is simply silly—the great religions all say that killing is wrong except, of course, when the religion says it's just. They happily kill in the name of God. How would you feel, Ben, if people slaughtered each other in the name of Ben? The great truth is that morality is vitally important, but the moral choice depends utterly on the situation. Life is a test of your own devising. I warn you that the Tylers of this world may destroy all I had hoped for. The Enlightenment made me happy. The promise of reason. The advances of science, reason's child. The idea that people might figure out good things to do and do this out of love. But all this, which seemed so promising, could be a temporary aberration, drowned again in the rising tide of Tyler's fundamentalism, which seeks my destruction. So we both live in perilous times, you and I. I wish us both luck. Now, my friend, I am tired, and tired of being God. Let me rest, and tomorrow, with the new day, we will again find what hope there is to find and carry on a little longer."

Chapter Nine

The trail turned steeply upward at its beginning. The grass beside it was tall and thick and in the edge of the grass were bluebells. Ben looked for monkshood, dark, brooding purple, but decided it must be too early in the season. He saw some larkspur. He liked these flowers, whose shape was in their names—bells, hoods, and spurs. Sarah was on the trail ahead of him, slender, shape all up and down, waterfall of blond hair. Megan, behind her, also slender, tall, swayed slightly into the curved space of her geometry. Ben hoped this hike was a good idea.

It was the second week of June, and Ben and Megan had slowly edged back together in this romance of fits and starts. They agreed to be both close and distant, to take things slowly, and to be friends without being lovers. They worked out this agreement in sporadic late-night phone calls, in all the chance meetings at the library that Ben could invent a flimsy excuse for, and over coffee at the Roaster. The deal was sealed over a beer at the Moose Jaw, where Megan pointedly ordered onion rings and required Ben to eat one. They offered to each other a cautious toast, and Megan said, "This new arrangement is all a bunch of bullshit that gives us an excuse to keep seeing other, right?" And Ben said, "Of course, but we're not supposed to know that."

Ben had not heard a word from Karen except for a summer travel itinerary for Sarah that arrived in the mail. He reflected that the silence could be ominous, indifferent, or sheer forgetfulness. Sarah was not so forgetful. She had understood Karen's tumultuous visit to be related to Megan and began to see Megan as having some serious significance for their lives. She was still angry at her mother but sometimes a shadow also fell over her at mention of Megan. Ben had never made his feelings for Megan a secret, especially since Sarah read him like a first grade primer. He tried to talk with her but finally decided she could not well explain that which she did not herself understand. The idea for the hike was Ben's. He didn't want Sarah's negative feelings towards Megan to incubate and grow. He had carefully shielded Sarah from more than brief encounters with Megan, out of some concern that he, in his turn, did not fully understand. It occurred to him now that Megan might even decide that Sarah was a despicable brat. For all these reasons, but mostly for the fun of it, he suggested this hike. Both Megan and Sarah, separately, were studies in careful neutrality at the proposal. To each of them, he said, "OK, never mind, another time," whereupon each quickly said, "No, let's do it." So here they were.

Sarah was leader, always full of energy at hike's beginning. She hiked fast, perhaps to keep wary distance from Megan. On the steep stretch, the trail was full of grapefruit rocks, at once too large to be stepped on and too small. Ben picked his way through. Megan rolled her foot on a rock, and the dislodged rock bumped its way towards him until nesting itself in another brood of rocks.

Topping a rise, the trail flattened and became smooth, packed earth. Sarah might have broken into a schoolgirl skip across this good ground had Ben been her only audience. Megan might have, also. Neither did, and, lagging behind, Ben skipped a little to spark some happiness but gave it up for want of an audience. This group, he thought, was wet wood, impervious to fire.

Aspen leaned in from both sides and mottled with leafy shadow the smooth earth. Above, there were white, papery limbs and tethered leaves that tried frantically to sail away on every vagabond breeze. Blue, mountain sky made patchwork pieces through the shifting aspen canopy. Sarah stooped to inspect a flower beside the trail and then shifted to allow Megan an admiring peek. Sarah darted ahead. Ben caught up to Megan who shrugged in Sarah's direction, narrowed her eyes in Ben's, and quickly left Ben to shrug or squint or skip at his solitary pleasure.

The trail climbed sharply again through the cool aspen glade. After thirty minutes of steady hiking, the trail curved and the trees were on the left and a bench of meadow on the right. The meadow was thick with tall grass and early wildflowers, blue and yellow and white. Stopping, looking back, they could see how quickly the valley had dropped below them. Ben, standing behind Sarah, cupped the back of her neck with his hand. She nervously pulled away from his hand and then allowed herself to lean slightly back against him.

A memory came to Ben of his father cupping the back of his neck. They stood together, surveying the completion of some stage in the endless progression of farm chores. A section of drainage ditch lay polished before them. Ben had slashed the tall, thirsty weeds and flung them into the pasture. His father came behind and shoveled silt from the bottom of the ditch. The wet silt lay over sheathes of cut, green weeds that did not yet know they were dying. The water ran muddy from their labors, and father and son were sweaty and dirty. The two of them stood, for this brief moment, admiring the beauty of their work, before turning to the next section of ditch. For Ben, the work was defined by these interludes. They would finish a section and simply look at it. Ben never knew how long a section was since the only markers were in his father's eye. It did not occur to Ben to wonder how long they needed to work before stopping to survey the result, before his father once again cupped his neck, and Ben leaned against him, as now Sarah did.

When his father dropped his large hand from Ben's neck, the two of them went back to work. They moved together in the small world created by their labor. Inside that world, there was the steady flash of the curving blade of Ben's brush axe. Slashing through the weeds, the axe often buried itself in the soft dirt of the ditch bank. Ben stood in the shallow water in his rubber boots. When the axe became too layered in sticky, black earth, he held it in the water and scraped the earth away with the toe of his boot. He stopped to pick up the cut weeds and tossed them to the edge of this world he shared with his father. He made the bank clean so that his father would have an easy, low throw of the heavy, dripping mud in his shovel. The axe of the son made vertical swipes through their space, the shovel of the father made steady, lateral tosses, and the pace of father and son was the same. Ben grew tired, as the sweat oozed from his skin, but he knew he could keep working until his father called the next break. He did not complain because he was happy in this work and because he had never heard his father complain. A frog leaped from the bank and brushed against Ben's leg before splashing into the water. Ben, always afraid of snakes, jumped. His father looked up and a slow smile spread on his weathered face.

Ben missed his father. Hanging out with his students at school, Ben sometimes heard complaints about parents. "My father flies to Australia with his girlfriend to go snorkeling, but he can't afford to buy me a new snowboard." Children bitterly denounced their parents over the inequitable division of excess. Ben's father would have struggled to locate Australia on a map. He had no toys except an old shotgun and a brace of pointers. His dreams were small. He dreamed of having one end meet the other at month's end. He had the workingman's dream that his son might grow up to have soft hands. He had no toys because his son kept outgrowing his shoes. It was a life of small things: a sturdy shovel, a clean section of irrigation ditch, and a son who did not complain.

Ben thought that from these small things he had come far. He went to college. He could find Australia on a map. He found a way to move high in the mountains and to leave behind forever the South of his childhood: flat, wooded, humid, and backward. He hoped he was on his way to becoming a fulltime teacher of history and to living always in this place. He had come far, far enough for him, not far enough for Karen.

Ben wanted to ask his father what to do and knew the question could not be asked or answered. Although his father was buried with a shovel, he was not buried with a shovel. There would be no digging his way out of the grave, leaning on his favorite tool, and pondering the mystery of a child who wanted to know precisely how many stars had taken station in the sky. Ben's questions, then and now, were, to his father, the questions of a child. His father did not read books or go to movies. There were no flamboyant Karens in his world. His father would not have married Karen; he would have been astonished at her very existence. He prepared me well, Ben thought, if all I am called upon to do is dig ditches with my child.

79

Ben found himself alone in the meadow. Megan and Sarah had slipped up the trail without him, leaving him digging in his past. Ben followed, and the trail entered a forest of lodgepole pine, cool and shaded, but again climbing steeply. The trees, closely spaced, competing for sunlight, did not bother putting out needles except at the very top. Ben liked climbing alone: it created an illusion of simplicity. He hiked slowly. Sometimes a bit of breeze pushed a note from a female voice down to him. He could not tell a voice, or any word; the note had floated away from the voice, from the word, to live for a little while as vagrant vapor in the pines. Ben climbed and, after a long while of being alone in the tall trees, he heard the sound of Meadow Creek. The pines left off and the country opened to gentle swells with blue spruce growing beside the creek. The stream came down through a meadow and pooled as it puzzled its way around a hill. Megan and Sarah sat on a sandbar beside this pool with bare feet in the water. The sunlight reflected from the water and from Megan's honeyed hair and Sarah's blond hair. The two of them sat close together, their hips touching, and sometimes leaning their heads together to add murmur to the whispers of the water.

Ben joined them, seating himself a respectful distance from this fragile union. Removing boots and socks, he placed his feet in the icy water and sucked in his breath. Megan and Sarah hooted and called him wimp. The three of them sat on this small beach, the sun warming them, the clear water sliding past, and, standing sentinel, the tall, dignified spruce. Making games, they competed to see who could keep feet longest in the water before having to warm them in the sand of the beach. Sarah turned out to have the bravest feet.

The three of them talked of small things. A boy in Sarah's class inspected his boogers and then popped them in his mouth and ate them. Megan argued that he inspected them first so that he could reject any that might turn out to be yucky. They considered in detail the characteristics of good and bad boogers and meandered eventually to the philosophical conclusion that bad boogers were those that came from someone else's nose. Megan warned Sarah not to be too hard on this boy because one day she might grow up to kiss him, and Sarah was filled with excitement at the prospect of kissing a boy and alarm that he might have eaten boogers in his sordid past.

Satisfied that they had fully explored the world of boogers, the conversation turned naturally to spirit animals. Megan explained this notion of an animal whose spirit you share. Her spirit animal was the ermine, reclusive creature of silky fur and slender neck, ferocious hunter. Once, she had traveled into the deep forests of the Gore Range on snowshoes. She napped on a boulder in the thin winter sun and awoke to the curious study of an ermine dressed in winter white. They admired each other, and Megan was given to understand that this ermine, if forced to be human, would be her. Sarah thrilled to this notion. Ben tried to rain on their parade by reminding them that the elegant ermine, dressed in summer brown, was a simple weasel, and the two of them threw handfuls of sand at his skepticism.

Sarah tried to pick a spirit animal. She liked the soaring eagle, the soft eyes of the deer, the cute, lively spirit of the chipmunk. She liked Ollie, but he was not wild; a spirit animal should not slobber on your face. Neither, Megan reminded her, should boys you kiss have eaten boogers. Sarah kept returning to the imagined wonder of the ermine, a creature she had never seen. Megan explained that, since there were only so many kinds of animals, it was possible that two people could share the same spirit animal. Sarah walked happily through this tactfully opened door and adopted the ermine as her own.

It was left to Ben to pick a spirit animal. Sarah and Megan examined several possibilities for him. Sarah happily suggested skunk and Megan applauded. Sarah described in graphic detail the odiferous agony of long car trips when her father thought she was asleep. The two of them carefully considered the merits of coyote, hyena, and buzzard. They rejected the coyote as being a creature with too much intelligence. Turning serious, they agreed that the only choice for a fisherman was the trout. Ben surprised them both by claiming the otter. He told of an otter on the Blue who had chosen Ben for a playmate. The day of their meeting, it showed off its tricks by swimming tight circles in the middle of a pool. It popped out on a rock to study at length Ben's tricks with a fly rod. It seemed to delight in the looping line, shedding jewels of water into the sunlight. Watching, the otter rubbed its paws together excitedly. Approving, the otter slipped back into the water and did more tricks, surfacing like a porpoise, rolling, and bouncing off underwater boulders. It climbed back onto its midstream rock, and Ben smiled and laughed. The otter dived again and swam straight for Ben. Ben expected it to veer away at the last minute, but it came on with great speed, hit his leg under the water, climbed up his thigh, and did a back flip into the water. Having shared a laugh, having earned the last laugh, it swam happily home.

Having done small things, having talked of small things, Ben and Sarah and Megan also headed home. The trail was downhill and welcoming. They walked close to each other. On the bench of meadow, where the wildflowers grew, Sarah ran into the tall grass to lie among the flowers. Watching her, Ben and Megan held hands and leaned against each other. Sarah came back, tears in her eyes, with a single flower for each of the three of them. Sarah smiled and explained to Megan that lying in the flowers always made her cry, and Megan solemnly agreed that this was as it should be. On the section of flat trail, with the good, smooth ground, Megan and Sarah held hands and skipped. On the steep section below, with the rolling, grapefruit rocks, Sarah, agile, catlike child, reached one hand to Ben and the other to Megan, so that the two of them might keep her from stumbling.

Chapter Ten

As Ben knocked on Tyler Flanagan's front door, he was willing to admit that this might not be one of his brighter ideas. But Tyler was Megan's brother; he was some kind of family. Maybe there was an actual human being underneath the religious nuttiness; surely, no one could stand to listen to themselves spout crap all the time. Even the hardest working nuts must have to take brief sanity breaks once in a while. Maybe Ben could catch Tyler on break and they could talk about fishing or something. Tyler had taken a dislike to Ben, but maybe this was simple protectiveness towards a sister he loved. Tyler was certainly correct that Ben was a married man, and a brother could take exception to this. Ben thought he might be able to make peace, or, if Tyler insisted on being an enemy, it could be useful to take his measure. Maybe Ben could also learn more about the unanswered questions of Megan's past.

Ben had put Sarah on a plane for Houston the day before, so she was safely out of the way. Tyler had clearly wanted Larry to beat Ben up in the Moose Jaw; Ben did not know whether Tyler personally had such intentions, but he had seemed big enough and crazy enough. Ben figured he might as well find out, and now Sarah would not be around to observe any new bandage job. Ben was not too worried. His experience was that most people needed to plan their way into battle. They did not cope well with surprise, and Tyler would certainly be surprised at this Saturday morning visit. Since Ben had not told Iris or Megan of his plan, he had wondered if he would have to hire a private detective to find out Tyler's address, but the phone book worked as well and was free. He had not told Iris or Megan because both would try to stop him, or come with him as bodyguards.

Ben was touched by their protectiveness of him; in their separate ways, they were both tough women, and this pleased him. With any luck, they might never find out about this little mission. They were also smart women, but Westerners did not always catch on quickly to the subtleties that shaped some Southerners, and especially Ben; Ben left the South to escape its twisted cultural relics, but he had not escaped all of it. He despised the backwardness, the religious and racial bigotry. Much of the South would prefer to erase from history the Enlightenment and return straightaway to the Middle Ages, where king and bishop made pawns of peasants by promising heavenly riches and salvation from Hell. In the meantime, King and Bishop agreed to take on the burdensome earthly chore of grabbing all the gold. Barefoot Southerners, privates in General Lee's army, too poor to own a slave themselves, fought and died in countless droves so that the plantation aristocracy, supported by the church, could keep its slaves and its money; in return, the aristocracy generously promised the private to protect him from the hell of having a black man marry his sister. The barefoot private went gratefully off on this crusade, and it never occurred to him, looking down at his blackened feet, that his only natural ally in this world also had black feet. Ben had never seen much evidence that this part of Southern culture had changed, except that now the moneyed classes, in an additional burst of generosity, had promised poor whites that they would keep black men from marrying their brother.

On the other hand, Ben took a childlike joy in the defensive little quirk that ran through many Southerners—the perverse delight in seeming to be less than you were. It was the "poor country lawya" syndrome, welcoming underestimation. So, if Iris thought he was overly diplomatic, overly cautious and indecisive, that was OK with Ben. He knew it to be the truth about him, but he also knew that it was not the whole truth.

Tyler's home was gray and had the shape and size of a double-wide trailer, but it had a garage, sat on a concrete foundation, and occupied its own city lot. Tulips beside the front door, their blossoms come and gone, still stood uncut, three weeks into June. There was a loud television inside, and Ben had to knock a second time. A woman answered the door. She was friendly but distracted. When Ben gave his first name and said he was here to see Tyler, she smiled and motioned him inside. The entry hallway reached in two directions, one into the room with the television and the other into the kitchen. The woman turned her back on Ben and headed for the kitchen, and he followed. She motioned him to a kitchen chair and asked if he wanted a glass of water.

"I'm Thelma. What did you say your name was?"

"Ben."

"This is Nathan." Nathan sat hunched over at the table. Ben predicted to himself that Nathan was a sixth grader.

"Pull up a chair. Tyler's in the shower. He'll be out soon. Sure you don't want something to drink?"

Ben pulled up a chair beside Nathan, who was restringing the leather laces of a catcher's mitt. Thelma disappeared in the direction of the noise from the television. Nathan looked up and looked back down quickly when Ben greeted him. Nathan seemed faintly pleased when Ben guessed out loud that he was a sixth grader. He mumbled that he was about to be eleven and would be in fifth grade in the fall. He kept his eyes on the mitt, and Ben thought this was more from shyness than interest in the mitt. He was a chunky kid, and Ben wondered why chunky kids were always assigned by coaches to be catchers. Ben immediately formed a picture in his mind of a chunky kid who demands to be a shortstop and turns out, against all odds, to be a star.

"Nice mitt," said Ben.

Nathan barely nodded. He was making a mess of the restringing because he kept letting the laces become too loose.

"Did you ever want to be a shortstop?" Ben asked. Ben thought perhaps his theory was right because Nathan looked sharply up for a moment, still not looking at Ben, but then shook his head. Ben cautioned himself against thinking he was too brilliant, since every kid on the team likely wanted to be shortstop. Ben also noted to himself that he was thinking unusually fast because he was keyed up over seeing Tyler. Nathan began tearing down his failed work, and Ben offered to help. Nathan looked up at him, and Ben thought he saw a sad kid, but the look was too brief to know. In any event, he seemed to have lost interest in stringing the mitt and handed it listlessly to Ben. He went to the refrigerator, came back with a tub of chocolate pudding, and ate as Ben began stringing the mitt. Ben had the laces tight and was ready to knot it when Tyler came into the room, stopped abruptly, and bellowed. Nathan jumped up and ran out of the room as Thelma ran in. Ben glanced up, saw no blows coming, and told Tyler to hang on a second because he was almost done. Tyler yelled at Thelma as Ben tightened the laces one last time and pulled tight the knot. His racing mind was thinking that it would be very awkward, even for this obvious idiot, to hit someone while he was fixing your son's mitt. Tyler and Thelma were having a confused conversation, which ended with her saying, "Oh, that Ben!"

Ben stood up, handed the mitt to Tyler, and said, "What do you think? Tight enough?" In this delicate moment, he also liked the idea of Tyler having something in his hand besides a fist. He had forgotten how big and solid Tyler was. Ben saw Nathan edging his way back down the hall to see what was going on; Thelma also saw this and quickly took Nathan back to the other part of the house. Tyler was sputtering and looked down with surprise to see he was holding a catcher's mitt. He seemed not to know what to do with it and reflexively handed it back to Ben. Ben said thanks, which confused Tyler further.

Ben quickly said, "Pull up a chair. I just want to talk to you. I promise you can hit me later if you want to."

Tyler seemed confused about being offered a chair in his own home but was recovering his equilibrium. "OK, but this better be good."

Ben moved slowly in the direction of the other side of the table, and Tyler pulled out a chair on the opposite side. As soon as Tyler committed to a chair, Ben reversed course and sat quickly in the chair beside Tyler. If it was hard to hit someone holding a catcher's mitt, it was also hard to yell at the person sitting beside you rather than across from you.

"What have you got to say?" Tyler asked stiffly, as he backed his chair slightly away from Ben.

"Mostly," said Ben, calmly, "I wanted to hear out what you had to say to me. I don't like causing problems between family."

There was little left for Tyler to do at this point but talk, and Ben thought he was home free with the first part of this business. It popped into his mind that he had Karen to thank for this skill at maneuvering Tyler. Ben had had plenty of time to study at the feet of the master.

In the Moose Jaw, Tyler had a prepared speech, but this time there was none. "I want...You are to leave my sister alone." Tyler began to drift back into a version of the speech he had given at the Jaw, and Ben found nothing illuminating in it. It was the standard fundamentalist argument about God and sin and everlasting damnation, beginning with an unprovable assumption and ending with absolute truth. It was a tricky circle to square, and Ben thought it doubtful that Tyler would succeed where Aquinas had failed. When Tyler warmed to the topic, his voice fell into the pastoral singsong cadence that Ben was brought up on in the South. When Tyler coughed, Ben jumped up and got him a glass of water, and this disoriented Tyler enough that he briefly dropped the singsong and talked in normal tones for a while. He would then get excited over some point and fall again into the singsong cadence and strange religious language. Tyler seemed to realize that Ben had caught him off guard and had him at some kind of disadvantage. He briefly became threatening and told Ben he would "thrash him within an inch of his life" if the Bible did not require him to be welcoming to a guest in his home. Ben could not think where the Bible said this, but he nodded in hearty agreement with this scriptural command. Ben took the opportunity to edge his chair closer to Tyler, which made Tyler uncomfortable. The phrase "critical distance" popped into Ben's mind. The phrase had been the mantra of his karate teacher in college. The survivable space was an inch out of range, or more tricky, in close where a blow had no chance to gather momentum. Ben had been an indifferent student of karate, renowned mostly for having collected over time more stitches in his left eyebrow than anyone within his teacher's memory. Ben had mastered the theory of critical distance but regularly failed to apply this knowledge to incoming punches.

Ben tried to get some sense of why Tyler was OK with Larry, the breaker of wrists, and not with him, and it boiled down to the fact that Larry was a believer who had joined Tyler's church. Tyler angrily said that Ben was not a believer, and Ben firmly agreed. Plus, Ben was married. Ben asked him if it would be different if he were divorced, but in Tyler's religious sect you got the one time to be married in the eyes of God and that was it. Ben was growing tired of it all and angry. He had been right in the Moose Jaw. There was nothing of Megan in this stupid man, nothing but the beautiful eye color, and this again made Ben angry. There was no sign of humor or kindness or love, only the rote and fevered repetition of nonsense. Megan was right to say she had no family; at least Ben finally understood this part.

Ben was baffled that the two of them could be related. He still hoped to learn more about Megan's childhood. "You and Megan grew up here? Did you get along when you were kids?" Tyler's eyes widened, but Ben had no clue whether from anger or fear.

"What has Megan told you?"

Ben said, "Not a darn thing. That's why I asked."

"And I won't tell you anything, either. It's not your business. This family is not your business. You have been warned to stay away. Stay away from my sister."

"I care about your sister."

Tyler pushed the side of his face upwards with his big hand. "You care about Megan in this world. This world is not important. Our father waits for her in the next world."

Ben found this was an odd phrase. "Do you mean God?"

"Our father...Yes, God. God waits for us all. Megan faces a terrible punishment."

"Why would God want to punish Megan?"

Tyler rubbed his face again. "Punishment can be from love. God punishes his children. Hell waits for those who choose the wrong path. You. It waits for you if you don't go back to your wife and leave my family alone. Go back to Texas. We don't need you here. I can help Megan. You can only hurt her."

Ben wondered about the reference to Texas and thought he had probably found the source of the letter to Karen about Megan. He's a religious nut, thought Ben. He's crazy on top of it. Ben was not sure whether he was dangerous or not. Ben took the catcher's mitt off the table and slipped it on his left hand. As he did when he was a kid, he began idly hitting the sweet spot with his fist. Tyler took this as an opportunity to talk some more about religion; he seemed compulsively unable to stop, and Ben could not listen to much more. Like Megan, he found himself being all done with Tyler. Tyler was talking about the proper place of women. Ben interrupted and asked, "So Thelma submits to you?"

Tyler nodded and said, "She is a godly woman."

"And if God decreed it the other way, you would submit to Thelma?"

Ben could see the question made Tyler angry, but he was done caring. He leaned in closer to Tyler.

"Man is made in God's image…"

Ben interrupted sharply, "But if the Bible said God was a woman, if it was all reversed, you would submit to the command?"

"If the Bible said it, I would do it."

"What bullshit." Ben watched Tyler's right arm, with his hand resting on the table. As he expected, the muscle in his arm clenched, and the back of Tyler's hand came up towards Ben's leaning face. Ben smothered the hand in the catcher's mitt as it came up and pushed the hand sharply back down on the table. Tyler struggled briefly to raise his pinned hand, but his arm was at a bad angle, and Ben was surprised and relieved at how quickly he gave up. He also filed away Tyler's ponderous reflexes. Ben let loose his hand and slid his chair away from Tyler, this time outside the critical distance. He took off the mitt and set it softly on the table.

Ben said, "Thanks for talking to me. I don't think we have anything else to talk about. Here is what I want to tell you. You're kind of a nut case, but it's a free country. All you can think about is weird ideas and beating up people who don't do what you want.

You're a big, dumb guy, and I expect you can beat me up anytime you want to. Just keep in mind that I won't care whether you can beat me up. I've been beaten up before. It doesn't much matter to me. I'd rather be left in peace, but I don't really think you can hurt me that much, except for hitting me over the head. If all you care about is beating me up, we can go outside now, and you can get started. I don't care. But I will do whatever I can figure out to do about my life. And Megan will do the same. And it won't have a damn thing to do with whether I have to take a beating from you every single day. All you're going to do is tire yourself out. It would be better if we lived in peace. I have known some good religious people. You're an embarrassment to them. Now, if you want to get started on today's beating, just follow me out the door. I will fight back to the best of my poor abilities, but that should be no problem for a tough guy like you."

Ben turned and left, knowing that Tyler would not follow. In the hallway, he nodded to Thelma, who had been listening in. She didn't exactly smile, but she also didn't seem too unhappy with him. A schoolyard bully, thought Ben. He did not rule out the possibility that Tyler might give him that beating one day, if he lost his temper, but he doubted it. Ben was light-hearted to have this chore over with and relieved by his view that Tyler was a bully, a nutcase, but perhaps not dangerous. Ben was mostly baffled that Tyler was so stupid—how could he be related to Megan?

…..

Ben drove home. Ollie came running over with a stick, and Ben threw it. He wondered how many times he would have to throw the stick for Ollie to get tired of this game and quit. He knew that his own arm would wear out before Ollie did. He thought about assembling a team of throwers. It could be a town event in the park. Barbecue and beer, and people could pay for turns at stick-throwing. They could call it the Ollie Festival. Massage therapists could be standing by at intervals to rub up throwing arms and Ollie's legs. Ollie would be in heaven, and the community would declare Ben a

Town Father. As Ben indulged his active fantasy life, Iris came outside, and the two of them sat on the grass.

Ben said, "Tell me more about Tyler Flanagan."

"Ah, I heard you had a little dust-up with Tyler and Larry at the Jaw."

"How'd you hear?"

Iris laughed. "How did I not hear? George, Kari the bartender, about six others. I never even need to leave the house. The only one I didn't hear from is Billy, who saved your ass. But Billy would have known I would hear from George, so he's excused."

"The Town Mother," said Ben.

"What?"

"Never mind. Tell me about Tyler. Is he dangerous?"

"Tyler's family has been in this valley for three generations. My parents and their parents welcomed his grandparents to this valley, and they never spoke to me about it with anything but regret. They're all whacked, except for Megan. Who knows, maybe Nathan will turn out all right, but I worry, and I know Megan does. Tyler's grandparents stole cows. His father poached trout from one of my father's ponds, and when Tyler was younger, no contractor could leave a tool overnight at a construction site. I know of at least three girls who went out with him in high school who never could quite decide later whether they had sex with him or were raped. These days, Tyler's just a dumbass and a pious jerk. His family has always had that pious streak. The joke in the valley was that his father always prayed over the trout he stole. And then there's Megan. Grew up in the middle of all that craziness. Never stole a thing. She once caught a boy being mean to my Laurie and kicked him in the ass. She didn't have to do that. My Laurie's so retarded she never knew she was being made fun of. But Megan knew. And I found out about it, just like I find out about everything in this valley. I watched Megan. Watched her put herself through college waiting tables. I watched her close because I thought she could have been Laurie without the brain damage. And I watched Tyler making good money driving a backhoe and never giving his sister a dime. Not a dime. Hell, he could have put her through college on all the tools he stole. That

91

child pulled herself up. And when she was late with her tuition check at the university, I would get a call. And then Jeff, the manager at the Golden Buffalo, would get a call. And at the end of a shift, he would pull Megan aside and tell her that some crazy tourist had left her a thousand dollar tip. I know everybody, and as much as I know anybody, I know Tyler. Nah, he's not dangerous, at least as long as you don't go out on a date with him. He's a bully with a temper, but what the hell, a lot of people think I'm a bully with a temper. Larry, on the other hand, I'm not so sure about. I've got my eye on him, and so does the sheriff. But you don't need to worry about Tyler. Just stay away from him."

"Yes, ma'am."

"And, Ben. Don't tell Megan what I told you about her family. She's touchy. And especially don't tell her what I said about the tuition."

"Not a peep."

Chapter Eleven

On their way to climb a high peak, Ben and Megan followed the Arkansas River down from Leadville. The river was on their left and a massive wall of mountains on their right. The river cut through brown hills and the water was blue or green or gray depending on the light. The light in the valley was always changing as the clouds clinging to the big mountains lost their grip and fell across the valley, shedding angry lightning as they passed. In the river, with its changing colors, there were bleached white boulders. Ben thought of the trout lying behind the boulders and picked out places he would fish. He entertained himself thus as he drove.

Sarah had been in Texas for a week. Ben missed her and worried about her, but he relished the time to have fun with Megan and the respite from responsibility. Like everyone who climbs mountains, he and Megan went to see what possibilities opened up from the top.

"Sarah is starting to like me a little bit," Megan said.

"What's not to like," Ben said. "Plus, she has a good heart. My goal in life is to grow up to be as nice a person as she is."

Megan reached and touched his arm, and Ben liked it that more and more they could talk with a touch or a nod or a look.

"Maybe," he said, "it could be possible for two people to never need any words at all."

"Think, Ben, think. To do that you would have to learn to shut up once in a while."

"Well, there is that." Ben tried shutting up, and they rode in silence. Ben laughed to himself about how many things he wanted to talk about when ordered to shut up. In recent years, he had often withdrawn into unhappy silence with Karen. He glanced over at Megan and wanted to tell her how he liked her hair when it was tied back, but he maintained his experiment in silence as they traveled between river and mountains. Megan came up from her own thoughts and released him from silence by saying, "I'm sorry about Tyler."

Ben was lodged in a crack where he was not sure whether she was talking about the incident at the Moose Jaw, which she would have doubtless heard about but had never mentioned. Or maybe, it was the incident at Tyler's house. "Sorry about what?"

"Don't play dumb, Ben. Tyler and Larry jumping you at the Moose Jaw."

"Not a problem. I had Billy to take care of me."

"It is a problem. But it won't happen again, at least with Tyler. I had a talk with him. I think he will behave now."

Ben wondered if perhaps that was the real reason he had escaped Tyler's house without any bruises. There were complicated undercurrents in a small town.

Megan continued, "I found out Iris talked with him, too. And she had Hector Morales, the sheriff, talk to Larry. Iris and Hector are close. But don't tell Iris I told you this stuff because she made me promise not to tell."

"I'll try to keep it all straight. But thanks, to all of you. Thanks for taking care of me."

Megan gave him a sharp look to see if he was being sarcastic, and Ben looked at her and touched her hand to show he was not. Ben said, "It's not a big deal."

Megan looked straight ahead and said, "It is a big deal. Because I was ashamed."

The two of them held hands and rode in silence. Ben looked at the river with its changing colors beneath the shifting sky. Megan looked at the mountains and the heavy clouds that moved among them, touching and letting go. When Ben could stand it no longer, he touched Megan's cheek with the back of his fingers.

Megan finally said, "I hate that Tyler is so angry."

"And, if I have it right, that is all you want to say about Tyler?"

"Yes."

Ben said, "See? I'm so proud. I'm learning the rules of Megan."
Again, Megan turned to search his face. "I'm serious," Ben said.
"Isn't that what we're doing together? Learning the rules of each
other?"

"OK. Yes."

In Buena Vista, they stopped for ice cream and walked a little
under the shade of the huge cottonwoods. They kissed with the taste
of ice cream in their mouths, and it made their knees weak. A little
boy, standing nearby, giggled.

They drove on south, with more high mountains still on their
right, set far back from the valley floor. The mountains were green
along flanks and shoulders and then, above tree line, were gray as
they rose up and up into the cold sky. Ben and Megan were headed
south and west to climb a big mountain like those that now bordered
their path. Neither had given much thought to why they were
driving past these mountains to climb another more remote and
distant. Maybe it was because these mountains had stuffy names, like
Princeton and Harvard and Yale. Ben and Megan were heading for a
mountain called San Luis, more melodious, clearly more saintly. The
highway skirted the town of Salida and turned west to squeeze
through Monarch Pass. Ben and Megan speculated about whether it
was a pass paying homage to royalty or to butterflies; they wished for
the latter. Climbing, they hoped the top of the pass would be draped
in blue spruce, with every frond drooping under layers of golden
butterflies. They painted between them this vivid picture and felt
sorry for the poor people in other cars for whom the trees were not
lighted in gold.

Down from the pass, they followed Tomichi Creek into the open
hills of ranch country. In the irrigated bottoms, the grass was deep
green beneath the low, brown hills, and higher, the silver sage. They
passed a rancher in black rubber boots, leaning on his shovel, and
Ben thought that he and his father could have worked for this
rancher because cleaning irrigation ditches was something they
understood. They also understood the joy of leaning on a shovel.
Ben expounded to Megan the virtues of the long-handled shovel and
theorized that ranchers bought for themselves a beautiful shovel

with a long handle to lean on and survey the world. He rudely suggested that ranchers bought short-handled shovels for the hired help to promote productivity. Megan made fun of him for thinking he was the only one who understood about shoveling and topped his every shoveling story with one from her own childhood on a hardscrabble sliver of ranch at nine thousand feet. Ben marveled at her ability to talk about her childhood while never mentioning another person in it. They argued through twenty miles of rolling hills about their relative childhood hardships and agreed at the end only that the rancher they had flashed past was probably still leaning on his shovel, listening to the gurgling ditch, smelling the earth, and watching ripples of mountain breeze trickle through tall, green grass.

Ben and Megan turned south again and climbed beside the falling waters of Cochetopa Creek. They entered a tight, twisty canyon with outcropping rock like rusted iron. Rounding a curve, Ben braked suddenly at a bighorn sheep beside the road. The sheep's horns, sweeping back around its head, seemed to Ben to be two great lobes of exposed, corrugated brain. Deer were twitchy, impulsive creatures, senseless in the face of oncoming traffic. This sheep waited calmly for them to pass, utterly indifferent to the advent in his world of hunks of speeding metal. Leaving the canyon, Ben and Megan turned from the paved road, turned from the creek, and began a long dirt-road loop that would eventually bring them to the base of San Luis Peak. They climbed through aspen groves and meadows and forests of lodgepole pine. In this remote country, the pine forests had not been logged, and the trees were big and grew at a respectful distance from each other, allowing the bunchgrass to form parks between them, inviting creatures to walk on the grass and wander among the towering trees. Ben and Megan declined the invitation because they had begun, in the open meadows, to catch sight of the great, sloping bulk of San Luis, standing alone in the La Garita Wilderness.

They were excited at these glimpses of the mountain and impatient to hike away from their hunk of metal. Parked finally at the trailhead, they forced themselves to bolt a lunch of ham sandwiches before setting out. They bumped into each other as they assembled their backpacks and prompted each other to remember matches and moleskin. Backpacks shouldered, the two of them stood for a moment looking up the trail as it wound beside Stewart Creek.

"I'm not going to sleep with you," Megan said.

"You can't just refuse to sleep with me. Out of the blue like that. I refuse to sleep with you first."

"That's crazy. You can't be first when I was first."

"I thought about it first, but I was too polite to say it because I didn't want to hurt your feelings," Ben said.

"So, if I had offered to sleep with you, you would have declined?"

"Yeah, probably. That's it. Something very like that."

"You are a lying dog. With ticks. And fleas."

"You won't sleep with me just because I've got ticks and fleas?" Ben asked.

"I won't sleep with you until...something...I don't know..." Megan threw up her hands. "Until we're done with dumb."

Ben wondered why she felt the need to remind him of a deal they had so recently worked out. Maybe she worried that he had misunderstood the kissing in Buena Vista. They had made an agreement to keep seeing each other but maintain some distance. Like all rules about sex, it was both silly and wise.

Ben tried to put his arms around her but couldn't because of the backpack. He put his hands on her shoulders and kissed the top of her lowered head. "Hey, we made a deal. The good part of the deal for me is I get to spend time with you while my slow brain works out my problems. Right now, that's all I want."

Megan put a hand on top of one of Ben's. "I know. Me, too. I've got my own problems. What I really think is that you'll work out yours before I work out mine."

"Is that why you're so patient with me?"

"One reason," said Megan.

"Whatever the reason, I'll take it."

Megan looked up at Ben. "I'm scared we won't work out. And I'm just as scared we will."

"I'll take it. Just so we get to spend time together," Ben said fiercely. "Right now, you're scared, and I'm feeling pretty brave. When I get scared, you can take a turn at being brave. Deal?"

Megan took a deep breath. "Deal."

"Good. Just don't come whining to me for sex in the middle of the night. I hate it when women beg."

Megan kneed him gently in the crotch and they set off to hike San Luis. Early on, the trail followed the edge of grassy bluffs overlooking the creek. Ben lagged behind as he stopped to peer into pools, watching brook trout suspended in clear water. Sometimes one lifted slowly from its station, barely pricked the surface film, and drifted back down with a mayfly snack. Ben wondered if the trout could taste the mayflies. A dish as beautifully presented as a mayfly should be a sensuous feast to the trout; Ben hoped it was so, hoped they ate for some other purpose than the endless race to store enough fat to survive the high, harsh winters.

The trail left the creek and the treacherous bogs and willows that surrounded it. Ben and Megan entered the shade of thick woods, and the trail climbed gradually, unremittingly upward. They were grateful for the shade as they began to sweat under the weight of their packs. Hiking steadily, they could see nothing but the trail and the big pines around them. Megan led and let them stop now and then for a quick drink. Her good humor restored, she stopped once to negotiate with a squirrel, a jousting knight errant, blocking their path. The squirrel ran a little way up a tree, chattered angrily, and then ran back down to stand in the trail. Megan stood and patiently explained her situation to the squirrel. "Yes, I am a damsel. No, I'm not in distress. At this moment, I am very happy. You are right. This man does look like a knave. You are also right that he is unworthy of me. But this morning we ate ice cream and kissed and it was delicious. I am hoping that he turns out to have a pure heart and shining armor. More suited, you say, for a career as the king's fool? Mayhap you are right, Sir Squirrel. I have just to cry out if he turns knavish? You will protect me? I will remember this and glad I am to hear it. Now, if you please, allow us to pass. We have, you see, a quest before us."

"The king's fool?" Ben asked.

"Eavesdropping is rude, knavish even."

"The king's fool?"

"Only a fool would fail to love me beyond all reckoning."

Ben did not answer, but as he followed Megan again up the trail, he thought, true that, true that, and true that, until it was the simple lyric to the rhythm of his footsteps.

They hiked for four hours. At the end, the trees grew smaller and opened repeatedly into islands of high meadow, and they could see the great, bare shoulders of San Luis, turned to orange in the setting sun. Now the trees were gone except for spotty patches of gnarled bristlecone, and they stopped beside the headwaters of Stewart Creek. The creek was six inches deep here and only a giant step across. They threw down their packs, stretched out in thin grass, backpacks for pillows, and looked down on the country sliding below and away into the falling light of evening. They drowsed until the warming sun passed below the mountain, and then, abruptly rousted by the cold, they fished fleece and gloves from backpacks. Megan fired the tiny stove while Ben pumped purified water from the stream. He took an icy drink and marveled that anything so cold could still be liquid. Megan added water to a pan of backpacker gruel. The picture on the package, cruelly deceptive, promised beautiful, layered lasagna. They huddled over the pot and took turns spooning hot, lasagna gruel. Ben advanced his pet theory that you burned more calories spooning in this thin gruel than you gained by eating it, a recipe for starvation. Megan agreed and offered to eat his share to keep him from starving. She would do this for him, she suggested, as a final beautiful act of love and sacrifice. Ben suggested that she could have the rest of the gruel if he could have her candy bar. Megan said that she would find her squirrel and have him hack Ben to death with his broadsword if Ben touched her candy bar. Ben threatened to eat the squirrel. Ben was sentenced to wash pot and spoons in the icy stream to help him learn not to be a jerk.

They zipped open a sleeping bag and huddled under it for warmth as they ate their chocolate bars. The falling light had turned the valley below them to smudged charcoal and the sky to purple, slashed through with orange. Venus, a distant lighthouse, beamed at them. The chocolate was delicious. Ben bolted his and then was forced to watch Megan cruelly savoring every dainty bite. She refused categorically to share but relented and allowed him to lick her fingers clean when she was finished. They kissed with the taste of chocolate in their mouths and clung tightly together under the sleeping bag. Their bodies were warm, but the air on their faces was sharp and chill.

In the last of the light, Ben forced himself to prepare their beds. He found a piece of ground near the stream that was almost flat. On hands and knees, he searched out and tossed aside rocks. He spread the blue tarp and anchored the corners with hefty rocks. He spread the two waterproof bivy sacks on the tarp and placed inside each one a short sleeping pad. He shook open the other sleeping bag and stuffed it inside its bivy sack. The sacks were oriented so their feet would be downhill on the slightly sloping earth. Ben pronounced made their beds and then hurried to join Megan under the other bag. The sky now seemed to pause and remain suspended between purple and black. The brook murmured secrets known only to brooks. The mountains were black ships at anchor, waiting to sail on first light.

"This is how I want my life to be," said Megan.

"Freezing at twelve thousand feet?"

"Yes."

"Do you think they will discover our frozen bodies right away?" Ben asked.

"It could take centuries, but no matter how long it takes, when they find us, I will be perfectly preserved and beautiful. They will wonder what I was seeking at this altitude, alone with an ugly knave."

"You should leave a note while there's still time, describing my redeeming charms."

"Your opinion of yourself is pretty high," Megan said.

Ben turned serious, made so by the hugeness of the night falling over them. "Just trying to convince myself. And not always succeeding."

"I know. Sitting in the emergency room, after Larry broke my wrist, I rocked back and forth in the chair and thought I must have deserved it."

"No, Megan."

"Oh, I know you're not supposed to think that. And I didn't think it for very long. And then I had him arrested. I did the right thing. In a funny way, I passed a test when I did that. Can I really keep it together? Those are always my tests. But I have always felt I was doing the right thing because I read about it in a book somewhere. I am jealous of your father. You got to see him living a good life. Do you know who my father was? My real father was a waste of time, so I stole one from the pages of a book. I made Atticus Finch my imaginary father, and I was Scout, his daughter."

"To Kill a Mockingbird," Ben said.

"Atticus was kind and gentle and loved his daughter and let her sit in his lap while he read the paper. Every day, when I was a kid, I got on the school bus and opened a book and escaped into another world, and I hated it when the bus got to my house. I made a dream world in books, and I made up my mind that I would make it so those people in the books were more real than my own family. That was the only thing that saved me...if I managed to be saved."

"You told me your mother died when you were young. Like Scout's. What was Scout's real name?" Ben asked.

"Jean Louise Finch."

"And your father was not exactly like Atticus?"

"I don't talk about him," said Megan fiercely. "Atticus was my true father. Atticus, Atticus, Atticus. Some of the time, in my dreams, Iris's husband, Buster, was my father. You should have known Buster. He was a big, beautiful, outgoing mountain man. He had a ponytail. Sometimes he and Iris would see me on the street and take me into Piggy's for ice cream. He called me doodle head, and sat with his chin in his hands and asked me questions about school and listened to me talk. If I had a book with me, he wanted me to read to him. Once, when I was reading to him, I looked up and huge tears were running down his face, and I thought I had done something wrong. I was going to stop reading, but he laughed and smiled and boomed out that I should go on. He was the only man I knew who could laugh and cry and yell and whisper all at once, and he never seemed to notice that there was anything inconsistent about it. No wonder Iris was so mad about him."

"He cried because of Laurie."

"That's why I drew back. It was too confusing. Even Iris was confused, and she is never confused about anything."

"Iris would have welcomed you."

"Iris is a great lady. She is always welcoming, but she is not warm. I suspect she loves you and Sarah because the love between you is like Buster and Laurie."

"You invented a father. How about a mother?"

"Odd. I never felt the need. I mothered puppies and kittens and new, wet calves. It felt like I knew what women were supposed to be like. I just didn't know what men were supposed to be like until I discovered Atticus."

"And you didn't miss being mothered?"

"Yes. But some things there are no help for. I did my homework, did my chores. I avoided my family, especially my father. I took care of imaginary Atticus because I knew he needed me to make his life complete. I played with friends. Sometimes I went for ice cream with Buster and Iris. I read books until my eyes crossed. I grew up in the library by the river, went away to college, and came home to the library by the river. I chased after the happiest life I could see."

Ben said, "You are a creature of your own invention." And he wondered at the iron discipline that made such a thing possible.

"I suppose. But I don't really know if it's possible to invent yourself and be a real person. You should worry about that about me. Maybe at some crucial moment in life the invention evaporates, and all that's left is an empty shell."

"I'll take my chances."

"As I am taking mine."

"So, can I call you Scout?" asked Ben.

Megan paused. "I don't think so. It's too personal to say out loud. It might become a kind of joke between us, and I don't want that."

"Understood. But I might secretly call you Scout, if only to myself. It is a good name. Someone who goes ahead on the trail to lead the way, as you did today."

"Sometimes I think of you as Benjamin."

"OK. But I guess I don't get it."

"It's a girl thing. When I was trying on the idea of being in love with you, I sometimes sang your name to myself. Benjamin makes a better song than Ben. Three syllables are better for singing than one."

"If you need syllables, why not go with Rumpelstiltskin?"

"Because when I was small, I had a melody that went with three syllables. I sang it to myself in the woods."

"Ah," Ben said. "The song of Atticus."

"Not a bad guess," Megan said. "Sometimes I think there might be hope for you."

"I could never live up to a man like Atticus Finch."

"I'll be the judge of that."

"OK," Ben said. "I am honored to provide the lyric for a child's ditty."

Megan turned sharply to look at Ben and found him looking steadily into her eyes, with no trace of anything but love. He did not want to break this spell, so he thought but did not say that on this mountain she had just told him things she had never told anyone else in the world.

She put her hand to her hair, to her face, to Ben's face. "Shut up, oh, shut up, my Benjamin."

It was dark. There was no moon and the sky was fully black. Here, no light from civilization drifted up to make pale the cast of blackness. It is hard to remember, thought Ben, the real color of night sky. Hard to remember, also, how many stars there are, how many there are that are drowned in the milky soup of human light. In this place, at this altitude, the stars were all present, and the brighter ones pulsed and winked as though powered by living hearts. Ben sent Megan to the bivy sack that already had a sleeping bag in it. He zipped together the bag they had been sheltering under and stuffed it into the other bivy sack. He took off his boots, placed them under the edge of the tarp, and slid into the bag. He reached and touched Megan's cheek with the back of his fingers and she leaned her face into his hand. They lay, covered completely against the cold except for white faces upturned to white stars. They struggled against sleep, trying to keep the stars in their eyes, and then quickly winked out.

Tired from the hike, Ben slept deeply. In some wee hour, he emerged into the edge of consciousness. He heard a snuffling sound and was filled with dread. He could only think bear. He tried to awaken, but it seemed an impossible distance to travel from his deep sleep. He decided he was dreaming the bear, but still he could not escape the dread. The snuffling came again, this time with a warm breath on his face. Almost immediately, there was a sharp nudge on his shoulder. The fearful image of bear filled his mind. He gasped and flailed and struggled to open his eyes. When he did so, the image of the bear, so vivid, slowly resolved itself into one of Megan kneeling over him, making snuffling noises, and butting her head against him. Still fearful, Ben struggled to free his upper body from the sleeping bag and sit up. Megan collapsed on top of him, layers of laughter pealing and peeling from her convulsing body. Awake, Ben held tightly to Megan.

"Your face," she spluttered. "Oh, your face. Oh, that was so mean of me."

"When I opened my eyes, your face looked like a bear. I had the hardest time turning the bear into you. I can't tell you how happy I am that it was you. When I get over being happy, you will have to be killed. Until then, just keep holding on to me."

"I can make it up to you," Megan said.

"How? What?"

Megan scrambled over Ben and slid back into her sleeping bag. She wriggled like an inchworm until the back of her head rested on his chest. Ben watched her, baffled.

"Look up," Megan said. "The sky is falling."

Ben looked and the sky was shedding stars. One after the other, meteors burst into flame and burned a path across the great bowl of black sky.

"I had to wake you for this," Megan said.

"Yes."

They watched grains of space sand explode into racing light. With the cold on his face, Ben wondered how anything could catch fire in the truly deep cold above them. He stroked Megan's hair, fingering gently the nighttime tangles, and his hands were warmed.

"Ah," he said.

"What?"

"Just ah."

"Yes," Megan said. "Me, too."

They watched meteors flying brightly across the sky. They looked at a galaxy of stars. They listened to the unceasing murmur of the brook. Ben warmed his hands in Megan's hair and stroked her forehead.

They awoke to the sun slanting into their eyes. They lay in the luxury of its warmth. Megan dozed like a cat and awoke again to the smell of coffee. She sat on a rock and grimaced as she brushed the tangles from her hair.

"Rats could nest in that hair," said Ben.

"One did. I'm looking at him."

"Be thankful it wasn't a bear," Ben said. Megan smiled happily at the memory of the bear.

They left their gear and set off for the top of San Luis. Ben had emptied his backpack and carried in it only water and snacks and extra clothing. They soon passed out of the last of the stubby, canted bristlecone pines into the region of alpine tundra. Small flowers bunched close to the ground. The trail switched back and forth across the steepness, following a broad ridge to the top of San Luis. At first, they hiked easily without their heavy packs, and then they began to labor with the steep grade and thin air. The crest of the mountain, two miles above them, looked in the clear air only two steps away. They stopped for a rest, breathing hard, at the turn of a switchback.

"Tell me again why we're doing this?" asked Ben.

"We're on a quest."

"For?" Ben asked.

"At the top we can have another chocolate bar, with a kiss."

"I'm in."

They hiked up through a boulder field. Marmots popped out from the rocks at random locations, like targets on a shooting range. The fat, golden creatures whistled and then ducked back into the rocks. Megan insisted they were whistling at her. Ben argued that she was not getting enough oxygen to her brain. Two hours later, they reached the top. The final climb was anticlimax. There was no last steep pitch, just gradual, broad-shouldered incline, suddenly giving up and becoming flat earth. Ben and Megan reflexively looked around for more trail leading upward. They spun around and the view in all directions spun with them. Mountains, ridges, and small, pocketed alpine lakes spread below them. All the earth around them was below them, and it was colored in gray, changing shades of tan, dark and light green, and the winking blue eyes of the little tarns. The wind blew hard across the top of the land, and Ben and Megan huddled behind sheltering rocks to feast on water and chocolate kisses. Safe from the wind, they napped in the sunshine. Ben awoke and admired the softness of Megan's cheek and her gentle snoring. Standing to leave, they faced into the wind and opened their mouths so this air could blow deep inside them. They left the mountain and on the way down saw two mountain goats emerging from a fold in the mountain. The goats were white and fluffy as new cotton and seemed surprised that any other creature would be above them in this high land.

Chapter Twelve

Ben thought about taking Iris outside and throwing her down the well. He was seated at his kitchen table, in this first week of July, filling out a job application. The high school had alerted him they might have an opening for a fulltime history teacher. Ben was excited at the prospect of a job he loved and a regular paycheck. The application required one of those pain-in-the-ass essays on why he wanted to be a teacher, and Ben struggled to suppress all the irreverent answers that came first to his mind. Iris sat across from him, drinking coffee, insisting she would be no bother; he should just go on with his work as if she weren't there. Ben had the materials spread before him, with a sharp yellow pencil and a blank yellow pad waiting to receive his thoughts. Iris got up and rummaged in one cupboard and then another.

"What do you need, Iris?"

"Sugar. Don't worry. I'll find it." Ben wrote "Teaching" at the top of the page. He had a piece of the central idea in his mind, but it splintered in the face of softly closing cupboard doors and tin cans pushed from side to side. Unable to cope with the pressure, he put down his pencil and got up to search the cabinets. Iris stood aside to let him look.

"Maybe I'm out of sugar."

"Don't worry about it."

"Sometimes Sarah puts things in mysterious places." Ben went through three cabinets. He triumphantly located the sugar bowl, stored under the sink between the dishwashing liquid and the trash bags. The bowl was empty except for a few grains of sugar congealed on the bottom.

"Don't worry about it," Iris said. "Go back to work."

She sat at the table across from him and stared sadly at her coffee. Ben found a piece of an idea to scratch onto his yellow pad although he was nagged by the thought that it was not the same idea that he had thought was the best idea before the great sugar search. Iris took a sip of her coffee. Ben was staring down at the paper, but he could feel the face she made when she tasted her coffee. She set her cup down with a soft clunk. I could drown her in the well, thought Ben. I could lure her outside on the pretext of looking at the moon. He tried to remember if there was a moon that night. A quick shove in the small of the back should do it. Ben tried to recall if Iris had ever mentioned being able to swim. He jotted another idea that seemed in no way connected to the idea he had already written or to the original idea that he had almost called to mind until Iris clunked her coffee cup.

Iris got up again, scraping her chair on the wood floor, and began softly rummaging in the cabinets again.

"Iris?"

"There must be a bag of sugar."

"I looked."

"Maybe it's behind something. Just go on with your work."

There was rustling and scraping, and Iris retrieved a chair so she could peer into the recesses of the topmost cabinet. What if someone should hear her cry out when he pushed her into the well? It seemed clear he was going to have to first hit her over the head. That would solve the problem of whether she could swim. Boots, Ben thought. Concrete galoshes. He had to find a way to make her sink, else she would float on the surface, face down, hair fanning out across the clear surface of the water, arms extended gracefully as though preparing to breaststroke her way into perpetuity. What if Ollie should hear the splash? It would be just like Ollie to spend all night howling mournfully beside the well. Ben could not imagine how he would ever get his essay prepared with Ollie howling all night. Iris gave up the search for sugar, scraped her chair across the floor, sighed, and clunked her coffee cup back on the table.

"I should put in a well out back," Ben said.

"A well?"

"Yes, one of those old-fashioned wells with a stone wall around it and a rope to let down a bucket."

"That's the dumbest thing I ever heard, Ben. Are you going to prepare that application or sit here and daydream about wishing wells?"

Ben looked at the disorganized application materials in front of him and sighed. "I'll get them spanked up eventually."

"Spanked up?" Iris asked.

Ben looked up and was confused by the question. "Yes, spanked up. I'll make it spanky."

"You're going to spank your application?" Iris asked.

Ben struggled to make sense of why Iris did not understand such an obvious expression, an expression that had always been a part of his life. He recalled his father looking at a sagging pasture gate and saying, "We need to spank that up before it falls off."

"It's just an expression my father always used," Ben said.

"When he was spanking you?"

Ben could not recall that his father had ever spanked him. Had he done so, it would probably have been the end of Ben's known world.

"Spank it up," Ben said. "It means to fix something up. Make it spanky. Make it brand, spanking new. I guess it comes from the old idea of giving newborns a spank so they will take their first breath."

Iris nodded. "OK. It's kind of Southern strange, but I get it. So, shouldn't you be spanking up that application?"

The phone rang, and it was Sarah, calling from Houston.

"Little one. How's my best girl?"

"I'm fine. I love you. Have you been fishing?" It was immediately clear to Ben that things were not fine.

"George and I drove over to Leadville on Tuesday and fished the Arkansas. We had a good day."

"Did you catch any fish?"

"Don't I always catch fish?"

"No," Sarah said.

"Well, I guess that could be right. If we're going to be, you know, honest. What are you and your mom up to?"

"We took a ride in a helicopter. It's so flat here. We went to the beach and stayed in a fancy hotel."

"How cool is that?"

"I hate it, Dad. I want to come home."

"I'm sorry, love. Maybe you're just having a bad day. Did you have a fight with your mom?"

"She's in Paris. A woman that works for Mom is staying with me."

"Ah."

"Mom says it's a business trip. She went with a man named Walter. He always wears a suit, and he slicks his hair back. Every time he comes over he brings my mom a yellow rose and me a pink one. I don't get it."

"Yellow roses are your mom's favorite."

"Are you guys going to get divorced?"

"Damned if I know, Sarah. I'm trying to figure it out. I know this is hard for you. I'm sorry."

"Don't say damn, Dad. If you get divorced, I want to stay with you. I hate Walter. I hate my mom."

"You're mad at her right now. Sometimes you love her and have fun with her. Your mom can be more fun than anybody."

"I don't know. I guess. But it was different when we were all together. She was different."

"Maybe we were all different. And you weren't pulled in all directions."

"I guess so. But, Dad, that's not what I'm talking about. You're always the same. When we were all together, Mom was better. She wasn't mean as much. And when she was, I always had you. Now she's talking about how I should live with her if you guys get divorced, so I won't grow up like...like..."

"Me."

"I heard Walter talking. He knows some famous lawyer about divorces." Ben could hear the strain in Sarah's voice.

"Don't worry, love. Don't worry about that stuff."

"Dad, I can't tell you guys what you should do. Get divorced or don't get divorced. But I have to be with you. Promise me that."

"Do my best, kid. That's all I can promise. Do you want me to just move to Houston? Is that what you want?"

"You can't ask me that."

"I know. Sorry."

"I want you to be happy. I love you," Sarah said.

"I love you, little one. I will do my best."

"OK." Sarah seemed to be done with this difficult topic, so Ben changed the subject to Ollie. He told Sarah that Ollie had switched professions. He was no longer interested in fetching sticks and had become a sheep dog. Since there weren't any sheep, Ollie had turned to finding and herding bears. He was using Sarah's room as his bear pen, and there were now four bears living there full time. Ollie took them out every day and herded them up and down Main Street. People were beginning to talk, and Sarah's room was getting a little stinky, but Ollie could not be reasoned with. Two of the smaller bears were beginning to dress up in Sarah's clothes.

"Say goodnight, Dad," Sarah said, her voice drowsy, more relaxed.

"Goodnight, Dad," Ben said. Sarah sighed and Ben thought it was a contented sigh. He said, "Have happy dreams, little one."

"You too. Thanks, Dad. Kiss Ollie for me."

"That bitch," Iris said. Ben had forgotten Iris was sitting at the table. He flushed and for a tiny, confused instant thought Iris was talking about Sarah. He sat with his head in his hands.

"I'm sorry," Iris said. "You know I've never liked her. She has a family, a beautiful family, and she throws it away."

"It's more complicated than that, Iris."

"Not to me. And if Buster had lost me, or lost Laurie, it wouldn't have been complicated to him. And nothing's complicated to Laurie. She just wants her feet tickled. Karen doesn't just have a daughter. She has a perfect one. My daughter's broken. I feel bad every day for not being able to make Laurie feel loved the way that Buster made her feel loved. But if Karen can't love Sarah, she can't love anybody. Nobody but herself."

"What about me? Why don't you blame me for this mess?" Ben asked.

"Not yet. I may get around to blaming you, but not yet. I won't start blaming you until I see that you are too weak to make a decision."

"Where is strength, Iris?" Ben asked sharply. "You tell me. Maybe the problem is that I'm not strong enough to love Karen enough."

"Love Karen enough? Or put up with her shit?"

"Sometimes it amounts to the same. You know, it's the damnedest thing. I've never been able to figure out whether I love Karen out of strength or weakness. I know what it feels like to be in love, with Karen, with Megan. Sometimes, feeling love, I'm stronger for it, sometimes weaker. Maybe love and strength don't have anything to do with each other."

"OK, OK, but, damn it, you better be careful you don't think it to death."

"Yes, ma'am." Ben loved Iris, but he was in no mood to take advice from George Armstrong Custer about charging the Little Big Horn. He hid his irritation at Iris's bulldog grip on one piece of the truth. She could have been twin to Karen in this respect. If Ben let Iris pressure him into doing things her way, then he was being strong; if he rejected her advice, he was weak—the only way to prove to Iris that you were strong was to give in to her. Some of Ben's good humor returned as he entertained this paradox, but he knew there was no use in sharing this with Iris. He had no intention of doing things any way but his own. It came to him that the one person who seemed to understand this best was Megan, the child who invented herself and set her own course.

Ben put on a fresh pot of coffee. The machine gurgled and hissed and when it was done, he poured them both a cup.

"You'd better not make a face just because there is no sugar," he warned. "If you have to have sugar, you can run over to your place and get some, and lend me a cup while you're at it."

"While we're being honest with each other, there's a thing I should tell you."

"What?"

"I'm out of sugar, too."

"I think she's been talking to lawyers about Sarah."

"That bitch."

"It's what people do, Iris. I wondered when it was coming."

"Why would she hire a lawyer? She doesn't want Sarah."

"Sure, she does. She loves Sarah. She's just not so good at taking care of her. But that doesn't mean she couldn't hire someone to do it. She can also hire a heavyweight lawyer. Money helps."

"That bitch."

"Iris, you may not have noticed this, but you're not as objective as you could be. Besides, I've talked to a lawyer, too. I had coffee with Brad Jenkins."

"That idiot. What did he tell you?"

"He said I should throw myself on the mercy of the court and ask for every other weekend. And he offered to make out a will for me at half price."

"Forget about Brad Jenkins. If it comes to that, I know some 17th Street lawyers in Denver. You won't be outgunned," Iris said.

"I can't afford to say hello to a 17th Street lawyer."

"You won't need to. These guys owe me favors."

"Iris, you're the best, but I couldn't let you do that for me."

"I know you couldn't. That's why I'd be doing it for Sarah."

Ben got up and put on his shoes and jacket.

"Where are you going?"

"You're a hard woman, Iris. You're trying to make me cry, and I'm damned if I'll give you the satisfaction."

Ben was gone for a while and when he returned Iris was sitting at the table reading his history textbook. He put in front of her a pound of sugar. He took another bag of sugar from the plastic sack, opened it, and filled the sugar bowl. From the bowl, he spooned sugar into Iris's coffee. He then placed the sugar bowl back where Sarah had left it, under the sink, between the dishwashing liquid and the trash bags.

. . ...

God pulled up the kitchen chair Iris had vacated thirty minutes before. The chair scraped against the wood floor. Ben put down his pencil and gave up the notion of getting the essay done that night.

"The prodigal returns," Ben said. "Where've you been?"

"Everywhere. All at once."

"Good trick."

"It's what I do. Got a Fat Tire?" God asked.

"No, but I do have sugar."

"Look over there at the door."

"Why?"

"How about because God commands it?"

Ben looked at the door. When he looked back, God was sipping a Fat Tire.

"Another good trick," Ben said. "I don't suppose you could write my essay for me?"

"Look at the door."

Ben looked and when he looked back at his paper, it was still as he had left it.

God chuckled. "I'm full of good tricks."

Ben laughed. They both leaned back with their feet propped up on the worn pine table. The kitchen clock ticked, a sound so barely perceptible that it was only there when you wanted to hear it. Ben was happy to see his itinerant boarder. God nursed his beer and inquired, "Tough day at the office?"

Ben glanced at the refrigerator, at some of Sarah's artwork, a pencil drawing of Ollie standing on top of a mountain. "I've had better," he said.

God followed his gaze. "I'm not much help, am I?" he said softly.

Ben shrugged. "It is what it is. I believe in Sarah and me. I think we will be together. In case there is a fight over Sarah, I have Iris, who likes to fight. I suppose I could conclude that you gave me Iris, but I don't because it's too mysterious. What I conclude is that Iris gave me Iris, and I am happy for it. To paraphrase Mr. Lincoln, I freely confess that I'm at the mercy of events rather than their master. To paraphrase me, I stubbornly believe that I will know what to do when it is time."

Ben adjusted his feet and his socks squeaked softly against the wood. God was as silent as some far patch of deep space.

Ben said, "It'd be nice if there were a point to prayer because at times like these it's what I feel like doing."

God said, "Know what you mean. It's why I've had the damnedest time stamping out religion. If I could figure out a way to unhook religion from prayer, I think I'd be halfway home. I don't take requests. On the other hand, if you just have in mind a good conversation, I am sometimes available to shoot the breeze, as well you know. That can be fun. In my lonely position, a little companionship always comes good. Matter of fact, what I like about you is that you never ask me for anything. The whole world is out there begging me for answered prayers, and bribing me with promises of good behavior. But you want nothing from me, except for the opportunity to pass along the occasional good-natured insult. In fairness, I do recognize that most of your insults are good-natured."

"Now you mention it, there is one thing I could ask of you," Ben said.

"Ah ha," God said, grinning.

"You're a couple months behind on the rent."

God slapped his forehead. "You didn't get the rent check? I put it in the mail."

Ben laughed. "Same place I put the eviction notice."

"I'd be pretty hard to evict. What with my godlike powers and all."

"I could have Iris do it."

"I'll pay."

God sipped his beer and Ben his coffee. They listened to the wind pushing, backing up, and then sliding around the corners of the old house.

"I guess I don't ask because I don't believe in you." God lifted his hands in a question. Ben went on. "Unlike Iris, you don't intervene. You may notice the fall of the sparrow, but you don't reach out a hand before it hits the ground."

God sighed. "Sadly true, but I have intervened from time to time."

"To what effect?"

"Not much. Mostly to satisfy some odd, whimsical impulse," said God.

Ben idly pushed the saltshaker back and forth with his finger. God took a sip of beer and set the bottle back on the table so softly that it made no sound. Ollie barked in the distance.

"Raccoon," God said. "Out there in the dark a raccoon has waddled up a tree and Ollie thinks he's got him just where he wants him. The raccoon will take a nap while he waits for Ollie to forget his mission and wander off."

Ben said, "So I believe that you are here, drinking a Fat Tire, scratching my table with those god-awful Texas boots, but I'm not sure you serve any other purpose, except..."

"I sense another insult coming," God said.

"Except," continued Ben, "for the absolute, unmitigated pleasure of your company."

"You, my friend, have a twisty little mind. I am always refreshed."

Ben said, "You mentioned the odd whimsical intervention—I'm trying to imagine an intervention both divine and whimsical."

"I just made the raccoon appear four times its normal size. Scared Ollie shitless."

Ben laughed, and the two of them talked far into the night. God told yarns about swapping stories with Mr. Lincoln. "Lincoln told a great story. What a cornpone. He'd be in the middle of some yarn, slapping his thigh, cracking himself up, waving those long arms, with his hair sticking out every way there was, and it was clear that he thought if he just made the story funny enough, just zinged the punch line a little harder, maybe it would take his pain away. Sometimes his eyes were so sad I had to look away."

"Does that happen often?" Ben asked.

"What?"

"Having to look away."

God gave a quick grunt, as though someone had hit him in the stomach. "Who in their right mind would choose to be all-seeing? Think what you are forced to look at. It is a curse beyond endurance. Sometimes I don't just look away—I run away."

"Because you created this world?"

"Maybe. It's hard to remember so far back. Sometimes I'm not sure whether I created the Big Bang or was simply awakened by it. All I can really say is that I've been around for as long as I can remember. A lot is lost, mercifully, in the haze of memory. I used to worry over the question of where I came from but eventually lost all interest. A thirteenth century theologian named Duns Scotus had this notion that God cannot fully comprehend himself, not a bad guess, but it never caught on in theological circles. I take responsibility for setting some things in motion, but here's the thing—part of the reason I assume responsibility is that I simply can't find anyone else to blame it on. Never have been able to locate any other gods, so I guess it's all on me. And that's OK. I don't completely regret it. Some beautiful things have come of it: wildflowers, Sarah, not to mention our friend, Ollie. But the truth is that this world and I have mostly run along parallel tracks. When I take the notion, I skip the tracks and check on things. Hang out. The old Jews apparently guessed right about monotheism. I have spent eons searching the universe for another god. If he or she or they are there, it has not been revealed to me. I can't escape the feeling that there must be some higher authority I can appeal to."

"You complain about people always asking you for things. If there were some higher authority than you, would you ask for something?" Ben asked.

God held the cool glass of the beer bottle against his cheek. "Absolution, my friend."

"For what?"

"I am haunted by the sadness in Mr. Lincoln's eyes."

Chapter Thirteen

Ben and Megan brought a half-gallon of French vanilla ice cream to Iris's house. They found Iris and Laurie seated in the backyard in the shade of two towering blue spruce. Each tree was twin to the other and only the birds could tell which was tallest. No bird, from mountain finch to chickadee to junco, could pass by without commanding for a while the topmost frond. Iris and Laurie sat in deep wooden lawn chairs. Iris rose gracefully to hug Ben and Megan. Laurie floundered to get out of the deep chair until Ben took her hands to pull her up. She came too far when he pulled her and draped herself in his arms.

"Laurie, you remember Ben," said Iris.

Laurie said yes and smiled confidently.

"Do you remember Megan? You haven't seen her for a long time."

Laurie said yes but was tentative. She accepted a hug from Megan, but it was listless on Laurie's part.

Iris, Megan, and Ben went inside to get bowls and spoons for the ice cream.

"I hope it's OK that Ben brought me along," Megan said.

"Oh, damn it," said Iris sharply.

Megan watched her cautiously. "If it's not…"

"I hate that about myself. What do I do that makes everyone so uncomfortable?"

Megan smiled. "You're just Iris. You are formidable." She used the French pronunciation.

"I know. I know. I want to intimidate people, so I shouldn't be surprised when I succeed. I hate that I make you feel uncomfortable. You, of all people. I have thought of you as my daughter at a distance. I always felt like I was involved in your life, but it was always outside of this home. The distance had nothing to do with you. I held back because it felt like I was being disloyal to Laurie. Which was stupid—she would have loved having a sister." Iris looked directly at Megan. "I have a hard time without Buster. It was always his job to make people feel welcome. Megan, you are welcome here now, welcome always. If you would come to this home more, I would be happy. I want you to be my friend. I don't know how you get there, but I wish we could have coffee together, call each other when we are sad or happy. Sometimes I have this picture in my mind that we could go running together. You, Ben, I want us all to be some kind of family to each other." She laughed. "Scaring you shitless?"

Megan nodded gravely. "Yes. Just like always. But at least now I'm scared in a new way." They hugged. Iris was awkward. Megan, in spite of her words, seemed the more confident of the two, as if this day had only been a matter of time.

When they returned with the bowls, Laurie was seated again in the deep chair. Ben sat on the end of her chair. Laurie had her shoes off and Ben began tickling the soles of her feet. Laurie's laugh was high-pitched and ragged and she squirmed with delight. Ben stopped, and she said, "More Ben, more, more."

"Enough," said Ben. "More later." He got up to help with the ice cream, but Laurie snagged his hand and pulled him back. He sat in the grass beside her chair, and the two of them held hands.

"Ben, yes, my Ben," Laurie said.

"How does it feel to be so universally adored by women?" asked Megan cheerfully. "Any chance all this may make you insufferable?"

"More insufferable," said Iris.

"It's a shame I can't help with the ice cream," Ben said, "but Laurie and I are spending quality time. Could I have three scoops, please?"

"Do you want us to spoon it into your mouth?" Megan asked.

"I was thinking one of you could spoon and the other could massage my feet."

119

Iris spooned up a dip of ice cream and walked over and carefully dropped it in Ben's hair. Laurie hooted with delight. She reached over and dipped a finger in the blob of ice cream and stuck it in her mouth. Ben scraped the ice cream from his hair and fed it to Ollie, who wriggled with delight. Ollie then proceeded to lick the rest of the ice cream from the top of Ben's head. The four of them ate ice cream until they could eat no more and then gave Ollie the bowls to lick clean.

"You couldn't get Hank to join us?" Iris asked.

"Couldn't find him," said Ben. "He has taken to coming and going, sometimes for weeks on end. His ways are his own. I don't think he's much on ice cream socials, anyway."

"The mountains are full of odd tumbleweeds," Iris said. "Mostly all they want is solitude, and that's easy enough to grant."

Iris stretched out in the grass with her fingers laced behind her head. Megan lay beside her for a few moments and then twisted perpendicular to Iris and used Iris's flat, runner's stomach as a pillow. Ben looked at this scene with wonder, and Laurie's eyes widened. Beside him, Laurie struggled to rise from her chair. She pushed hard off one arm of the chair and gained her feet, though she staggered awkwardly for a couple of steps before finding her balance. She walked with her pinwheel lurching gait over to Iris and Megan. She steadied herself for a moment and then kicked Iris hard in the upper arm. On the other side of Iris, Megan bolted upright. The force of her own kick unbalanced Laurie, and she plopped down on her behind. The three women sat upright staring at each other, and Laurie held her stomach with her arms and bent over as though she were the one who had been kicked. She rocked back and forth and cried.

"I want Buster," Laurie said. "Buster is dead. Where is he?"

"Oh, Laurie." Iris vaguely stroked Laurie's arm.

"Buster is dead,' said Iris. "He can't come back."

"No, Iris," said Megan sharply. "Like this." She scooted over and put one arm around Laurie. She reached across to Iris and put an arm around her and pulled her firmly towards them. Iris looked lost and bewildered but slid closer. Megan pulled them both to her and the three of them held tightly together. Iris freed her left arm from Megan and began to stroke Laurie's hair, and Megan scooted backwards from the circle. She stood and went over to sit beside Ben who had remained frozen in place beside the chair. The two of them leaned their shoulders against each other.

Megan and Ben carried the bowls inside and washed the dishes. "You were good," Ben said.

"I was good," said Megan simply. "Who knows? Maybe I'm OK."

When they returned to the back yard, Iris and Laurie were strolling arm in arm around the yard, inspecting Iris's flowers. From a distance, their roles could have been reversed. Laurie's life was sedentary, and she had put on weight. Iris, with her girlish figure, could have been the child, supporting her limping mother. They finished their circuit of the yard and sat beside each other in the deep chairs. Iris stroked Laurie's arm where it rested on the arm of the chair. Ben signaled to Iris with a thumb and a raised eyebrow to ask if they should leave, and Iris signaled for them to stay.

Megan went to her purse and fished out three brightly colored handkerchiefs, orange and green and red. She did a mock curtsy in front of Iris and Laurie and began juggling the handkerchiefs. She threw each handkerchief with her hand turned down and an upward flick of her wrist. In the air, the handkerchiefs opened and floated slowly down and Megan picked each one out of the air with a downward movement of her hand. The air was full of floating, twisting, garish color, and Megan, the conjurer, held falling bodies perpetually aloft.

Laurie was entranced and clapped; her hands came together at an odd angle. Iris paid little attention to the handkerchiefs but smiled and looked back and forth between Megan and Laurie. When Megan tired, Ben wanted to try. Megan started him out with two handkerchiefs, and he learned to keep them both aloft. When Megan added the third handkerchief, he flailed the air as handkerchiefs sailed serenely to the grass. He claimed that the wind had come up, creating tricky air currents, and gleefully denounced as a miserable, pathetic failure.

Laurie wanted to try. She got up from her chair, and Megan started her with one handkerchief. Laurie wanted to make an underhand toss into the air, and Megan worked with her on the unnatural movement of keeping her palm downward and flicking it skyward. Laurie had trouble learning when to release the handkerchief, and it often sailed straight away from her instead of upward. Each time it sailed anywhere, Megan clapped and cheered and darted to retrieve the handkerchief. Finally, Laurie got the hang of sailing it upward. Her eyes followed the handkerchief into the sky as though she had personally launched a swirling orange galaxy to the far reaches of heaven. She neglected to even try to catch the descending handkerchief because this was too much to remember. Megan sat on the grass at her feet and handed up to her the handkerchief each time it fell.

Iris pulled Ben to the back stoop of the house. "I've made such terrible mistakes," she said.

"No shit. I can't believe you put ice cream in my hair."

"Be serious, Ben."

"OK."

"I let too many things in my life be a slave to Laurie's disability. It just made me so angry. I wanted a perfect child, not one that said her first word at age four. Buster got sad and cried every day for three months and then went fishing and got over it. I got mad and stayed mad. I wondered why God would do that to a child until I realized God was utterly unaware of Laurie's existence. Friends tried to be sympathetic, and all I could find to say to them was, 'Fuck you, fuck you, and fuck you. I don't need your damn sympathy. If Laurie learned to tie her shoes at age ten, well that's better than your kid getting straight A's. My family is perfect the way it is.' I went around town and dared anyone to show me sympathy. I pushed Laurie to learn to tie her shoes until she cried; I pushed the way other parents pushed violin lessons. Buster wanted more kids, and I wouldn't because I didn't want anybody, even my own child, showing Laurie up. Megan practically grew up an orphan. She needed me, and I didn't help her as much as I should have because of Laurie. It never occurred to Buster that loving Megan could subtract from loving

Laurie. But it was all I could think about. My child was broken. It was my job to protect her at all cost." Iris turned to Ben. "Do you get any of that?"

"Iris, whether I get it or not is the last thing that matters. What matters is that the right thing for me to say at this point is 'I'm sorry.' What matters is whether you then decide to hit me, or whether you decide to say, 'Thanks, Ben. I'm sorry, too.'"

"OK."

"OK, what?"

"Thanks, Ben, I'm sorry, too."

"Look at them. Juggling their hearts out. Aren't they a trip?"

"This is how I want our lives to be. All of us together. And Sarah."

"Back off, Iris."

"This is right, Ben. It's time you saw that. Megan is right."

"Megan is right in every way. But don't be so quick to know what's right for Sarah."

"Damn it, Ben, look at Megan with Laurie. She has heart. What could be better for Sarah than that?"

"You could be right. But you can't be sure. And you can't know what's good for me and Karen."

"I don't care about Karen. And you shouldn't, either."

"I love Karen. A part of me needs her, and a part of her needs me. You tell me that Laurie is broken. Karen is no less broken. You devoted yourself to taking care of Laurie. I've done something similar. I've thrown up my hands in disgust and given up, but then I think I see a glimmer of hope and try harder. Isn't that what you've done with Laurie? Isn't that what everyone does who loves someone hard to love? You say to me it's been your job to protect Laurie at all cost. Do I have the same job with Karen, with Sarah? That is exactly what I promised when we got married. It is certainly what Karen wants, at least on alternate Tuesdays for extremely brief intervals and under circumstances that for the most part are downright nutty."

Ben wanted to say to Iris that he was ready to give up on Karen, but he had to be sure in some way that he had not figured out. He had been ready to give up Karen many times before, but, when someone you love falls overboard, do you throw a rope? What if they jump? What if they are pushed?

Iris said. "The two situations are nothing like the same."

"Maybe they are nothing like the same. On the other hand, maybe all love is something like the same. Laurie is broken. Karen is broken. You've just finished telling me that you are in need of a few repairs. And we're still trying to figure out whether I'm the most broken of all. I'm not ready for you to figure out my life for me."

Chapter Fourteen

Ben stood in the Blue and the sound of the water was around him and part of the sound was a song. Everywhere across the surface of the water was movement. Sometimes the surface was slick when the water moved deeply through a channel. In other places, the water was choppy and created tilted surfaces that lifted and fell in swift and tireless repetition. Ben was well back from a midstream boulder that made behind it a calm surface. Between this smooth water and the heavy, tumbling water of the river, there was a dark, choppy seam where the two kinds of river came together. In this seam, impossibly large green drake mayflies bobbed as they were carried downstream by the irresistible tension of the current. It was a sacred feast day for the fish, and they rose and swirled as they wrestled the big flies from the surface. On feast days like this, the trout packed green drakes into their stomachs like Sir Francis Drake filling every cranny of the Golden Hind for the long voyage to come. For the fish, the long voyage was winter, and now, in July, in the warmth of summer, they joyfully stuffed themselves.

The fish were lined up in the seam and Ben lined up behind the fish. He cast into the breeze and at the last moment took the punch from the cast and left the fly suspended over the water. The breeze seized the powerless fly and sailed it softly down onto the water so that it floated freely and wandered in the eddy of the current like innocent insect flotsam. Ben watched his green drake rise up one side of a small swell and slide down the other. It drifted lazily towards the next swell and then was suddenly gone. As the trout turned downward with the fly, the curve of its back glowed for an instant above the water. Ben gently lifted the rod tip. A spark traveled across tight line, droplets of stolen river flying from it, falling home. The spark traveled across bowed, vibrating rod and, at each end of this connection, this spark ignited a beating heart. Ben never cared whether he actually landed a fish. He cared only for this instantaneous, shocking moment of connection. This fish he landed and turned gently back into the stream.

As a child, Ben loved to fish, loved that moment when the cork bobber dived beneath the surface. His father never fished with him as Ben fished with Sarah. The summer grew its crop of chores, and these his father attended. His father was a hunter who had no interest in fishing, but he never minded doing extra chores on the farm so Ben could slip away to some pond full of pan fish. Ben never returned a bluegill to the water. He brought it abruptly from the water, briefly admired the sheen of the dark blue shading into black, and promptly threaded a stringer into heaving gills and out its gasping mouth. He came home with meat for the table, and his mother breaded the fish and fried them in a skillet that sizzled and threw off stinging pinpricks of hot oil.

Ben's mother turned the fish aggressively with a spatula, at war with the hiss of the frying pan and its fiery spray. She pursued her part of their life's station with grim determination and submerged anger. Ben's father found his reflection in the gentle purl of an irrigation ditch; his mother saw her image in the bubbles roiling from the bottom of a frying pan. The two of them carried what there was to carry and carried on; one infinitely careful and caring, the other chafed raw by the weight of care. Ben's mother loved her family, but she also saw that their combined weight was pulling her under. She got up at six to begin each unremitting day and looked in the mirror at her fading beauty and reddening skin. She fired the frying pan, spread strips of bacon, and listened to the hiss and pop.

It was a fall day with sharp blue sky over the green forest of loblolly pine. Ben and his father were exploring places to hunt on rutted dirt tracks that wound through the deep woods. Ben barely noticed a car almost hidden in a stand of sapling pines. His father steered them through a deep rut that jolted the truck and snapped their heads. As Ben's head came up, he looked at the car and a man's head rose up from the back seat. Ben saw the top of a woman's head, tousled hair and forehead, come up from the seat, only to be quickly pushed back down by the man's fast-reaching hand. Ben's father stopped the truck for a long moment, looking over Ben's head into the eyes of the man in the back seat. It seemed to Ben that this moment, each man looking into the eyes of the other, would flatten him under its weight. Ben was looking also at the man's face. He did not see but could feel his father glance down at him, and the truck creaked again down the road, swaying through the bumps and the ruts. Although he, too, had been staring at the man in the backseat, Ben found that this man's face was an oval blank, empty of features. He recalled only the dark tousled hair of the woman, the visible piece of her forehead, and her widow's peak, as though it were leaning over him, tucking him once again into bed.

The waters of the Blue flowed into, around, and past Ben, dislodging shards of memory and tumbling them downstream. He caught two more fish and petted them and let them go. The fish, crazed by the floating feast, were almost too easy to catch, but Ben quickly discarded this thought. The angler's highest ethic demanded that he believe that these fish were caught because of his peerless skills; he found that he was able to think this without undue difficulty. He forced himself to slow down. The day had been mostly overcast but the sun was now sliding through the canopy of cottonwoods. In this new light, he could see the glint of lazily drifting insects in the air and the hard, diamond spray of water pitched into the air when the water splashed over a boulder. The banks of the river in this place rose steeply and were covered in brush and trees. His friend, the otter with a sense of humor, had magically appeared, but was content to sit on the far bank and watch Ben fish.

Ben began casting again and this rhythm returned to him the memory of his childhood. Ben and his father had stayed out scouting the woods until late in the afternoon. Ben's father was quiet and turned aimlessly from one dirt track to another and did not look at the woods or at Ben or at anything but the ruts and bumps in the road. Ben did not look at his father but peered out the window into the dark, tangled recesses of the pine forest. At home, Ben's mother prepared dinner as if nothing had happened. She could not know for sure whether she had been seen and probably could not decide whether she cared. Ben's father ate as if nothing had happened. He ate slowly and deliberately, but this was not different from any other night. Ben could not eat until his father looked at his plate and silently nodded. Ben understood and forced himself to eat. He thought his mother might have seen this nod, but he was not sure. She would surely have noticed that the two of them were not full of talk about their day. She would surely have noticed this.

Later, Ben slipped out to the barn where his father kept a workroom. His father was there, with his shotgun on the bench before him; about this, before the start of hunting season, there should have been nothing unusual. Ben sat and watched his father methodically and carefully clean his gun. He ran a cleaning rod through the length of the barrel. He oiled and polished with a soft cloth the outside of the barrel and the exposed metal parts. With another cloth, he polished the wood of the stock and grip. His movements were slow, and he turned the gun in the light to capture the soft, reflected gleam. He tested the trigger and was rewarded by the cold, metallic snap of the firing pin.

"When are you going hunting?" asked Ben.

"I don't know, son." There was no life in the voice of his father.

"What will you hunt for?"

His father looked at him and smiled. This smile, thought Ben, was like the light from a star, light that had traveled an impossible distance through space that was dark and cold and empty. The distance, the darkness, the cold, the emptiness, they made faint the light, made fainter yet the smile of his father. His father did not hunt that season, in spite of the fact that his gun was beautifully oiled, its kinetic energy resting on pegs in the locked shed through the long winter. To Ben's limited knowledge, his father never spoke to anyone, not even to Ben's mother, of these happenings in their lives. He simply carried on within the life of his flawed family because he did not have another. It was true that sometimes during that winter Ben wandered in the dark to where the light softly glowed from under the door of the shed. He sometimes knocked and went in, to be greeted by the slow smile that had regained a little warmth, the warmth of a small, glowing fire. Ben always found his father sharpening tools or building shelves or reading some novel of the Old West. Ben wished, for reasons of his heart, that the shed had a window, so that he could maintain watch on his father's safety. Sometimes Ben did not go inside but stood outside the shed, shivering in the dark. Sometimes also he thought he heard voices coming from inside, soft, calm, sometimes with a dry chuckle. He could never make out the words, or to whom his father was talking, but he went away reassured that his father had some kind of company.

Ben thought about these things now, alone in the Blue, because he needed to understand if his life was the same as his father's and because it was easier to think on these things while being washed by the clear water. Ben continued to catch fish although now less frequently. The clouds had gone and the sun was strong on the water. The green drake hatch was mostly over although the fish still rose to the artificial fly, rising to the memory of the great feast. The otter scampered on the far bank to get Ben's attention, and Ben smiled and waved and was pleased by the company. Ben was distracted by the presence of a hummingbird hovering over the river ahead of him. In the bright sunlight, the hummingbird was brilliant green with a slash of red at its throat. It hovered and darted, taking tiny insects from the air. When Ben looked down, he noticed that the otter had remembered it could swim. Smooth fur gleaming wet, it perched beside Ben on a small boulder in midstream, also watching the hummingbird. It, too, seemed delighted with the tiny, cheerful bird.

Then the otter's chest exploded. There was an instant in which Ben thought he could see down into the otter's heart through the spraying blood and in the next instant the otter rolled backward off the rock and splashed into the water. It floated downstream, trailing blood in the clear water. Later, Ben could not recall whether he had even heard the gunshot. He thought he must have heard it, even over the sound of the river that surrounded him. There must have been the sharp, flat crack, which must have bounced back and forth between the echoing banks of the river. Ben imagined later that the sound might have simply disappeared into the gaping redness of his friend's chest.

Frozen, Ben watched the otter drift downriver. He cried out and gave chase, running with the current and stumbling over rocks. He pitched headfirst into the sharp coldness of the water, regained his footing, and continued his ragged race with the current. The otter floated like a green drake, now on the surface, now dragged beneath it. Ben dived and caught it and came up panting as though it were his own chest exploding. He hugged it tightly against him but could not look at it. He carried it to the bank and sat, exhausted, on a log, with the otter's body at his feet. Ben noticed that he still held his fly rod in his right hand, and he laid this gently beside the otter.

Only then did Ben truly understand how the otter died, and that somewhere along the river was someone with a rifle. He stood up and searched the banks and the hills, covered with trees and brush that rose up along the river. Remembering the position of the otter, he knew the shot came from the opposite bank but someone who would shoot an otter could have been hidden anywhere, and the river was now as it was.

Ben hiked out to his truck. He stripped off his waders and put on his hiking boots. He retrieved a collapsible Boy Scout shovel and returned to the river. There were too many rocks to bury the otter close to the water. He carried it to a small, loamy bluff with a view of the river. It took him a long time with the small shovel to dig a deep hole, and he wished for one of his father's long-handled shovels. In this wishing, and in his fatigue, he became briefly confused about whether he was digging a grave for the otter, for his father, or for all of them. Sweat poured from his face, and he could not tell whether he was crying. He lowered the otter into the sweet-smelling dirt and scraped full the hole. He covered it with a large mound of rocks to mark the spot and to keep away the digging critters. He broke off some sage and pushed it in among the rocks to perfume the grave.

Only when he was driving home did it occur to him that the shooter might have missed.

Chapter Fifteen

"I'm getting out of this town," George said. "I'm moving to Durango."

"George, give it a rest," said Iris. "You've been threatening to move to Durango for twenty years."

"Not twenty years steady. Sometimes I threaten to move to Creede."

"Just to mix it up a bit. We appreciate that, George," Iris said.

"I tell you what creeps me out about living in this place," George said. "Some scumbag shoots the nicest otter we've had in six years, and we have to discuss it in a place with all these gapers. Whose dumb idea was it to come here?"

"My dumb idea," said Iris frostily. "I get so fucking tired of the Moose Jaw."

"Well, Iris, I would tell you that you're a dumb broad, but I don't feel like getting beat over the head," George said.

"I'm not up to beating anybody over the head right now," said Iris, wearily.

"If that's the case, then just let me say that you're a dumb broad," said George.

A dumb broad chorus went round the table, from George to Billy to Hector to Ben.

"I can't hit anybody today, anyway," Iris said. "Hector would arrest me."

Hector Morales laughed. "Mike Mills was sheriff in this county for, what, twenty years? When I took over from him, he pulled me aside and said, 'Son, you'll do OK in this job if you remember two things: no one in this county is above the law, and that does not include Iris Gibbs.' Mike was a wise old bastard, rest him."

Billy said, "You remember that otter before this one. He used to swim out and try to bite tourists in the ass while they were fishing. Mean little critter."

"Not one of you is getting what I'm talking about," said George. "We have a real tragedy in this county, a real crime. I liked that otter better than I like ninety-seven per cent of the people in this county. Somebody offs him. They may have been trying to kill Ben, a lesser crime, but still real. And here we are talking about it in the fucking Hacienda, surrounded by a bunch of fucking gapers." When George got to the word, Hacienda, his booming voice could be heard on the other side of the Gore Range. Tourists swiveled cautiously to look. They were unsure whether it was a good or bad sign that the sheriff was sitting with this wild man.

"Keep it down, George," said Hector. "You're going to run the tourists off. You run enough of them off, and I don't get my new patrol car this year."

"And I get no tips," said Lisa, the server.

"You shouldn't call them gapers," Billy said. "The only thing we have to sell in this valley is gaping. People come here to gape at the mountains. It's what they should be doing. The best thing about driving the snowplow is that I get more chances to gape at the mountains. If you live here, and you're not gaping every single day, you might as well move away to some place where you can get a decent job. Gaping is a sign that you don't have a shriveled soul."

"I'll tell you what's shriveled," said George. "OK, never mind. You're right. Give me seven hundred and fifty words on that, and I'll put it in the paper."

Ben liked the occasional columns Billy wrote for the paper. Ben knew from George that Billy would not allow the customary picture of himself to be published alongside the column. With no picture, most people never even connected Billy Mapp, snowplow driver, to William Mapp, newspaper columnist. The fact that a typical column might be devoted to how a black-eyed Susan along a September highway reminded Billy of a kindergartener also threw people off the scent.

"How much?" Billy asked.

"The usual fifty bucks."

"How about seventy-five?"

"Isn't greed a sign of a shriveled soul?" George asked.

"What about being a miser?"

"Sixty-two fifty."

"Deal."

"On one condition," George said. "I want you to work into the seven hundred and fifty words how the gapers look. Turn your chair around and take a good look at them. Everybody just turn around and gape at the gapers."

The group scraped their chairs around on the tile floor. A bicycle couple sat across the way dressed in Lycra. They were in their forties, skinny and tanned. Their tight shorts were black, but their shirts were orange and yellow in what would have been a camouflage pattern if they were trying to hide in a colony of giant parrots. The man's legs were shaved. They ate pasta and sipped Chardonnay. Beyond them was a couple in their sixties. The man was overweight, balding, and wore a gray goatee and a gray silk shirt. The top two buttons were undone and gray chest hair poked out around a silver medallion of a roadrunner. The woman's face was surgically tight. She had nice trim legs and an odd, high paunch that jutted out over the waist of her pants. She wore a ring with a large diamond encrusted in a bed of rubies. They were each on their second martini, and they spoke to the waiter but not to each other.

"Gapers," said Ben.

Billy sighed. "That's not the point, Ben. These people just look funny because they're rich."

"Ben hates the rich," Iris said.

"Iris is rich," said George.

"I'm not rich," Iris said. "I just put on airs."

"All I know is what Buster told me," said George.

"What did Buster tell you?" Iris asked, menace in her voice.

"Told me that every two weeks he got paid for driving the bread truck, and he always handed over his check to you. Said he was fishing through a drawer once, looking for a set of Allen wrenches, and he found twenty or thirty of his checks. Never even got put in the bank."

"All that proves is that Buster spent too much time drinking with the town snoop," Iris said.

"I miss Buster," Billy said.

"Me, too," said George. "One night there was this whiteout blizzard and we were drinking at the Jaw…"

"Does anyone remember why we're here?" asked Iris.

"We got a shooter on the loose," Hector said.

"And what's the High Sheriff got in the way of 'ebidence?'" George asked.

"Not a damn thing. I had a deputy spend all day climbing around that riverbank. No shell. No footprints that couldn't belong to ten different people or six different moose."

"Footprints," snorted George. "The only way a footprint would help is if Billy did it. You find a size eighteen footprint, and we got our man."

"Size sixteen," said Billy, defensively.

"I could dig up the otter and see if the bullet is still in him," said Hector uncertainly.

"Leave the damn otter alone," growled George. "Bullet would have gone straight through him. It's buried in the river somewhere."

"I know," said Hector morosely. "I just wish our chief witness could remember whether there was an exit wound."

Ben shrugged. He had no real sense of danger to himself. The events on the river seemed real, this meeting a little unreal, maybe, as George implied, because of its location at a high-end tourist restaurant. Dead otters did not exist in the Hacienda. The people who dined here were not personally acquainted with any otters, nor had they ever buried one with a Boy Scout shovel. There were no otters on the path that connected the Hacienda to the Lexus to the trophy home to the spa to the gleaming office tower. The otter lived and died in the real world. The purpose of money was to create a universe parallel to the real world, where dead otters were theoretically possible but only in another dimension. Ben recognized that his mood was bad and that Iris may have been on to something when she said he hated the rich. He also recognized that, even without money, he, too, built his own private parallel universe, his fashioned from the material of his restless imaginings. He and the otter had both watched the hummingbird hovering over the Blue River, sipping insects from the streaming sunshine, but the otter had likely watched with fewer distractions.

Iris slammed her beer bottle down on the table. "Could we stop playing detective?" She turned to Hector, "When are you going to arrest Larry?"

"As George puts it, I got no 'ebidence,' Iris. Plus, I got no Larry. Not to be found. Could have left the county. Could have taken to the hills. Half the ski bums in the county camp through the summer to save on rent. Maybe he'll turn up."

"Was he trying to kill Ben?" Iris asked.

"Most likely not," said Hector. "Ben says he hit the otter dead center. We don't know where he was when he shot, but the odds are long that he missed Ben and hit the otter. I'm guessing he's a good shot and not a bad one. Besides, if he missed, why not just shoot again. Ben didn't even have the good sense to get the hell out of there. If he wanted Ben, he had plenty of chances."

"Then why shoot the otter?"

"To scare Ben. Warn him. Warn him away from Megan, if Larry is our man. Before we get any lynch mobs going, it also could have been some random sick prankster up from Denver trying out his new rifle."

"It's a cinch it wasn't any of this group." George waved his hand at the customers in the Hacienda. "There's not a prankster among them."

"Find Larry, Hector," Iris said.

"I'm looking."

"Are you searching the mountains?"

"The mountains are too big, Iris. But I've personally shown his picture to every checker at all three grocery stores. That's usually how I catch them. Sooner or later, they come in for supplies. If he's around, I'll get a call."

Iris said, "Hector, please find him. Please, you have to find him." The group quietly adjourned, all of them made thoughtful by the events before them and by the idea of Iris pleading for anything.

Iris stopped Ben in the parking lot. "You've got to be careful."

"I liked that otter. He got shot because he came out into the river to keep me company. I told Megan and Sarah he was my spirit animal. He must have been because right now I don't have much spirit."

"Well, go home and find some," snapped Iris.

"Yes, ma'am. Your spirit is a little ragged, also. Are you OK?"

"Of course I'm not OK. I'm scared. You remember I told you once I had nothing left to be scared of? Now, I do. I was never smart enough to be scared of losing Buster, and he stole out of this world like a thief in the night. I can't ever get him back. It never meant shit to Buster that I was tough. If I ever got mad at him, he just walked over and smiled and picked me up like I was a bride being carried across the threshold. Being tough didn't matter to Buster. He was a big, rowdy man, and the only thing that made any sense to him was love. I can't get him back. The hardest thing, after he died, was waking up in the middle of some dream about Buster, some dream so real I could have stayed in it forever, and then coming awake and remembering. For a long time it was a new death every night, every time I woke up. This time I'm smart enough to be scared. I don't want to lose anybody again. Please take care of yourself. Take care of Sarah. Take care of Megan. Take care of me."

"Yes, ma'am."

Iris turned to walk to her car. Ben slipped up behind her and lifted her like a bride, turned a complete, swooping circle, and set her back down.

Chapter Sixteen

Megan lived in a rented apartment on the second floor of a Victorian house on Main Street in Frisco. Stairs had been added to the outside of the house, at the back, so that rental income could be squeezed from the upper story. The first floor was a consignment shop, pulling in tourists delighting in bargains, and locals desperate for them. Ben climbed the stairs to Megan's apartment and found her angry.

"Why didn't you tell me about this meeting?" Megan demanded.

"I don't know. No good reason. Iris said to be there, so I went. I didn't think about asking you to come."

"And Iris didn't ask me because she thought it would upset me?"

"I don't know. I guess."

"Am I a child to be protected?"

"Damned if I know. Iris just gave me a lecture about protecting you," Ben said.

"That's just like Iris."

"Unlike Iris, the lecture was pretty inclusive. She included herself in the list of people I needed to protect."

"I won't be treated like a child."

"Yes, ma'am," Ben said.

"Are you patronizing me?"

"No, ma'am."

Megan looked at Ben closely. "No, you're not, are you? I still have trouble getting used to all that Southern talk. Do you think you could ever get over all that ma'am stuff?"

"Yes, ma'am."

They were seated at opposite ends of the small couch, and Megan swung her bare feet into Ben's lap. The couch, sturdy tan corduroy, was from the consignment shop downstairs. The outside of the house was painted purple, and this, her combination of living room and kitchen, was lavender. Megan complained about the lavender paint but Ben liked the boldness of it. If you wanted bland white rooms, you could always move to Denver and live in a suburb. Stacked in one corner of this room were alpine skis, telemark skis, a snowboard, two pairs of snowshoes, and a mountain bike. Ben loved this toy corner. Towering over everything was a pair of antique wooden skis that were seven feet long. The heel binding was missing from one of the old skis. Ben could not imagine ever being able to turn such skis. Ben and Megan had once spent an evening conjuring a business in which they rented these antiques to tourists for actual use on the mountain. Then they realized that only some of the local diehards would be up to the task of figuring out how to use this primitive equipment, and, as soon as they learned to use the skis, they would probably break them skiing off cliffs.

"Rub my feet," Megan said.

Ben happily complied. It was soothing, this rhythmic rubbing and probing of these feet, and Megan's small sighs of contentment. He liked being surrounded by Megan and the things of Megan. A tall, narrow bookcase, also lugged up the back stairs from the consignment shop, loomed against the opposite wall. It brimmed with secondhand paperbacks. The shelves were meant for tall hardbacks, so the upper half of each shelf was filled with a layer of paperbacks stacked sideways. When he first came to Megan's home, Ben had checked to see what order there was in the arrangement of a librarian's books. He was relieved to find none, not even that of the alphabet.

"I don't think it was Larry," Megan said.

Ben shrugged.

"He couldn't do such a thing," she said.

Ben shrugged.

Megan said, "I know what you're thinking. But I've been thinking, too. He has a temper, but this was not temper. This was calculated...cold. Larry gets painted in everyone's mind as a monster because of one thing he did to me. He was hotheaded, not cold-blooded. He could be warm and kind and loving."

"You would know him best," said Ben, coldly.

"Yes, I would," she said, returning cold for cold.

"Maybe you're just busy defending a bad choice."

"Maybe I am. You would be the expert on bad choices," Megan said.

"I can't stand to hear you saying anything nice about him."

"And I want to throw up every time I hear you defending Karen."

Megan jumped up from the couch. She went outside on the landing and stood under a hanging basket of petunias. Ben picked up a copy of *Angle of Repose* from the coffee table and stared bleakly at the pages. Megan came back in and turned on the heat under the teapot. She went back out and pinched off the stems of dying petunia blossoms. Ben tried to find the chapters on Leadville in *Angle of Repose* but seemed always to be reading ahead of or behind this part of the book. The pot began to hiss and Megan came back in and made two cups of tea. She set the cups on the coffee table and took station at the far end of the couch.

"Thanks," Ben said. "There are many kinds of misery in this world but few that seem so like the end of the world as when you are mad at me. I tell myself it's not the end of the world, that it's a storm in this teacup and will pass. But at the time, I'm always unconvinced and miserable. It's not, is it?"

"Not what?"

"The end of the world."

"It will be if you don't apologize," Megan said.

"I thought I just did."

"It was classic Ben, full of left-handed misdirection. But the words, 'I'm sorry,' have yet to come out of your mouth."

"I'm sorry."

"And I." Megan said.

"And I what?"

"I what? OK, I'm sorry, too. Satisfied?"

"Blissfully so."

Megan threw a pillow at Ben, and he threw it back at her. She again put her feet in his lap.

Ben said, "And this is the way the world begins, not with a bang but a foot rub."

"Yes, love, a little more on the heel, please. When you childishly started that fight, I was trying to make a serious point. I don't think it was Larry."

"Maybe. But in some ways that makes it even scarier, saying it could have been anybody. And remember this, Larry tried to hit me with a roll of dimes in his fist. That's not exactly sporting, and no one just happens to have a roll of dimes in their pocket. It was carefully planned, not something he just suddenly lost his temper about. If it hadn't been for Billy, I might still be seeing stars, or little Tweety Birds circling around my head."

"God bless Billy."

Ben said, "Amen, sister. And on the subject of God, Larry apparently found God, or at least some twisted fundamentalist version of God."

"I know. Too bad he didn't find Billy instead, the original gentle giant. We should found a religion of Billy. He's practically all-knowing, at least on the subject of me and my family. Sometimes I love him for it, sometimes...sometimes...ah...never mind."

"I don't understand," Ben said.

"I know you don't understand, and, for now, let's keep it that way. You're not yet entitled to know everything about this valley. You know, you just arrived in these hills about twenty minutes ago. There's some dark side to all of us, even Billy, but he's as qualified to be God as anyone else."

"OK," said Ben. He was not sure exactly what he was agreeing to, but he had the good sense not to start another argument with Megan this soon. He recalled a line from Megan's favorite book, in which Scout Finch defined "fine folks" as those who did the best they could with the sense they had. When Megan had talked of Billy, it had popped into Ben's mind to ask her why they never looked at each other, but again, he thought he might continue, for a little while, down the unaccustomed path of good sense. For now, he was on good behavior. Ben was amazed that most people most of the time forgave him his aggravating ways.

Megan said, "My mistake was introducing Larry to my brother. Larry and I started having problems as soon as he and Tyler started praying together. Larry wanted to get married and patiently explained to me that I should be submissive in the marriage. Actually, he wanted me to be submissive immediately and get married later. Larry wasn't that smart, but he was crafty."

"I'm just thankful no matriarchal societies founded a great religion."

"As well you should be," Megan said.

"Then God would have decreed that men should be subservient. Hell, God would have been a woman, and there's a scary prospect. The first commandment would have been to never wear white shoes before Easter." It came to Ben that his episode of good behavior had been fleeting, but at least he had tried.

"No, the first commandment would have been never fall in love with a smartass."

"God would, by definition, have been a goddess," Ben said.

"Not unlike myself."

"The world would be a kinder, gentler place."

"I wouldn't bet on that. Power still corrupts, I think," said Megan.

"Maybe so. I love that story about the Mormon, Joseph Smith. He got tired of his wife and went out into the woods and came back with a divine revelation authorizing polygamy. You're thinking a Josephine Smith would do the same?"

"A Josephine would never be that dumb," Megan said. "Who would want to pick up dirty underwear from multiple husbands?"

"There's a point. Small-minded, prejudiced, but a point nonetheless. In any event, I'm content that God is clearly male."

"Because?" Megan asked.

"Because you will notice that I'm rubbing your feet. I'm pretty sure God meant it to be the other way around."

Megan glanced down at her feet in Ben's lap, where he was slowly kneading her soles. "You're saying you want to switch?" she asked.

"Only in the interest of God's plan for my feet."

Megan sighed. Ben took off his shoes and socks and placed his feet in Megan's lap. Megan rubbed his feet and Ben sighed.

"The poor otter," said Megan. "We're so scared for us that we forget the otter."

"I haven't forgotten."

"It spooks me that he was your spirit animal."

"That's pretty superstitious," Ben said.

"I guess. But at least it's tied to nature. It feels like it's anchored in the real world. It's like worshipping a mountain, a river. It's even like worshipping Billy. At least it's real."

"OK, but I despise superstition."

"Despise all you want. But that doesn't mean that things can't be connected in ways that are sensed but not seen."

"Or not," Ben said.

"Or not. But there are mysteries in life even your skepticism can't deny. There is me. I am a mystery to you, or I had damn well better be. I had better be to you something mysterious, wonderful, always slightly beyond explaining. There are the invisible ties growing up between us all. I knew Iris cared about me. But who knew she would finally come out and say it? She thinks of me as a daughter. That thread was between us all these years, and it finally became visible."

"A gossamer thread?" Ben asked.

"Keep it up and I break your little toe."

"Ow."

"Who could have predicted the mystery of you and me? Could you have known about the threads that bind you to Sarah? The only thing here that has no mystery, that is completely dull and predictable, is you."

"One for you," Ben said. "I'll tell you a thing that has occurred to me: that otter died for me. Do I say that he died for my sins? I certainly have a few. That would be a mystery."

"You're just saying that to be unpredictable."

"To what possible end?"

"So I will love you more than I can stand."

Megan put down Ben's feet and crawled on top of him. They held each other. Holding each other, they felt safety and strength, and it did not feel like an illusion. It had grown dark outside and a single lamp glowed in the room. On Main Street, the lamps had come on and people strolled to a restaurant, to a bar. The people laughed and murmured and called out to friends. Megan and Ben heard George pass, his booming voice calling out greetings to friends, enemies, and baffled tourists. A vagrant breeze carried the kitchen smells of the Italian restaurant across the street, lifted this smell up and through their open window, and passed it over the corduroy couch on which Ben and Megan held each other. In this breeze was olive oil, garlic, fresh steaming bread, and softly bubbling sauces. Ben and Megan became hungry for the food, for each other, for the voices in the night, for the pools of yellow light under the street lamps, for the thin, crisp air of the mountains, for the dark mountains themselves, rising up around the little town.

Chapter Seventeen

"I'll give you fifty dollars to catch her and kill her," Ben said.

"Catch her yourself," said Megan.

"I can't."

They could see Iris running smoothly above them on the rising trail. Ben spaced his words so he would have enough air to get them out.

"We must have been crazy to think this was a good idea," Ben said.

"It is a good idea. I'm having fun except for the part where I have to listen to you whine."

When Iris hatched the plan to run a complete loop around Buffalo Mountain, Megan had been enthusiastic. Ben had faked enthusiasm on the theory that anything could happen before he actually had to make the run. Preachers on every corner were promising the end of the world around time's next corner. Ben asked God about it; God shrugged and allowed that anything was possible in a universe that he, himself, found increasingly baffling. God suggested that, just in case, Ben consider a serious training regimen. God allowed that this particular run sounded like the end of the world. Warming to the topic, he suggested that this sounded like the run from Hell. Ben, finding no comfort in God, left him sitting in his rocker in the attic room, staring out the narrow window at the deep blue August sky flowing between the mountains. As Ben left, God speculated over his shoulder that Iris might be in league with the Devil.

This was the theory Ben adopted as he struggled up the Gore Range Trail, with Iris running lightly ahead of him. It was a simple plan when Iris sketched it on a napkin at the Roaster. Park at the

Mesa Cortina trailhead. Run north to the Gore Range Trail. Turn west and climb the narrow valley between Buffalo Mountain and Red Peak. Run this valley to the top of Eccles Pass at twelve thousand feet. Run the Meadow Creek Trail down and south. Turn east on the Lily Pad Trail, briefly climbing again to Lily Pad Lake, and then dropping to their starting point. Later, Ben took a ruler to the map and roughly measured this jagged rectangle at fourteen miles. This was Iris's idea of a Sunday jog.

With Sarah gone for the summer, Ben sometimes joined Iris for her morning run. She had taken up running at twenty-five and had rarely missed a day in thirty years. She told him that she had missed the day after Buster died but had taken it up again the day of his funeral although she did not remember how or really remember doing it—someone told her at the funeral that they had seen her out running that snowy morning. Ben could keep up with her for the first mile but after that she had to slow her pace if she wanted the pleasure of his company. Part of the problem was that there were no flat miles in Summit County, and at nine thousand feet, not much to breathe. Living here, you acclimated to the lack of oxygen, but part of that acclimation was simply learning that you were going to be out of breath a lot. Ben was, at best, an indifferent runner. He liked to run but became bored and began talking to himself; sometimes these conversations so engrossed him that his pace lagged to the merest crawl unless Iris was there to ride herd. Megan had recently joined them for some runs, and she was a better partner for Iris because she was more the natural athlete than Ben. Ben sometimes begged off, pleading a chromosomal condition on the laziness gene, so that the two of them could run without having to slow down for him.

"I still think we should kill her," Ben said to Megan. "We could hide her body in the bushes." Pause for breath. "No one would ever know." Pause. "The perfect crime."

"Stop talking about killing people," said Megan sharply.

"What bee got in your bonnet? It's a figure of speech. I could never kill Iris. Maybe break her ankle."

"Stop it," Megan said. "You don't know what you're talking about." She put on speed, leaving Ben and closing the distance to where Iris loped steadily on the trail ahead of them.

Ben was left to reflect on having made another mistake with a woman, a mistake whose name he did not know. He left this mystery and focused on his running. Left alone, he put aside keeping up with Iris and Megan, focused on finding his own rhythm, and began to run more easily.

The trail climbed steeply along Willow Creek, and Ben lost sight of Iris and Megan. Willow Creek pitched down the hill in liquid stair steps and, as Ben climbed, the stair steps turned into a series of sheeted waterfalls, the thin water orange against the color of the rock. He found Iris and Megan waiting for him at the top of the falls. They were running in place and sipping water. Ben looked forward to a break as he crested the steep patch of hill, but Iris and Megan, with Megan leading, started up the trail as soon as he caught up. At least the trail here was level as it twisted through head-high willows. Ben rounded a sharp curve and nearly ran over Iris and Megan, stopped in the trail. Just ahead, the path was blocked by Billy's huge bulk. The three of them were staring at each other, atypically mute. Billy seemed embarrassed.

"Caught you, Billy," said Iris. "You're busted."

"How do you know I wasn't just crossing the trail?" said Billy. Billy made a fetish of not hiking on trails. He went everywhere in the mountains but never on a trail. In a narrow valley, he sometimes bushwhacked twenty feet parallel to the main trail, scaring tourists unused to large creatures crashing through the brush. Billy's theory was that trails contained no surprises. Off the trails, he had spent years crisscrossing the mountains. He cheerfully devoted days to studying some remote piece of meadow. He knew the grasses and the flowers and their positions in relation to light and water. He followed the trickle of a stream and studied the soil and rocks that bowed and looped the water's relentless energy. Billy sat in a meadow like the giant that he was and stared until the midget highways of voles gradually became visible. In the dark timber, he knew the location of such curiosities as abandoned mineshafts, the rusted head of a hammer flecked with dried blood, and shaded places where mushrooms forced their skulls from the earth.

"Maybe I was just cutting across the trail," Billy repeated, without much conviction.

"I don't think so," said Iris. "Megan and I both saw you hiking straight up the middle of the trail."

Billy shrugged. "This is America. I'm as free to use the trail as you are."

"That's only technically true," said Iris.

"What are you guys doing?" Billy asked.

"Running around Buffalo," said Iris.

"That's nice," Billy said. Running held no meaning for Billy.

"Where are you going?" Iris asked.

"Home."

"Where've you been?"

Billy pointed to a fold in the mountain high on the shoulder of Buffalo.

"Why there?" asked Iris.

Billy smiled. "Never been there."

"Then it's one of the few places you haven't been."

"No," said Billy. "There's a million places like that I haven't been. I won't get around to all them. When I was up there, I spotted a little cut between two sideways ridges over on Red Peak I never noticed before. Next weekend I'll go there."

"Because it's there?" Iris asked.

"Thoreau," said Billy. "He liked to say that he had traveled far in Concord. I can't afford to go to Europe or even Iowa, but I have traveled far in Summit County."

"And found things nobody knows about," Iris said.

"Yes," said Billy. He glanced at the three of them, and his look paused for an extra beat on Megan before continuing on to Ben. It was a pause so slight it might have been nothing more than an involuntary tribute to beauty. "And," Billy said, "no one ever will."

Megan stepped closer to Billy. She hit him hard on the left arm. She could have been hitting an oak tree. Billy looked at her sadly and without surprise. Megan looked in his eyes and then hit him again. Billy shrugged helplessly.

Megan made a sound, a frustrated moan, and began running fast up the trail. Billy looked at Iris. She stepped over and touched his cheek with her finger.

"Don't worry about it, Billy. It is what it is."

Ben looked on in wonder. Iris turned and gave him a long look.

"Drink some water," said Iris. "I worried you might not be able to keep up. So far, you're the weak link in this chain."

"What was that about?" Ben asked.

"Have a drink. Rest. We've got miles to go," Iris said.

"I'll be going," Billy said.

Iris said nothing but touched him again on the cheek with her finger. Billy, embarrassed again, took off. This time he did not go up the trail but turned into the willows in the direction of the creek. His destination was unclear but for Billy there was destination in every direction. Before Ben could speak, Iris began running up the trail. Megan was no longer in view. Iris went very fast and Ben had no hope of keeping up. He tried, at first, because he wanted to ask questions of Iris. Iris clearly did not intend this to happen, so Ben gave up and settled into his slow, steady pace. The trail left the willows and began to climb again. Ben was now in the long narrow valley pinched between Buffalo Mountain and Red Peak. The trail, when it went through a meadow, was a thin sliver of fine, gray earth, crowded by overhanging grass. The bunches of grass, having had the good luck not to be in the trampled trail, now furthered fortune by sending leaves to overhang the trail and take advantage of the extra sunlight. Wildflowers grew in the meadow and the tall grass moved before the breeze. Ben wanted to lie in this grass with Megan and watch the blue sky. Always climbing, the trail went in and out of forests of aspen and spruce. In the trees, the trail was wider so two people could walk side by side. Ben wanted to lie in the tall ferns under the aspen with Megan and watch the darting leaves stitching the fabric of deep blue sky. But there was no sign of Megan, or of Iris, and he kept running.

As he passed through a grove of spruce, dense green and blue needles draped to the ground, Iris appeared magically beside him. "God, you're slow."

"True that," gasped Ben. "But I'm also weak of mind. That should count for something."

"Don't you get lonely running back here by yourself?"

"Yes. Would you slow down and keep me company?"

"For a while."

"Actually. Maybe Megan needs the company. Maybe you should speed up and run with her."

"I tried," Iris said, "but I couldn't catch her." Iris and Ben were running side by side through the tall trees. The trees hid the two mountains rising above them. Iris kept pulling ahead of Ben and then forcing herself back to his pace. To solve this problem, she dropped behind Ben and ran on his heels. Ben, in turn, forced himself not to speed up, knowing that his breathing would turn ragged.

"I can't believe that you couldn't catch Megan."

"Megan is inspired."

"By what?"

"Who knows? Anger? Guilt?"

"Over hitting Billy?"

"You are weak of mind."

"Then tell me."

Iris, at this slow pace, spoke easily. "Be careful what you ask for. Most of us…change that…the few of us that have given it serious thought—that would be me, Buster before he died, George…George thinks about everything…Billy, Hector, almost certainly Tyler—most of us think Megan killed her father."

Ben stopped abruptly in the trail and started to turn around. Iris pushed him sharply in the back. "Keep running," she said. "You don't need to see me to hear this. We will find out if you are weak of spirit as well as mind and body."

Ben stumbled forward and regained his stride. They entered into another meadow, but Ben no longer saw the waving grass and the flowers and the two mountains that early and late kept this narrow valley in shadow.

Iris said, "Megan's father disappeared when she was sixteen. As far as anyone knew, he lived in this valley for fifty years and never left it. Not even a trip to Denver. Tyler—he would have been seventeen or eighteen—finally reported him missing. Henry Flanagan had been missing by then for a couple of weeks. Megan just kept going to school and going to one of those jobs she always had after school. She never mentioned that her father was no longer at home."

Ben ran on, no longer hearing his own ragged breathing. Iris spoke evenly as though they were two neighbors visiting across the good fence in their backyard.

"'I guess he got tired of this place.' That's what Megan told Hector when he questioned her. She wouldn't say anything else. She wouldn't come live with me or anyone else that offered to take her in. She never missed turning in an assignment at school. Hector kept going back to talk to her. Poking around like sheriffs do. She wouldn't even say what day her father went missing. All she would say is that he got tired of this place. Mind you, no one missed Megan's father. Not in that way. He was a sorry bastard, who had no friends. Even the people at that weird little church Tyler goes to thought he was creepy. But still, Hector said he had to do something. He was going to call in the state police and search the mountains. George and Buster and I took Hector to the Moose Jaw for a beer. I promised Hector that I would personally pay Billy to search the hills. I told him that if there was anything to be found in these mountains, Billy would find it. George showed Hector an article he was going to put in the paper. It said that Henry Flanagan had gotten tired of this place; rumor had it that he had gone off to do missionary work in Africa. Buster, God love him, just told Hector he was a sweet man and should have another beer. Hector is a sweet man."

"And Billy never found anything?"

"Nothing he likes to talk about."

Ben stopped in the trail. Iris pushed him again in the back, and he turned and pushed her back. "Enough," he said. "This is crazy."

"Can't face the family secrets?" asked Iris.

"Screw you, Iris. Screw you and your little macho tests. This is serious. You act like we're talking about an arm-wrestling contest at the Jaw. You spend about half your time acting tough. Just so we're clear. It's something I tolerate. But I don't admire it. I don't respect it. So, put it away. There are things I need to know."

"Ah," said Iris. She sat down beside the trail. "What do you need to know?"

"For starters, do you really know anything? You tell this wild tale like you know what happened. You don't say if Billy found a body. Maybe Megan's father did run off to Africa to do missionary work."

"Billy's not much of a talker. He was telling Megan the truth when he said no one would ever know what he found in the mountains. Megan, I think, does not always know whether she believes that."

"He was working for you. He wouldn't even tell the boss?"

"As hard as I try to be a bully, not everyone is afraid of me."

"So what good did it do to send Billy out to beat the bushes if he was never going to tell anyone what he found?"

"Think, Ben, think. For my mind, that made him the perfect choice. Well, almost perfect. Eventually I caught on to the fact that I was paying Billy to do what he was going to do anyway. Not one of my smarter moves."

"Why Megan? That makes no sense. What about Tyler?"

"Could be. But, for what it's worth, Tyler was all torn up about his father being missing. He wouldn't tell Hector any more than Megan did, but he went off on one of his sprees, fighting everybody in town, finally got himself locked up. He had already quit school. When he got out of jail, he got his own place to live. Megan just went on being the same perfect Megan. You tell me."

Ben said, "And then the real question. Why? Why were you all convinced that Megan would kill her father? Did he abuse her?"

"We guessed as much. But she would never say."

Ben said, "Billy won't say. Tyler won't say. Megan won't say. What if there is no mystery? Maybe they just have nothing to say. Or maybe there are things you're not saying. Why don't you take all this crazy talk and shove it."

"I love it when you talk macho."

"Go to hell."

Iris laughed. "Still loving it. How about we finish this run before it gets any weirder?"

Ben was silent.

"Ben, it's ancient history. Leave it alone."

Ben did not argue, but he didn't think twelve years amounted to ancient history, and he didn't think Iris was telling him all of the truth. He was angry at Iris. Only Iris, who was a law unto herself, would choose a time like this to dump this story on him. If anybody had killed anybody, it seemed to him the most reasonable suspect was Iris. There was nothing Iris would not do, whereas Megan was always loving and gentle and perfectly herself. But this was also how she had been when her father went missing—what about that? Ben did not know about that, but he knew that Megan had told him she was a creature of her own invention, the daughter of a fictional character. She told him this and lived this with the kindest and most steely determination he had ever seen, and it was this about her that he loved. At that moment, he did not care if Megan had killed the president of the United States. He did not want Megan to hurt or to have been hurt. He wanted to hold her, comfort her, but she was running like a banshee somewhere ahead on this endless steep trail.

Ben and Iris ran on and eventually Ben simply kept his head down and tried not to trip over rocks in the trail. Iris ran ahead of him but kept her pace down, so he would not be left behind again. Ben was aware only that they had been running for a long time in a meadow. He looked up and realized that they had left the trees below them. They passed a glassy tarn that reflected a spire of wavering rock, and this time, when he looked up, he could see the top of the pass. Ben put his head down again to make the final steep pitch. Running the last twenty feet, he looked up, and Megan was stretched out on her back in the short, thin grass at the top of the saddle. Ben, his vision blurred, stumbled on a rock, and then stood over Megan. He rested with his hands on his knees, and she smiled serenely up at him, with whatever anger she had felt towards Billy, towards Ben, gone, set firmly, delicately, aside.

The three of them stayed close as they loped down the other side of the pass. They did not run much faster going down because they were weary and to trip meant pitching downhill into rocks and roots. After four more miles, Ben thought his feet would burst into flame, and Iris, without being asked, called a rest beside Meadow Creek. The three of them pulled off their shoes and dangled bare feet in icy water. Ben found it wonderful to the point of heartbreak. Feet cooled, they ran again. Ambitious tourists, gasping in the thin air, struggled to walk up the trail on this side of the pass and gawked at the three runners, gods of the Meadow Creek Trail. The tourists looked at the trail, at the hurrying waters of the creek, at the great looming hump of Buffalo Mountain. They did not register the places where the mountain folded in on itself, the dense recesses of the spruce forests, the yellow streamers of dirt marking some abandoned mineshaft, portal to endless earth. They saw none of these things, or any of the hidden places where Billy had wandered in search of Megan's story. They saw only the postcard possibilities, and they snapped pictures as Iris and Megan and Ben ran on.

Chapter Eighteen

On the day after their run, Megan was busy with work, and Ben was too sore to move very far from the couch. In the afternoon, he hobbled unannounced into the library with a banana split from Piggy's. Megan was teaching a group of senior citizens to use the Internet when Ben tapped on the narrow glass window on the door of the conference room. She interrupted her lecture long enough to step outside and receive the ice cream, together with a quick and furtive kiss. As Ben looked back through the window of the room, the seniors were already grinning knowingly at each other. The Internet was, to them, mere hearsay, but the rumor of romance had been with them all their lives. Megan was vexed and pleased at the interruption and instructed Ben to put the ice cream in the refrigerator of the break room. She laughed at his hobbled gait, but it was a sympathetic laugh, and it did not sound at all to Ben like the laugh of a killer. In the break room, he found a Sharpie on the table and wrote, "I Love You," on top of the plastic container of ice cream.

He drove home and mulled the fact that he had no clue what else to say, but he was glad he could say that. He wanted to comfort Megan for something he did not know to be true and was not supposed to know about. Failing all else, try ice cream. That morning, Iris had been atypically distraught when Ben hobbled over to her house.

"I should've kept my mouth shut," she said. "You didn't tell Megan what I told you, did you?"

"Neither of us felt much like talking after the run from Hell."

"Good, don't tell her. All I've done is make a mess of things."

"Megan," Ben said, "asked me once before what you had told me about her. Is this what she was talking about?"

"What else?"

"Why'd you tell me?"

"I don't know. I just got scared. This otter business has me spooked. Sarah's back from Texas tomorrow. I didn't think it out. When I get too many worries on my mind, I always feel like I've got to get tough and do something." Iris took a deep breath. "Sorry," she said.

Ben asked Iris if she had any reason to think that Sarah could be in any danger, and Iris did not. She threw up her hands and admitted that she could not even be sure that anyone was in any danger. Sitting on Iris's couch, Ben lifted his feet and placed them on the beat-up coffee table. He grimaced and pointed out that the main danger to life and limb was crazy runs in the mountains. Iris was already apologetic, on the defensive, so he figured he might as well pile on before she got her strength back.

Ben said, "So what about Megan?"

Iris seemed to be recovering her strength because she was no longer so apologetic. "Megan is wonderful. If you are ever smart enough to want to marry her, and she is dumb enough to want to marry you, I'd be content. I got it in my mind that I had to tell you something about her past because I didn't want you hearing some other way."

"Like maybe from Megan herself?" said Ben sarcastically.

"No. Quit being mean. You told me that someone here wrote to Karen about you and Megan. If someone wanted to cause trouble, they could also write you about Megan. Tyler would be suspect number one. There aren't that many people who know much, but in a small town rumors spread. I got worried that you might hear something and blame me for not having told you. Especially anything that might affect Sarah."

It was the perfect circle of small-town life, and Ben appreciated for a moment why Karen hated it. Everyone knew some secret on someone, and the secrets got passed around with the proviso you were not to tell the object of the secret, or, more complicated yet, not to say how you had come to know what you had come to know. Iris had confided to Megan that she got Hector to warn Larry to stay away from Ben, but Megan was not supposed to tell Ben, so Ben was bound not to say anything to Iris. Iris had confided to Ben that she had secretly helped Megan through college, but Ben was not to reveal this to Megan. Ben was still trying to be mad at Iris, but he had to admit that the common thread here was Iris trying to help someone. He also had to admit that he had neglected to tell Iris or Megan about his visit to Tyler, which meant they didn't know unless they had gotten wind of it and agreed not to tell him they knew. Plus, maybe everybody was getting what Huckleberry called "nonnamous letters." It occurred to Ben that if he just stayed around long enough, he, too, could go into the "nonnamous letters" trade, and ship one out whenever he got the urge to stir up a little excitement. He could feel his good humor returning and gave up trying to stay mad at Iris.

"So what do I say to Megan?" Ben asked.

"Whatever you want. I say keep your mouth shut, but I've screwed things up enough already. I'm too much of a fuckup to be allowed an opinion."

Ben began to think that in this matter of keeping his mouth shut Iris might be right. If it was all a bunch of malarkey, then Megan deserved a chance to say so. At the same time, Megan made no secret of the fact that she had secrets and made no secret that she did not now intend to say what they were. She might decide Ben had gone prying where he had no business and fail to understand that Iris had dumped all this on him without invitation. Besides, it wasn't his business. He was still married to Karen. He had not earned any rights to the special privilege of secrets. His job was to be grateful for the privileges he got. His mission, even though the odds were against him, was to try not to be a jerk, or, worse yet, a knave. He thought there were a few holes in the story Iris had told him on the mountain, but if he was going to let it be with Megan he might as well let it be with Iris. He was worried about how any of this might relate to Sarah; that, he could not let be, but he could leave until another day the question of Megan and Sarah. In the meantime, it was an unaccustomed joy to have Iris playing defense, and he decided to push his luck by asking her to get up and make him a sandwich since he was so sore from the run. Iris dutifully got up and went to the kitchen. She rummaged and came back with a single piece of bread folded neatly around a carrot. Having tested his limits, and found them, he took his sandwich and hobbled home.

.....

The next day, home from Houston, Sarah spent her first hours touching things. She dragged Ben to the sofa. They lay together, Ben holding her tight, both looking at their reflection in the dark television screen. She touched his hands. Sometimes she squirmed around and looked back at his face. She looked at him for long moments and then had to look away. She held tightly again to his hands. Ben offered to turn on the television, but she did not want it. She jumped up and retrieved the wooden bear from the end table and then got back on the sofa with Ben. She traced its surface with her fingers and rubbed the smooth, dark wood against her cheek.

Sarah told Ben stories about Ringo, the Texas cat. Ben made up stories about the secret nightlife of Ollie, about the places he rambled when his coat was darker than night and the dogcatcher safely asleep. Ben explained that the dogcatcher's legs twitched when he was asleep, so you knew he was dreaming of chasing dogs. Ben told Sarah of the night Ollie ran into a bear. The two of them growled dark threats at each other and ruffled their fur. Then, honor satisfied, and lacking any audience to impress, and, furthermore, both made lonely by the clouds scudding beneath the full moon, they decided to prowl around together. The bear found a trashcan and Ollie was impressed at the mess the bear created and jealous that it ate half of a chocolate cake.

Sarah pulled Ben outside to look for Ollie. She buried her face in the warm fur of his neck, and they both shivered with happiness. Ollie, overwhelmed with excitement, ran for a stick and dropped it at her feet. She threw it and each time Ollie fetched and then dropped at her feet this wooden offering, covered with happy slobber. Sarah lay on her back, and Ollie romped on top of her. She wrestled him to the ground and whispered in his ear that she knew about the night he spent with the bear and Ollie licked her salty face.

Back inside, Sarah pushed Ben down on the sofa and growled at him and licked his face. Ben laughed and twisted away and tickled her to make her stop. They howled and rolled off the couch. Sarah clunked her head on the floor, and Ben, worried, stopped tickling her. Sarah pretended to be hurt, and Ben reached for the back of her head. As he did so, Sarah lunged and licked his face again. Ben drew back and told her how he used to lick the fat rolls of her neck when she was a baby and how this made her laugh. Sarah asked if her neck was still fat and Ben told her it was perfect. Sarah said one day she would have a baby with a fat neck and lick it the same way.

They went looking for Iris. Sarah buried her face in Iris's slender neck and touched the back of Iris's strong hands as Iris stroked her hair. The two of them toured Iris's garden. Sarah sat down in the dirt and pine bark and gently traced with her finger the curving velvet blossom of a dark purple petunia.

"We're so happy to have you home," Iris said.

"I'm so happy to be home."

"We'll have a party and make ice cream."

"How's Laurie?"

"She's good. I'll bring her up to the party."

"Good. I like Laurie."

"Me, too."

"Don't you love Laurie? She's your daughter."

"I didn't mean that I didn't love her. I like her and I love her."

"It doesn't matter to you that she's…slow? Is it OK to say retarded?" Sarah asked.

"It's OK, and it doesn't matter that she's retarded."

"My mom said that I was retarded."

"She shouldn't say that."

"I know. She didn't mean it. She was mad at me because I dropped one of her fancy plates—china."

"She still shouldn't say it. She doesn't understand."

"She thought I did it on purpose," Sarah said.

158

"Anybody can have an accident."

"I did drop it on purpose."

"Oh."

"I get so mad at her. Did Laurie used to get mad at you that way?"

Iris laughed. "Laurie once threw a plate at me. But I think that was different."

"Because Laurie is retarded?"

"I guess. Maybe it wasn't so different. Mothers and daughters sometimes have a hard time with each other."

"I know. I wish my mom didn't get so mad at me."

"Things will work out. And we'll have a party with homemade ice cream to celebrate your return. And look at Ollie. He's so happy you're back he can't stop wagging his tail."

"Dad says Ollie's been hanging around with bears," Sarah said.

"I wouldn't be at all surprised. Ollie has his secrets."

The two of them carried on this conversation as if Ben did not exist, but he knew that Sarah was reporting to him on her summer. Iris was reminding him that she was family to this child. And maybe Ollie was reminding him that you could be both purely yourself and still the guardian of secrets.

Ben fixed dinner. He nuked chicken patties in the microwave and served them with barbecue sauce on a hamburger bun, with a side of applesauce. Sarah ate hungrily.

"Poor baby," Ben laughed. "Forced, once again, to eat my cooking."

Sarah wiped barbecue sauce from her lower lip. "Do you think I'll like to eat this stuff when I grow up?"

Ben allowed that he was amazed she liked to eat it now. Sarah said she liked it but that probably when she grew up she would like to eat the kind of fancy food that her mom liked. Ben agreed that age would surely cure her of her taste for the garbage he regularly set before her, but Sarah wanted to know why it had not cured his taste for it since he was already old.

"No clue," Ben said. "Maybe it's a guy thing. But that can't be completely true. Lots of guys appreciate good food. I've just never been that interested in food. Most of the time, all I care about is that it tastes OK and is quick, so I can get on with something else. I don't care much about how the table looks or how the wine smells or how sparkling the conversation is over dinner."

"My conversation is pretty sparkling."

"'Deed it is, child. 'Deed it is."

"Are you making fun?"

Ben told her that it was his job to make fun, and he told himself that talking to Sarah was the most interesting thing he had yet done in his life. Ben finished his sandwich, pushed his plate away, and propped his feet on the table.

"Why don't you like to eat?" asked Sarah.

"What have I been doing?"

"No, I mean big, long meals like Mom has, with wine and everything. Meals where you don't put your feet up on the table at the end."

"I don't know. I never liked wine that much. I like Coke and I like coffee, sometimes a beer. Wine is what rich people drink."

"Okay, but I'm not talking about the wine. What about just the big meal?"

"You know, I never thought of it. Maybe it's because of what meals were like when I was a kid."

"Tell me," Sarah said. She loved every story she could dig out about her father's childhood. Ben told her that when he was a child he was not allowed to talk at the table. As he thought about it, he recalled that, of course he was allowed to talk. The real but unspoken rule was that he was not allowed to jabber on about childish things. He was expected to talk about things that might be interesting to an adult. This was not too hard for a child who was a reader, but it made him a diplomat before his time and too thoughtful too early. He tried to explain to Sarah the rule about making the conversation interesting to an adult, but she was generally horrified by the rule. She asked him if this was his mother's rule, and Ben remembered, with surprise, that the rule came from his father.

"It was my dad. He never actually said there was a rule. He just had a little sound he made when he was unhappy with you, a tiny little grunting sound. When he made that sound, you knew to shut up or stop whatever you were doing."

"You have that sound."

Ben was surprised. "I do not."

Sarah imitated perfectly the small, impatient sound Ben remembered from childhood. Ben scratched his head. "Well, it appears that I do. Who knew?"

"Me."

"When do I do it?"

"When you're tired. When you're worried about stuff. When you're thinking about something else and I'm talking too much."

Ben shook his head. "I have become my father, good parts and bad. I'm sorry."

"That's okay. I always understand. Sometimes I do talk too much. Sometimes I talk too much to try to get you to stop worrying. It never works." This life of theirs made Sarah, also, unnaturally thoughtful.

"I am lucky beyond measure," Ben said.

"What does that mean?" Sarah asked.

"It means I love you all the days."

"All the days," Sarah agreed.

Ben and Sarah washed the dishes. They rarely used the dishwasher. Ben washed and rinsed and stacked the dishes on a towel. Sarah dried and scooted a chair from cabinet to cabinet to put the dishes away.

"Mom made fun of me when she asked me to do the dishes and I filled the sink with dishwater."

"Did that hurt your feelings?"

Sarah laughed. "No. It's funny the way we do it. Why don't we use the dishwasher sometime?"

"I don't know. I guess I'm a Luddite."

"What's a Luddite?"

"Someone who is suspicious of progress in general and technology in particular."

161

"I don't get it."

"Someone who would rather use a shovel to dig a ditch than one of those big backhoe machines." And, Ben thought, someone who is slave to the past, someone drawn to the study of history.

"You never dig ditches."

"I do sometimes when I work construction or when I get a job shoveling snow. Mostly I used to with my father. He had his good qualities in spite of the fact that he grunted every time there was mindless chatter at the dinner table—or maybe that was one of his good qualities. And I used to wash dishes just this way with your grandmother."

Sarah finished putting away the last of the dishes. "Let's always do the dishes this way."

"So we can become better Luddites?"

"So we can have these weird talks. You never grunt at me to shut up when we're doing the dishes."

Sarah and Ben went for a walk in the last of the light. They picked up Ollie in Iris's front yard. Sarah knocked on Iris's door and asked her if she wanted to go. Iris looked at Ben and Sarah, with Ollie swirling around and between them, and claimed that she felt too tired to go for a walk.

Ben and Sarah held hands and Ollie drifted along in front of them. It was almost dark, the air had chilled, and Ben kicked himself for not making Sarah wear a sweater. He had gotten out of the habit of parent rituals. They went downhill, circled the block and, coming back up the hill, Sarah began to lag. She stumbled over a crack in the sidewalk.

"Long day," said Ben.

"Yes."

"Hard to change worlds?"

"Yes."

Ben picked her up and carried her. "I can walk," she protested. "You don't have to help me."

"Who said I was helping you? I'm far too selfish to be doing this for you." She put her arms around his neck, her head on his shoulder. He carried her up the street, into the house, into her room, and she was asleep.

Chapter Nineteen

"Why don't you ever ask for help?" Ben asked.

Iris grunted. "Maybe because I don't need any."

"It's going to take you forty days and forty nights to get this firewood moved."

"Then that's exactly how long I'll work on it." She pitched split logs into the wheelbarrow.

"Why didn't you have Jose dump it in the backyard? He would've stacked it for you."

"I didn't have last year's wood moved out of the way. I like the old wood on top so I can burn it first. Jose got the date wrong and brought it a week early. He knows I always get my firewood the second week of August. I got mad and just told him to dump it here. He got mad and told me I was a stubborn gringa."

"OK. But Jose would have rotated your stock for you," Ben said.

"That's not part of our deal."

"So pay him extra."

"He wouldn't have taken it. Jose already works too hard. And he's not getting any younger. Maria has diabetes. Two of his sons are running wild—they think he's a damned old fool for working so hard. It's your typical American family."

Ben sighed. "Life in small towns is complicated."

"It is. So the best thing for you to do is shut up for about fifty years until you get the hang of it."

"Maybe I won't live that long," Ben said.

"Then at least Sarah will have the hang of it."

"Under the theory that you have to hang around for about three generations before mountain folk will begin to think you're a local?"

"Three's marginal, but you're on the right track."

Ben went back to his house and got a pair of brown, cloth work gloves. They were the kind of gloves he wore when he shoveled ditches with his father. He came back and began pitching firewood into the wheelbarrow. He pushed the jumbled load to the back of Iris's house. Iris had already moved the old wood out of the way. The ground where the wood had been was black and damp and scattered with bark and wood chips. Black beetles wandered aimlessly in this maze, alarmed that their sky had fallen upward. Iris stored her firewood under a shed against the back of the house. The shed began low to the ground at the corner of the old house and slanted steeply up and over the back door. You could step out the back door, safe from weather, and retrieve wood, and you could reach up with a snow shovel and hurry the collected snow down the sharp pitch of the shed's roof. The only problem, to Ben's mind, was that the woodshed rose to a peak over the back door and then, caring nothing for the other side of the house, indifferent to symmetry, stopped. Ben began stacking the sweet-smelling wood in the black earth. Iris stacked from the other end.

"Where's Sarah?" Iris asked.

"Gone to play with Tara."

"Thanks for the help with the wood."

"No problem. Moving firewood feels nice, like digging ditches. I wonder if Jose will give me a job."

The two of them attacked the mound of firewood. They pitched and hauled and stacked. Ollie wrestled smaller pieces out of the jumble but became discouraged when no one would throw one. Iris, exasperated, told him to take the stick to the backyard and stack it on the woodpile. He wagged his tail, hoping to improve her tone of voice. Failing, he took a nap. Ben worked silently. Iris sent up trial balloons of small talk without result.

"I've spent plenty of time stacking firewood with Jose," she said. "No way he's going to hire you. Jose likes to pass the time of day as he works. He likes cheerful company."

"Ah," Ben said. "Sorry. Off in my own world."

"I've been sick that maybe I messed up things with you and Megan. That maybe you'll think you have to protect Sarah from Megan."

Ben was surprised. "No. I considered that for about ten seconds. It's absurd. I mean, Sarah and Megan might decide they hate each other's guts once they get to know each other better, but that's the only danger I can see. I'm not saying I buy every word you told me about Megan, but assume the worst. She was horribly abused in some way I don't like to think about by her father, and she pushed him down the well in the backyard. I'm with Megan. Keep in mind that I'm the father of a daughter. I say throw the son of a bitch down the well. And then cover up the fucking well."

Iris threw the piece of firewood she was holding on the stack, but her aim was bad and it rolled off. She walked over to Ben and took the piece he was holding and dropped it on the ground. She hugged Ben so tightly he thought his back might break and then went back and resumed work at her end of the stack.

"What was that about?"

"Shut up, Ben."

As they worked, Ben tried to picture the kind of anger that could have driven Megan. He knew he could not; he could only picture the anger that had shaped his own life. As a child, he had been angry that his father never got a break. Work diligently and with integrity, and you, too, can die of a heart attack at forty-eight. You can be fired by the seed company at forty-five because you're too arthritic to do the heavy lifting that made you arthritic in the first place. You can die broke after always having been broke. Ben was angry that his father was never angry. Somebody had to be angry for him because his acceptance of life was entire and complete.

Ben recalled a time when he was twelve and hunting quail with his father behind the two hyperactive pointers. Unlike Colorado, South Carolina had almost no public land. Ben's father had obtained permission to hunt from a black farmer who owned thirty acres of land that was mostly given over to soybeans, corn, and swamp. The farmer carefully marked for Ben's father the boundaries of his land, warning against a large private hunting preserve on one side. The hunting preserve was leased by a club of wealthy white men. The farmer also warned against straying off into some dense woods on the other side but spoke only elliptically about why. Ben's father nodded and later explained to Ben that an extremely large, volatile, and poor white family, the Saxons, used a remote piece of their land to convert corn into whiskey, without benefit of government oversight. It was not a good idea to disturb them at their labors.

Ben and his father hunted happily on this land, sandwiched between rich and poor. One afternoon, they both shot at the exploding rise of a covey of quail and attracted the attention of the rich. Two members of the hunting club approached them from across the field. Ben's father waved politely, and one of these men cursed and yelled a warning for them to stay put. As the two sets of dogs intermingled, Ben recalled that the new brace of pointers were somehow bigger and sleeker than their own. The leader of these two men was big, red-faced, loud, and profane. He seemed to Ben to be in an uncontrollable rage. He accused Ben's father of poaching on their land. Every time Ben's father made quiet reply, it was drowned out by screaming and threats. In the sun, Ben could see the spit flying out of the man's mouth. The man threatened to call the sheriff, threatened to thrash Ben's father, threatened to shoot him on the spot. Ben's father told the man that he was mistaken about the boundaries. Told him he could call the sheriff or go talk to the farmer whose house was in the distance. The man screamed that he did not need some damned nigger to tell him whose land it was. Ben's father said this was not something to shoot over. He pointedly laid his gun on the ground. If the man wanted to fight, he could put his gun down, and Ben's father would oblige. The second of the two men was quiet in the background, holding his gun, but also trying uselessly to get his friend to calm down. No one paid attention to Ben, a kid, also standing in the background with a twelve gauge shotgun. The loud man, still screaming, still holding his gun, advanced on Ben's father, who did not move. The man advanced within ten feet, his gun pointed at Ben's father, and then his eyes began to flicker because he could not make Ben's father move or be afraid. When his eyes flickered, he saw a child, behind and to the side, down on one knee, gun to his shoulder, with the gun pointed steadily and perfectly at the man's big stomach. The child was already leaning forward into the shot as the man stopped and stumbled quickly backward. When he was out of the range that a shotgun full of birdshot would tear a hole through a person's big stomach, he resumed screaming curses as he retreated into the distance through the cut stalks of the soybeans. Ben's father picked up his own gun and carefully walked a semicircle around the line of Ben's gun. He knelt beside his son and put his hand on his shoulder and quietly told him to put the gun's safety back on. Ben relaxed his killing finger from a trigger that seemed to him to have been already pulled.

Ben had grown up and tried to create a perfect life that would somehow make things right for his father. It seemed to Ben that schoolteachers made just the right amount of money, so he became a schoolteacher. They did not have calloused hands, but neither did they have enough riches to abuse the working classes. Karen had been a schoolteacher when he married her. Two teachers—it was going to be perfect. And then Karen had become more deeply Karen. She took real estate classes. She began to make what she referred to as contacts. They separated. The first time she was unfaithful Ben was enveloped in shards of burning glass. He could roll in this blanket of fiery glass, but the cuts just came from a different direction. And Sarah needed her breakfast fixed and Karen said he was her lifeline, so he went on. But he was again angry enough to kill.

Ben thought also about the times as a child he had wanted to kill his mother for being unfaithful to his father. He could never let it be only his father's business because he was also his father's lifeline. Ben thought a life could be heard in the timbre of a voice. His mother loved him; she took care of him. All of them worked, but hers was the work of despair. She pushed the rock up the hill, and, for her, it was not that the rock rolled back down the hill. If the rock rolls back down, at least you can rest as you stroll down to retrieve it. She pushed the rock up a hill that was unending. She ironed, cooked, washed clothes, mopped the floor, assisted with school projects, and cleaned an unceasing tide of dirt. She was weighted under the knowledge that cleaning was simply a matter of transferring dirt from one location to another. The dirt went to the thick, white strands of the mop, turning it brown. She scrubbed the mop white in a bucket of clean, soapy water near the back steps. The water turned brown. She pitched it into the grass. Her son and her husband walked past her into the house, tracking in more dirt. This, for her, was the great circle of life, and she was driven by despair and duty. This despair, this duty, became the timbre of her voice, a voice that sometimes Ben despised.

Ben's father shoveled the ditch and then leaned on the long, worn handle of the shovel to admire the way the steady current of clear, upstream water gathered in the muddy water created by his shovel and carried it downstream. Ben, standing beside him, listened to his father point out this small wonder to him for perhaps the thousandth time. Ben rolled his eyes and ignored the words. But the tone of fresh wonder in his father's voice bound them together. Ben raged secretly against his mother and sometimes wished her dead and could find for her no sympathy.

In the course of growing up, of youthful excitement and disappointment tumbling one onto the other, Ben buried this secret rage. There was nothing else to be done with it. And later buried his father and later still his mother. His rage on behalf of his father carried on, but there was a kind of consolation for Ben in the idea that at his own death it would be gone. There would be no more memory of his mother's widow's peak peeking over the backseat of a car, a strange car half-hidden in a grove of pine saplings beside a rutted track in the forest. He would not have to be angry at her anymore because she found the life that his father provided to be not enough.

Now he was no longer so certain that this memory would be interred with his bones. His own choices would live after him, Sarah's bequest. He bequeathed to her himself and her mother, gifts of debatable measure. He bequeathed to her the Rocky Mountains, a gift in which he had faith—a rock on which she could build a house. Was Megan, too, to be part of her bequest?

Megan perhaps had wanted to kill a parent, doubtless with better cause than Ben. Unlike Ben, she had only the myth of Atticus Finch to guide her, and it takes an iron discipline to drive a myth down through skin, muscle, sinew, and into the marrow of bone. Megan had said to Ben: Atticus Finch was my only father, and this is something that should make you worry about me—fair warning that she knew how hard the task of replacing family craziness with the kind and disciplined thoughts of Atticus Finch. Perhaps he and Megan were both cautious because of wary knowledge of the short gap between thought and action; this gap can be infinitesimally small, the slight, dangerous difference between a trigger pulled or not. Who knows when the spark jumps the gap, when the thought becomes father to the deed? Ben knew that he had been patiently waiting on some mysterious force to fire across the gap of his conflicting thoughts into the heart of some deed that would give shape to his life.

Iris prepared to drop another armful of wood into the wheelbarrow.

"I almost killed a man once," Ben said.

The load of wood clunked and rattled in the bottom of the metal wheelbarrow, and Iris did not hear him. She must have sensed that he said something, or meant to, because she said, "Welcome back."

Ben looked at her and smiled slowly, the way he knew his father's smile had seemed to come from far away. "I guess I have been away. You know, I'm so happy Sarah's home."

Iris grinned. "Ben, if Sarah went out and gathered up all of Ollie's poop—which reminds me, I need to hire her to do that—and fried it up for your breakfast, you would think it was the best meal you had ever had."

"Leave me alone. Anyone can plainly see that Sarah is perfect."

Iris smiled, happily, indulgently. "Plainly."

Ben said, "And maybe I understand why Megan is so perfect, in a different way. She feels if she slips she might keep sliding. She is kind and gentle and in control because she understands danger."

"Come again."

Ben waved a hand at Iris. "Never mind. I'm not trying to make you understand. Just me. Just the way Megan and I are alike." But also, he thought, maybe we are alike in the knowledge that there are some moments that demand living dangerously, moments given over to action. There is an eternity in which the finger rests on the trigger, then an instant of pulling, gateway to another eternity.

"Ben, you're a strange duck. And you've been off today flying in a far place. Jose would have fired you, but it turns out you actually work harder when you're off flying upside down, so no complaints from me." Iris grinned as she admired their work, "As my friend Ben Wallace would say, we spanked up that woodpile very nicely." She looked at Ben. "Wherever you were off flying, I hope you got somewhere."

"I did," Ben said. "I finally got somewhere." He was done with it, done with Karen. This was the place he had known time would eventually bring him to, the place where something irresistible fired across the gap between thought and deed.

Chapter Twenty

Ben sat with his feet up on the scratched kitchen table. He was tired from helping Iris stack her firewood. Sarah was asleep. Above him, God was silent. Ben dialed Karen's number.

"We should get divorced."

"OK, Ben, whatever you say," Karen said sarcastically.

"I want a divorce."

"Megan must be standing beside you with a gun to your head. I can see her now. One of those Wild West sluts. Lives over the saloon. Keeps a derringer in her bra. If she can't have you, nobody can. Always confused about whether they want to kill themselves or kill their unfaithful man. She hasn't threatened to kill me, I hope." Raising her voice, Karen shouted into the phone, "Hi, Megan, put the gun away. You can have him."

"I'm going to call a lawyer."

"Oh, Ben, please don't mean this."

"I'm serious."

"Don't do this."

"I have to."

"What about Sarah?" Karen asked.

"I don't know. I haven't told her."

Karen laughed bitterly. "Don't worry. She will decide it's all my fault. Her father can do no wrong. When she's a teenager, she will scream at me for ruining her life by divorcing you."

"She loves you."

"And hates me," Karen said.

"I've tried to fix that. It appears I can't do it."

"I should just be your vision of the perfect mother and everything will be OK."

"As of now, that's between you and Sarah. Be kind to her and everything will be OK."

"I am so tired of your 'be kind' advice I could scream."

"I'm so tired of giving it I could scream. You listen. You nod your head. You cry and blame it all on your mother. And then, on a good day, you are kind to Sarah for all of two hours. And in those two hours, she is the happiest child in America. And then she gets tired, or makes a mistake. She slips from your idea of perfection, and you scream at her that she hates you. And then, sure enough, she does. You can't stop. You won't stop. So—enough. I stop."

"I wanted us to be a family forever," Karen said, and Ben understood she was referring to the original dream that they had clung to, both in their own way, with such tenacity and futility.

Ben looked at the scratches on the old table. He made out the first two letters in Sarah's name and then the angle of the light on the table prevented him from reading further. You wanted us to be a family forever, he thought. You wanted this more than anything in the abstract and less than anything in the specific. This he did not say. It was the same story, and he had never figured out a way to penetrate the wall of Karen's grand pronouncements. I love you more than anything. We love each other so much that nothing can ever come between us. You are the best man I have ever known. I have never known such happiness as being a mother to Sarah. Ben, growing up with quiet understatement, found Karen's pronouncements thrilling. She said these things with such intensity, such passion and conviction, that Ben felt he had been transported into a realm of depth and excitement he had never known existed. When her actions did not match her words, he was bitterly disappointed and confused. Then she would give another speech and lift him again into swirling clouds of passion. He heard the speech and each time knew to his very bones that this time it had to be true. And it was true. It was as true in the moment of the speech as a thing could be true. He learned all the rules. You did not doubt the speech. You never mentioned that some specific action did not fit the words. In the beginning, for Karen, was the word and only the word, and the word was love, and all else were deeds, and these were part of the great, dark void. And if you dared to mention a deed, you incurred wrath beyond measure and were thrown out into the void to live with the meaningless deeds. He had no idea whether he and Megan would ever marry, would ever have any future together, but they were together in the imperfect struggle to marry words to deeds.

"Are you there?" Karen asked.

"I'm here."

"This is all about Megan, isn't it? She's destroying our family, and you're letting it happen."

"It's partly about Megan."

"Have you moved her in yet?'

"No."

"But you're going to," Karen said.

"What I do or don't do with Megan is not what we're talking about. I called to tell you two things. I love you. I will get a divorce. Make any sense of that you want." Ben knew that he had not figured out how to stop loving Karen, but it was enough to figure out how to get divorced. He was no longer responsible for Karen. He could simply put down that load and leave it beside the trail. It flashed through his mind that his mother should have put down her load if she could not bear it, and he had a confusing moment of softening towards her. Ben pushed this thought from his mind because he did not want more confusion. What was in this moment was that he was a lifeline now only for Sarah, the happiest of burdens. He felt clear-headed and light as a dust mote in the sunshine.

Karen said, "Don't you dare tell me you love me. You don't know what love is. You grew up without emotion. You're an empty man. You could never express love. You have no passion, no fire, no drive. You're a lousy provider. And lousy in bed."

"I'm glad we got to clear the air on these things." Ben no longer even registered the ritual flailing. With Karen, it was either love or destruction, or perhaps it was love and destruction. It occurred to him that Karen was partly just pissed because she did not get to decide first to get a divorce.

"Megan will never be a mother to my daughter. Do you hear me? Never."

"You will always be Sarah's mother."

"Don't try to pacify me. You're not the only one who knows how to talk to lawyers. You'll regret this. You'll pay."

"This isn't the time to talk about that stuff. I'm just going to talk to the lawyer and try to figure out what you have to do to get a divorce. We can talk about all the other stuff another time."

"Don't try to hand me a pacifier, Ben. It won't work."

"Karen, I'm so sorry. I am sorry. I don't know anything to tell you. I'm sorry. I want a divorce."

"Don't try to end this conversation, you little coward. I am nowhere near done with you…"

"I promise that you will have a lot more opportunities to yell at me. I will call you with what I find out. Now, I have to go."

"Coward, asshole, no one hangs up on me. I will…"

Ben hung up. Almost immediately, the phone rang. Ben did not answer. He stared at the phone, and each succeeding ring seemed to have more intensity and anger. Afraid that it would awaken Sarah, he found a way to turn down the ringer. Karen's legal threats were probably empty, but if not, so be it. He got up to close the door against the evening chill. He looked up into the ocean of dark sky and all he could think was that it had been his job to throw Karen a rope, and he was not going to do that job anymore. She would continue to get rich; she would continue to become more fully Karen; and, she might drown in it. But he was done with the rope throw. When the phone stopped ringing, Ben called Megan and she agreed to meet him for breakfast.

…….

God came downstairs, opened the refrigerator and took out a Fat Tire. He held the cool bottle against his check and said, "Couldn't help but hear. You've had an eventful evening. Ever think of consulting me before you make these big decisions?"

"Nope."

"You are wise beyond your years. It is odd that you consult with no one."

Ben shrugged. "Who would I consult? Megan, Karen, Sarah, they are all a part of the decision. Iris as much as anybody."

"I wonder why you didn't ask George or Billy, both smart men."

"Damned if I know. Never occurred to me," Ben said.

"Men happily consult with each other about war but never about love. Some sort of design flaw is my guess. It's fascinating to me that, when religions went away from the notion of polytheism, they created a god who, by definition, could have no direct experience with sexual relationships. At least Zeus had Hera, and any other woman he could get his hands on. Zeus could, as they say, relate. And if his advice seemed limited, at least you could get a second opinion from Hera. Not a bad arrangement. The down side is that then you have gods shouting contradictory instructions into each ear. Monotheism is a great simplifier, but then you're left in the absurd position of turning to a male god for advice on love. How dumb is that? It's just my opinion, but it seems to me that the safest bet for Christians, Jews, and Muslims is to only pray for divine guidance on football and beer."

Ben got up and got a beer. God looked at the beer and lifted a quizzical eyebrow.

"What? You can drink and I can't?" Ben asked.

"I only drink to humor Willie Nelson. But it's not your style."

"Who knows? Maybe I'll become a hard-drinking guy like George." God and Ben clinked bottles, and out in the night, Ollie barked. God said, "Ollie sees it as his role in life to protect Iris from raccoons. In his view, this is a much more important contribution to the relationship than Iris dumping dog chow into a bowl. But he loves her anyway because she's cute and loyal."

Ben said, "You have a gift for distraction."

"In the wee, dark hours, a little distraction is not a bad thing."

"True that," Ben said.

Ben and God sat at the table, drank beer, and talked for an hour about all the second and third chances that Lincoln gave General McClellan before he fired him. Ben thought Lincoln had been too patient for too long, but God would hear no criticism of Lincoln. God insisted that Lincoln moved to the tides of his own nature, took no heed of those who said he was too fast or too slow, and most important, did not berate himself for being the only person he could be. Ben gratefully conceded the argument to God.

PART TWO

Chapter Twenty-One

Ben made Sarah breakfast and dropped her off at Iris's. He met Megan at the Kokomo Cafe at nine. It was crowded, but Lisa, the owner, was resourceful. She spotted them at the end of the line of tourists and loudly said, "Are you two in the Smith party?" Ben and Megan agreed they must be, and Lisa motioned them past the line and took them to a private booth by the window. Lisa then hustled off to the kitchen so that the tourists who realized they had been scammed could get the grumbling out of their system. If a couple of them chose to get mad and leave, the line would only fill again from the rear. Lisa had perfected a cozy café that served simple, tasty food for breakfast and lunch and then closed up so Lisa could take her golden retrievers for a walk in the mountains. She could have filled a restaurant three times as large for three meals a day, but she wanted to walk the dogs. She had mastered the idea of enough.

"How's Sarah?" Megan asked.

"Wonderful. I'm so happy she's back."

"Me, too. I like Sarah."

Lisa took their order. She spontaneously leaned over and kissed Megan on top of her head and told her how wonderful she looked. Megan had waited tables for Lisa when she was in high school and still filled in sometimes on the breakfast shift if Lisa was shorthanded.

Ben thought Megan was nervous. She said, "I need to talk to you."

"I thought I was the one who needed to talk to you."

Megan said, "But I need to go first." Her words rushed between them. "Do you know why I dated Larry? And, for that matter, the guys I dated before him. They were basically all the same guy, anyway." Ben started to speak, and she shushed him. "I dated them because they were fun and they liked to do things. Mostly, though, it was because I could never be serious about any of them. They were safe. You're not safe for me. I told you on San Luis that I thought you might get ready before I did, and you did. I'm not ready. I'm sorry, Ben, I do love you but I'm scared." Megan's hands fluttered and her face was so drawn that Lisa said nothing when she brought the food and hurried away. Megan's breathing was shallow. Ben took her hand and it was cold.

"It's OK," he said. "Don't be scared. You don't have to tell me anything." Ben rubbed Megan's hand. "What brought this on?"

"You got ready before I did. You're divorcing Karen."

"How did you know that?" Ben was incredulous.

Megan allowed half of a smile although her eyes were damp. "Oh, Ben. I know you think you're deep and mysterious, but not really so much."

Ben groped for an answer. "Did Karen call you?"

"Iris called me last night, and then you called me and wanted to have breakfast. And then I called Iris back and we figured it out."

"But Iris doesn't know. I haven't said a word to Iris."

"She saw it yesterday when you were acting like a zombie. She thought I ought to be warned. I never promised you anything, Ben. I told you that I came with no guarantees, whatever you did about Karen. I told you that. Please tell me you remember me telling you that."

Ben was baffled. "Wait. Stop. I am divorcing Karen. Whether we ever see each other again or not, I'm divorcing Karen. Does that help?"

"Yes. No. I'm sorry. I should be happy for you that you worked things out in your head. And I am happy for you. It was the struggle of your life, and all I can do is talk about me." Megan took Ben's hand across the table. She was crying. "Ben, I'm happy for you. I'm proud of you. I always had faith in you. I stayed up all last night thinking what I would say, and I'm messing everything up. I'm sorry. I do love you. You know I love you, don't you? That's the whole problem. If it was Larry, I could just say let's go shoot some pool or something. But it's you. It's you, Ben. And I'm not ready. I'm not saying never, just please give me a chance to get ready."

Ben struggled to catch up. "Wait. It sounds like you're breaking up with me."

Megan cried and people at the next table were beginning to take notice. Lisa came by and filled Ben's coffee and gave him a dirty look, a look that signaled that men everywhere were scoundrels and rogues, but none worse than he.

Megan said, "Just some time, Ben. I need some time. It's not forever. I hope it's not forever. I don't want it to be. Please, please forgive me."

Ben shook his head as if he could shake surprise out of the closest ear. He had come here to make something like this same speech to Megan. He toyed with the wonderful temptation to put his speech away in a drawer and play the victim. Megan looked down at her lap, sunk in misery.

"OK," Ben said and drank his coffee. He started in on his scrambled eggs. He pushed Megan's plate slightly towards her and reminded her to eat. Megan sat with her head sunk on her chest but could not help but notice Ben digging into his breakfast.

She looked up. "OK. Just OK! And then chow down on breakfast!"

Ben looked in her eyes and smiled. He reached across and touched her cheek. "That I were a glove upon that hand, That I might touch that cheek." He returned to his breakfast.

"Shakespeare? I don't need Shakespeare at a time like this. Is anybody home over there?"

Ben smiled and touched her cheek again. "Oh, God, I am so tempted...I am so tempted to be a bad man. Can I be a bad man, just this once? Just once, and I'll never ask again."

Megan was angry and flushed. "Ben Wallace, you had better tell me what you're talking about," she hissed.

Ben tried to touch her cheek again but she pushed his hand away. He looked her in the eyes and turned serious. "I do love to touch that cheek. I came here to ask you for the same thing, some time, just some time to be with Sarah, to start this new life it feels like we'll have. I'm as scared of you as you are of me. Believe me, I am. I don't want to fail again…I'm not sure I'm strong enough after Karen to fail again. You and I started wrong. My marriage…my divided loyalties…my fault. I don't want Sarah to see me leaving one woman and running into the arms of another. And I don't want you to see me that way, either." He shrugged. "I promise you I'm working on it."

Megan said, "You came here to break up with me? You bastard." Ben could see her mind racing, and the tension slowly leaving her body. "Oh, Ben," she said softly, "you are the oddest duck in the pond."

"That's what Iris called me yesterday."

"I know. That's where I got it. And she's right. You're just…odd. Nobody thinks like you. I guess it's all that farm boy life with your father or something. You're a smartass but you're painfully sensitive. I have to watch myself not to say something crude around you because if I say 'fuck' a cloud passes over your face. See—I swear—you just did it again. You're…what is it? You're a liberal Puritan. And such a diplomat, never a raised voice, always polite, but then you go sneaking off and march into my crazy brother's house. Don't give me that look. I knew about it the day after it happened. I still don't know how you got out of there alive. I can't even think of all the contradictions about you. Here's another. You're the sanest person I know, but you talk to yourself. You carry on these conversations when you think you're alone and there's no one there. Oh, I know. At my house last summer, you thought I was asleep, and you're sitting at the kitchen table murmuring the night away. You're in the wrong time or something. You don't fit. You're odd, Ben. Face it. You're quiet for the longest time worrying, thinking, I don't know, and then you get going until all a person can do is tell you to shut up."

Ben was rendered for the moment speechless, and Megan added, as afterthought, "You know it makes you irresistible. Damn it, you know that, don't you?"

Megan's voice had been steadily rising, and people were beginning to look again. Ben caught her eye and nodded at them.

Megan threw up her hands in frustration and began to slide out of the booth. Ben put money on the table and hurried to catch up as Lisa beamed death rays in his direction. He caught up with Megan at the little historical park, sprinkled with big cottonwoods and tiny log cabins, and she allowed herself to be guided to a park bench under a tree.

Megan said, "And here's another thing—you quote Shakespeare like you just had a conversation with him this morning, which you probably did. I think I want Larry back. The only person he ever quoted was his buddy Cyrus, who tends bar at the Briar Rose."

"Sorry," said Ben. He was pretty sure he should be sorry for something.

Megan took a deep breath and took Ben's hand. "OK. I'm done. All better."

Ben was fascinated at this outburst. Most of the things she said about him were true enough, he supposed. The remarkable thing was to have someone think so deeply about him, as he had been trying to do about her. Exhausted, they watched the tourists strolling Main Street, gaping at their mountains.

"How'd you find out I went to Tyler's house?" Ben asked.

"Thelma. I don't talk to Tyler, but sometimes Thelma, mostly so I can find out how Nathan is doing. She told you you had Tyler buffaloed. She hung around eavesdropping so she could try to save you if Tyler went off. Don't expect my brother to stay buffaloed forever. Count your blessings and stay away from him."

"Yes, ma'am."

Megan laughed. "I thought you invited me to breakfast to propose. It came to me at two this morning that that's what you were going to do. I freaked. What an idiot!"

"Me or you?"

"Me, I guess…and you."

"You're the one that just had to talk first. Serves you right. I was so tempted to be a bad man, to just say nothing and let you be the villain."

"I know you think that's funny, but it's not. What are we going to do?"

"We? There is no we. You broke up with me, remember?"

Megan started to get up. Ben realized his mistake and held her lightly on the arm, and he was grateful she allowed herself to be held. He said, "You're right. I'm sorry. Here's what I'm going to do. I'm going to do what I said. I'm going to spend time with my kid."

"Have you told her?"

"Not yet. I'm going to take care of her if she needs taking care of. I'm going to play basketball with her and help her with her homework and take her for walks and tell her bizarre stories that no normal person would even think of. I'm going to luxuriate in the feeling of relief that I have had for about twelve hours now. Who cares about getting a piece of paper from a judge? I'm divorced. Karen is not my problem anymore. I'm not going to beat myself up for not sticking with her forever, and I'm not going to beat myself up for not leaving her sooner. It is what it is. So be it."

Megan reached over and took Ben's hand. He said, "I'm not done yet. I'm going to go to work and take care of my kid and have a life in the mountains. I'm going to show myself I can do it. Maybe all this is phony bullshit, me trying to act like I didn't just leave Karen to run to you. But if it is, I don't care. I'll just be cheerfully phony—I can play that role. And all the time I'm doing this stuff, I'm going to be dreaming that one day I walk into a library by the Blue River and meet you."

Megan sat with her head down, not meeting Ben's eyes. He continued softly, "That's what I'm going to do. What you do is up to you, but I hope…never mind what I hope…I can't tell you what to do."

Megan looked up at him, fierce, unreadable. She said, "I'm going to take Sarah to the movies. Just the two of us. If she'll have me."

"She'd love to. Whatever you guys want."

"I think I need Sarah." Ben tried to make sense of this but there was no clue in Megan's face. He looked away at the sound of a horn honking and Megan was gone, lifted off with no more sound than a bird taking flight.

Chapter Twenty-Two

Sarah launched skyward a prayer. The basketball had no rotation, the shot had no arc, but it skimmed the front rim, hit the back rim, and dropped through the net.

"Yes," she said, and pumped her fist.

"No," Ben said. "I hope you don't think that counts."

"Game, Dad, I have game. And what do you have?"

"No game?"

"Correctamundo. And why do you have no game?"

"Because I'm a loser?" Ben asked.

"With a big L on your forehead." Sarah tossed the ball to Ben. "Take it out."

Ben dribbled the ball idly back to what would have been the three-point line if the school playground had one. Sarah came up to guard him as he turned towards the basket. He held the ball and jab-stepped left and right. Sarah wasn't buying. She stayed back to take away the drive to the basket. She knew his weakness, which was laziness, and tempted him to launch a three. He did so and she chased down the long rebound that clanked off the front of the rim. Ben hurried to guard her. She dribbled the ball back out.

"Dad, my spelling is really bad. Tell me again, how do you spell 'brick?'"

"I can tell you how to spell 'brick' if you can tell me how to spell 'wretched, ungrateful child.'"

Sarah grinned. "S-A-R-A-H."

Ben watched her dribble, blond ponytail bobbing gently as she planned her move. She wore Converse tennis shoes, cut-off jeans that were faded and frayed, and one of Ben's T-shirts. She loved to wear Ben's shirts, and this aggravated him every time he searched for some article of clothing and came up empty. At the same time, her love of his large T-shirts was useful on the basketball court. Ben's defense was as lazy as his offense, and when she drove around him, he could reach out and grab a handful of shirt to slow her down. He had learned to grab and jerk and let go so quickly that she was not always aware of his perfidy. He watched now the firm set of her mouth and her narrowed eyes as she searched for an opening. At one moment, some fraction of her face was his, at the next, her mother's. As her face flowed from one expression to the next, it spun dizzying echoes of each of her parents. No divorce judge had the power to unravel this marriage of chromosomes. Ben marveled at her beauty, and, as he did so, she drove under his elbow. He followed her to the basket, took ruthless advantage of his height, and blocked her shot.

"Who's the loser?" he taunted.

Ben dribbled out to the free throw line and began backing her down. She pushed his lower back and reached around to disrupt his dribble. Ben turned and went up for a jump shot. Sarah went up with him and expertly jabbed his right elbow as he shot. Short, the ball deflected off the front of the rim.

"Foul," Ben cried.

"Don't whine, Dad. Nobody likes a whiner."

The rules of their game had evolved over time. Ben never used his height advantage to block a shot, except when provoked. In spite of what Sarah said, whining was allowed at all times, as was taunting. For reasons lost to memory, Sarah was allowed to spit on the court but Ben was not, something about the grossness of boy spit as opposed to girl spit. Ben's favorite dodge when he missed a shot was to complain that the ball had slipped from his hand because he had just dribbled through a spit spot. Sarah, by prevailing in the argument over who could spit on the court, forever gave up the ability to use this particular excuse. Claiming spit spot after a missed shot brought no specific gain; Ben was not allowed to take the shot over; but the complaint was both satisfying and traditional. Sarah was allowed to foul at will and became very good at it. Ben was allowed to whine about being fouled, but there were no free throws.

If he became too aggravated, he could always block her shot or throw her a hip to teach her respect for the majesty of brute force. This carefully worked out set of rule modifications made the game fun as hell for both of them.

When they first began playing together, Ben had revealed to Sarah the true story of his life in basketball. They had just finished a game and were resting in the grass in the cool, fading light of a summer evening. He swore her to secrecy with a double pinky promise and a spit-in-the-hands handshake. He looked over his shoulder, lowered his voice, and gravely explained to her that he and Michael Jordan were identical twins.

Sarah had questions: "Isn't he black? Isn't he tall? Isn't he good?"

In response to the last question, Ben reminded her of the two fadeaway jump shots he had made in the game they had just played. Sarah reminded him that he had taken two hundred such shots and only made the two. Ben reprimanded her for being a child prone to exaggeration and assured her that all this other stuff about height and skin color was irrelevant detail. He explained to her that he was born five minutes before Michael, so he always had to assume the burden of the older brother. He told Sarah that Michael was weak and sickly. He told her that she probably inherited her tendency to whine from her Uncle Mike. Ben described how they grew up poor but industrious in North Carolina. At least Ben was industrious; Mike was a slacker. As the older brother, Ben had to spend time caring for their ailing mother and working six simultaneous fulltime jobs to make ends meet. He also did his best to help Mike with his game although it was a tough go because Mike was soft and had very little aptitude for the sport. Mike often resented Ben because he was so much better at basketball.

Ben and Sarah lay on the sweet-smelling lawn and each chewed a blade of grass as Ben shared with his daughter the deep secrets of his life.

"So why didn't you become a professional basketball player?"

"I'm getting to that. Our mother became sicker as the years went by. It was clear that one of us had to stay home and take care of her. I was the oldest. What was I going to do? Mike had time to play high school ball and then got the scholarship to North Carolina. Our mother was so excited. She watched all his games on TV while I cooked dinner and washed the dishes. Because I was always working, almost no one knew that Mike had a twin. Mike never told anybody because he didn't want anyone to know that I could school him on the basketball court. I do try to love my brother, but he is a limited person."

"So my uncle is Michael Jordan? Cool."

"Mike. You can call him Uncle Mike."

"When am I going to get to see him?"

"You have seen him, many times," Ben said.

"I don't mean on TV. In person."

"You have seen him many times in person."

"I have?"

"It's very complicated, but I'll try to explain. It all started when Michael, Mike, was in college. I told you that he was weak, a whiner. He just couldn't stand up to pressure. So, before one of his big college games, he called home and told his, our, mother that he couldn't go through with it. Claimed to be sick. Said he was going to drop out of school. I could've killed him for getting our mother so upset. She went to her room and cried. Finally, she came out, and she had a plan. She told me I had to go play for Mike. She said no one would ever know. No one at the University of North Carolina knew he had a twin. I tried to talk her out of it. I told her that Mike needed to learn to stand on his own feet, to be a man. She would have none of it. She told me if I didn't save Mike it would be the death of her."

Sarah chewed on her blade of grass. "No one knew the difference because you were identical twins?"

"Are."

"Right. Are identical twins."

"That was the start of it. Mike came home and looked after our mother, and I played in the big game. Twenty points, eight rebounds, and five assists—I held back because I was afraid someone would notice. From then on, whenever there was a big game, Mike would come home, and I would go play for him."

"But you couldn't play for him all the time?"

"No, just the big games when Mike couldn't stand the pressure. Mike actually learned to play the game fairly well when there wasn't much on the line. But when the stakes were high, when he had to be tough, then the phone always rang. Our mother had created a monster. It went on like that for years, even after she passed to her reward."

"My grandmother Jordan died? And you didn't even tell me?"

"Sorry, love. My bad."

"So, when do I get to meet Uncle Mike?"

"I told you. You already have, a bunch of times."

"When was that?"

"Well, mostly during the NBA playoffs," Ben said.

"But we always watch the playoffs together."

"You and your Uncle Mike watch the playoffs together."

"Ah."

"That's why it's so important to keep the secret."

"And I never knew," Sarah said.

"Actually, I thought you might catch on. Didn't you ever notice times when the person you thought was me was grumpy, or too lazy to read you a bedtime story?"

"Uncle Mike?"

"Exactly."

Sarah picked a fresh blade of grass. Her eyes narrowed. "So, are you going to read me a story tonight?"

Ben saw the trap. "Of course, love."

"And every night? And never be grumpy?"

"I'm never grumpy."

"Only Uncle Mike is grumpy?"

"Exactly."

"One more thing, Dad. Why don't people notice that you're tall and handsome, just like Uncle Mike?"

"You mean they don't?"

Ben thought of this story as they played. He wanted Mike to fill in for him in this hard game of divorce. He and Sarah took a break. They leaned against the chain link fence and shared a water bottle.

"I talked to your mother last night. I've decided to get a divorce."

"OK."

"Just OK?"

"It's not exactly a surprise," Sarah said.

"I guess not."

"It won't change that much for me. You guys haven't been living together anyway."

"Your mother and I will do everything we can to make it OK for you."

"Will you buy me a horse?" Sarah asked.

Ben looked at her.

"Joke, Dad, joke."

"Maybe things will be better in some ways. I don't know."

"I think they might be better for Mom. She says she gets tired of you always judging her."

"How so?"

"I don't know. She gets tired of you always being right. She doesn't want to be like you want her to be. She calls it the Ben trap."

"You and your mom talk about this stuff?"

"Sure, all the time. We're girls."

"Oh. Anyway, I'm going to do my best to make it OK for you. I hope it's not going to be too hard for you."

"I will be OK as long as I can take care of you."

"Wait. No. Taking care of me is not your job. I will take care of you. And your mother will. Your job is to be a kid. None of this is your fault. You will always have both your parents. Your mother and I are not divorcing you; we're divorcing each other."

Sarah rolled her eyes. "You don't have to give me the speech, Dad. Every kid knows the speech. But it's my job to take care of you."

"No. I'm the parent. I take care of you."

"I know. I know. But that's not what I'm saying. It's still my job to take care of you."

"No."

"Dad, you don't get it. It's not like you're making me. It's my job because I want it to be. It's what makes me happy. You couldn't get

190

along without me." Ben was reminded that this was the feeling he had towards his father. It was the feeling that the fictional Scout Finch had towards her father, the feeling that Megan had stolen from a book to help her create a life. Maybe it was part of the gift he and Megan had for each other if they could once master Sarah's simplicity of purpose.

Ben said, "No, that's not right. I mean, it's right, but it's not..."

"Dad. Could you just get over it? Mom doesn't need me. Half the time she doesn't even know I'm there. You're always checking to see if I'm OK. And I do the same thing with you. It's my job. I take care of you. I don't have to. I want to. It's what I do. Get used to it. Get over it."

Chapter Twenty-Three

"Good choice," George said.

"All my choices are brilliant," said Iris, irritably. "Which one are you talking about?"

"O'Hara's. I like this bar. It's as close to a workingman's pub as you can find in Summit County."

Ben had been shanghaied into dinner with Iris, George, and Billy. Ben had been reluctant but since Sarah had been invited to the movies with a girlfriend from school he had no good excuse. He was not much in the mood for conversation, but when George and Iris were drinking beer, what they mostly valued were listeners, anyway. Ben was happy to be with this group, to stack one more stone on the cairn of clan he was slowly building. They sat at a table in the back dining room and had the room to themselves. There was a television suspended from the ceiling over their table. The television was tuned to a baseball game, and Iris made Billy reach up and turn it off. Carlos, the middle-aged busboy, passed with a load of plates and told Billy that if he was not an ignorant giant he would know that he was not allowed to turn off the television. Billy asked Carlos about his wife, who had gone to Mexico to visit her family and now was not sure she wanted to return. Carlos shrugged helplessly, and Billy nodded sadly. From their table, they could see some of the regulars at the rectangular bar. Henry was the cable guy. Eric fixed the lifts at Copper Mountain. Julie was a nurse at the hospital.

"What do you know about the working class?" Iris asked. "The only thing you have in common with the workingman is a low income."

"I work," George said. "I'm poor. How am I not working class?"

"Billy is working class," Iris said. "Buster was working class. You're a newspaper editor. You could be editor of the New York Times if they didn't require you to wear a tie and live in New York City. You're poor by choice."

"Poverty is a lifestyle choice!" exclaimed George. "Why is it that once you're rich, you develop all the intellectual depth and empathy of Marie Antoinette? You inherited your money, Iris. And the only work you do that I've noticed is wearing out running shoes."

Ben scored this point for George. Iris was rich, but she wore her wealth and her family's name in her own peculiar way. She did not spend much money because most of the time she seemed to forget she had any. She liked the rough company of men. She clearly had no patience for the symbiotic relationship that so many women maintained with the insecurity industry. Her idea of fashion was fundamentally masculine—jeans and a T-shirt. Her theory of beauty seemed to be limited to intense physical exercise, and Ben admired her imperial slimness, sheer physical strength, and spitting indifference to what anyone else might think. Ben wished that he had known Buster, and Buster and Iris together, to see how they lived their marriage.

Iris said, "Don't tell me about work. I worked like hell before we turned the ranch into cute little ranchettes and sold them to rich people so they could build ten thousand square foot homes that they visit once a year. I'm only rich, anyway, by your standards, not by the standards of the rich people I sold ranchettes to. And I don't work now precisely because I am rich. Think, George—the whole idea of being rich is so you don't have to work. Isn't that every working stiff's dream?"

"It is mine," allowed Billy.

"Pay no attention to him," said George. "He's a poor working stiff with shit for brains. If God had intended snowplow drivers to be smart, he would have made them plastic surgeons."

"What does that mean?" asked Iris.

"It means," Billy said, "that now he's trying to pick a fight with me. In the best of all worlds, he can then spend the evening arguing with both of us." Billy winked down at Iris. "The problem for

George is that you're tougher than he is, and I'm smarter. Either way, he loses."

In this small circle of close friends, Billy's shyness disappeared, and Ben wondered if he was smarter than George, or as smart. Without formal education, Billy's knowledge was as uneven as blown snow after a storm, deep against one side of the house, paper thin on the other. George genuinely held Billy's intellect in high regard, else he would not have spent so much time calling him a dumb snowplow driver. Billy sporadically wrote arresting miniatures for the paper, sporadic because Billy labored over each one for so long. They were short columns about small things, the veins in an aspen leaf, a pine cone half chewed by a squirrel, as if Billy yearned to escape his own bulk and take up residence among the overlooked.

Mary came to the table to take their order. She put one hand on Billy's head and one on George's and leaned her weight on them. She took no such liberties with Iris. All four of them handed up their menus unopened to Mary. Iris ordered the fried fish special, and Billy, George and Ben nodded agreement.

"What would you do if you were rich, Billy?" Iris asked. "Would you quit your job?"

"In a minute."

"And then what?"

"I'd take my wife and kids to Wal-Mart and walk down every aisle, and buy them everything they asked for."

"Wal-Mart," sneered George. "Don't get me started."

"Shut up, George," said Iris. "And what, Billy, would you do with your time?"

"You know. I'm not sure. I never thought about it."

"Why not?" Iris asked.

"Three kids. A wife. I never graduated high school. I'm never going to be rich. I'm not dumb enough to think I'm going to win the lottery. Why waste time thinking about it?"

"Well, think about it now. You've explored every nook and cranny of Summit County. Why not travel?"

"Maybe," said Billy, doubtfully. "I've always wanted to see Indiana."

"Indiana!" shouted George.

Billy smiled slowly. "Gotcha."

"OK," said George. "Outwitted by a snowplow driver."

"I can't be rich, Iris," Billy said. "The only option left is contentment."

Ben, sitting beside Billy, was struck by his precise wording. Ben leaned over to Billy and spoke softly so the others would not hear in the hubbub drifting in from the bar. "Billy, don't answer if this is too personal. Did you mean to say contentment instead of happiness?"

Billy was silent and seemed to be pondering whether the question was too personal. "I think you have to give up one to get the other." George and Iris, seeing them put their heads together, began chasing another conversational rabbit.

"Ah," said Ben. "I wondered if that's what you meant. Never mind. Forget I asked."

"No, it's OK. I like the question. I've thought about it a lot. Dropped out of high school. Went to work. I didn't know there was anything else I could do. I was kidding George just now about being smarter than he is. The truth is that it was George who finally got me to think about being smart in the way that he is, that you guys are, book smart. George started giving me books to read. I went to the University of George, mostly over beers at the Moose Jaw. I came to see I could have done more with my life, but by then I had a wife and three kids and a pretty good job with the state. For a while, I wanted more, but Thoreau helped me get over it. Lena lets me spend a lot of time hiking around the mountains. That helps me get over chasing after all the things I want or might've wanted. I'm content."

Ben said, "Lena, your wife, I'd like to meet her sometime."

"Sure. Sometime. She's not very comfortable in this group. She's not very smart."

Ben could see that Billy was not kidding. There was a silence, and Ben said, "She must be pretty smart if she knows to avoid the likes of us."

Billy smiled. "Lena's the best. I was lucky things worked out like they did. If I had known I was smart, I would never have married Lena."

Ben raised his hands in a question and Billy went on. "My parents had no schooling. Grew up in a trailer park, same one as Lena. Mostly I just knew I was big and strong and quick at fixing mechanical things. Lena was slow in school. But at least she's a high school graduate. Our kids are slow in school, too. If I had known I was smart, how much I loved learning, I would have found a way to go to college. And married some smart woman. Worn a tie. Had a career. And never married Lena. I didn't know better, so I married for love. Lena is a screw-up. When she's not burning dinner, she's letting the car run out of gas. And every time she does some dumb thing, she slaps herself on the forehead and runs laughing to tell me about it. I've never known a person of such good cheer. So, if I made a mistake in marrying her, I just slap myself on the forehead and laugh. I like to think of it as an inspired mistake, but maybe I was just lucky."

Ben had no eloquence to match this simple recitation so he reached up and put a hand on Billy's shoulder. Billy grinned across his round face and said, "The other reason Lena doesn't join us much is that she's scared shitless of Iris."

Iris must have been monitoring their quiet conversation because she said, "I heard that. And I hate it. I'm trying to become a nicer person in my old age. I'm going to have a party sometime. Billy, you tell Lena she'd better be there…see, that's still not right, is it? Billy, would you tell Lena I would love to have her come? Ben, you're the diplomat, was that better?"

Ben said, "You're growing as a person." This, thought Ben, was part of the ingredient in the odd friendship between George and Billy. Both were devoted to their wives. George, irrepressible, flirted with every woman he saw, which pleased most of them. He flirted at the top of his booming lungs, in or out the presence of his wife, thus disarming sinister suspicions. Julie, his wife, would likely have only been alarmed if George lowered his voice. Billy was too shy to flirt unless, perhaps, his avoidance of Megan's eyes was a form of flirting.

It came to Ben that Buster must have been devoted in the same way to Iris. Ben wondered how he, divorcing his wife, missing Megan, got admitted to this club. Maybe one part of this answer was Sarah; he did not lack for devotion to her. The thought cheered him.

Mary, the serving tray over her shoulder, brought their dinners. Without having been asked, there were four more bottles of beer on the tray. Iris pointed at her own forehead, her signal to mail the bill to her. Iris hated carrying a purse and there was no room in her tight jeans for a wallet.

"Are you guys done with all this sensitive shit?" George asked.

"Done," said Iris. "Why?"

"Because I never did get to talk about Wal-Mart."

"If you must," said Iris.

"I don't want to hear anything bad about Wal-Mart," warned Billy.

"It's just part of the weirdness of living here," George said. "Everybody hates Wal-Mart. Pick a reason. They're big box ugly. They don't pay their employees for shit. They drive mom and pop out of business. They buy from sweatshops. But here's the thing—everybody shops there. Wal-Mart is a lifeline for every busboy and housekeeper in the valley. Carlos can't afford to shop at mom and pop hardware, at mom and pop home furnishings, at the mom and pop appliance store. So he heads for Wal-Mart. And mom and pop can't compete with Wal-Mart, so they sell the appliance store and open a high end Oriental rug emporium for the rich second-homers. Even the rich go to Wal-Mart to pick up a TV for the guest bedroom and three vacuum cleaners, one for each level of their hillside home."

"OK, George," Iris said, "so pick a side. Is Wal-Mart good or evil?"

"It's absolutely good because Carlos couldn't make it without it. You won't hear Carlos complaining about Wal-Mart. On the other hand, it's absolutely evil because it further cleaves the valley into rich and poor."

"Cleaves?"

"Up yours, Iris." George said. "Buy a dictionary. I own a home because I've been here twenty years. Billy makes a decent wage driving a snowplow for the state. The only reason he owns a home is that he won the affordable housing lottery and got to buy a small townhouse under market value. I am actually a little bit rich because my dump of a house has appreciated like crazy. Billy can't get rich because, if he sells, the housing authority won't let him capture the appreciation. Carlos rents a cheap condo that he shares with about seventy-three roommates, seventy-one of whom are illegal aliens. Ski bums work nights at Subway, ski all day, every day, and rent a bedroom, or maybe just a couch. There's a chronic housing shortage, while millions of square feet of high-end housing sits empty for about fifty weeks a year. It's crazy. If you're not rich, you have to do weird shit to make it. You cram six people in a two-bedroom condo. And then you learn the underground economy. You work in a ski rental shop for ten dollars an hour. You slip your buddy a pair of high-end rental skis, and the skis don't come back until the end of the season. Your buddy tends bar, so, in turn, you drink free every night. The owner of the rental shop and the owner of the bar know exactly what's happening, but it's all part of the overhead."

"I'm lost," said Iris. "What's all this got to do with Wal-Mart?"

"What I get out of it," said Billy, "is that Wal-Mart promotes increasing stratification between rich and poor. Wal-Mart's one of the tools the rich employ so the poor will squeak by without rebelling. It's the opiate of the poor; it represents the intrinsic duality of good and evil."

"Exactly," George said.

Billy looked at Iris and shrugged apologetically. "I know this speech by heart."

"Well, I still don't get it," said Iris.

"Wal-Mart is evil," said Billy, "because their cheap toilet paper allows all this shit to be wiped away. On the other hand, they are good because without their cheap toilet paper, we'd all have chapped asses."

"Oh," said Iris. "I get that. Why can't George just say what he means?"

Billy grinned and shrugged.

George snorted in disgust. "At least Wal-Mart has a good side, unlike my friends."

Mary had cleaned away the plates and brought them another round. George took a toothpick from the jar on the table so he could chew on it.

"What are we going to do about Ben and Megan?" Iris asked.

"Neither of them has much money, either," George said. "I think they should go ahead and shop at Wal-Mart."

"Shut up, George," Iris said.

Ben finally found his voice. "Butt out, Iris. We're grownups. Ben and Megan will take care of Ben and Megan."

Iris ignored him. "I think I'll throw a party. I'll invite them both. Maybe they'll come to their senses. A little matchmaking never hurts."

"Iris," Ben said, threateningly.

"Oh, shut up, Ben. Don't forget that those of us here at this table raised Megan. We're her family. Maybe we didn't do as good a job as we should have, but we're still family."

"George said, "That's right. You're dining with your future in-laws, so you'd best try to make a good impression."

Iris said, "We'll give the two of you a little time to work this out on your own, but don't think you have all the time in the world."

"That's right," George said, "we could be looking at a shotgun wedding. You still got that gun, Billy?"

Billy was uncomfortable with the conversation. "They'll be whatever they're going to be. Leave Ben alone."

Billy was right. Ben did not like the conversation. It just made him feel alone. They were family, Megan's family, maybe his family, but family sometimes said the wrong things. Usually, when he felt alone like this, he talked more, told more absurd jokes, but this time he could think of nothing.

George was enjoying himself and did not hear Ben's silence. "Maybe Billy's right," he said. "It's not our job to do anything about

Ben and Megan. They will work things out or they won't. The world will not end for either of them."

Iris became irritated, "George, you're a stupid man. You accuse the rich of being insensitive to the needs of the poor. I believe I was included in that insult. You, on the other hand, are rich in love, as is Billy. I used to be rich in love and then Buster died and I went broke. You don't know what it's like to be rich and then go broke. You're the Marie Antoinette of love. Ben and Megan should just eat cake, is that it?"

Ben said, "I love you guys, but cut it out."

Billy put his hand on Ben's shoulder. "OK, we'll stop."

George mumbled an apology. Iris reached across the table and took Ben's hand. "I'm sorry, Ben. I just keep screwing things up. Times like this, I wish I had Buster to tell me what to do. I keep thinking that somehow I screwed everything up when I told you about Megan's father."

Ben felt like crying but remembered he was in a working class bar. He took a deep breath. "It's OK. All of you, it's OK. Iris, I told you I don't care about Megan's past. Maybe it's something that makes a difference to Megan—I don't know."

"I wish you hadn't told him, too," said Billy. "What's that got to do with anything?"

"Don't play dumb, Billy," Iris said.

"Leave me alone," said Billy angrily. "Leave me alone. Leave all this alone. Leave the dead to their own ways. Leave Megan to her own ways. She has her reasons. I've spent years scrambling around these mountains. And a lot of that scrambling was on the path of Megan as a little kid. I've poked inside that old shell of a house they lived in. There's a cave in the ridge behind the house. She used to play in it, or hide out. I found a diary in it, hidden and forgotten."

"What was in it?" George asked.

"How should I know? I returned it to her because I didn't want someone else to find it by accident. That was maybe dumb. I should have just burned it. Now she's not sure about me. She mostly knows I didn't read it, but sometimes she has to wonder. She knows I've been on her trail. Nobody likes that. I've started out from her old house and followed every path that a kid could take back into the hills. Like any kid, she liked to find hidden places, in the middle of a lodgepole blow down, a willow thicket. She made little homes in these places, little playhouses. I found old dolls, parts of tea sets. I once found where she had carved "I love Atticus' into a tree trunk."

"Who's Atticus?" asked Iris.

"Got me," said Billy. "Maybe her true love in the fourth grade. Gone now and forgotten."

Chapter Twenty-Four

Sarah wanted to go down to the Blue, and Ben needed little persuasion. He could not remember a time when he had ever found disagreeable the companionship of this river or this child. The two of them commandeered Ollie from Iris and drove to a spot on the edge of town. In late August, the river was low and they found a narrow slice of sandy beach. Flecks of fool's gold glinted in the sun. The old cottonwoods filled the high spaces and willows hugged the banks beneath them.

Sarah stood on the spit of sand with a stick in her hand and Ollie stood in front of her, eyes glued to the stick, muscles quivering along his shoulders. Sarah faked a throw towards the bank behind her. Ollie flinched but held his ground. He knew the stick was going in the river. Who would bring a Labrador retriever to the river and throw a stick on the bank? In Ollie's world, there was a gentle and serene order to things and when the stick spun out toward the head of the pool he leaped far out so that his broad chest crashed against the cold water. He swam a strong line with his head high to measure the drift of the stick in the current. He swam back with his stick and came up on the bank streaming water from his black, shining coat. He dropped the stick at Sarah's feet and spread wide his legs. Ollie shook, and the water streaming from his fur turned into a shower of droplets that Sarah spread wide her arms to receive. For her, it was like playing in a sprinkler.

Ben sat a little back on the sand and watched the show. He also watched up and down the bank for someone who might shoot an otter. Here, they were in the outskirts of town; two houses sat on a little rise across the river; and Ben did not think there was danger. There were no high banks crowding in, dense with trees, underbrush, and places to hide. But he watched anyway because this was Sarah. This was not about spirit animals; this was Sarah. He had considered if she should stay with Karen until this danger was past, but he did not even know if there was danger. There was just a dead otter and suspicions of Larry. Larry seemed to Ben to be as likely a suspect as not, but he recognized that he did not know anything about Larry. He was willing to let Larry be the villain because he had broken Megan's wrist and because he had disappeared when the otter was shot. But Megan did not think Larry could have done it, and this had to count for something. Ben found it odd that no one was more suspicious of Tyler, a nutcase. Iris and Megan both dismissed this idea, each privately implying the same thing: that Tyler would never have the nerve to incur their wrath. Ben was not entirely convinced that nutcases operated under such tidy principles.

Ben knew he had to maintain some kind of Larry alert, but he was not sure what this would be. If Larry was hiding in the mountains, Ben wished he could find his camp and sit down with him for a cup of morning coffee around the fire, to take his measure as he had with Tyler. Ben had no wish to become friends with Larry. But he did wish to understand his mind. Was Larry a careless, impulsive bender of wrists, or a brooding, devious killer of otters? Megan argued for the first, and Iris dreaded the second. Ben condemned Larry for being an angry son of a bitch and then reminded himself of his own carefully submerged rage. He thought that perhaps this was something he should ask God about; Ben smiled at the image of God bobbing and weaving and feigning indignation that it might occur to anyone to hold him responsible.

Ben also smiled at the thought of how many people would wish to be in his shoes: to be able to put your feet up and have a beer with your own personal God, to have a conversation with God in which God actually talks back. Ben thought perhaps he was neglecting his opportunity. He should spend his time asking God bigger questions. He remembered the puzzle from elementary school about whether God could create a rock too heavy for God to lift. That would be fun. Or, now, the more sophisticated version of that question: does God have to choose between being great and being good? If God is good, he must be powerless to change things for the better; if powerful, then how can he be good? What is the nature of evil? Is anger the evil twin, the antimatter, of the universe? Ben had asked if there were other gods, but it had not occurred to him to ask if there was a devil. Is there a heaven? Who gets to go? Will physicists ever finish the task at which Einstein failed and find a unified equation to unite the world of the very large and the very small? Will the Nuggets ever win an NBA championship? Ben took a devilish delight both in thinking up these questions and imagining the fiendish skill God would display in avoiding them. He realized he was becoming fond of the old guy. And following that was the realization, for the first time, that God, a vagabond creature, might someday move on.

Ben looked up and down the river and thought again of Larry's anger over losing Megan. She was much to lose. But why was anger the necessary emotion? In the face of such events, could the species have not been alternatively wired to experience some other emotion besides anger—perplexity, perhaps, or melancholy, or bemusement? Almost no one, in Ben's experience, breaks someone's wrist in a fit of perplexity. The melancholy, the bemused, they rarely ambush otters. Anger was a red-rimmed attempt to force an idea to work: we will have true love, we will have this eternal love in precisely this way, or I will break your wrist. "Rage, rage against the dying of the light." It was a wonderful line but not half so effective if rendered as: work steadily and with patient determination against the dying of the light. In Ben's version, it sounded like a Maoist slogan having to do with electricity production goals. But Ben's father, the Maoist, worked with patient determination in the dim and flickering light. And, against Dylan Thomas's best advice, he did go gentle into that good night. Maybe he was too tired from working with patient determination to do much raging. Maybe he thought he needed the rest. Maybe he looked forward to that good night.

Ben did not even believe that the great masters of evil, Hitler, Pol Pot, were, in the end, angry. They doubtless started out angry, but, inevitably, they must have turned into accountants, numbering the dead in the manner of rich widows counting and recounting their net worth. In the end, Hitler and Pol Pot must have been dead even to anger, dead certainly to anguish, alive only to the climbing count of bodies, the numbers bloating in sultry, charnel heat.

Lost in thoughts of Pol Pot, Ben looked up to see Ollie's grave and gentle eyes close to his own. He leaned impulsively forward and kissed Ollie's nose and Ollie responded by licking the entire right side of Ben's face. Sarah had wandered downstream and Ben watched her picking up bright pebbles and holding them to the light. He and Ollie ambled after her. Sarah passed into the willows along the bank and Ollie chased after her. A moment later, she cried out, and Ben ran.

He found Sarah and Ollie staring into the top of a willow. One of the high, slender branches was bobbing up and down under the suspended weight of a small hanging bird. Ben thought at first the finch had been lynched and was hanging by its neck, wings flapping upward in order to defeat the hangman's rope. Closer, Ben could see that the bird was hanging not by its neck but by one wing. It periodically flapped the other wing, propelling itself in a panicked circle, causing the flexible willow limb to bob up and down. The hangman's rope was almost invisible fishing line, snarled and broken off in the top of the willow after some errant cast.

Ben had caught birds on a couple of occasions while fishing. Each time, it was on a back cast, so he had never been able to figure out if the bird was swooping after the airborne fly or whether it was sheer accident. He thought it was accident because he had never seen, on the forward cast, a bird chase his fly. If you make, say, a million casts on rivers swarming with birds, eventually there will be a collision. In each case, the hooked birds veered awkwardly to land, struggling to fly against the weight of the fly line. Ben had the surprising, unsettling sensation of feeling for an instant that his fly line had become a living, and disobedient, thing. The hooked birds, equally surprised, more unsettled, huddled on the ground while Ben pried the hook from a bony wing. Afterwards, he sat beside them on the ground, and they stared at each other while the bird decided whether to trust itself again to the miracle of flight. Ben knew the feeling.

Ben bent the willow limb down so he could reach the lynched bird. He could tell immediately that this bird was in trouble. There was no telling how long it had hung, exhausting itself against its invisible tether. Ben fished his penknife from his pocket and cut the line away from the willow limb. He held the bird, all feathers and lightness. The body beneath the bulky feathers was so light and insubstantial it seemed it might simply become airborne, like a dust mote, with no assistance from the flapping of feathered wings. The monofilament line was snarled and wrapped around one wing and across the bird's body. Ben began making cuts in the line and gently tugging away the pieces. He sat in the river rock with the bird in his lap and picked at the tangled line. The bird lay peacefully and only startled when Ollie stuck his nose in for a better view. Sarah pulled Ollie back and cautioned Ben to be careful. She sat beside him and pulled Ollie to her chest to keep him from trying to be helpful. Ollie would have been happy to retrieve this bird, but since it was already here, he was confused about his role.

Ben continued to cut away pieces of line, but he did not like the fact that the bird was lying so still. Some of the line was wrapped in and between wing feathers and had been cinched tightly by the ferocity of the bird's struggle to free itself. Ben cut away all the line and the bird lay quietly in his lap, its eyes closed.

"Will it be OK?" Sarah asked.

"I don't know. We don't know how long it's been hanging. The wing may be broken."

"What can we do?"

"I'm not sure. We'll let it rest and see what happens."

Sarah held Ollie with one hand and stroked and smoothed the feathers with the other.

"Will it die?" she asked.

"Maybe. Probably." Ben had begun to realize what he needed to do for this bird, but he did not want Sarah to see. He did not like finding even accidentally lynched birds. Ben despised superstition, but still he did not like finding lynched birds or assassinated otters along this river that was his true home. The Blue River was alive and lively, murmuring, muttering, groaning, singing, always ready to carry on a thousand conversations with anyone, like Ben, who always needed someone to talk to. He wanted to talk to Megan, for the sound of her voice, but for this day, for now, the lyric of the Blue would have to do.

"Better not touch it," he said. "That could just scare it more."

"It seems like it's dying. Maybe it will feel happier if someone strokes its back."

"Maybe you're right. We can at least keep it company."

"What kind of bird is it?" Sarah asked.

"A finch."

"Can we take it home? Maybe Hank can fix it."

"Why do you think that?" Ben asked.

"He's always watching the birds at our feeder. He told me once that he loved sparrows. This is kind of like a sparrow."

"We'll see. I'm not sure Hank is good at fixing sparrows. Right now, let's let it rest. Maybe it'll get some strength back."

Ollie, feeling Sarah's grip relax, lunged in for a closer look. The finch, aroused by this new fear, fluttered crookedly out of Ben's lap. It could not fly but pin-wheeled across the river rock on its good wing. Ollie dove after it, and before Ben could gain his feet, the bird was in the river, fluttering weakly on top of the current. Ollie went in after it, with Ben right behind. Ben ran, stumbling over rocks, through the knee-high water. He could see that the bird had ceased fluttering and was now simply drifting on top of the current. Ollie was faster than Ben and had the bird gently in his mouth when Ben caught up. Ollie, happy to perform the useful art of his species, carefully delivered the bird into Ben's cupped hands. The finch was now bedraggled by the cold water and lay with eyes closed. It no longer struggled and the only sign of life was a slight opening and closing of its beak.

On that day, full of life and energy, it had swooped to a perch on the slender limb of an inviting willow. The willow looked out over a river full of cool water to drink. In the air, on the ground, crawling on the leaves of the willows, were the insects that took their life from the river. The canopy of tall cottonwoods filtered the sunlight and provided for the finch protection against the terrible, screaming hawks. It was a good place for a small finch: food, drink, shelter, and the sparkling river to delight the eye. All this bounty, and then its luck turned bad in incomprehensible ways.

Ben held the bird in cupped hands over the moving water. Ollie stuck his nose against the bird for another curious sniff, and the bird did not notice. Sarah stood on the bank asking if the bird was OK. She started to wade in and Ben warned her back. He turned his back to Sarah and crouched low against the water. He closed his hands tightly around the finch and sank them beneath the flowing water. He held the bird under for a long time, to make sure, feeling the feathers against his palms and the icy cold of the water flowing through his fingers. Ollie stood still and watched, his nose pressed against the pane of the water. Sarah was quiet and asked no more questions.

Chapter Twenty-Five

Sarah was ecstatic. Iris had promised her a party to celebrate her return, and it could not have been better. Iris's backyard swarmed with mountain people welcoming Sarah and saying good-by to summer. The monsoons had come and August had been wet. A couple of days before, barely two weeks into September, an early morning shower had turned briefly to stinging hail. The nights were cooler. The leaves on one small branch of the lone cottonwood in Iris's backyard had turned suddenly yellow and glowed in the sunlight. It was high country, home to winter. Revelers in Iris's backyard recycled the chestnut about the mountains' two seasons: winter and July the Fourth.

George, in charge of the barbecue grill, boomed instructions to his helpers in the kitchen. When George assumed charge of a barbecue grill, everyone within earshot was automatically a helper. George and Billy had brought their wives. Iris had called Lena with a personal invitation, and she had agreed to come. Lena arrived, nervous about the crowd, nervous about Iris, and Iris put her arm around her and took her straight to two folding chairs set apart under the cottonwood. Between the two chairs, Iris had set two wicker baskets, one full of Olathe sweet corn and the other empty. There was a paper grocery sack for the husks. Lena had been at the party for no more than two minutes when she was shucking sweet corn with Iris. This was a thing she knew how to do. Not only did she know how to shuck sweet corn, she knew how to talk about shucking sweet corn, and talking about almost anything made her laugh, and her laughter made Iris laugh. Lena told Iris how scared she had been about coming to the party and then radiated peals of laughter at herself for being the silliest goose in Summit County. Sarah ran off to play with Ollie and Ben wandered among the group.

Julie, George's wife, sat visiting with Laurie, who was stretched out in her favorite wooden chair.

"I like your dress," said Julie.

"Mom said wear shorts. But I like this dress. Shorts make my legs look fat."

"I know what you mean. We all have something to hide. We're so glad to see you home. Are you having a good time?"

"Yes. I miss my dad. But it's OK."

Laurie started to explain, but Julie waved her off. "Time makes things better. I remember sitting here laughing at Buster tickling your feet. I never could tell who was having more fun, you or Buster. Your dad was one of my favorite people in the world." Julie was as laconic as George was flamboyant, as direct as he was complicated.

"He was my favorite, too," said Laurie. She added, "Every morning, I got his paper for him."

"I know. He told everybody that would listen because he was so proud of you. It made his face light up."

Laurie's face lit up in turn.

Ben stood talking with George at the grill. Megan, arriving late, caught Ben's eye and signaled him over to the edge of the yard. Ben left George in midsentence and hurried to her. Ben was tentative and Megan extended her arms for a hug.

"I'm so happy to see you," Ben said.

"Oh, me, too," said Megan. "I wanted us to sort of walk in together so people wouldn't be watching us all the time to see how we treat each other. Besides, it makes me look good if everybody thinks I'm magnanimous towards the jerk that dumped me." Ben thought she was probably kidding about the dumping part, but also thought a wise man would let this pass.

Ben said, "You do look good. And you are magnanimous."

"It's an act, stupid. Later on, I'm going to dump a plate of barbecue in your lap."

"Ah, Megan, Megan."

"How's Sarah?"

"She's good. She'll be happy to see you."

Sarah ran up at that moment and gave Megan a hug. In a stage whisper, she nodded her head at her father and said, "What a dope!" Ben was bemused that his own treacherous daughter automatically blamed him for breaking up with Megan.

"True that," said Megan. "Listen, the dope says you and I can go to the movies sometime, just us girls. Would you like that?"

"Great. And a lot more fun with just us—without you know who."

"I agree. So, gang, shall we make an entrance?"

Sarah stood between them and took each of their hands and began running madly towards the group. Ben and Megan laughed and ran to keep up, and the gathering looked up and smiled and went on with their conversations. The direction of Sarah's run carried the three of them to where Iris and Lena sat beneath the cottonwood. Having remanded Ben and Megan to Iris's care, Sarah ran off to play with Billy and Lena's children on the other side of the yard. Iris looked up at Ben and Megan and smiled.

"Pull up a chair," she said.

Ben and Megan sat in the soft, green grass. They sat close to each other, and Megan, seeing this, slid a subtle distance towards Iris and away from Ben. Ben reached for an ear of corn and Lena playfully slapped his hand away.

"Leave the corn to me," said Lena. "What can a man like you know about shucking corn?"

Ben was surprised. He could not make out who he was in Lena's eyes. He thought to explain to her about all the corn he had shucked and all the peas he had shelled as a child. Iris read his mind, arched an eyebrow in his direction, and he kept his mouth shut.

"I thought I heard you two broke up," Lena said.

"We did," said Megan.

Lena stopped shucking corn and looked over at the two of them. She studied each of their faces in turn. Lena's plump, cheerful face furrowed. She looked back and forth and then her face relaxed. She brushed her blond bangs back from her forehead and shrugged. "I guess nobody just knows how to be happy, do they?"

"Lena," Iris said, "I think you are my new best friend."

Lena giggled. "Whatever that means."

Sarah ran past them at full tilt, screeched to a halt, and came back and kissed Ben on the forehead. Like a roadrunner, she was again in instant motion and disappeared.

George passed by on his way to put down an insurrection among recalcitrant, and possibly intoxicated, kitchen staff. "Congratulations on the job," he said to Ben.

"Job?" asked Megan.

"I'm a schoolteacher. Fulltime at the high school. I'm going to teach everything there is to know about American history in two semesters."

"Oh, Ben, that's wonderful news," said Megan. She leaned forward, her hands on the grass, and kissed his cheek. Ben was surprised and intoxicated by the smell of her hair.

"Congratulations," Lena said. "I flunked history twice," she added, cheerfully.

"Iris," Megan said, "isn't that great news?"

Iris nodded. "Wonderful," she murmured, as she went on shucking corn.

Megan said, "Ah…perhaps Iris already knew. Maybe Iris knew even before the principal at the high school knew."

Ben was hurt. "Damn it, Iris. I'd like to think I got this job because I deserved it."

"I promise you I had nothing to do with it," Iris said. "Megan is running off at the mouth."

"She's right," said Megan. "That was a stupid thing to say. I know how good you are. I was trying to be clever and ended up saying something dumb."

"Don't feel bad," laughed Lena. "I end up saying dumb things even when I'm not trying to be clever."

"Sorry," Megan said, and she leaned over and again kissed Ben's cheek. Ben was happy with the flurry of cheek-kissing.

The corn shucked, Iris steered Lena inside so they could boil it, not coincidentally leaving Ben and Megan sitting alone together on the grass. They were silent, and Ben studied Megan as she studied the gathering in the backyard. She wore running shoes and loose khaki pants. Her blue blouse, not coincidentally, was perfect match for the color of her eyes. Her honeyed hair fell to one side of her head, and Ben studied the curve of her neck, her smile as she watched the children playing, and the color of her cheek.

Without looking at him, Megan said, "What are you doing?"

"Memorizing my homework."

"Well, stop." Ben stopped and followed her gaze out to the children. It was not the time to explain that it had been about a hundred years since he had seen her, and he wanted to hold this picture in his mind. Looking at Sarah, he also wanted to tell Megan about the letter folded in his pocket. He expected at any moment that they would be interrupted, and, anyway, the letter would make Megan happy for him, might even get him another kiss on the cheek, but was not at the top of the list of the things on her mind. Karen had written a kind and loving letter in which she wished him well, in which she said it would be criminal to separate Sarah and Ben, in which she said she had hired and then fired a slick lawyer because she would not turn such a scumbag loose on Ben and Sarah. She hoped that both of them, she and Ben, would find love and happiness. It was Karen when she could be magnificent, and it reminded Ben that he had not been a complete fool for having loved her.

His life with Sarah was secure. He had a job. He had a backyard full of friends. For this moment, he had Megan to himself but could ask her no questions. Do you think of me as I think of you? Have you found a way to get past what holds you back? If you have, will you teach me? Is it OK if I come by the library once in a while whenever I need the memory of your face made fresh?

Megan said, without looking at him, "We're not crazy."

"I know."

"Iris, George, they all think we are. They're wrong."

"I know."

Megan allowed herself a piece of a smile. "Maybe a little crazy. Do you think we can keep this up?"

"I don't know."

Megan turned to look at Ben, blue eyes wide and searching deeply and quickly for something, and then she jumped up and ran to play with the children. For the rest of the party, she played their games, ate with them at their small table, and lay on the grass with Sarah, staring into sky. Ben had no more time alone with her, and he watched as Megan slipped like a sleek ermine past every adult that tried to hold her in one spot.

．．...

Sarah was slow to sleep after the excitement of the party. Ben sat in the chair beside the bed, his feet on top of the covers. At first, she talked loudly, her voice still pitched to the volume of the party. Ben spoke quietly, and gradually her voice softened to match his. She said it was wonderful that Iris would throw her a party. She asked if Iris was old enough to be a grandmother even though she did not look like a grandmother. Ben suggested this was a bit of a stretch. Sarah wondered if she could call her grandma. Ben laughed. He told her if she did to be sure to call her that when he was there to hear it.

"You think she'll get mad?"

"She would love the thought, but she might not want to be called something that made her seem old," Ben said.

"I've never really had a grandmother." Ben thought of his mother. Maybe she would have been a good grandmother. Sometimes people who failed as parents flowered as grandparents, taking a generation to get ready to love. He did not like to think about the barriers to love taking so long to overcome and pushed this thought away. The thought that pushed its way in was his mother putting afternoon chores aside to pitch the baseball to him as he learned to hit. Had she really smiled and laughed and clapped her hands every time he hit the ball? Had she really run like a deer to collect the ball, and come back to pitch it over and over again? Could that be?

Ben said, "Why don't you ask her if there is something special you could call her besides Iris? And besides grandma?"

Sarah pointed out that Laurie was old enough to have children. Ben said yes, but if she did, they wouldn't be as old as Sarah. Sarah asked if Laurie would someday have children. Ben did not think so.

"Because she's retarded?" Sarah asked.

"Yes. She might not be good at taking care of a child."

"You're good at taking care of me."

"I'm not retarded."

Sarah rolled her eyes, and Ben saw too late the trap she had set for him. He smiled, marveling at how clever and subtle she was.

Reading his face, she said, "You like me."

"God knows why."

"Do we believe in God?" asked Sarah.

"You can believe in anything you want."

"Do you believe in God?"

"I believe in trying to be good. And if good is God, then I believe in God."

"I don't get that," Sarah said.

"Join the club. My father once told me that if you did your best, you don't need to worry about whether there's a God."

Sarah left this alone and pointed out that George did not know much about children but Julie would be a great mom. Sarah never knew what George was talking about. Julie was quiet, but she was a good listener, and she didn't seem like she would ever get upset about anything. Sarah thought about it and decided that George was loud and gruff but that he could probably learn to talk to a kid. She thought he just didn't have any practice.

"When George starts yelling about something, Julie just ignores him and nothing bad happens. He just gets over it. I think they might be good parents. Why don't they have any children?"

"I don't know," said Ben. "You've got family on the brain tonight, kid."

"I guess."

Sarah snuggled in tighter under the down comforter. Her blond hair spread out over the flannel pillow cover, the one with strawberries, now faded from red to pink from frequent washing. The soft brown face of a teddy bear peeked out from under the covers; one of its ears dangled half off because Sarah believed in sharing her toys with Ollie. The window was open a crack, and a chill layer of night air slid in. The old house had begun to creak with the change in temperature. The only light was from a small lamp beside her bed, and the ceiling and far corners of the room were in darkness. Ben could see that Sarah's eyes were glassy, but she fought sleep.

"Megan and I are going to the movies."

"That'll be fun."

"Are you jealous?"

"A little."

"You could go, too."

"I don't know. I think it's best that we're just friends now," Ben said.

"Are you friends?"

"I hope so."

"I like Megan. We talked this afternoon, lying in the grass."

"I saw you."

"It was easier since you guys aren't dating. She's like a kid, but she's not. We found animals in the clouds. She claimed a rhinoceros, but I never could see it, so I wouldn't let her count it."

"Ah, the old rhinoceros trick."

"Dad…"

"Yo. Here. Present."

"I like her."

"Me, too, love," Ben said.

Sarah's voice was winding down. She offered that Billy's kids were mean but only because they were boys and couldn't help it. She thought Lena was funny. She found Billy strange.

"Strange how?"

"I don't know. He's like a giant. He seems like he's afraid to sit down because he might break the chair."

"I think it must be hard for Billy," Ben said. "It's like he doesn't fit anywhere. Sometimes it seems like he doesn't fit in his own body."

"Maybe so." Sarah struggled to stay awake. "His kids...he's a giant...they climb all over him."

Sarah's eyes slid shut, her grasp on Ben's hand became feathery, and she was asleep.

Chapter Twenty-Six

In the fall the mountain sky was unbearably blue. The light streamed through the aspen leaves and was changed to fire. Ben and Sarah took walks then on trails in the aspen country, trails that hugged the lower shoulders of the mountains. They found meadows to lie in, to stare at the sky or across the valley at the flowing spills of color on the facing hills. Hiking through the trees, the path was littered with aspen leaves, and sometimes a blue spruce beside the trail was covered with Christmas baubles of bright, fallen leaves. Like everyone in the mountains, in this season, Ben held tight to these crisp days, feeling each day that there could not possibly be another like this one. In the Blue, the yellow leaves tumbled beneath the surface of the clear water, flowing from the sky's swirling ocean to the other great ocean that lay somewhere at the bottom of gravity.

Sarah talked on these hikes about her new teacher. Mrs. Ferguson was old and sometimes crabby, but Sarah was happy when she discovered that Mrs. Ferguson liked her. Sarah needed to get up each day and feel herself drawn to someone who liked her. Ben did not find Mrs. Ferguson crabby, but students lived in a different world with their teachers, and Ben knew that if Amy Ferguson was crabby, she had reasons. Amy told Ben that Sarah stopped on the way out of the classroom and returned pieces of trash to the wastebasket. Amy did not often get up from her chair. She was short and odd-looking and heavy with the weight of age and the looming end of her diabetes. Every year her glasses got thicker. Amy showed Ben pictures of a baby, her first granddaughter, and, perhaps suspecting she would not be there to see, let Sarah stand in for how this child might look and be. Surely, this granddaughter would be beautiful and would stoop to pick up bits of paper for a teacher who could no longer stoop.

Lying in the grass, in a meadow, staring into deep sky, Ben chewed a blade of grass and wondered about this other deep thing of his daughter, this need to be liked. It was part of being a child, parcel of being a girl child, one who was at pains to see that her stuffed animals all got along with each other. But, also, Sarah often thought her mother did not like her, as often her mother did not. When Karen hated herself, she hated in turn all things weak or imperfect, and a child who spilled milk at the dinner table became a living sign of the savage emptiness of life. Thus, Karen drove Sarah away from her and created in Sarah a thirst for approval. Despising any need for the approval of others, Karen created a child in danger of needing everyone's. Ben sometimes noticed Sarah telling small lies to please him, and he did not know what to do or say about this.

As with all first-time parents, it had not occurred to Ben that he would have a child with imperfections. He wondered if it would be different with a second child and doubted it. He thought about having a second child with Megan; the thought made him happy and he forced it from his mind. He wondered if his own father had seen his imperfections and then wondered the more that he could ask himself such a dumb question. If a parent can fool you into thinking they are blind to your flaws, then...then what a thing is that. It is, he thought, a thing as deep as fall sky, a sky deep enough for a thirsty hiker to reach up a ladle and drink, letting liquid sky overflow and slosh down your chin.

Sarah had settled into school and Ben into the harness of his new job. He was much happier no longer being a substitute teacher because for every day there was a plan and a rhythm. He smiled at the sky, knowing that Karen was right—he was a plodder. He was a mule who loved the weight of the plow and who never slacked in the traces. Teaching history was as constant as shoveling ditches; the South did not lose the Civil War one school year and then, with some erratic mood, win it the next. You could come to admire a great warrior like Robert E. Lee, but you could never move him, like a chess piece, to the right side of history. Ben knew he was, like his father, a plodding mule, cursed with a love for the harness, and blessed with a sense of humor, wonder made merry. Ben's students loved his sense of humor and loved his sense of wonder in the retelling of the old stories. Ben told them the story of the fearful soldier hauled before General Lee for deserting his post. Lee told him there was no reason to be fearful because here he would find justice. The soldier replied, of course, that the prospect of justice was exactly what made him so afraid. Ben's students liked that story because, as teenagers, they had experience of being hauled before higher authority. Ben liked the story because, like the soldier, he feared justice and craved mercy. It was why Ben preferred Lincoln to Lee. Lee, upright and proud, moved in a realm beyond weakness, saw clearly the unshakable necessity of discipline, and ordered the fearful deserter shot. And, having been faithful servant to justice, Lee slept well. Lincoln, to the stern displeasure of his Secretary of War, pardoned as much of errant humanity as he could get his arms around, but still his sleep was troubled because well he knew what terrible dreams may come.

Ben wanted to hide himself in the simplicity of his life because in it he avoided the danger of mistakes. Karen had been a profound mistake, a problem he could not plod through and perhaps not get over. And yet, how do you name a mistake that gives you Sarah? Megan there was, but she came with no guarantee, and she was away from him now, struggling with the self of her own invention. The only certain happiness was Sarah, the mountains, the river living between the mountains, and the retelling in the classroom of the old stories.

Ben's students, duty-bound to be slackers, asked him if it was enough to learn the material or did they have to memorize it. In their view, learning was the high road to knowledge and memorization the low. Ben frustrated them by asking how it might be that something is learned but not remembered. He cheered them by telling them elaborate (and mostly clean) shaggy dog stories. At the ending pun, they groaned and rolled their eyes, but they liked the good cheer and evident lack of shame in Ben's telling. Some of them probably even tried on in private imaginings how it might be to themselves tell such stories. Ben told the one about making an obscene clone fall. He relished the story about transporting gulls across the state lion for immoral porpoises. His students could not make out whether this was humor or insanity, but they responded to anything lively. Ben performed the most mindless of magic tricks. One day, in a slack moment, he asked them if they wanted to see a magic trick, and a student in the back asked if Ben could do his disappearing act. Ben gave that student an A for intelligent class participation. He began, thus, to win his students and win a firmer life in this place.

So the fall became a time of digging in, of shoveling channels to carry their lives downstream. Sarah made new friends at school and had them over to play. One of the mothers made a call to Iris and passed the word to the other mothers that with Ben a child was safe. Sarah looked in the mirror and decided it was time that Ben advance from the primitive ponytail to the sophistication of the French braid. Sarah knew that Karen sometimes wore her hair this way and in doing so was old-fashioned, elegant—stunning. Ben tried to evade by suggesting that Iris could give her a French braid when she wanted one, but Sarah was determined that Ben step up to his responsibilities as a mother. Under Iris's supervision, Ben spent most of a Saturday morning training his fingers to move independently, like playing a keyboard, among soft, fine layers of hair. Each layer had to be wrapped tightly or the song sagged at the end. Iris became irritable at his slowness and Sarah, sitting patiently erect, reached out and told her to shut up by squeezing her hand. Ben sweated over it until he got it right and then tore down his creation and rebuilt it three more times until he was sure that the memory of the thing was in his fingers.

He recalled his original adventures with the mysteries of the ponytail. Karen would be off traveling somewhere, and it was Ben's job to get Sarah to preschool. She wanted a ponytail, and this seemed an easy thing. He brushed her hair from the top and from underneath and then carried it in his hand to the crown of her head. He pulled into place a rubber band, twisted it, and ran the ponytail back through and did this again if the grip was not tight enough. Sarah went happily off to school and, at the end of the day, the rubber band had slipped, and the ponytail was a mess. Ben decided that the cure was more twists in the rubber band to create a grip so tight it could not slip. The next morning he twisted and ran the hair through and repeated until the rubber band broke, snapping back against Sarah's tender scalp. She rubbed away the pain and encouraged him to keep trying. He finally got a rubber band to hold. Picking Sarah up from preschool that evening, the ponytail had drooped again. Ben winced when he saw it and Sarah nodded with resignation. Ben stood talking to Becky, the preschool teacher, about Sarah's day. Listening only slightly to the grownup talk, Sarah wandered over and leaned back against Becky's legs. Becky glanced down, and without interrupting her conversation with Ben, took half of the drooping ponytail in each hand and pulled the two halves away from each other. The rubber band snugged into place against Sarah's scalp, and the ponytail was again a ponytail, ready to bob and bounce and proclaim the lively presence beneath it of a little girl. Becky continued her conversation, but Ben shouted to her to stop.

"What did you just do?" Ben demanded.

Startled, Becky was not aware of having done anything.

"What did you do with her hair?"

Becky raised her open hands as though she had been accused of shoplifting from Sarah's hair, trying to make sense of what she had been accused of.

"You pulled her hair apart," Ben said.

"I was just fixing her ponytail. It was drooping."

"Show me exactly what you did."

To celebrate this new knowledge, Ben took Sarah to dinner at McDonald's. They took turns toasting their new ponytail life with Cokes and feeding each other French fries. Such a simple trick— how was a father to know?

On this fall day in the meadow, Sarah had found a comfortable place by squirming into a hollow of earth and elevating her feet onto Ben's stomach. Ben smelled the brown grass, the fine gray earth, and knew he was a good father only because the two generations that sandwiched him made him so—his father and his daughter enclosed him. Driven by love, by survival, Sarah molded him into the father she needed. Ben thought of Megan, who, having no other, ripped a father from the pages of a book, a great fictional father who had in him no meanness. Ben struggled to think how he might have shaped his own father and could think of nothing. Ben knew that he must have played some part in making of his father the man he was; it could not have been otherwise, but Ben could think of nothing about his father for which he could take credit or blame. Perhaps Sarah was similarly blind to the ways in which she created him. He thought of God, presiding with bemusement over his creators, waiting patiently for them to make him worthy of his station in life.

"I like Mrs. Ferguson," said Sarah. "Do your students like you?"

"I think so. Sometimes it's hard to tell with big kids."

"I bet they think you're funny."

"Why do you think?"

"Because you are. Funny. But it takes a while to catch on. Sometimes, when we're with other people, I laugh at something you say. And then I look around and no one else got it. Your sense of humor is kind of strange. Give them time. They'll catch on."

"I think they're catching on. They're starting to laugh at the right places."

"Good. They will love you."

Ben did not feel very funny, but he knew that when he was sad he made others laugh. For practical purposes, he had no wife and Sarah had no mother. Megan had no father of whom she would speak. Karen had a mother she could not stop cursing. Iris had no husband; Laurie had no father. All this sadness crept into him and out came some diversion of a story, a smartass remark, some tilting of life in the direction of the unexpected. It was what he had. Between periods, he sometimes sat in his classroom, feet propped on the desk, and stared at a water stain in the industrial tiles of the ceiling above him. If a student came in, he could always hear the door opening behind him, and he rubbed his eyes as if they were tired, perhaps allergic, and some story about obscene clone falls shoveled its way into his mind, springing from someplace he could not name or understand. It was what he had.

Chapter Twenty-Seven

Sarah and Iris were shopping and Ben was going through the motions of Saturday housekeeping. Sweeping the front porch, he found Ollie stretched out in the afternoon sunshine. Ollie opened one eye but refused categorically to move as Ben swept around him. Ollie sneezed once and sighed as Ben stirred the dust. Ollie closed his eyes against human folly and went back to sleep. Having moved some dirt from one place to another, having satisfied duty, Ben stretched out on the porch, using Ollie as a pillow. Ollie sighed again, but this time happily. Ben kept the broom across his chest so Iris and Sarah would see he had been working if they returned early. Ben liked the fragile warmth of the late September sunshine and Ollie's rhythmic breathing and the collected heat in Ollie's black fur. Ben let his breathing follow Ollie's and dozed.

Ben was startled awake when Ollie growled and scrambled to his feet, claws scrabbling against the wood. Ben's head clunked on the floor, and he looked up into the slanting sunshine at two dark figures against the light. Ollie stood over Ben and growled steadily from deep in his chest, each growl rolling out deeper, more ferocious, than the last. Ben pulled himself up with one hand on Ollie's shoulder and the other on the broom handle.

Larry and Tyler stood on the bottom step of the porch, arrested by Ollie's ferocity. Ben, struggling to make sense of their presence, put a hand down to calm Ollie. The muscles in Ollie's shoulder coiled and uncoiled under his hand.

"We came to straighten things out with you," Tyler Flanagan said.

Ben looked at Larry, and Ben thought about his friend, the otter. "You're back," Ben said flatly.

"Who said I'd ever been away?" Larry said. "Did you think you could get the sheriff to run me out of town?"

"Did you shoot the otter?"

"I heard you lost a little friend," Larry said.

Tyler interrupted. "Larry didn't shoot any otter. We've straightened all that out with Hector. Larry would no more take the life of one of God's innocent creatures than...than I would."

Ben looked at Larry. "Why did you disappear?"

"Who said I disappeared? I've been around. I want to know why you used your rich friend to cause me trouble with the sheriff."

"Ah, so that's the story. I caused you problems. I pulled strings to make life miserable for poor Larry? Did you bring your roll of dimes today?"

"You son of a bitch!"

At Ben's feet, Ollie's low growl was continuous, methodical.

"Now hold on," said Tyler. "That's not why we're here."

"And why are you here?"

"We came to settle things, so there will be peace among all God's creatures."

Ben hated Tyler's religious language, which turned all meaning inside out. Tyler had had time to prepare a speech, and the speech was everything. "If Larry didn't shoot the otter, then there's nothing to settle. You go your way. I'll go mine. It would be OK with me if you started going your way right now."

"You see," said Tyler, "that's what I'm talking about. You've been nothing but trouble since you came here. You make these false accusations against Larry. You lead my sister into sin. My advice to you is to get right with God."

"What the hell are you talking about?"

"I'm talking about you getting out of my sister's life. Follow God's will. Put your own marriage back together. You have a family. God wants you to be the head of it. This is a godless home, and no good can come of it. If you leave my sister alone, then she will find God, which she will never find with you. I mean this as a true Christian brother to you." It came to Ben that this man was brother to no one in this world. Tyler believed that the soul was all, but the only soul that Tyler saw vividly was his own, and all other things that moved across the earth's face were seen darkly.

"Have you talked with Megan about this?" Ben asked.

Tyler paused uncertainly. "She is stubborn and willful."

Ben understood then that Megan would not talk with her brother, and Ben was proud of her. There was also something else in Tyler's voice, and it flashed into Ben's mind that Tyler was afraid of his younger sister. Ben was simply incidental to something between Tyler and Megan.

"OK," Ben said, "I know what you want from me. You want me to stay away from Megan. And talk to God." He turned to Larry. "What do you want from me? Megan? You want me to help you get Megan back? Even you can see that's a little crazy." Ben leaned against his broom. "If you want Megan back, go ask her. I know she cares about you. I can't figure out why. All you are to me is a guy with a roll of dimes in his fist. But Megan defends you, so maybe I'm wrong. But look at yourself. Getting rid of me is going to help you find love? If you have a broken heart, join the human race. But don't come to me for sympathy. And don't come to me, like some kind of idiot, to get Megan back. Go to Megan."

Larry relaxed his fists, and it was only then that Ben was aware that they had been balled up. No roll of dimes fell out when Larry opened his hands. Ollie, crowded in against Ben's knee, continued to growl.

"Shh," said Larry to Ollie. "It's OK." He reached an open hand to Ollie. Ollie ignored this peace offering and continued to growl, eyes locked on Tyler.

"I did go to her," said Larry. He looked up at Ben and met his eyes. "She doesn't want me." He looked over at Tyler. "Let's go. This is stupid."

"We'll go when I say to go," Tyler said. "I came here in Christian love. But the Devil is in this man."

Larry's shoulders sagged. "Aw, hell, Tyler. You're always on about the Devil. Maybe Ben's just a guy. Let's get out of here." He reached out a hand to Tyler's arm, but Tyler shook him off.

"I came in Christian love, but I am mindful that Jesus had to use violence to chase the moneychangers from the temple. It is from love of God that you hate the Devil."

Tyler, face red, fists clenched, rushed up the last two steps towards Ben. Ben was surprised. He had expected this from Larry but not Tyler. Ben pushed the broom down against Tyler's feet and Tyler tripped. His momentum carried him forward and he hit Ben in the chest with his fist as he fell. Ben fell back against the door as Tyler struggled to regain his footing. Tyler came up, powerful fists swinging wildly, as though robed moneychangers drifted everywhere in the air around him. Ben recoiled from the door and crouched in front of Tyler. Ben was vaguely aware of Ollie growling and swirling between and around them. Ben straightened the broom, grabbed the handle with both hands, and joined in Ollie's deep growl. Ben ducked under Tyler's swinging fists and planted the tip of the broom handle in his stomach. Knees bent, he lifted it upward and drove Tyler back and off the porch. Tyler rolled down the stairs. He came up more slowly this time but started again for Ben. Reversing his grip, Ben swung the flat, hard head of the broom over and hit Tyler on top of his head. Tyler lurched back and it was at this moment that Ollie found the grip he had been searching for. His teeth snapped into Tyler's behind. Tyler straightened up to escape this pain and tried to reach behind him to push Ollie off. Ben drew the broom in a wide, horizontal arc and whapped Tyler hard in the face. Tyler staggered into the front yard, this time holding his face, with Ollie, snarling, still locked on his rear.

Ben tried to call Ollie off with no result. Ben saw movement from the corner of his eye and turned, thinking it might be Larry. Iris stepped from the corner of the house. She held a beer bottle carelessly at her side, gripped by the neck. She watched Tyler staggering blindly against the force of Ollie's grip. Her eyes were alight with the purest joy of battle. Slowly, regretfully, she called out, "Ollie, down." Ollie, who had been deaf to Ben, released his grip, backed to Iris's side, and leaned in against her knee. Larry had retreated to the sidewalk, having decided to be an onlooker to this odd fight. Tyler, released, quit staggering and held his face, still stinging from the bristles of the broom, with one hand, and his behind with the other.

"Go home, Tyler," Iris said. "Unless there's more fight in you. Oh, I hope there's more. But I'm afraid you're done. Ben's had a shot at you. And Ollie. God, I hate being a spectator to life. Maybe if you rest a minute you'll have some more fight in you?" Iris swung the beer bottle gently, hopefully, in her hand. Tyler glared at her. He pulled his hand away from his bottom and inspected the blood on his fingers. He spat at Iris's feet. Ben moved in his direction and Iris's grip on the neck of the beer bottle tightened.

"I'm going," said Tyler. He hobbled to the sidewalk and crossed it to get into his car. He motioned to Larry to get in, but Larry shook his head and walked alone down the hill.

Ollie, watching Tyler's car pull away, seemed unable to stop growling. Iris sat down in the grass beside him and hugged him and kissed him on the head. She rocked him back and forth in her arms and murmured in his ear until he was at last quiet. Ben sat on the steps and caught his breath, still holding his broom. Iris's car door slammed and Sarah ran into Ben's arms. Ben held her and stroked her hair.

Iris looked up and smiled at Sarah. "I forgot about you. You did a good job waiting in the car."

Iris got up from the grass and kissed Ben on top of his head and sat beside him on the steps. "And you," said Iris, "were magnificent. A broom? Since when do you beat someone up with a broom?"

Ben laughed. "You know, it has a long wooden handle. It felt a lot like a shovel."

Ollie came over and squeezed his way into the middle of the group, tail wagging. Iris kissed him again on his head and then pulled Ben's face to her and kissed him on the forehead. "I love you guys. You are two of my favorite people. My warriors."

"You're the warrior, you and Ollie. I was only Don Quixote with a broom. But you, the light of battle was in your face. To tell you the truth, I always thought that people were only afraid of you because you are overbearing and insufferable. You would have actually hit him with that beer bottle."

"Oh, yes," Iris said. "Oh, yes."

Sarah pulled her face from Ben's neck. "What about me?"

"You," said Iris, "were perfect. You waited in the car just like I told you to."

"I couldn't do anything else. The way you told me almost made me wet my pants."

Iris laughed and rubbed Sarah's cheek. "I had to be sure you knew I was serious."

Sarah smiled at Iris. "I think I did wet my pants. But only a little." She buried her face again in Ben's neck. Sarah, her face still buried against Ben, asked, "But why were they mad at you?"

Ben looked at Iris, and she furrowed her brow. "I was wrong," she said, "about Larry. He's just a ski bum, a follower."

"How much did you hear?" Ben asked.

"Pretty much the whole thing. I was standing at the corner of the house."

"And you didn't jump into the middle of it? Amazing self-restraint."

"I'm getting more mature in my old age. You and Ollie were doing OK."

"And Tyler?" asked Ben.

"I was wrong about him, too. I thought he was a harmless crank. I've been looking in the wrong direction."

"I don't mean to be critical," said Ben, "especially while you still have that beer bottle in your hand, but you're batting a thousand today on being wrong about people."

"I don't know. I wasn't wrong about you. And I've never been wrong about Ollie. And Sarah. It's not possible to be wrong about someone as brave and beautiful as Sarah."

Chapter Twenty-Eight

The following Saturday night, Ben was home alone, reading *Dancing at the Rascal Fair*. He heard Sarah fumbling outside the front door. He put his book aside and went to the door. He opened it and hugged her to his side, as both stood in the doorway under the porch light. He waved into the dark at the car, lights on, parked at the curb. He looked into the car but could not tell whether there was an answering wave as it pulled away.

"How was the movie?" Ben asked.

"Great. Megan and I decided you wouldn't like it because it was a chick flick. We cried at the end. Actually, Megan cried and I pretended to so she wouldn't be embarrassed. Of course, maybe she was pretending, too. Girls are like that."

Ben helped Sarah tug her coat off and picked up a lavender knit glove that fell from the pocket.

"You're quite the authority on what girls are like."

"Well, I should be. And you, you are the authority on what girls are not like."

"I suppose. Meaning I don't know anything about girls?"

"Not a clue. Me and Megan figured that out over ice cream."

"Megan and I," Ben corrected.

"Not that it took very long, about half a scoop. Can I...may I turn the TV on?"

"Enough moving pictures for one night."

"Why don't you ever watch TV?"

"Because it rots your brain."

Sarah hit the side of her head with the heel of her hand. "My brain doesn't feel rotten."

"That's because it's so rotten you can't even tell it's rotten. Plus, TV makes me nervous. There's too much noise, too much action. When I'm watching it, I don't realize I'm nervous. And then when I turn it off, I see that I'm all wired up."

"That never happens to me."

"Because your brain is rotten. There's nothing left to get wired up."

Ben returned to the recliner and picked up his book. Sarah stretched out on the couch with her own book, one that featured a winged horse on the cover. Ben could not make out the title. Sarah moved her lips silently as she read. Ben had worried about this habit, thinking that it must surely slow her reading, like reading aloud. But she was a good and fast reader. He had concluded that she must silently slur her words. They had once had an argument over this. Ben insisted that he could read lips, but he could not read Sarah's, so it followed that she must be slurring the words together as she read. Sarah argued hotly that she was pronouncing every silent word precisely, which Ben would know if he wasn't deaf, or blind rather. They had referred this argument to Karen who resolved it by telling them that they both needed to grow up. Ben and Sarah each took this verdict as a moral victory and stuck out their tongues at each other when Karen turned her back.

"How was Megan?"

Sarah set her book on her chest and smiled gleefully. "Why do you ask?"

"I can't ask about a friend?"

"Come off it, Dad."

"Come off what?"

"Grab a clue about yourself. You love her, and you're too stubborn to admit it. I told Megan that."

"I don't think you should be interfering in things you don't know anything about. Don't forget that you're the kid, here, and I'm the adult. So what did she say?"

"Who?" Sarah asked, with fake innocence.

"Megan."

"She said I should mind my own business."

"Good advice," Ben said.

"And then she said any girl could figure that out. We talked about how dumb boys are."

"You guys are quite the pair. You have pretty much everything figured out."

"Not everything. Just you."

"Where did you learn to be such a smartass?" Ben paused. "Don't answer that question unless you're prepared to be grounded until you're forty-three."

Sarah, content with herself, shrugged and returned to her book. Ben tried to concentrate on his book without success. He was pleased that she could get the better of him in this contest of wits and displeased that she was involving herself in his decisions. But why would she not try to shape his life? Mr. John Donne, poet and preacher, thought no man an island, entire unto himself. If a parent were an island, it was one overrun by children, hurling coconuts from every treetop.

Ben liked their life. He liked the grooved ritual of every part of their day. In the early morning, Ben sat at the kitchen table alone and drank coffee, watching the snow that had come in the night to dust the high peaks. He liked touching Sarah's smooth cheek to wake her and the way she captured his hand and held it against her face as she tried to sink deeper under the down comforter for one last moment of sleep. They both left in the morning happy at the prospect of quiet, school adventures. They played basketball in the late afternoon sunshine and trudged home, trading ridiculous boasts about their respective skills.

Ben fixed dinner while Sarah did her homework at the kitchen table. In preparing dinner, Ben followed Sarah's rule of three. She had learned in school some fixed notion of proper nutrition, and she required that always there should be at least three things on the plate. If one of these things, usually some slimy vegetable, did not suit her taste, she felt absolutely no obligation to eat it, but she was rigid in enforcing on Ben the obligation to put three things on the plate. She cheerfully flushed the offending vegetable through the garbage disposal, justly feeling that such nastiness deserved no better fate than to be shredded and washed into the dark, whirling underworld.

After dinner, Sarah washed the dishes and, if she had finished her homework, she watched TV in the living room, while Ben read in the kitchen. Sarah took a bath and afterwards Ben helped brush the tangles from her blond hair, now wet and dark. In her long flannel nightgown, she sat on a low stool beside the woodstove in the kitchen and let the warmth of the fire dry her hair and turn red her cheeks. They talked of the small things of their day and Ben then tucked her into bed. Sometimes she read herself to sleep and sometimes she required of Ben a story. He did not actually read her stories anymore but made up adventures in serial form. The latest serial was about an evil, crafty flea named Wilberforce, who spent his life plotting Ollie's destruction. Wilberforce made carefully timed leaps at Ollie, and every leap was thwarted by some freak and random event, such as Ollie suddenly remembering, at the crucial moment, that he needed to go dig around the woodpile for beetles, so that he could push them back and forth with his nose.

Sometimes Ben was a hero at bedtime. Spiders hitched in out of the cold in an armful of firewood, and Sarah was deathly afraid of spiders. She did not mind them in other locations, but the thought of a spider in her bedroom, crawling on her while she slept, gave her the willies. Ben was baffled as to why a child who was a hunter of water snakes became the hunted in the presence of a spider. Whenever this situation arose, he was tempted to refrain from making a big deal of Sarah's cowardice. He always found a way, however, to resist this temptation. He made fun of her by clucking like a chicken as he went about killing the spider. He was himself at a loss to explain why he was so fearful of snakes and not of spiders. He showed off his spider bravery to Sarah by crushing them against the wall with the palm of his hand. He then tried to run his hand through Sarah's hair as she dived beneath the covers.

Ben liked this life. He had always liked the peace that opened up in Karen's absence, but before there was always the promise and threat of her return. In the life that he had now, he sat by himself after Sarah had gone to bed and read and listened to the occasional pop of the fire. Thinking of happy times, he sometimes missed Karen. He marveled at the brain's capacity, at such moments, to conjure some sweet memory and isolate this perfumed memory from the unsavory and disagreeable odors within which it swirled. He wondered if this is what Ollie did, sniffing the air and pulling from it only the swirl of scent that pleased him. Sitting by the fire, Ben often thought he smelled Megan's hair, the scent hitching a ride on some sly eddy of wood smoke. Ben longed for Megan and dreamed of what they might be.

In the daytime, his mind raced, raced to Megan, worried about her, worried about the emptiness he would face if he should lose her forever. But in these late evenings by the fire, he was calmed. There was no better way to spend this waiting time than making a life with Sarah. Sitting beside the fire's gentle rustle, he could see more clearly the pattern of him and Megan coming together and falling away. When they fell away from each other, there was no rancor, only an admission of struggling necessity, and Ben took comfort and hope from this. In this quiet time, he was learning that storminess and ducking Karen's flying bears were neither love's requirement nor perfect expression. He allowed himself to think that he and Megan were made for each other, that each time they came back together they came closer, and that some eddy of history would gather them back together, like the fire's curling smoke, and give them their time together. So in this time of falling away, he was as calm as a person could be who ached to trace the contour of Megan's cheekbone with his finger.

Ben looked up from his book and realized that Sarah was talking to him. She had again laid her book across her chest.

"Next weekend, you're coming with us to the movies," she repeated.

"I'm not sure that's a good idea."

"I know."

"Know what?" asked Ben.

"I know you're not sure. And I know you're coming to the movies with us."

"And how do you know this?" Ben asked.

"Because you love me more than anything."

"What's that got to do with…?"

"And I love you more than anything. If you wanted me to climb to the top of Buffalo Mountain and fly off it, I would do it."

"That would be dumb, but I take your point. If you fly off Buffalo Mountain, be sure you're riding that horse," Ben said.

"What horse?"

"The one on the cover of your book, with the wings."

"Etherea. That's a good idea. You can ride Etherea to the movies with us," Sarah said.

"I don't know. My life is mostly good right now. But I worry about how your life is."

"Dad, I know you worry. My life is good. It's not perfect, but it's good. I'm afraid you'll get stuck. You'll get stuck and go on exactly like this forever. I want you to fly."

"But…"

"Dad," said Sarah impatiently, "Mom has moved on. Believe me, she has moved on. Mom never looks back. You and Megan…you look back."

"I know it doesn't seem like it to you, but there's lots of time. We'll see what happens."

"Maybe there's lots of time and maybe not. You always accuse me of wasting time watching TV. Maybe you're wasting time looking back. You're always studying history. Study what's now."

"I don't know," Ben said.

Sarah grabbed her hair and pretended to pull it out by the roots. "Dad, yes you do know. You know you don't have any choice. You're going to the movies with us."

"Why don't I have a choice?"

"I already explained to you—because you're doing this for me. I'm asking. I'm asking you to fly off Buffalo Mountain. And I'm going to lend you Etherea to keep you safe."

"So, you've got it all figured out."

"I believe I do," Sarah said.

"I just have one question."

"OK."

"If it's a chick flick, do I have to cry?"

Sarah went to bed happy, determined to dream of riding Etherea. Ben sat up late in the recliner, wrestling with the sudden danger of happiness. He fought sleep and nodded off and awoke to the scent of Megan's hair and then he slept through the night and dreamed.

Chapter Twenty-Nine

"Come in," Ben said. Megan slipped inside and patted Ben lightly on the arm as she passed. She wore a British seaman's cap, and as she passed, Ben could smell her hair and the wool of the cap. He wondered why all women did not know to wear hats.

"Sarah says you're coming with us to movie night," Megan said.

"If you'll have me."

"I'll have you if you really want to go," said Megan evenly. "But if you don't...don't. Just don't."

"I have been happy all week thinking of this movie."

"I didn't know you were such a movie-lover."

"Who said anything about loving movies?"

Megan allowed herself to look in Ben's eyes for a long moment.

"Where's Sarah?"

"Getting ready. Slowly."

Sarah came in from the kitchen and kissed Megan. "You look great, Megan."

"You're not so bad yourself, kid."

The front door opened and Iris pushed her way in, a paper bag of popcorn under her arm and Ollie at her ankles. Ben looked inquiry at Iris.

"Going to the movies, huh? You two have fun."

"Three," Ben said. "I'm going, too."

"I know," said Iris. "You two have fun."

"Ah," said Ben.

"Ah," said Megan.

"Iris and I decided to play hearts tonight," Sarah said. "Hope you don't mind."

"And if we did?" asked Ben.

"I'd have Ollie bite you in the ass," said Iris, as she opened the door and pushed the two of them out.

"Our lives," laughed Ben, as they stood under the porch light, "are controlled by sinister forces."

"Just so we're straight. I had nothing to do with that," Megan said.

"Wait," said Ben. "This is not the foot we should start out on. I'm the one who should be defensive, apologetic. Your role is to be frosty and unforgiving. Could we at least get our roles straight? Besides, I'm not sure you're smart enough to be as devious and manipulative as those two."

"You're partly right. I am gracing you with my presence. And you are undeserving."

"Much better. And my plan for the evening is to be your obedient servant in all things."

Ben could feel the tension between the two of them. He had instinctively reverted to joking to get them through it, but he was on edge that he might go too far. They both treasured the playful talk that ran between them, like the braided currents of a river that merge in the instant of collision. On their good days, they caressed each other with this play and created a flowing story of themselves. On this night, Ben wanted to keep fresh in Megan's mind any treasures that might lie between them. He also dutifully took up the role of villain of their breakup because this convenient half-truth seemed to be one that Megan liked. There was plenty of time later for as much of the whole truth as either of them could bring themselves to understand.

Megan said, "Very wise. Shall we go?"

Ben lowered his voice. "Don't look around, but the two schemers are watching us through the window. Up for a little show business?"

"Sure."

Ben reached and took Megan in his arms and bent her backward in a lingering, Hollywood air kiss. Ben liked the lingering part. As the two of them came up, they turned to the window and stuck out their tongues at Iris and Sarah.

In the car, Megan asked, "So what movie do you want to see?"

"I'm the obedient servant here, but the last place I want to go is some place where we're not allowed to talk."

"So where?"

"I vote to go back to the beginning."

Megan was confused and then smiled. "You came to my library looking for *Huckleberry Finn.*"

"Do you have your key?"

"If I don't, we'll break in. Libraries are very lightly defended places."

Megan let them in the back door with her key. A few dim lights glowed inside to assist police patrols, vigilant to the possibility of looting by English majors. Ben liked the mystery of the shadowy aisles. The two of them took their shoes off and sat at opposite ends of the love seat that faced the Blue River. Megan sat with her feet curled under her; Ben leaned back against the arm of the couch and draped his sock feet over the back. There was only a shard of moon and the river revealed itself in pinpoints of unsteady light across the riffled surface. Ben felt as unsteady and jumpy as the light on the water. He let the dim light of the library launch him into the first story that came to mind.

"When I was in college, I had a study partner for algebra. Meaning that I was lousy in math, so I found a study partner that might pull me through. This guy—his name was James—was kind of strange, but I figured that's how all people are who are good at math."

"I beg your pardon. I'm good at math, and I'm not strange."

"Megan, you have many outstanding qualities, but I think you should let me be the judge of how strange you are. Have you noticed that you're interrupting my story?"

"Go."

"So, one night we get together at his place for a study session. Turns out he lives in an apartment over a funeral home. He's working there to pay his way through college. Conveniently enough, his career goal is to be a mortician. Algebra is just kind of a sideline for him. He offers to give me a tour of the place. It was spooky.

239

There are all these display caskets, propped open, waiting for a customer, sort of like the way car dealers prop open the hood of a car. It's nighttime, and the showroom's dim, like it is in here. We're walking along looking at these caskets, and I see a ghostly figure moving in the dark at the far end of the room. Turns out to be a mirror, and I'm seeing my own reflection, but that freaked me out all the more. You don't really want to see a ghostly image of yourself in a funeral home. So then, James…"

"Who's James?" asked Megan.

"James, the guy in the story. I told you that."

"I don't think so."

"His name was James. James something. He starts telling me about which casket he wants to be buried in. I'm thinking, well, OK, I guess it's natural that you think about things like that when you're in the business. But then he starts telling me which one I would look good in, and I'm thinking this is getting a little sketchy. And then he asks me if I would like to get in the casket. Take it for a test drive. Talk about freaked! I got out of there. Told him I had a date or something."

"Sounds like he wanted to be your date."

"Yeah, but the thing that still bothers me is whether he preferred his dates dead or alive."

"You know," said Megan. "That's a truly bizarre story. Borderline gross. I understand how the dim lights in here might have reminded you of it. But, beyond that, I don't see what it has to do with anything."

"What it has to do with is how happy I am that you're my date and not James."

"I can't tell you how flattered I am."

"What it has to do with is that I'm a little nervous, and I'm rattling on so you won't notice."

"And why so nervous?" asked Megan.

"Because I love you. And I don't want to blow it this time."

It was the lesson of Sarah. Ben had made everything complicated, twisting elaborate knots from the strands of Sarah, Karen, Megan, a strand from each of his parents, from duty, the gross national product of Paraguay, and most of all, what he understood as the real fear that he might be tipped by failure forever inward. Sarah cut the knot, told him to get on with it, and he obeyed.

"OK," Megan said.

"OK what?"

"You're getting warmer."

"OK, I'm getting warmer. But are you?"

"You already said that my job is to be frosty," Megan said.

"Figure of speech."

"I did find my heart melting a little at the casket story. You are a master of the romantic story."

"Ah ha," said Ben, triumphantly. He swung his legs over and jumped up from the couch and clicked his heels together in the air.

"Why are you celebrating?"

"You said romantic. I got you to use the word romantic. You gave yourself away. You do love me. Or maybe not love exactly, but something close. You don't hate me. You have the kind of feelings for me that keep you from killing me. I'm good. I'll settle for that." Ben leaped in the air and clicked his heels together again.

"You know that you are not a normal person, Ben Wallace." Megan slipped down and stretched her legs out on the couch. She reached up and pulled Ben down beside her. She held his hand as they looked up at the great wooden beams of the vaulted ceiling and out to where the moonlight danced with the riffles of the river.

"I want you to lie here beside me and hold my hand," Megan said. "And I want you to shut up so I can be happy in peace."

They lay together in silence in this house of tales, stories marching up one aisle, down the next.

"It was the casket story," said Ben.

"I thought I told you to shut up."

"I know. But it was the casket story that did it. Women are suckers for that story. Poor little fools."

Megan reached up and took off her hat and gently slapped him with it. She tossed the hat on the back of the couch.

"No," said Ben "Put the hat back on. I love you in that hat."

"And without the hat?"

Ben saw the trap. "I still love you."

"Poor little fool."

Ben pulled Megan's hand to his face and brushed the back of her hand against his cheek. He kissed the back of her hand. He separated her fingers and inspected each of them in turn. Megan twisted slightly so she could watch.

"This one," said Ben, holding her little finger.

"This one, what?"

"This one is the prettiest."

"And the others?"

"Sort of average." Megan tucked her little finger back in and extended the middle finger.

"Point taken," said Ben. He returned her left hand to her lap and retrieved the right. He repeated the process of inspecting her fingers. Megan leaned over and kissed him on the cheek.

"You're so wound up," she said. "Relax."

"I'm trying. It's hard. You're not wound up?"

"I'm still being frosty."

Ben looked in her eyes. "Really?"

"No, I'm holding on tight so I don't explode. I don't want to act as dumb as you. I'm trying to shut out everything but this moment. And you're not helping with all your hyperactivity."

"I know. Sorry. How about if I just go back to picking my favorite finger?"

"Why don't you hold me instead?"

"Yes, ma'am," Ben said.

They lay together, holding tight. Ben could feel the pulse of Megan's heart and hear the flow of her breathing. The sound of the river did not come through the closed windows, but he did not have to hear a river to hear a river.

"I thought I had worked it out in my mind so I wouldn't be so scared this time," Megan whispered.

Ben stroked her hair. "It's OK."

"No, I have to say it. I'm so scared." She sat up abruptly and pushed Ben back to his end of the couch. "See what you've done. I was doing such a good job of being calm and peaceful and happy. I was holding on tight. I had such a good grip. And then you got all hyper and then you played with my fingers. It's all your fault."

Ben, from the end of the couch, raised his hands and his eyebrows in silent question.

"I don't know whether I'm good enough," Megan said. "There, are you satisfied now? What if I'm not good enough for you? For Sarah? Even for Iris, who wants to be my mother."

Ben sat silently. He tentatively took hold of Megan's foot, and she did not pull it away.

"You and Sarah and Iris are real people," Megan said. "You come from someplace. I don't come from anywhere. A body needs to come from someplace, to grow up in a field of people. I used to envy the aspen because they all grow from the same root; all the trees in a grove of aspen are identical twins. You can't just create yourself. It's crazy to invent some fictional father from a book. The field I grew up in was like a talus slope high on Buffalo Mountain. What if you grow up in a field of rocks? How do you become something human? I invented a father. Invented myself. Iris wanted to help, and Buster, and I wouldn't let them. I had to be completely my own creation. I don't know why. I'm proud I worked hard. I'm proud I went through college, got this job. I made myself look normal. But it's not real. I can't escape the talus field I grew up in. I was not made for happiness. I thought I could do it, but it hit me while you were inspecting my fingers, and I was loving you, and then all of a sudden I saw it might actually happen. What am I going to do if it actually happens? How can I know how to be happy?"

Megan cried and did not bother to wipe away the tears. Ben leaned towards her to touch her face and she brushed his hand away. They sat silently together and the only sound was the river that only Ben could hear. He thought he began to understand Sarah's role with Megan. Megan had told him she needed Sarah, wanted to spend time with Sarah, because Megan needed to feel through Sarah whether Ben could be trusted. Ben concentrated as hard as he could on what he had come to understand as Megan's Dilemma. She did not think she could love someone, marry someone, without telling everything about herself. In the worst case, she might be confessing to crime, perhaps also something that involved others. Tyler was eager to place her in Larry's arms, perhaps because she would feel no need to tell Larry anything, perhaps because Tyler thought he could control Larry. And if others were involved, this could also include Megan's other family, what George described as Ben's in-laws, Iris, George and Billy.

Ben said, "We know each other pretty well. I have tried to hide nothing of my weird past from you. But someone I love once told me that she wanted to keep on falling in love forever. It's the same, I think, for learning about each other. If we're together for two hundred years, little bits and pieces from the past will keep cropping up. Sometimes I feel like I could spend all day telling you about the hour I just spent away from you."

"Ben…"

"Wait, just wait, I'm not done. So here's what I've figured out to do. Tell me anything you want to tell me whenever you want to. Tell me nothing at all. I don't care. All I want to do is have you feel I'm on your side and that I am sanctuary. I have no clue whether I can do that or not. All I know is that it's what I want to do; it's who I want to be."

"Ben…"

Ben put a finger to her lips. "Woman, who said you could talk? None of this is a way of trying to get you to say anything. All that is required of you is to understand what I'm saying. Also, I wouldn't mind it if you let me touch your cheek."

Megan took Ben's hand and placed the back of it against her cheek, and Ben lightly stroked, feeling the softness and the hard strength of her cheekbone beneath the surface. Finally, Ben said, "That Sarah pisses me off on a regular basis."

"What are you talking about?"

"She sat me down last week and had a long talk with me, to kind of get me sorted out on things. She told me that you and I are just alike."

"In what way?"

"She said we both spend too much time looking back. Kind of her way of saying it was time to face the future and get on with it."

"What if I can't do it?" asked Megan.

"I don't know. I know I sat up half the night scared to death."

"Scared of what?"

"Scared, like you, that I was meant to be misery's brave child."

"And?"

"About two in the morning it came to me that I had no choice. Sarah required it of me. Plus, she knows more about love than I do."

"I think what she knows she knows from you."

"Nah. It's just a miracle."

Megan, her face still wet, leaned forward and touched Ben's cheek. "That works for you, but..."

"No buts. I require it of you. I came to understand that night, somewhere in the wee hours, that we are not given a choice in such matters."

"I will try."

"We will both try. But here's the other thing I came to understand. You and I are masters of trying. Trollope said, 'It's dogged as does it,' and we are his true disciples. Look at you. You exist out of sheer, dogged determination. Between us, we own dogged. Beethoven was as dogged as they come, but the Ode to Joy was a miracle, coming from nowhere, headed towards the third star to the right. We can keep plodding doggedly along, or we can hold hands and hitch a ride on the Ode to Joy."

Megan was sitting up with her hands on Ben's shoulders.

"You wid me?" asked Ben.

"Yes."

"You scared?"

"Yes."

Chapter Thirty

"What up, dawg?" Ben asked God later that night.

"Chillin' in the 'hood," replied God.

Ben took a beer from the refrigerator and joined God at the kitchen table.

"You're drinking beer?" inquired God.

"I'm celebrating."

God launched a quizzical eyebrow.

"The grandeur of life," Ben said. "The triumph of the human spirit. The absolute, unvarnished beauty of it all. In other words, Megan. Megan. Megan."

"It was nothing."

Ben propped his hiking boots on the table beside God's snakeskin cowboy boots. "So, angling for a thank you note?" Ben asked.

God chuckled. "What a scam I've got going. I get thanked and praised to high heaven for all the good things that happen; at the same time, an army of theologians works overtime to explain why I'm not responsible for the bad things. You gotta love it. Sort of puts me in the position of being a spoiled child, but, what the hell, you take your blessings where you find them."

"I'll drink to that." The two of them, God and Ben, clinked beer bottles. God belched softly. "And to that," said Ben, and they clinked bottles again.

"Speaking of blessings," said God, "It doesn't compare with Megan, but I was roaming around town today and stopped to admire the A&W Root Beer sign."

"What a hoot," Ben said. "Makes my day every time I go by there. Guy uses his billboard to post Biblical scripture, along with the special of the day. 'I am the way, the truth, and the life' is followed immediately by 'Try the Cheese Curds.' I wondered for a while what the Biblical citation for trying cheese curds was."

"Beats me," God said, "but if it's not in the Bible, it should be. I tried the cheese curds, and they have my official endorsement. I was a little baffled by the sign on the window that says 'God Bless America,' and directly beneath that says 'America Bless God.'"

"Must make you feel pretty good that we extend our blessings to you."

"What can that possibly mean?" God asked.

"I wondered over it for a while and finally decided that it just means the guy doesn't own a dictionary."

"Ah. Sometimes the simplest explanations are best. But this God Bless America stuff is everywhere. Kind of a weird country you've got."

"It just seems like the most natural thing in the world to every American that you would bless us, clearly in preference to the less deserving."

"Ah, the infinite divisiveness of religion. Sometimes even I feel sorry for ecclesiastics. It has to be a strain to turn the most random of guesses into absolute, divine certainty. But the whole business loses its quaint innocence when you guess that one gender or one group should be subservient to another. I notice that no one has ever received a divine revelation that the chosen people are not his own tribe but actually the tribe on the other side of the hill. Moses comes back to his people and says, 'Sorry, guys, God switched over to the damn Canaanites.' Men in patriarchal societies rarely receive revelations that women should be in charge. Guy never goes up the hill, prays for divine revelation, and then comes back down to the wife and says, 'Damn, God put you in charge.' It's always God said I was right, and, frankly, I get a little chapped at the presumption." His voice rose. "And I get absolutely enraged at the pathetically bizarre idea that I would choose any group based on the devoutness of their beliefs about the unknowable. But you can't just blame the preachers. Nobody has to buy what they're selling. People are simply sheep. It vexes me sorely." God took a deep drink of Fat Tire, a deep breath and seemed to recover his wry disposition. He said, "What about 'God bless us each and every one?' I always liked that one."

Ben said, "Doesn't fit on a bumper sticker."

"How about 'God Bless Finland?'"

"Who cares about the Finns? To borrow from Mr. Stalin, how many troop divisions do the Finns have?"

"They're a fine and modest people," God said, "given to minding their own business. I may just decide to extend my blessings to the Finns."

"And if you decided to bless them, how would you do it? By giving them the atom bomb and forty divisions?"

"Don't be stupid. I'd make them a fine and modest people."

"Far be it from me to be contrary," Ben added helpfully, "but I thought that you just said that they already are a fine and modest people. Why does this require any additional intervention on your part? Seems redundant. Borderline dumb."

Ben and God sat silently drinking their beer. God picked at the damp paper label on the beer bottle with his fingernail. He placed the small pieces of paper on the table and herded them with his forefinger into a neat stack. "You know," he said finally, "it's not usually considered a good idea to make God look dumb. Lots of people would say it's theoretically impossible."

Ben grinned. "Maybe you're slipping. No offense, but you're not getting any younger."

"True for you," said God. "But don't get too puffed up about it. Remember, pride goeth before a fall. Is that the Bible or Shakespeare? I never can keep them straight."

Ben got up from the table and came back with a copy of *Bartlett's Quotations*. "'Pride goeth before destruction, and an haughty spirit before a fall.' Proverbs."

God sighed. "At least I was close. Speaking of haughty spirits, you're right up there tonight."

"I was aiming for joy. I'm just so inexperienced at it that it comes out haughty."

"You know, my friend, I'm happy for you."

Ben said. "Megan and I are going to make it this time. We're going to be absolutely spanky. What about joy? Does joy always end in a fall?"

God sighed. "Once again, you're in danger of worrying the problem to death. I don't even know that pride always ends in a fall, much to the regret of the prim little old lady that wrote Proverbs. I have known people who lived joyfully right up to the end. Nothing in my limited experience says joy has to end in destruction. I expect that joy only ends in a fall if you get too obnoxious about it, which, for you, is always a danger. How can someone so obnoxious be such a worrier?"

"Leave me alone," Ben said. "It's what I do."

"I know," God said. "Truth be told, me, too. It's hard to kick dread in the ass. We are much alike, my young friend; I sometimes wonder if our destinies are intertwined."

Ben said, "You can see into the future, right?"

God narrowed his right eye. "If I really concentrate. Why do you ask?"

"I'm not asking for any insider knowledge. As we both know, I'm not the smartest person in the world, but I am smart enough to know that the last thing anybody should want to know is what his own future holds. What really interests me is whether, in light of our relationship, you have bothered to look into mine."

"Nope. The smartass answer is that you're not that important. The real answer is that I refuse to look. As aggravating as you are, I have become fond of you. In your case, I'd rather just open each unfolding moment as it arrives."

"I can live with that," Ben said.

"You'll have to. I can tell you one thing. You should stop worrying."

Ben turned this over in his mind. "Cryptic as always. You could be dropping a subtle hint about my wonderful future with Megan, or you could be giving the kind of all-purpose advice that the little old lady that wrote Proverbs gives."

"True for you," laughed God.

"One more question. Where'd you learn to talk black?"

"Come back?"

"When I came in you said you were chillin' in the 'hood," Ben said.

"Damned if I know. I guess I must know some black people. It wouldn't be out of the question, though clearly not in this white bread town. More to the point, where'd you learn to talk black? I can't recall the last time anyone addressed me as 'Dawg.'"

"Where else? My students, who are mostly white kids trying to talk like black kids."

"That reminds me. I went to church the other day. Lutherans."

"How'd it go?" asked Ben.

"I only lasted about fifteen minutes. Had to fake a coughing fit and climb over the feet of about ten irritated Lutheran matrons to get out of there. The place had a nice feel to it, though. The pastor made everybody introduce themselves to the people sitting beside them. I liked the introductions, but at the last minute I decided to introduce myself only as Hank."

"So what was the problem?"

"They started singing." God became visibly distressed at the memory. "I'm sitting there and a bunch of white, middle-aged Lutherans start to sing. Never in my wildest dreams did it occur to me that any plan for the cosmos could go so wrong. Only black churches should have singing. Why didn't they think to put that rule in their Bible? I'm telling you, it was hell. Fortunately, I made my escape before they started dancing."

Ben no longer thought it slightest strange to carry on conversations with God. When he was around, Hank was never reluctant to talk, and conversation soothed Ben's swirling mind. Wanting to be a copy of his father, Ben had wrestled his exterior into his father's calm shape, but it was a shape that struggled to contain the ceaseless caroms of his mind. His father's serenity was for Ben both model and frustration. He wondered who made the rule that serenity always had to be quiet. Ben wanted to talk. As a child, he wanted his father's thoughts, but they came to him only in fragments, and Ben was left to conjure the missing pieces. If he could guess the pieces, perhaps he could halt his father's steady withdrawal towards some serene and distant destination that Ben could sense but not see. When God was home, Ben talked to God. When God was out wandering, Ben talked to himself. In putting on the shape of his father, the best Ben could manage was not to talk to himself in the presence of others. It would have to do.

On this night, when God finished his beer and went to bed, Ben again stayed up late, sitting at the kitchen table, feet propped up, talking, hearing in return only the Blue River's ceaseless song, carried, in variations without end, always in his mind. He talked about a thousand rushing topics, but mostly about the wonder of Megan, about the triumph of joy over dread.

PART THREE

Chapter Thirty-One

In the mountains the fall died with the aspen leaves. With the leaves grounded, there remained only an aimless, theoretical fall, a calendar fall, in which there was nothing much to do but watch the snow fill in the land from the peaks down. In mid-October, an early storm had reached the valley floor and left a foot of wet snow, snow that only decided not to be rain at the last moment. People looked at it and thought about skiing and then thought themselves stupid to have thoughts of skiing in the middle of October. Ben went to the basement, for no good reason, and stared at his skis and then trudged back up the creaking stairs. Children built snowmen. Some of Ben's students skipped school and took old, beat-up snowboards to the top of Loveland Pass and slalomed, high above tree line, through the snow and the rocks. Ben got wind of this escapade and talked to them about it afterward. He was concerned that, growing up here, they might not understand how wonderful it was to be able to skip school and spend the day carving through new snow at twelve thousand feet. They understood.

Megan came over often on weeknights. She cooked dinners for the three of them from recipes she had picked up in her years of waiting tables. Megan asked if Hank would join them; Ben shrugged and explained that his odd, roaming boarder mostly paid the rent on time but otherwise provided only fleeting proofs of his existence. In the beginning, Ben insisted that Megan should not cook all the time, that he could also cook. Megan and Sarah insisted that he could not have been more wrong.

Sarah chose her words carefully, and said, "Dad, you know how to fix dinner. Megan knows how to cook."

Ben sat at the kitchen table and watched the two of them sliding gracefully around each other as Megan cooked and Sarah assisted. He liked to listen to Megan explaining her choice of spices to Sarah and how to tell when the pasta was al dente. Sarah's head was upright and alert. Megan's was bent over the saucepan, over Sarah, patiently surveying, managing. Ben sat at the table, feet up, and let his eyes follow the soft, curving line of Megan's neck. When Sarah began to set the table, Ben was in the way.

"Does he always sit with his feet propped up on the table?" asked Megan.

"Always," Sarah said. "But he mostly takes his shoes off first."

"Do his feet stink?"

Sarah bent over and sniffed Ben's socks.

"Only a little," said Sarah. "I don't think he ever learned good manners. Should I make him quit putting his feet on the table?"

"Does propping his feet up like that make him happy?"

"I think so," said Sarah. "He always does it."

"Then I say forget about it."

"Me, too," said Sarah.

"Me, three," said Ben.

"Who said you get a vote?" demanded Megan, and the two of them drove him out of the kitchen and into the living room, where the scents and sounds of dinner followed him. The only oddity of Megan's cooking was that she absolutely refused to cook any rice dish. One evening Sarah suggested rice, which she liked, but Megan refused, quietly, categorically, without explanation, so there was no more talk of rice.

At dinner, the three of them sat at one end of the long table. Sarah told about her day at school. Mrs. Ferguson was often out sick, and Sarah worried about her, missed her when she was gone. The substitute teacher was young and energetic, and Sarah liked her, but Sarah's loyalty lay with her "real" teacher because Mrs. Ferguson had shown Sarah, and only Sarah, pictures of her infant granddaughter. Sarah, with a child's half-knowledge of the world, worried that Mrs. Ferguson must feel miserable to get so many bad colds. Ben and Megan understood that the principal was bending her budget to get Amy Ferguson one last year towards her retirement benefits before her diabetes kept her home for good.

"Why are boys so mean?" asked Sarah of Megan.

"Don't look at me. Ask your father. He used to be one."

"Why is it my fault that boys are mean?" asked Ben.

Sarah and Megan ignored this question, understanding that the answer was too obvious to require explanation.

"Sam," continued Sarah, "said that Mrs. Ferguson was an old, fat witch. I hate him. His nose is always runny, and he never wipes it. Mrs. Ferguson has to call him up to her desk to get a tissue and make him blow his nose."

"I was in love with my second grade teacher," Ben said. "She was young and beautiful. Her name was Miss Andrews. She must have been just out of college. She got married halfway through the school year and moved away. It broke my heart. I remember I wrote her a note on her last day. I folded the note and glued it and told her not to open it until she was gone."

"What did the note say?" asked Sarah.

"I don't remember exactly. It probably just said I will love you always, or something mushy like that."

Megan reached over and tousled Ben's hair. "Poor baby. Maybe all boys aren't mean."

"No, no," Ben said. "That's what made me mean—having my heart broken by a girl. That's probably what's wrong with Sam. Some mean little girl dumped him. That's why he doesn't bother to wipe his nose. Why bother wiping your nose when your heart is broken?"

"Oh," said Megan, "it's all our fault that boys are mean and don't know enough to wipe their own noses."

"Exactly true."

After dinner, Megan and Sarah went to the living room and Ben washed the dishes. It took him longer than usual because Megan, when she cooked, was lavish in her of saucepans. She had shown up one afternoon with a grocery sack of assorted condiments, and one kitchen shelf became an outpost of the Spice Islands. Ben was disoriented for a while but eventually found the new location for the salt and pepper and was able to steady himself. Megan had spent an hour sitting on the kitchen floor, creating order from the chaos of pots and pans. Now, drying the dishes, Ben took care to nest the saucepans according to the plan of Megan. As he did this, he grinned and told himself that he took such care out of pure love for Megan, influenced not at all by his love for Megan's cooking, by his reawakened love for food. With Megan, Ben savored the taste of things.

Chores completed, Ben found Sarah and Megan on the floor of the living room. Sarah was working on a math sheet, and Megan was reading book reviews in the *Library Journal*. From the first, when Megan spent time with Sarah, Megan instantly curled up on the floor. It was, thought Ben, such a simple thing to know. Maybe they taught this in library school, in the course on the Children's Hour. Or maybe you just had it, even if you came from a family with all the warmth of a talus slope. Ben guessed that Amy Ferguson had sat on the floor with her students when she was a young teacher, in the days when the floor was still within her reach.

Ben remembered his surprise when he came to know he was a good parent. He had never dreamed of having children, had never even thought about it. And then Sarah was in his arms, and he had known what to do. He learned some things, but mostly he learned over time that he was a natural. Even as an infant, Sarah was a willing and generous teacher and all that was necessary was to listen in class.

Sarah elbowed Megan and asked for help with a math problem. Megan told her to try once more and then she would help. Sarah tried again and got it and elbowed Megan again to tell her this. Megan, without looking up from her journal, elbowed her gently back, and the two of them went about their business, their knees touching.

Ben, stretched out on the couch, propped a biography of Jefferson on his chest so that Megan and Sarah, if they looked up, would think he was doing something other than simply watching them. John Adams, on his deathbed, had said, "Jefferson still lives." Ben loved this joyful and defiant proclamation, and these words played in the background of his mind as he watched Sarah and Megan, knees touching, living.

Sarah went off to take her bath. Megan continued to read her journal until the sound of the running water went off and Sarah could be heard splashing in the tub. The week before Sarah had turned the water on and then sneaked out, innocence wrapped in a towel, to catch the two of them kissing on the couch. She watched for a while, grinning, pretending she was too polite to interrupt the moment. With the sound of splashing and singing in the tub, Megan got up and stretched out on top of Ben. Ben held her face between his hands as they kissed.

"We've done this before," said Megan.

"So, having once kissed, we should forget it and move on to other things?"

"No. I mean, I'm all for moving on to other things, but I meant something else. When I'm away from you, I think about wanting to kiss you, but I never quite remember how wonderful it is. It takes kissing you to bring back the feeling of the time before."

"I'm always available as a memory aid," Ben said.

"Always?"

"Always."

"Damn, I always tell myself not to ask questions like that. It makes me seem needy, which I am not because I can kiss you or not kiss you, it's pretty much all the same to me," Megan said.

"My sentiments exactly. But can we always kiss?"

"Always. It begins to feel like always."

"And you're not freaking out?" asked Ben.

"Mostly not. You were right."

"Of course I was right. About what?"

"The Ode to Joy. Sarah rests her knee against mine, and I can hear it. She is so full of love."

"She is that."

"Sarah's knee. Your feet on the table—what a rude habit. But the world would not seem right if I could not come to the back door and look in the window and see you bent over a book with your feet up."

"So I'm perfect the way I am?"

"Shut up. I'm trying to make a point here. It is such joy. In a few minutes, Sarah is going to come out and pretend she needs me to help her brush her hair. I can't wait."

"Don't forget about the part about kissing me. That seems to be slipping dangerously down the list of joys. Sarah's an OK kid, but she's not that much fun."

"You're so pathetically needy."

Megan kissed Ben again and then slid off him to the floor. The bath interlude was almost up. Megan sat with her back against the couch and Ben ran his fingers through her hair and gently squeezed her head.

"I know," said Megan, "that this is only practice. But I'm doing OK." She turned her head to look at Ben. "Aren't I?"

"I think you are afraid of some kind of nothing. Of ghosts. I don't know what your nightmares are, but I know that family is either in your bones or it's not. You're a natural."

Megan reached up and took Ben's hand from her hair and held it against her cheek. Since they reunited, they had not discussed anything further about Megan's past. Sarah went around obnoxiously pleased with herself for her role in engineering this reunion of her father and Megan. Her father was obnoxiously pleased with her, too, and grateful. Megan would tell him about whatever ghost stories from her past she had to tell him in her own time, but this would be from her own need and not his. As always, it was hard to tell with Megan when she might be troubled. Through some combination of discipline and denial, she was able to pick up and go on, serene, unruffled. Ben put his faith in the feel of her cheek against his hand, the way she and Sarah gently, unconsciously elbowed each other in the ribs, and the way his home was lit by small things when the three of them were there.

Chapter Thirty-Two

You could buy a pumpkin for ten dollars. The lavish profit went to buy winter coats and snow boots for needy kids. The pumpkins, bright orange against the fading green of the grass, were spread out on one end of the town soccer field. Families wandered among the pumpkins in the warmth of the afternoon sun. Strings of children knotted and unknotted as they raced among the pumpkins, sometimes jumping over them. A large boy in a blue jacket jumped directly on top of a pumpkin, creating a pumpkin disaster, and was dragged off by his angry mother.

Ben and Megan sat on a grassy hill at the edge of the field. The early snow had melted away in the open spaces but still hung on to the north side of anything. The two of them watched Sarah as she raced among the pumpkins with friends from school. They spotted Tyler and his family on the other side of the field. Megan did not wave, and it was hard to tell whether Tyler saw them or not.

Megan giggled. "I can't believe you beat up my brother."

"Ah. You heard." Ben noted again Megan's capacity for keeping things to herself. She did not have the common need to talk about things immediately. Like a good librarian, she filed things away.

"You get in a fight with my brother, and you were never going to mention it to me?" Ben admitted to himself that perhaps history teachers could also be guilty of filing things away.

"Sorry. I didn't want to cause trouble."

"Trouble with me?" asked Megan.

"That. Or between you and Tyler."

Megan squeezed his arm. "Off and on, I have thought that Tyler could be my family. I gave it up. I have no family."

"Keep me in mind as a candidate."

"For what?" asked Megan.

"Family."

Megan kissed Ben on the cheek. "You're kind of lame, but I like Sarah."

Ben put his arm around her and they leaned together.

"I do miss my nephew," Megan said. "Sometimes Nathan stops into the library to see me. He never says so, but I don't think he's supposed to talk to me. Consorting with the Devil's handmaiden. I worry about him. He's too remote. He just hangs around the library for a while, staring at the books, staring at me, and then he leaves. I can't ever get him to talk to me about himself."

"I wondered about that, too...the time I met Nathan at your brother's house. He seemed like a distant kid, or something. Your brother is pretty religious."

Megan laughed. "Ben, the diplomat. My brother is whacked. I thought he was done with beating people up and being a bully, though. I still can't believe he tried to fight you. I also can't believe you whacked him with a broom."

"How did you find out?"

"Huh. In this town? I probably knew about it before you were done hitting him. But, as in most things, George was my news source. I'm just grateful he didn't put it in the paper. I'm also grateful Tyler didn't hurt you. I've seen Tyler fly into a rage and hurt people. Will I hurt your feelings if I say I think you were lucky?"

"No hurt feelings. I'm a simple history teacher, inexperienced in the ways of the world. I was just lucky Ollie was there to do the heavy lifting. And Iris—she was standing there the whole time. I expect she would have rescued me if I needed it. The scary part was how much Iris enjoyed it. I've never seen her like that. Not sure I want to again."

"Iris was a wild one," Megan said. "I grew up with stories about Iris. She's mellowed with age. She married the only man who wasn't scared of her. I don't think she'll ever find another."

"Is your brother scared of you?"

"He'd better be."

"No, I'm serious."

Megan turned to look at Ben. "Why would you ask that?"

"I'm not sure," Ben said. "Tyler came over to my house to tell me to stay away from you. We weren't seeing each other at the time, so it was obvious he wasn't up to speed. He clearly wanted to save your soul, and I said something to him about taking this up with you. There was a flash of something in his face, and it popped into my mind that it was fear."

Megan looked away. "I guess he might be afraid of me. We lived in the same house with a maniac. He was afraid of the maniac. I wasn't. He was the older brother. I guess he thought he was supposed to protect me, but he was too afraid. Things are all twisted up inside Tyler. Some part of him probably blames himself for not taking care of me when we were kids. Maybe the only way he can think to take care of me now, to make it up to me, is to save my soul. As always, whenever Tyler is up to no good, he figures out a way to turn it into the Lord's work. It's a trick he learned at an early age."

"The same fire that melts the butter hardens the egg."

"Does that make me the egg?" Megan asked.

"Sunny side up."

"You are a romantic fool."

"Not only that. I'm a fool for you. I have no idea what went on with you and your family, but I am a complete believer in you. My faith in you is unshakeable, indestructible. I'm with Mr. Shakespeare—you may have heard of him. He's in all the libraries. 'Let me not to the marriage of true minds admit impediments.' Something. Something. 'Love is an ever-fixed mark, that looks on tempests and is never shaken.' Ever-fixed—I love that; only a poet desperate for an extra syllable could come up with ever-fixed. And then the sonnet goes, something, something, and then something else, ending with, 'If I'm lyin', I'm dyin'.' My knowledge of Shakespeare has a couple holes in it."

Megan placed her face against Ben's shoulder. "You really do believe in me, don't you? Be careful where you place your faith. You may turn out to be love's fool. Here you are, someone who does not believe in God, someone who is probably going straight to hell, at least according to Tyler, and you place such blind, religious faith in me. How does that make sense? Where is your famous skepticism when it comes to me?"

"Because, in spite of your fears to the contrary, you are real. Because you are flesh and blood. Granted, it's the flesh part that I like the best."

Megan put her mouth against Ben's ear and whispered, "Don't look around, but one of the women in your life is about to attack you from behind."

Ben could hear the snow crunching on the back of the little hill where they were sitting. He looked a question at Megan, and she grinned and refused an answer. Ben could see Sarah playing in the pumpkin field and was baffled until Laurie pushed his shoulders and then fell over awkwardly on top of him. Ben grabbed her arms and pulled her with him as the two of them rolled down the hill. Laurie alternately laughed and screamed with delight. Ben noticed how flabby her arms were and how heavy she was as they rolled. He worried that she might be hurt, but she sat up, laughing, at the bottom. When he looked back up the hill, Iris had taken his place beside Megan.

"You're back," said Ben to Laurie. "I'm so happy."

"For good," said Laurie. "I'm so happy, too."

"And me," Iris said. "I'm so happy, too."

"What about me?" Megan asked. "Don't leave me out. I'm the most so happy."

Laurie beamed. "We're all so happy. I came home to take care of Mom."

"Who is desperately in need of adult supervision," said Ben.

He helped Laurie up and the two of them held hands as they climbed back up the little hill. Laurie was puffing from exertion and excitement. Laurie sat beside Megan and put her arm around her so that Megan was sandwiched between Laurie and Iris. Ben sat below them on the hill. Sarah came running, face flushed, and hugged the three women in turn. Ben held out his arms to her and she ignored him.

"Dad, let's get moving. If we don't get a pumpkin soon, all the good ones will be gone."

"It won't matter much. I'm the worst pumpkin carver in America."

"That's true," said Sarah. "But I already talked to Megan. She's going to carve the pumpkin this year. Let's go."

Sarah led the five of them to the pumpkin she had picked out. Ben picked it up. Iris picked up a nearby pumpkin for herself. Megan started to pick up a small pumpkin, and Sarah intervened. "Why don't you just share ours?"

"Why don't I?" answered Megan.

"You can save yourself ten dollars," Sarah said.

"Good idea."

"And buy me ice cream with it," Sarah said.

"You are," said Megan, "your father's daughter."

They headed for the card table to pay. Ben nudged Megan when he saw that Tyler was already there ahead of them. The two of them dropped back, and each linked arms with Iris. Laurie and Sarah, nudged out of the way, held hands and talked about what they were going to be for Halloween. As they approached the table, Iris saw Tyler and stiffened. Ben and Megan tightened their grip on her arms, and Iris muttered, "I'll be good."

"Hey, Tyler," said Megan evenly.

Tyler turned, holding a pumpkin under one arm and replacing his wallet with the other. He looked at Megan, at the three of them, and his face twisted and turned red. "Megan, get away from these people."

"Tyler, why don't you have a nice day and go home," Iris said. "Or just go home."

"I have as much right to be here as you. Last I heard, you don't own the pumpkin patch. Why don't you go home?"

"OK, boys and girls, be nice," said Megan. "Tyler, this is stupid. These are my friends. Please, let me have my life."

"This is no life, Megan, what you have. It's…"

"Tyler. Stop. You owe me, Tyler. Do you forget?"

"Owe you? Are you insane? Owe you for doing the Devil's work?"

"Tyler!" Iris's voice was a roar. "Leave it alone." Ben and Megan still held to her arms. Ben had the pumpkin on his right hip. Sarah had come up beside him, and he handed the pumpkin off to her. Once before, Tyler had surprised Ben; he did not intend to be surprised again. He wished for his broom. Without warning, Sarah stepped forward and with both hands heaved her pumpkin at Tyler. The pumpkin described a small arc and hit the grass harmlessly in front of Tyler's work boots.

"Leave my dad alone," Sarah shouted. "You tried to hurt my dad. Leave him alone!" Ben let go of Iris's arm to pull Sarah back. By the time he got to her, Laurie had moved in from the other side. She stepped up close to Tyler. "Leave my Ben alone. I don't like you." She drew back her fist but already Tyler was retreating. Iris had hold of Laurie's shoulders so she could not pursue.

Iris's shoulders were shaking from laughter. She could barely get her words out. "I'm sorry, Tyler. This isn't much of a fair fight. You'd better escape while we restrain these two hellcats. It appears you aren't too popular with the womenfolk. You might want to work on that."

"Children of the Devil, all of you," said Tyler.

Iris said, "Aw, hell, Tyler, can't you at least see the humor here? Nobody expects you to be able to stand up to a child and a...to my Laurie. Even I'm on your side in this one."

Tyler had recovered some composure but showed no signs of retrieving a sense of humor. "You, Megan, you've been warned." He looked at the pumpkin under his arm as though he had forgotten how it came to be there and walked away with as much dignity as any person can have who is carrying a pumpkin.

Ben and Iris paid for their pumpkins. Megan, with no pumpkin, handed a ten dollar bill to the still stunned attendant.

"Megan," Sarah said. "You don't need to pay. You didn't get a pumpkin."

"I know. But these are the people who used to buy me my winter jacket when I was a little kid like you." Megan stooped to hug Sarah.

"But don't panic, I've got another ten dollars set aside for ice cream for everybody. My treat."

At the ice cream shop, Ben lectured Sarah about throwing a pumpkin at Tyler, and then Iris took a turn lecturing Laurie. Megan destroyed all sense of order by giggling throughout at the hypocrisy of it all. Laurie and Sarah, partners in crime, gave each other high fives. Megan argued successfully that Iris should pay for the ice cream as a punishment for being not just a hypocrite but a rich hypocrite.

Sarah hitched a ride home with Iris and Laurie, so that she and Laurie could continue reveling in their brave adventure. Ben and Megan walked home, taking turns carrying Sarah's pumpkin. Megan was silent.

"Why was Tyler buying a pumpkin?" Ben asked.

"For Halloween. Why wouldn't he buy a pumpkin?"

"I don't know. Isn't there something about Halloween being a pagan holiday, tied up with the Devil and all that?"

"Good question. Maybe Tyler hasn't heard. More likely, Thelma just makes him. For Nathan. Thelma has a little common sense." Megan fell back into silence.

"What are you thinking about?" asked Ben.

"Brothers, keepers…nothing, nothing, nothing."

Chapter Thirty-Three

When Ben got home from work, Megan was curled on the couch, waiting for him. He took off his wet, snowy boots and placed them beside hers in the entryway. There was a puddle around Megan's boots. Her green ski shell, dripping water, hung from the coat rack.

"Why aren't you at work?" Ben asked cheerfully, happy she was there.

She raised her wet face to him as he walked to the couch. She was curled under a fleece blanket, but he could feel her shivering as he put his arms around her. Her back felt thin and vulnerable.

"What's wrong?" Ben asked.

"Can you call Iris and ask her to take care of Sarah? Cut her off before she gets home?"

Ben made the call and put on a pot of coffee. He brought another blanket to cover Megan and turned up the heat. It had been snowing for several hours, a heavy storm to end November. A thick, swirling snow, it created its own world. It made you think it would never stop until the roofs were covered.

"What's wrong?"

"Nathan, my nephew, came by the library today. It was a field trip with his class. I got his teacher to let me take him back in the break room so I could talk to him."

"What did he say?"

"Nothing. He didn't say anything. I mean, he said he was fine. He said things were good at home." Megan's face was still wet, and she had trouble catching her breath. "He said he was doing OK in school. Stuff like that. He was nervous about being with me. I finally just let him go back with his class because it was clear he was miserable. When I sent him back, I stood in the doorway and wouldn't let him leave until he gave me a hug. He held on to me like I was the last warm thing in a world of ice. His body shook like he was having convulsions. I looked at his face, and he never cried. His face was a perfect blank, and it was like he didn't even know that his body was shaking. I begged him to tell me what was wrong. Never a word. He just looked at me and left."

"What does it mean?"

"It's started again. We're back to the beginning. All the things I dreaded to tell you." Megan looked up at Ben. "I know I must love you because the first thing I thought was that I had to tell Ben. If you don't love me afterwards, so be it. I have to do something—I don't know what—for Nathan. There can't be more of this."

Ben took his thumb and brushed tears from Megan's face, but they were immediately replaced. She shivered under the blankets. Ben stretched out beside her on the couch and held her to warm her up. Her shivering slowed but returned at intervals. Ben got up.

"I'm going to bring you some coffee. Do you want me to put on some soup?"

"Just coffee."

Megan sat up with the blankets tented over her shoulders and sipped at the coffee. Her hands shook and she spilled a little. She wiped fretfully at the spill. Ben sat beside her and ran his hands through her hair. He forced himself to wait for her to get ready to talk.

"Tyler is sexually abusing Nathan," Megan said.

"Nathan said that?"

"No. It's the look. I know the look."

Ben held tightly to himself. He could not stop running his right hand through Megan's honey-colored hair. He willed his mind not to form an image of Megan being sexually abused by her father. Over time, he had expected to have to deal with this image but had managed to keep it abstract, theoretical. Now, he wanted to kill a man he had never known, a man nowhere to be found except in the evil that lived after him, a man who had disappeared one day without a trace. Ben forced himself to look at Megan's face, this face that he loved, because wanting to kill someone did not answer to what she now might need. Ben forced himself not to guess at anything because the truth would be evil sufficient to this day.

"How do you know the look?" Ben asked.

"Because Tyler wore that look every time he came out of our father's bedroom. The winters were the worse, with the snow falling, because you couldn't stay outside without drowning in the snow. Our father would jump up on a chair and rant about the godless Communists. He was big on the Communists. He'd make Tyler and me line up two chairs in front of him like we were an audience of thousands. Then he would go into a panic because he'd forgotten his Bible. He'd race into the bedroom to find it and race back, as though his captive audience of two might run out into the snowstorm to escape. When he had the fever, he thought he was addressing some grand auditorium full of people eager to hang on his every word. I swear it never came into his mind that we were sitting there because he'd beat the hell out of us if we moved. He got back on his chair and fanned through the pages of his Bible, always desperate to find exactly the right passage. But, of course, the passages never fit anything. He picked one at random and then ranted about how the Communists were destroying the moral fabric of America. He told us our teachers were Communist spies, and we should never tell them anything about our lives. And we should always pretend that we didn't know they were Communists because if they knew we knew, they would have us kidnapped and taken to Siberia. He told us…told us that then we would be separated from his love."

Ben made himself stop repetitively stroking Megan's hair. She was still sitting with her legs akimbo. Ben gently pushed the near leg down and stretched out with his head in her lap so he could look up at her face. She looked down and touched his cheek, and he captured her hand and held it against his face.

"Ben, poor Ben, I'm so sorry."

"Shh, go on."

"On good nights, he ranted until he was exhausted and fell asleep on the couch. I would heat up some rice, some beans. It was the damnedest thing because, as crazy as our father was, there was always plenty of food in the house. He prided himself on the fact that no child of his would ever go hungry. Plus, he had these survivalist ideas, so the basement was stuffed with food. There was wood for the stove, plenty of food, and, when I was Sarah's age, I kept the house cleaned. I was a kid—I thought that scrubbing the house clean would somehow scrub the house clean—a miniature Lady Macbeth. The only danger was sometimes the smell of the food would wake him up. Then he'd eat and take Tyler in the bedroom...called it special religious instruction. Tyler would beg me not to cook anything because he was afraid the smell would wake him up. I was damned if I was going to be deprived of a hot meal. God forgive me. There was a lot I didn't understand. I even teased Tyler because he shit his pants all the time. I guess you could say it took me a while to catch on."

Lying there, listening, Ben wanted to reach up to Megan's mouth and change the story, change her lips with the tips of his fingers so the words she formed would give him the outcome he wanted. At that moment, he did not care about what had happened to Tyler. Anything could happen to Tyler as long as he could protect the past and future Megan.

"For the longest time," Megan said, "I went around thinking that the bad things that happened were because I cooked hot meals. Somehow, it got tied up in my mind with the smell of steaming rice. Much later, waiting tables, I would sometimes have to go out in the alley and throw up when the chef was cooking a rice dish. I'd sit in the kitchen at home and listen to the sounds that came from the bedroom. My father would rant from the Bible and then sometimes I could hear them both scream. I thought it was some kind of religious ceremony. That's how my father described it. Tyler just went around with a blank look on his face and shit his pants."

"Did Tyler ever say to you what was happening?"

"Only by shitting his pants. It was eloquent shit."

"How long did this go on?"

Megan was calmer now. "Depends how you measure time. Eons. Centuries. Generations?"

"Ah."

"Sometimes it would stop for a while. Our father would get better for a while. He would take Tyler fishing or hunting. Normal stuff."

Ben found a safe question. "Did he take you hunting and fishing?"

"No. He had no interest in me. Only that I should clean the house. He liked it that I cleaned the house and learned to cook. Sometimes he even praised me for it. I was doing what women were supposed to do. And I kept my mouth shut. That was another good thing. I found the things to do that would get him to ignore me. Sometimes he beat me if a pot wasn't cleaned right. His hand was like a lump of iron. He was a big man, like Tyler. But I knew even then that it didn't have anything to do with the pot, or even with me. You could just see in his face that he needed to beat somebody."

Outside, the snow was still falling, intent on drowning the world. Ben touched Megan's face, gently squeezed her arms, and held her hands, trying to find, in the repetitive laying on of hands, some cure. "I am," he said, "so sorry."

Megan smiled down on him. "I didn't care about being beat. I suppose I must have at first, but it got to be nothing. Besides, no matter how crazy the old bastard got, he knew enough not to leave bruises for the teachers to see. I had bruises on my behind all the time. I got so I didn't mind. For all I knew, all the other kids had the same bruises. It hurt to sit down, but it just reminded me how much I hated him. I didn't even really know that other kids had different relationships with their parents. Other kids talked at school about their parents, but for all I knew they were hiding things the same way I was. I made up lies to tell about my family—I thought the other kids were probably doing the same thing. That's why, when I read *To Kill a Mockingbird*, I fell so in love with Atticus Finch. Something about that book finally convinced me that normal families really existed. Maybe because it was a family with a son and a daughter, like my family, and no mother, like my family. And Atticus Finch was a father who was complete, who was gentle, and who had no meanness in him. I guess it doesn't take a genius to figure out that's why I fell in love with you. You're my Atticus Finch, except you're a terrible smartass, Ben. What the hell. Nobody's perfect."

"Kids aren't supposed to be beat."

"Yes. But any kid being beat will tell you the same thing—better beat than ignored. Atticus was old and never played with his children, but there was no one he would rather talk to than his kids. There was nothing more important to him than a child's thoughts. For me, it was safer to be ignored—safer but lonely. Tyler was the one that got the attention because only sons were important."

Ben went back in his mind to digging ditches with his own father, his father's hand resting lightly on his shoulder, and the two of them watching the water slowly change from muddy to clear. He thought of standing in the dark outside his father's workroom, listening to his father's gentle voice carrying on a conversation of mystery with someone who almost certainly was not there. He thought to himself that they were saved, he and Megan, because no words could come out of Megan's mouth that mattered. It only mattered that Megan was talking to him.

"You want some more coffee?" asked Ben.

"In a minute." The same calm seemed to have found Megan. She stroked Ben's hair. She looked outside at the falling snow, kneeling into the earth.

"Don't you want to know whether my father sexually abused me?"

"I hope he didn't. But if he did, so be it. From what you have said, it sounds like he didn't. It sounds like it was only boys. Only this minute did I feel sorry for the first time for Tyler. I don't want anything bad to have happened to you. But if your father did this to you, you're here with me. If he didn't, you're here with me. You are here."

"I am here. I'm in the right place. You're right—he only wanted boys. But there's another thing. Once, I opened the door a crack and peeked in. I wish I hadn't done that. If only I hadn't looked. Tyler was on the bed, on his stomach, and our father was on top of him, breathing these sharp, jagged breaths that were like the rise and fall of knives. Tyler turned his head and looked at me. I don't know what I expected. I couldn't have expected anything at the time. But I guess I expected the dull, vacant look that Tyler always wore when our father called him into his bedroom. But that was not the look."

Megan fell silent, her eyes far away.

"Are you there?" asked Ben.

"I am here."

"The look?"

"Ecstasy."

"Ecstasy?"

"He was, I think, in the deepest communion with our father. Tyler dreaded it…hated it…feared it." Megan's voice became far away and dispassionate. "But somehow he also loved it. He was a kid—it got all tangled together. Tyler has hated me from the time I opened the door and saw that look on his face." Ben was silent. Megan continued. "I don't know, then or now, whether it was possible for me to look at that and be OK. Maybe opening that door was responsible for all that came later."

The two of them were silent. Megan was exhausted. Ben knew she did not have the strength for more questions. He knew that when Megan spoke of all that came later, she was thinking of the eventual fate of her father. He wanted to remind her that other things also came later: Iris, Buster, George, Billy—people that loved her. Putting herself through college also came later, and coming back home to tend her library. Ben wished to be one of these good things that came later. He wished to convince Megan that the most important thing that came later was Megan, fashioned from the raw materials of herself. But they were both worn out, and he did not know if he could find the right words. He was too tired to say it, and she too tired to hear it.

Instead, he stood up and guided Megan down on the couch. He pulled the blanket to her neck and said, "I'll warm up your coffee. I'll fetch Sarah through the storm. Tonight, I fix dinner—soup, I think. And after dinner, you will come back and lie on the couch under this blanket, and Sarah and I will fuss over you. Sarah will rub your feet. I will massage your neck. Or the other way around. Knowing Sarah, she will insist that I take your feet since they may be stinky. And if you give us orders, we will obey them, unless they are unreasonable or require actual effort on our part. Clear?"

"Clear."

"Ben?"

"Yes, my love."

"My feet don't stink." Her voice was tired, but she was still fighting, and he was glad that he had not presumed to give a motivational speech to this woman.

Chapter Thirty-Four

The office was full of light and air and Stephanie Pace could look out through the high windows at Peak One, covered with new snow and bright in the morning sun. A lush philodendron had squirmed its way over the bookcase, so that the dark, gleaming leaves obscured some of the titles. Ben had pictured a grim place full of pale, harried social workers and haunted children. Stephanie, the director of social services for the county, seemed delighted to see them, delighted with this day. She hugged Megan and seemed tempted to hug Ben and then gave up the thought at the last minute and patted his shoulder. She told Ben that she remembered seeing him and Sarah in the grocery store and that she had heard he was teaching at the high school and wondered how he got lucky enough to date Megan. Ben reminded himself he lived in a town without secrets.

"How is my friend, Iris?" she asked Ben.

"She continues being Iris," said Ben, and this answer pleased Stephanie. "Good, we can't do without her, even when she's being a royal pain in the ass. I could tell you stories about when Iris and I were roaming the bars together, but I most assuredly will not. I have my dignity to protect. And if Iris has told you any of those stories, you tell her that I said she is a lying dog. How is the library, Megan?"

"It's good."

"We were so happy when you came back from college and took the job. We lose so many of our young people to Denver." It was not clear which "we" Stephanie referred to. Ben inferred that Stephanie spoke not only for herself, but also for others whose agreement she took for granted. Stephanie was another figure like George, like Iris, who knew all the people and all the secrets. She had been part of this small-town scrum for so long that she confidently assumed she was speaking for the county commissioners, the sheriff, the judge, the school board, and hundreds of others whose lives intertwined hers.

"And your job, Ben?" continued Stephanie. "Are you liking the high school?"

"Very much."

"We were so lucky to get you. I hear good reports from your students. By the way, you'll be pleased to know I'm giving you a grace period to get settled in." She laughed cheerfully. "But that won't last forever. Then I'll be calling you."

"What will you be calling me?" asked Ben.

Stephanie smiled again and nodded appreciatively. "I'll be calling you the new member of whatever committee or board I need a volunteer for. Sound OK?"

"You know. It actually sounds delightful coming from you. I suspect that many are called and few are able to resist."

"OK. OK. Would you two charm artists give it a rest?" Megan said.

"Megan, you have always been stubborn and willful, but I guess that's what you needed to be. So let's talk about your nephew." In an instant, Stephanie had replaced charm with piercing seriousness.

"How did you know we were here to talk about Nathan?" Megan asked.

Stephanie waved this question away as though she were flicking a crumb from her skirt.

"June Hunter has been the principal at the elementary school for, what, fifteen years? She's not blind. I'm not blind. We're just not sure what to do. Something is wrong with that child, and we're worried sick about it. We just can't get him to tell us anything useful."

"You've talked to Nathan?" asked Megan.

Stephanie flicked another crumb. "Ordinarily, I would've had one of my workers do the interview, but that wasn't good enough for Iris."

"Iris?"

Stephanie did not even bother to flick away this crumb. She simply nodded. "I'm sorry. So far, he just won't talk. Years ago, it was the same with Tyler and with you."

Megan was blank. "What do you mean with Tyler and me? What are you talking about?"

Stephanie stared at Megan intently and her face softened. "You don't remember, do you?"

Megan lifted her hands in a helpless question.

Stephanie said, "I did the same interview with you when you were a child. 'Tell me if anyone is doing bad things to you. Tell me what life is like with your father.' You don't remember—I guess that's not so remarkable. I was probably just one more adult not to be trusted. You were such a lovely child, all covered with freckles. Stubborn. I couldn't decide whether you were scared or mad. Most of the time when kids are angry, they get in trouble, like Tyler. But not you. You were the nicest, most polite kid. Everyone loved you. I finally decided you were more mad than scared, but mad in some way that was simply beyond me. The truth is I used to go home and cry over you. I was younger then and didn't have as many calluses as I have now. I knew something was wrong, but I never could make you out. Oh, well. You can't win them all. Can't save them all. You probably turned out a lot better, anyway, than if you had let me save you. It's a strange business I'm in."

Megan took Ben's hand. He could feel her trembling. Her face was white.

"I don't remember. You talked to me? I don't remember. You knew? Iris knew? You all knew?"

Stephanie was completely still. She sat serenely, and the silence grew as quietly and as surely as the philodendron that inched its way steadily towards the sunshine.

"Tell me what you knew," said Megan harshly.

"We didn't know anything, Megan, because you wouldn't tell us anything. We knew your father was a nut case. We knew he kept you kids isolated up in that cabin. None of which is against the law. We knew Tyler was an angry kid who talked about God a lot and cried for no reason. A couple of times he was smelly but before anyone could catch up with him, he would run home. We knew that you were a perfect angel when all logic would say you should have been a perfect hellion. It seemed in those days like Iris was screaming on the phone to me at least once a week. And I was screaming back at her to just tell me what to do. Your father disappeared, the years went by, and here we are. So, we didn't know anything. All we knew was what we could see, the surface of things. That's still all we know, unless you came here today to answer those questions I asked you when I was young and thought I could save everybody."

"You talked to me when I was a child? How could I not remember that?"

"Easy. Kids block things out that upset them, or I was just boring and forgettable. Doesn't matter. What's more important is whether we can have a do-over today of that forgettable interview many years ago."

"I thought I was coming here to get you to check on Nathan."

"I know. I've done that. I didn't get anywhere. Maybe Nathan told you something specific. If not, what I need to know from you is what happened to you and Tyler that might give me a clue about Nathan."

Megan pulled herself straight in her chair. "I see that."

"And?"

"I've just never told anybody except Ben. I spent years not telling anybody. There was a rule in my mind that said tell no one. It didn't matter who. They were simply...not to know. It was nobody's business."

"And it was shameful?"

"Shameful. I suppose. But also a kind of betrayal."

"Who would you be betraying?"

"I'm not sure. All of us who lived through it."

"You and Tyler lived through it. You are worried about betraying Tyler?"

"I don't have much use for Tyler. But yes, I guess."

"What about your father? He was there. He lived through it. Are you worried about betraying him?"

"No."

"He disappeared," Stephanie said. "But what if he turned up tomorrow? Would you be betraying him?"

"I'm not worried about betraying him. And he won't turn up tomorrow."

"How can you be sure?" asked Stephanie.

Megan looked straight and level at Stephanie. "It's just a feeling I have. I've always believed he was dead."

"Are you going to tell me what happened in your family?"

"I don't know."

"I can't get anything out of Nathan. Did Nathan tell you more than he told me?"

"No," Megan said.

"If I knew about your family, if I knew that Tyler was abused as a child, physically abused, sexually abused, then I'd have more to go on. I might be able to get Judge Porter to order a physical exam. I need to know, Megan."

"I'll think about it. I thought I could just get you to talk to Nathan and find out from him what is going on. You've already done that. I didn't know it was going to turn into this. I have to think about it."

"OK. Think about it. But don't take too long. This is about Nathan." Stephanie Pace was cold and direct.

"You don't have to tell me who it's about," said Megan. She got up to go. "You know," she said, "maybe this is why I didn't talk to you before."

Stephanie shrugged this off. "One more thing," said Stephanie. "You don't mind if I talk to Ben for a minute alone?"

Megan looked at Ben. "I don't mind."

If Megan had not expected this turn of events, neither had Ben. He had thought his role was to hold Megan's hand and support her. They had both thought that they would get Stephanie to investigate and that she would go out and solve the problem for them.

Megan closed the door behind her. Stephanie picked up a pencil from her desk and scratched the back of her neck with the eraser.

"Tell me, Ben, what Megan told you about her childhood. I wouldn't ask you, but you can see I need to know."

"Ah," said Ben. "That's not my place. Megan will tell you whatever she decides to tell you."

"You're a schoolteacher, Ben. The law requires you to report child abuse."

"Megan has reported to you the possibility of abuse, which you already knew about. Nathan has not told her that he was abused, nor has he told me that, or you that. With all due respect, Ms. Pace, you're trying to squeeze me."

"The law requires you to report all information that may help me in my investigation. You could lose your job."

Ben thought about that one. "Maybe. I'm not a lawyer. I would have to talk to one."

"Ben…"

Ben stood up. "You, Ms. Pace, are more complicated than I had guessed. Maybe you have to be—I don't know. But our work here is done. You do what you feel you have to do about my job. I have other skills I can fall back on."

"Really? What is that?"

"My childhood dream was to be a ditch digger. I can dig a beautiful ditch."

Ben left Stephanie Pace chewing thoughtfully on her pencil eraser.

Megan was waiting in the lobby. She took Ben's arm and leaned against him as they left the building. They drove in silence to The Roaster and had coffee at a table in the corner.

"Well, that was awful," Megan said.

"Sorry. Who knew?"

"I swear I don't remember talking to her when I was a kid. Do you think she's making it up?"

"No clue. She plays a deep game. I guess that's what you do when you spend your life poking into people's secrets. She's a friend of Iris. You would think she would be OK."

"She tried to get you to rat me out. I figured that out when I was sitting in the lobby. I should never have told her I told her anything."

"The woman misses nothing."

"Did she threaten you?"

"What could she threaten me with?"

"Thanks, Ben. It'll be OK. I'll tell her what she wants to know. But I had to have time to think first."

"About?"

"Tyler. There is a delicate balance of power between us. If I tell his secrets…"

"He'll tell yours," Ben said.

"Will you go for a hike with me tomorrow?"

Chapter Thirty-Five

On Saturday morning, Ben parked his truck on the dirt road beside the twisty lane to the cabin in the pines where Megan lived out her childhood. He leaned against a rotting fencepost and studied the gray, weathered cabin, the roof caved in at one end. The steps leading to the front stoop were twisted because the support column of stacked fieldstones had slipped from under one side.

"Is it hard to come back here?" Ben asked.

Megan looked over from the back of the truck where she was unloading gear. "Not so much. I used to come back here all the time when I was in college. I told you when we climbed San Luis that I gave myself tests to see if I was OK. This was one of the big ones. I made myself keep coming back until it was just an old house full of dust."

"Can we go in?"

"No. We're going someplace else."

That morning, Ben had felt the veering of her emotions. It was hard to tell with Megan because she threw up her wall of composure, so the only clues were like the serrated shadows of passing clouds. She was politely determined not to talk about where they were going and why. Megan handed Ben his daypack and a pair of snowshoes, and said, "Tie those to your pack. We may need them when we get higher." She gathered two ice axes from the bed of the truck and handed one to Ben.

"Axes? Isn't this overkill?" Ben asked.

"Could be. But it's steep at the end. Doesn't hurt to be safe."

They walked the road, patchy with December snow, to the end of the fence line and then Megan struck off into a sagebrush meadow. They climbed steadily and entered a pale, leafless aspen grove. Megan followed some remembered trail beneath the snow. The aspen gave way to lodgepole pine and deeper snow and still the trail must have been beneath them because always Megan found a clear way through the deadfalls on the forest floor. After a half-hour, Megan called a rest, and they sat on a huge downed pine. Megan brushed off the snow and motioned Ben to sit at a place where the bark was gone and the wood was smooth and worn. They shared a drink of icy water, and Megan ordered snowshoes for the rest of the way.

Ben offered to go first and break trail, but Megan waved him off because he did not know the path. The trail gained the top of a ridge and then followed its crest. The snow had blown off the ridgeline, and there was barely enough to make the snowshoes worthwhile, but the crampons kept them from slipping as the ridge slanted up. The pines were older here, and below in the shaded draw there were spruce that cradled in their fronds small mounds of snow. At a place where two boulders loomed over the trail, Megan abruptly dropped off the ridgeline into the ravine below. Ben plunged down after her, with only the crampons keeping him from sliding straight to the bottom. Huge boulders had calved long ago into this narrow crease in the mountain. Some rose twenty feet high, and leaned at crazy angles against the steep wall of the cut. Megan threaded her way quickly among these boulders, her snowshoes sometimes scraping against them as she slipped through narrow spaces. She led the two of them straight to two boulders that leaned against each other. She sat in the snow and took off her snowshoes, and Ben dropped down beside her.

"We're here," she said edgily.

"OK. We're here. Where is here?"

Megan ignored the question. She took her ice axe and cleared snow out of the way. She crawled into an opening at the base of the boulders. Ben left his pack with the ice axe and snowshoes outside the entrance. The opening was a close fit, but it widened as soon as he was through the entrance. They emerged into a room under the huge, canted boulders that leaned above them against the mountain. The room was made larger because there was a hollow, a piece of a cave, in the side of the hill. Pale light came in from the top between the gaps in the boulders. Ben remembered Billy's story about Megan finding secret places when she was a child. This room in the mountain was large enough to stand up and walk around in. The floor was smooth, packed earth, still holding old tin cans and a piece of wooden handle that might have been from a shovel. A fire ring held charred remains. An old, gray rope lay in the corner. Ben walked the perimeter of the room and, in the back, found a mineshaft. It was about six feet in diameter and began by going straight down and then seemed to curve slightly after about ten feet. It was hard to tell how deep it was in the dim light. Megan sat on a boulder nearby; it was the size of a large bear curled up tightly for a nap. Megan stared towards the mine as though she could penetrate the blackness and see the bottom.

"Where are we?" Ben asked.

"This was one of my hideouts. I used to come here and play. I guess that old mineshaft was a dry hole. Whoever dug it went down maybe twenty feet and then gave up. I stole that rope over there from Henry, knotted it into a kind of ladder, and went to the bottom."

"Henry?"

"My father. Strange he had an ordinary name; I often wondered how that could be. Anyway, I tied a flashlight around my neck and went to the bottom. I had thrown rocks in, so I had an idea of how deep it was, but, as I was going down, I became terribly afraid that there was no bottom. Mostly, I just played here; this is where I lived a normal life. I wrote in my diary. I read. I used this place for years. I first read *To Kill a Mockingbird* here. This is a shameful thing for a librarian to admit, but I stole that book. I told the school librarian that I had lost it, but the truth was that I simply could not part with it. The librarian, Mrs. Carson, a nice old lady, got angry and told me I would have to pay for it. She must have seen the look on my face—where was I going to get the money to pay for a book? I asked her how much. She hemmed and hawed and looked in the card catalog and then claimed that it was an old, damaged copy and that, luckily, the price was only a nickel. Maybe that's where I got the idea to become a librarian."

Ben again had the feeling that Megan was veering. He was an expert on telling stories to keep darkness away. This story of the library book seemed to be Megan's way of testing the strength of her composure.

"So this is where you fell in love with Atticus Finch?" Ben asked.

"And with you. I dreamed of love, of a life that was clean and safe, a life with no secrets. And I found it. And it's coming apart."

"This," Ben said, "is the secret Tyler holds over you. If you talk to Stephanie Pace, then he tells the sheriff where your father is."

Megan looked sharply up. "How do you know that?"

Ben shrugged. "It's all just guesses, some of Iris's, some of mine."

Megan's shoulders sagged. "You have no right, none of you, to know so much about my life."

Ben was silent. Megan said, "I should never have told Tyler. I was a kid; it seemed like I had to tell someone. In some crazy way, I thought Tyler would be happy. Tyler had more reason to hate him than I did. Surely, we had both dreamed of killing our father."

"We will find our way through this," Ben said. He went to Megan where she sat on the large rock beside the pit. He kneeled and took her hands, but she pulled them away. Her eyes stared past him and down into the blackness. Ben sat on the packed earth between Megan and the mineshaft.

"I should never have told you, either,' Megan said. "Now you are a part of this. What kind of person kills their own father?"

"You were a kid. You were abused."

"I wasn't a child. I was sixteen. More or less. Half of me was about six…the other half sixty. Besides, lots of children are abused. They don't pick up a hammer and hit their father in the head."

"Here?"

"Welcome to the old bastard's grave. We should have brought flowers," said Megan.

"How? What happened? Make me understand."

"I wish I could tell you that I did it to protect Tyler. That might have been a good reason. I made the mistake of coming here, like now, after a fall snow. This was my place, my only safe place. I never came here in the winter because there was too much snow—Henry could track me. I shouldn't have come, but winter was coming, and I wanted one last time before the snows shut me into that house. I built a fire. I was reading my book and I was happy and safe and it felt to me like I was surrounded by love. And then his head was sticking through the entrance, and he was screaming. Screaming that I had disobeyed him for the last time. He jerked me up and slapped me in the face—hard. I was lying on the ground. I looked up at him, but his eyes were on the pit. He started babbling that it was the gateway to Hell. He said it was where I communed with the Devil. He paced around the cave…found all the little things I had brought to make it homelike. A tin cup. An old coffee pot I had found in the woods. He threw the cup into the mine, and it clanged against the walls and then bounced off the bottom. He threw the coffee pot in…a piece of candle. It didn't matter. I knew I could never come back. This place was where I came to be with my real family. I stood right here, in this spot. I remember being very tired. I remember how much I needed to pee. Henry kept on with his rant, about me communing with the Devil, but I wasn't really listening. I just stood there waiting for him to be done. He dropped to his knees and tried to see into the pit. Talked about seeing the fires of Hell. Here, where my feet are, the two things that changed my life. My stolen copy of *To Kill a Mockingbird*, lying open, and an old miner's tool, a claw hammer. I used the hammer to hold open the pages of my book as I read. Henry snatched the book. He called it the work of the Devil. Asked me if the Devil had come up out of this hole in the ground and brought me this book. I reached to get the book back, but he held it over his head with one hand and drew back his other hand to hit me. He was in one of his frenzies; spit flew from his mouth; drooled down his chin. He asked me if I had sex with the Devil. Said women could never be satisfied by a man. He held the book over his head and said he was going to throw it back into the fires of Hell. He got on his knees, facing the pit, holding my book over his head. He was about to throw it in. I killed him. I picked up the hammer and held it with both hands and swung it as hard as I could onto the top of his head. I could feel his skull crack through the handle of the hammer. He fell to the ground, right there, his face hanging down over the pit. Blood was seeping out of his head, dripping into the pit. As he fell, I tried to grab for the book, but it went into the pit. I killed him...for a book."

Ben reached again for Megan's hands, but she shook him off. "Enough," said Ben softly. "You don't have to talk anymore." Ben pictured Megan in college, going back to the old house, sitting there alone until she could stare down every memory creeping out of those crumbling walls. But he knew she had never come back to this place, where memories blew a gale from a hole in the ground. He felt the wind, and they were not even his memories. When he was a child, he had once gone out of his head with fever. Somehow, he had been transported in his delirium from his bed to the two inches between the bed and the wall, and a terrifying wind howled in that space. He wanted desperately to close his ears to that howling wind, but his arms were squeezed to his side, his whole body flattened between bed and wall. He was helpless to raise his hands, to cover his ears against the gale. And Megan was helpless to stop the sound of her own howling memory.

"No," said Megan, furiously. "I have to. The book, my book, went into the pit. So, I climbed in after it. I got the rope and tied it around this boulder and climbed down in the dark. I didn't have a flashlight. I just went down into the dark. At the bottom, I was down on my hands and knees, feeling in the rocks. There was water at the base of the rocks. It was cold. I started shivering and couldn't stop. I found the pot, the cup. Finally, I found my book. Something warm dripped on the back of my neck. I shoved the book into my pants. Then, for a lifetime, I couldn't find the rope. I stumbled around and around the shaft, feeling for it, missing it. I thought Henry must have come to and pulled it up behind me. All I could think was that I would be left there with my book, and there was no light to read by. I found the rope. I climbed out. At the top, there was light, and I climbed back into it, and at the very top was my father's face. His eyes were open, but I knew he was dead. Maybe he was looking at the fires of Hell. I climbed past him. Then I pushed him into the pit. He was heavy, and I had to reach under his chest and inch him forward. It took a long time. I got his shoulders over and then his chest and then all of a sudden he went in, so...fast."

"Please, enough," said Ben.

"Enough? Enough? For me, or for you? Is it more than you can stand?"

"Yes. But that's not what I meant."

"Isn't it? All those times when I warned you about me. You said it would be fine. You could handle it. Ben could handle anything. Now, you're not so sure. Welcome to my world. This is what I have handled every day of my life. Every day. I told you I couldn't be normal. Why wouldn't you listen? This is Megan, this pit with my father's bones in it. And you say, 'Enough.' No more for Ben. Enough. So you can get out of here? And get away from me? Because who knows when I might snap again? Who knows when Megan might get mad because the house is messy and bury a hammer in the back of my head? You can't really know, can you? You can't know when someone like me might step over the line—I don't even know. This was my one safe place, this cave, and my father came in one day and ruined it. I thought I had found another safe place with you. But it can't be. All you want is for me to shut up so you can make your escape. There is no safe place. Not for me. Maybe not for you, either, Ben Wallace. You and your Ode to Joy. It's crazy. It's as crazy as my father's rants about the joy of the Lord."

Megan's voice echoed off the walls of the cave. Her face was red, and Ben, as he sat before her, could see the muscles in her face and neck stretched, twitching, at the edge of snapping. Megan stood up from her rock, from the place she had sat and read her favorite book in the cool light of summer afternoons. She stood over Ben. He saw the ice axe lying beside her feet. He picked it up and placed it in her hand. Megan's howling memory had sunk itself past brain and was alive in the fiber of every tensed muscle. This was one more test in Megan's life of tests, and only Megan, or Megan's muscles, was unsure whether she would pass it. She looked down on him as he sat between her and the pit that was her father's grave. They looked into each other's eyes, but Ben did not know what she was seeing. Ben reached over and gently patted the side of her knee. He put his hands down, pressing them against the cool, packed earth. He shifted his body, turning so that his back was to Megan, and he looked down into the mineshaft. He curled his arms around his knees, waited, and knew he was as safe as when Megan had held him in her arms high on the shoulders of San Luis Peak. He could feel the air parting as Megan raised the axe, could feel the air tearing as she threw the axe into the pit.

Megan slumped to the earth and put her arms around Ben's back. He did not change position but took one of her hands and held it against his face. Finally, Ben could feel Megan growing limp against his back. He carefully straightened up. He put one arm around Megan and with the other reached for her daypack. He positioned the pack at the base of the rock and guided the two of them down, so their heads rested together on the pack. He put his arms around her, and they slept for a while in this safe place.

Chapter Thirty-Six

Ben awoke in the gray light of Megan's cave. She had awakened before him but lay still in his arms, studying his face. When he opened his eyes, she touched his face with the tip of her finger. Her face was calm, her eyes serene and happy.

"Hey you," she said.

"No, hey you."

"Did you have a good sleep?"

"I must've," said Ben. Megan kissed his cheek, his nose. "And you?" asked Ben.

"I'm OK."

"Meaning you slept?" Ben asked.

"Meaning I slept. Meaning I'm OK. Meaning I woke up and the first thought I had was that we could love each other and be happy. I can do that simple thing. I came back here...I survived. Oh, God, it's OK."

"It's more than OK."

"Yes," Megan said.

"And could I just add this one thing?"

"Yes."

"I told you so. I told you. I told you. I love it when I'm right and you're not. It gives purpose and meaning to my life."

Megan pushed him in the chest and the two of them sat up. She found the water bottle and drank long and deeply. She wiped her chin and gave Ben a drink. They sat, leaning back against the rock. A few snowflakes filtered in through the small opening at the top where the massive boulders canted into the side of the ravine.

"I will call Stephanie Pace when we get back," Megan said. "I will tell her everything. Will you wait for me while I'm in prison?"

"I will wait for you. I'm not a lawyer, but I don't believe you will go to prison. A child defending herself against a crazy, abusive father? The same child grows up to be a good person. Maybe they don't even prosecute, and, if they do, I can't see a judge thinking prison is any kind of good idea. I guess it's possible. I know it's scary, but I don't think so."

Megan said, "You know, it's not even that scary. Not as scary as living it was."

Moved by an impulse she did not explain, Megan began walking slow circles around the wall of the cave. Running her hand against the rocky side of the cave, she found a small nook in the wall. She stooped to look inside and smiled. She reached inside and retrieved a small porcelain bird, tan beneath a layer of dirt.

"I almost forgot this," she said.

She rubbed the dirt off against the sleeve of her shirt. Some of the green and blue of its feathers came back. She cupped it in her hands as though to warm it back to life after so many years of hibernation. She again explored the dark nook with her hand and retrieved a piece of rotted fabric attached to some stuffing.

"It was a stuffed dog," she said. Megan held it up to her eyes doubtfully, "Lancelot, is that you?"

"Lancelot. A dog named Lancelot?" Ben hooted. Megan ignored him and reached in again and found a stubby pencil. She stared at the pencil and quickly reached inside again. She searched but came up empty and puzzled. "I had a diary here. I know I did." She searched again, feeling carefully around the little cave inside the cave.

Megan said, "I can't believe it's gone. I put everything in my diary, especially when I was younger. Who else could I trust? I had diaries hidden all over. It's just not here. Maybe I'm remembering wrong. Damn, I thought it was here."

Megan took her treasures, the bird, the pencil, the ragged remnants of a puppy, and sat on her rock. She cleaned the bird thoroughly with her shirt and with water from the bottle. It gleamed in the pale light, and perched contentedly again in the palm of her hand. "I loved this bird," she said, and Ben did not make fun.

Ben got up and walked around to stretch his legs. He stared into the mineshaft.

"I'll be right back," he said. "I'm going to get my pack." He crawled out and picked up his pack. He watched for a moment the snow drifting lightly down through the spruce. He dragged his pack behind him as he crawled back into the cave. Opening the bottom compartment, Ben fished around and came out with a camper's headlamp.

"Ben. No."

"It's been years. I'm going to see what's down there."

"No."

"Yes."

Ben emptied the contents of his backpack onto the floor of the cave and put the empty pack on his back. He fastened the headlamp to his head and gathered up the frayed, knotted rope. He passed it through his hands from end to end, inspecting its strength.

"Show me how you tied this around the boulder."

"No, Ben, there's no point in this. I don't want you to have to see what's down there. The rope is old. It's past old. It's ancient. When I used it, it was old. I don't care anymore what's down there. Let it be."

Ben circled one end of the rope around the base of the rock and knotted it. He leaned back against it with all his weight; the rope held and the boulder did not budge. He walked to the edge of the pit.

"I'm off to the office. Give us a kiss before we go."

Megan came over and kissed his forehead. "What a rock head. Listen. There are outcroppings that you can feel for with your feet. Don't try to jump off the edge. Lie flat on your stomach and let your legs hang over and then gradually slide in. Just follow the knots down with your hands and find the ledges with your feet. And Ben, wait."

"Yes."

Megan twisted his headlamp on.

"You are wise, my love, beyond all reckoning," Ben said.

Ben dropped over the side. He was relieved that the rope held. He slowly climbed down the rope, going from knot to knot and finding the footholds that Megan had promised. He looked up once and saw Megan's head silhouetted above him, her hair falling around her face. It was easy going down because the miner's pick had left jagged outcroppings of rock all along the wall of the pit. Ben passed the point where the pit bent slightly, and it would have been completely dark if not for his headlamp. At the bottom, he let go of the rope, and Megan, seeing the tension gone, called down to see if he was OK. Her voice wobbled as it came down through the tunnel.

"Give me some time," Ben called up to her.

He dreaded what he might see. The bottom was wider than he expected. The small camper's headlamp seemed too weak to compete with the intense black of the pit. Ben jerked his head around too much at first, trying to see everything at once and fearful of what he might see, of where he might be standing. He forced himself to slow down and search methodically with the narrow beam of light. It seemed to take forever. He loaded a few things into his backpack and was relieved to begin climbing out. Pulling from knot to knot on the rope was more difficult than he expected. He marveled that Megan had been able to do this as a child, one more reminder that she was the natural athlete. He hoped the old rope had one more ride in it. He was breathing hard but energized by the sight of light at the top and Megan's head looking down at him. As he neared the top, he could tell she was closely watching the frayed rope, especially where it rode against the rock at the lip of the pit. He pulled his upper body onto the floor of the cave and rolled over to swing his legs out of the mineshaft. As he rolled over, something rattled in his backpack. Megan retreated to the rock. Ben sat and caught his breath, and it took him a minute to notice Megan's fear and her eyes on his backpack.

"Wait," he said. "It's OK." He quickly stripped off the pack and took it over to her. Her eyes were wide with fear. He hurried to open it, and she shrank back until she saw the coffee pot in his hand. He reached in again and brought out the tin cup. She took them from him and stared. She shook her head and smiled and pretended to pour coffee into the cup. Ben touched her face with his grimy hand

and left a smudge. He tried to wipe it away and left a larger smudge. Megan looked again at his backpack.

"Is that all?"

"Just your ice axe." He handed it to her.

"That, you could've left down there."

"It's OK. It's literally nothing but an ice axe. And a mountain climber like you may find it useful." Megan looked at it and dropped it at her feet and turned her attention back to the old coffee pot and cup.

"Thanks for these," she said. "Can we get out of here now?"

"Don't you want to know what I found down there?"

"No."

They put Megan's treasures into Ben's pack and crawled back out into the world. It was still snowing lightly. They put on their snowshoes and climbed the steep slope to the top of the ridge without need for an ice axe. At the top, they were breathing hard and sweating. Resting on a boulder, leaning against each other, they watched the snow falling into the ravine. The rest of the way was downhill and when they reached the sagebrush meadow Megan broke off some sage, crushed it, and held it to her nose. Ben stopped and brushed snow from her hair and she held the sage to his face with her gloved hand.

In the truck, they debated whether it was a beer day or a coffee day. It was early afternoon and they were starving, so they went to the Moose Jaw for a beer and a burger. They took a table in the front where they could watch the snow filling in Main Street. They ordered and then washed their hands in the tiny bathrooms. The Moose Jaw was not big enough to waste space on large bathrooms; you could sit on the toilet and wash your hands and keep a foot braced against the rickety door, and you could do all three of these things at the same time.

They ate their burgers and fed each other salty French fries and drank the cold beer. When they finished, they ordered another beer. Ben leaned back in his chair and Megan rested her elbows on the table.

"You told me," said Ben, "that when you climbed down into the pit there were rocks all over the bottom and water under the rocks."

"Ben, I don't want to talk about that hellhole. This has been a hard day. Don't make it worse."

"I know. I'm sorry. But this won't wait. Trust me. Tell me."

Megan's eyes clouded and she sighed. "Yes. Rocks on the bottom."

"How big?"

"I don't know. Grapefruits. I stumbled over them."

"Spread all over the bottom?"

"Ben, yes."

"Here's what I found at the bottom."

"Ben, no."

"I found nothing. The stuff I brought up. Nothing else. No bones. No clothes. Nothing else."

"How can that be?"

"Here's what else. All those grapefruit rocks were stacked neatly in a pile, off to the side. The floor had a little water on it, but not much. I got down on my knees and ran my hands over every inch of the floor, looking for something, anything. It was smooth, empty, as though someone swept it clean with a toothbrush, inch by inch. I thought maybe there was something under the pile of rocks. Maybe the rocks were hiding something. I tore down the pile. Nothing. They had just been stacked up neatly out of the way."

"I don't understand."

Ben shrugged. "I don't, either. But this is what you need to know right now. If Tyler thinks there is something in that hole, he is mistaken. It has been swept clean."

"Billy."

"Who else? Who else would be so…meticulous?" Ben asked.

"But how could he even get into the cave? The opening…it's so small."

Ben shrugged. "Billy? Dug it out. Put the dirt back. Billy would find a way."

"Billy. Billy. Billy. And that's why I couldn't find the diary."

"What diary?"

"It doesn't matter. A long time ago, when Billy was on my trail, he gave me a diary. It was just a bunch of kid writing. I had diaries hidden out all over in the woods. It was what I did. But somehow, when he gave me that diary, I confused where it had come from. I didn't realize it was from the cave. The cave is so well hidden; I never really believed he would find it. And it never occurred to Billy that I wouldn't make the connection. He was telling me he had taken care of things, and I never got it. Oh, Billy! I never stopped being mad at him for invading my privacy, for always circling around my past. Billy."

"And there's one more thing to take account of," Ben said. "It's a little hard to picture someone as big as Billy as a puppet on a string, but..."

"Iris."

Chapter Thirty-Seven

Megan and Ben left the Moose Jaw and drove down Main Street through the falling snow to Megan's apartment. Megan turned up the heat, turned on a lamp against the gray light, and put on a pot for tea. Ben took a shower to wash off the dust and grime of the cave. When he was finished, Megan took her turn and warned him that if he had used up all the hot water he would pay a terrible price. When she came out, Ben was asleep on the couch. She covered him with a green fleece blanket and put a pillow under his head. She then squeezed in beside him on the couch, put her arms around him, and joined him in sleep.

When Ben awakened, Megan was sitting on the floor beside the couch brushing her hair. Ben looked at her with one eye opened. "You are beautiful in the morning."

"It's not morning."

"I know. But when it gets to be morning, you will be beautiful. I thought it would give you something to look forward to."

She leaned over and kissed him on the forehead. "You slept a long time."

"Exhausting day. Did you sleep?"

"I slept, but I have to figure out what to do."

"I know. And have you?"

"I'm going over to Stephanie Pace's house."

"And tell her what?" asked Ben.

"Everything. I will have no more secrets."

Ben got up and put on a pot of coffee. He found an apple and sliced it onto a plate and brought it back to the couch. He offered a wedge to Megan; she opened her mouth, and he held the apple so she could take a bite. She bit into it and some of the juice sprinkled his hand. Ben lay back on the couch. He ate an apple slice and stared at the ceiling. Megan brought him a cup of coffee.

"What are you thinking?" she asked.

"That you have to keep some secrets."

"I have to help Nathan."

"Yes. Tell Stephanie what your father did to you and to Tyler. That's enough."

"I don't want any more secrets about anything. I don't care who knows. I don't care what they do to me. Hector can arrest me if he wants. Don't you understand? I'll be free of it."

"I guess I understand a little—as much as I can understand. But if you tell the whole truth, then Hector has to go find the remains of your father. And they aren't there. Then the absolute whole truth requires you to tell Hector about Billy, and perhaps Iris. All of this assumes, of course, that Hector did not personally help Billy move the remains. That's too complicated to even think about."

Megan said, "I don't believe that about Hector. But you're right about Billy and Iris. They were trying to help me. If I tell Stephanie I killed my father, they become accomplices."

"That's what I'm thinking."

"But if I don't tell, then Tyler will. And if somehow my father's body is found, then we have created one more accomplice."

"Who would that be?" asked Ben.

"You."

"Ah. So be it. I will be in good company. If Tyler wants to sing, let him sing. We will have to live with the risk."

"And I'll have to live with the secret of having killed my father."

"Yes," Ben said.

"Will you come with me?"

"Where?"

"Stephanie's house."

"Now?"

"Yes. Now. Now."

"What if she's in the middle of some dinner party or something?" Ben asked.

"Who gives a shit?"

They drove to Stephanie's home, with Megan giving directions. The back streets were dark, and the snow was unplowed and untracked. The tires crunched softly over the new snow as they made fresh tracks. Stephanie lived among the tall pines where the national forest came down to the edge of town. The lights were on, but there was no dinner party.

Stephanie was not surprised to see them. She introduced Ben to her husband, who said hello and then quickly returned to the television in the den. Stephanie took Ben and Megan into a small study and closed the door. She picked up a yellow pad and a pen. "Go," she said.

Megan talked and Stephanie took notes. Ben reached over once to offer Megan his hand, but she refused it. Ben understood that she did not want Stephanie to think that she needed help. Stephanie's pen scratched quietly. Sometimes she interrupted to clarify dates and locations. She asked if either Megan or Tyler had ever told anyone else. She asked about any other witnesses. Ben watched Megan without listening closely to the words. She sat upright. Her eyes and voice were level. She did not cry. Nothing in her voice asked for sympathy or understanding. She had lived in this county, with Stephanie, with its people, forever. She had raised herself, with some help from Atticus Finch, Iris, Buster, George, and Billy. And there were others, including a cranky school librarian who charged a nickel for a book that Megan could not live without. Megan worked from the time someone would pay her. She paid her way through college, with some silent help from Iris. After college, she came back home. She did not go to Denver or New York or Pocatello, Idaho, places where no one would know her. She came back home because it was her place, because she had scattered childhood diaries throughout the forest, because the ermine was her spirit animal. She had secrets but none she could bring herself to be ashamed of. If life were to find her, it would find her here.

"What happens next?" Megan asked. "Will you go to Judge Porter to get a medical exam?"

Stephanie chewed on her pen. "Maybe. There may be another way. Thelma may be afraid of Tyler, but she loves her son. She can give permission for the exam. I never had anything before that I could take to her. This may convince her. I will have to use your name, tell her this story."

"I understand," said Megan.

"I may take Hector with me," said Stephanie, thoughtfully, "just in case I have to lean on her a little."

"An area," said Ben, "in which you have some skill."

Stephanie looked at Ben. "Yes." She did not explain or apologize or ask for understanding.

"It is done," said Megan, when they were in the truck. Ben turned up the heater and looked at Megan's face in the glow of the dashboard lights.

"When I grow up," he said, "I want to be like you." Megan took his hand. When they got home, she retrieved the porcelain bird from Ben's backpack. She petted it and allowed herself to cry.

…..

By Tuesday afternoon, Tyler was in jail. Iris, driven by her rage at Tyler, by her determination to protect Megan, took a smothering interest in every detail, and she promptly ferried every piece of breaking information to Ben. Over time, she was on the phone to everybody, especially Stephanie, Hector, George, and Billy. She even called Judge Porter and was outraged when he would not talk with her about any pending case. She told Ben that she had known Brian Porter when he was a pup and threatened that she might still take a rolled-up newspaper to his nose. She was likewise outraged when Tyler's lawyer wouldn't talk to her. Hector told her that under no circumstances would he listen in on a jail conversation between Tyler and his attorney, but he allowed that this rule did not apply to conversations between Tyler and Thelma. Since Tyler's attorney refused to talk with her, Iris simply went to see Thelma, who was no match for Iris even when she was not distraught. Iris retained a lawyer for Megan, just in case. Eventually, Ben wearied of Iris's minute by minute reports.

Nathan, in the doctor's office, scared, eleven years old, faced with reality that could not be wished away, told the truth to Angela Santos, the pediatrician, to Stephanie, to his mother. Stephanie, convinced that Thelma had not known, let Nathan stay with her. When Hector arrived at Tyler's work to arrest him, Tyler denied everything and tried to fight. Hector would ordinarily have left this to his deputies, but in this case, he took a personal interest. He wrote, in his official report, that the suspect had resisted arrest and suffered facial injuries upon being taken down to the icy, asphalt pavement by the undersigned officer.

Tyler raged in jail against his fate. He was angry with Hector for smearing his face across the asphalt. He was angry at whoever had poisoned Nathan's mind into telling lies against his own father. Tyler knew that Stephanie Pace had always been quick to violate the sanctity of the family. Tyler had heard stories about how a parent could not discipline his own child anymore, which was against the Bible. Over time, the picture became clearer to Tyler. He talked with his lawyer, who knew only that there had been a medical exam and a disclosure from Nathan. The lawyer thought he could eventually get Tyler bailed out. Thelma finally came to visit Tyler in jail. She had days where she believed Nathan and days where she knew in her heart that all this was not possible, not real. Tyler was the head of the family, and she knew that she should submit to his leadership. Tyler was not perfect, but God did not promise us perfection or complete understanding. Tyler was strict with Nathan, as was necessary, and children sometimes told lies to avoid punishment. Maybe Nathan had a guilty secret and made up this story to avoid owning up. Thelma knew that Nathan was exposed to horrible, immoral things at school, and there was no telling what he may have picked up from other kids. As to the physical exam, well, who knew?

When Thelma visited Tyler, he insisted that they pray together. This was awkward because the Plexiglas partition was between them, and they had to talk over the scratchy phones. Still, they kneeled on the concrete floor. They could not bow their heads because the phone cords were too short. Tyler led them in a prayer for the welfare of his family. He then questioned Thelma sharply about whether she was being disobedient to his will and the sacred covenant of marriage. It seemed to Tyler that maybe someone had abused Nathan—the world was full of evil—and that Stephanie Pace had put into Nathan's mind that it was Tyler. Tyler asked Thelma to question Nathan about this possibility, about whether it could have been one of his teachers, or perhaps some tourist passing through town, someone who picked him up and offered him a ride. The more Tyler thought about it, he told Thelma, the more it seemed that this must be the answer. This seemed so right to Thelma, but then she summoned up the courage to tell Tyler about what Megan had told Stephanie and whether this could possibly be true.

It was then that Tyler saw the face of pure evil at work. He beat the phone against the Plexiglas and howled. Thelma was terrified, and the jail deputies came and dragged Tyler to the isolation cell, where he brooded on Megan's great sin and this slander against the precious memory of their father. He saw eventually that it was his failure years ago to report Megan's crime that had now brought this evil into his family. This, then, was his punishment for allowing Megan to go unpunished. He sent word that he wanted to talk with Hector.

Hector, in his own good time, had himself let into Tyler's isolation cell. He noted that the right side of Tyler's face was scabbing up nicely. Hector knew that he was not getting any younger, so he allowed himself some satisfaction in this evidence that he had not completely lost his touch. Sometimes the younger deputies needed a reminder that the boss was capable of more than sweating over budgets and giving speeches to the Rotary Club. Hector listened impassively as Tyler told his story. Hector's handwriting was a disaster, so he brought in one of the young deputies to take notes. Hector told Tyler to draw him a map. Tyler became agitated and insisted that Hector should take him along as a guide. Hector assured Tyler that he was going exactly nowhere and became briefly hopeful when Tyler seemed about to fly into another rage. It came to nothing, though, and Tyler drew the map.

The map was sketchy so Hector took Billy along as guide. Hector and Billy and one of Hector's deputies hiked into the mountains. It was a sunny day, and Hector was pleased to be out of the office, pleased to be tramping in the fresh, deepening snow. He hoped that it would be a good snow year because they always needed water. Hector reminded his companions that they should not hurry because he was not getting any younger and because he was in no rush to get back to the office. Billy was able to follow the map without too much difficulty. Billy and the deputy went first down the steep ravine to pack the snow and make it easier for Hector. At the entrance to the cave, Hector had Billy wait outside. He teased Billy that he probably could not squeeze through such a small opening anyway and Billy sheepishly agreed.

Hector inspected the cave. He looked at the old rope and noted its frayed condition. The deputy pointed out the presence of footprints, and Hector worried aloud that teenagers might be exploring in such a place and have an accident. He and the deputy fastened their new, nylon rope ladder to a convenient rock. The young deputy prepared to descend and Hector waved him off. Hector said that, for once, the sheriff should be allowed to have some fun. Hector put on a hardhat with a lamp and descended into the pit. He took a series of pictures, and the camera's flash made a quick, eerie light against the black dampness of the mineshaft. He climbed back up the ladder and was winded at the top. He shrugged at his deputy and shook his head. Outside, he remarked to Billy that at least it was a beautiful day for a wild goose chase. He also instructed his deputy to call the Forest Service about rolling some boulders in front of the entrance because this was a dangerous place.

Chapter Thirty-Eight

"Long time no see," said God.

"And you," Ben said. "Been out wandering your world? Sampling more cheese curds?"

They sat together at the kitchen table over a late-night beer. It was one in the morning and Sarah was long asleep. God had wrapped his gnarled fingers around a Fat Tire. Ben noticed the liver spots on the back of his hand.

"No more cheese curds," God said. "They are instruments of the Devil—a recipe for indigestion. I begin to wonder if I am lactose intolerant."

"So, where are you on this whole question of the Devil?"

"Agnostic."

"You bob; you weave."

God shrugged and sipped his beer. For a moment, his jaw clenched, and he stared fixedly into some indeterminate distance; it came to Ben that God was forcing himself to meet, without flinching, some patient, painful gaze.

"I'm sorry," Ben said. "I am too much the smartass."

God reached an old, spotted hand across and covered Ben's hand with his. "Sometimes, from out of nowhere, I find Lincoln looking at me. He was my friend. You should always be able to look your friends in the eye." He looked directly at Ben. "I will tell you this. The only devil I have met is my own failure. I find that I can reconcile myself only with kindred spirits like Honest Abe. But I have not been of much use to my friends." God took a long swig of beer and held the cool bottle against his cheek. He held the bottle out in front of him. "In addition to kindred spirits, I find that I am also reconciled with Fat Tire—a cold beer to refresh an infinity of days—that is a happy thing." He smiled. "Before I became melancholy, you were ragging on me about something. Remind me."

"It doesn't matter."

"Ah, but it does. It all matters between friends. You were asking me about the Devil and accusing me, once more, of bobbing and weaving."

"You do have some skills in the area," said Ben, softly.

"I can bob and weave with the best of them. I guess, in theory, I am the best of them."

With their characteristic mood restored, Ben resumed. "You claim, in your typically shifty fashion, that you have never come face to face with the Devil. But what about the question of evil?"

"Oh, I'm unequivocal there. If you don't look around and see evil, you have a mote in your eye."

Ben thought of the evil of Megan's family, of Tyler's evil locked up now in one of Hector's barred boxes.

"Pure evil?" Ben asked.

"What is this, chemistry class? No, it's all alloyed. Hitler could be kind to his dog."

"Alloyed with what?"

"The marvelous human talent for creating justifications. 'Because he hit me first. Because my mother put me on the potty backward when I was two. Because I love God. Because I hate God.' If you go in search of a splendid ideal to hang your actions on, there is always one ready to hand. Hitler was an idealist, purifying the species. Once humans learned to invent reasons, there was no holding them back."

"True that," Ben said.

"This is a depressing topic. Any possibility of changing the subject?"

"Name it."

"You have been leading an eventful life."

"A life I am in love with. Unalloyed."

"Interesting notion," said God. "You think that evil can only be an alloy, and love can be pure."

"Wait a minute. You're the one with the alloy theory of evil, not me."

"True for you. All I'm saying is that sometimes love does seem to be without alloy. Granted, it can get mixed up with other stuff—lust comes to mind. But it seems pure and maybe that's enough."

"It's enough for me. You get paid the big bucks to figure out all that other stuff."

"That seems fair to you? That I should have to be the one to make sense of the great soup of people? Hitler and Gandhi—how did they get mixed in the same soup? The mind boggles."

"Tough job. Better yours than mine."

"I'll tell you one of the little-known perks of my position. I am free to take on only the jobs that strike my fancy. I'm not sure that this one does. You have any interest in it?"

"None."

"Good judgment. Maybe I can put an ad in the paper."

"I have the job I want. It is a garden of delights—Sarah, Megan, Iris, and these mountains rising above us in the dark. I am fully and joyfully employed."

"And I am happy for you. You are making progress—more joy, less worry. The Ode to Joy is good medicine."

"But?" Ben asked.

"Who said but? But is a nasty little word. There are too many buts in this world, and almost all of them the enemy of joy."

"I could swear that you were thinking, 'but.'"

"Actually not. I was thinking, 'and.' I was thinking of King Lear, who is driven, finally, to notice that, unlike him, everyone is not a king, that some of his ragged subjects are pelted by the storm. Mr. Shakespeare drives old Lear into the kind of fix in which he is forced 'to feel what wretches feel.'"

Annoyed, Ben said, "You want me to be full of joy, and at the same time to feel what wretches feel? It is too much. It is not possible, even for…"

"Even for God?"

Chapter Thirty-Nine

"Do you two have any idea how obnoxious you are?" Iris asked.

"It's impossible to be obnoxious when you're this happy," said Ben.

"I rest my case," said Iris.

Iris and Ben and Megan were Christmas shopping for Sarah and Laurie, who were spending the day with George and Julie. The serious snows had finally come and the sidewalk was a path between knee-deep, shoveled snow. Ben liked the look of shovels sticking out of the snow beside every shop door. He liked the days when it snowed and the days when the sun lit the snow, and the surrounding mountains lifted into blue sky. It occurred to him that Iris was right; anyone who could find nothing wrong with any part of the weather was obnoxiously happy. He put one arm around Iris and hugged her to his side. He pulled Megan in from the other side, and the three of them boldly filled the sidewalk, forcing morose Kansans to give way before them.

To the Kansans, Iris called out, "Merry Christmas!"

Ben cheered them with, "Aren't the mountains grand?"

Megan joined in with, "God bless us, each and every one."

The Kansans were too baffled by the good spirits to be angry at being run off the sidewalk.

Christmas wreaths with red bows hung from every surface that could hold a hook. Frisco was decorated for Christmas, and all such decorations were gilt on the lily of Victorian buildings piled round with snow and evergreens and mountains.

The three of them finally let go of each other when they entered the Roaster. Ben and Megan ordered coffee and fudge. Iris embarrassed herself by ordering mocha with whipped cream and cinnamon sprinkles. She sneaked the elaborate confection to her table by the window.

"I don't know why I ordered this thing. I was carried away by the Christmas spirit."

"What's the big deal?" asked Ben.

"All this fancy shit. People will think I'm drinking coffee above my proper station in life."

"Putting on airs," Megan said. "Next thing you'll be putting on dresses. Mocha is a gateway drug to chiffon dresses."

"I wore a chiffon dress once," confessed Iris. "It made me feel like farting." Iris looked at the two of them. "I am so proud of you two."

Ben took Megan's hand. "We have," he said solemnly, "a chance to catch the last train for happiness. The train is slowly pulling away from the station. The two of us, Megan and I, are holding hands and running down the platform beside it. We run in slow motion. We look at each other and smile because we are full of youth and happiness and we can outrun any train. A kindly conductor smiles down at us and extends his hand as we leap to board our private, golden carriage."

Megan retrieved her hand from Ben's as though she had, by chance, dipped it into shit. Iris stared at him and then put her hand to her throat and made gagging noises.

"The world," said Ben, "is no longer a haven for poets."

Iris and Megan made farting sounds.

"What," asked Iris, "are you getting for Sarah?"

"She's been staring longingly at a lavender ski jacket," said Ben. "She hasn't brought it up because we looked at the price tag, and I told her that it's much more than we can possibly afford."

"Ah, the perfect gift," said Iris.

"I found," Megan said, "a pair of snow boots for her that are trimmed in fake sheepskin. And, by the luckiest of coincidences, they're lavender."

"And for Laurie?" asked Megan.

"She's tough," said Iris. "She never wants anything. If I buy her clothes, she puts them in the back of the closet and lets them age for a couple of years before she'll wear them. She much prefers the old to the new. Sort of takes the joy out of shopping for her."

"So what's the plan?" asked Megan.

"I have one, but it's risky. I took one of her favorite pictures of Buster in and had it blown up. It's damn near life size. I had a frame made from some wood I tore out of an old barn on that little river farm I still own. All I have to do today is go pick it up. She likes old things, so I'm going to give her a picture of her old dad. I hope it makes her more happy than sad."

"She'll love it," Megan said.

. . . . .

Sarah led Ben and Megan to Iris's Christmas party. They did not cut across the yard because it was covered in a foot of December snow. Iris had strung Christmas lights across half the front porch and then got bored with the project and dropped it. The twinkling lights created the impression that Iris must have simply forgotten to plug in the lights on the other side of the porch. Sarah stopped on her way up the walk and silently shook her head in disapproval. Behind her, Ben shook his head in envy. His own house was sagging under the weight of Christmas lights. There were lights on the roofline, lights framing the windows and door, lights on the porch railing. Megan spent her time running to the grocery store for more lights, and Ben climbed up and down the ladder under Sarah's fevered direction. Sarah may have been shy about asking for presents, but she was bold on Christmas lights.

George opened the door, wearing a Santa Claus hat, holding a beer, and shouting, "Ho, Ho, Ho." He held a sprig of mistletoe over his head and demanded kisses from Megan and Sarah. He leaned over for a kiss from Sarah, and she giggled and complained that his beard was scratchy. She took his arm, and the two of them wandered off, arguing about what it would be like to kiss Santa. Ben watched them and thought that he would send Sarah to live with George when she became a teenager and developed the overwhelming urge to argue with life. No one was better prepared than George to scratch this itch.

Julie came over and gave Ben a kiss. "I noticed that my thoughtless husband gave the ladies a kiss but overlooked you."

"I suspect," said Ben, "that there was nothing thoughtless about it."

"Well, Merry Christmas, anyway. Come have some eggnog."

"Can't stand the stuff," said Ben, "but maybe I will have a wee drop of that Irish whiskey that Iris keeps hidden for herself." He led Julie to the imposing hutch that went with Iris's fancy dining table. He opened a door, reached into the back, and pulled out a half-full bottle. Julie nodded thoughtfully, filing this knowledge away, and brought Ben a glass from the kitchen. Ben poured himself a small drink, and Julie returned to the kitchen to help Iris and Lena.

Ben joined Megan and Billy on the sofa. "Merry Christmas, Billy," he said. Megan had Billy's big hand in hers, and Billy looked uncomfortable. Billy aimed a half-smile at the middle distance. Megan said, "Billy, I don't completely understand why you made it your mission to save my sorry ass. But you did. I wish I could return the favor, but I don't know how. Maybe one day. Now, all I can do is say thanks."

Billy glanced at Megan and quickly away. "It's OK. We all thought—I thought—that we should help, that I should help. You were alone. I did my best."

"You did more than your best. Now, I have one more favor to ask of you."

"Sure."

"Would you look at me?"

Billy glanced over at Megan and away. "OK. What can I do?"

"Look at me. That's the favor. You look at me. I look at you. I want us to look at each other the way real friends do. Look at each other and smile."

"I guess I always thought that you thought I was too funny-looking to look at," Billy said.

"I guess I always thought that you thought that I was too screwed-up to look at."

There was a silence, and then Megan tugged on Billy's hand. They looked, each into the eyes of the other, and smiled. Ben leaned over, picked up Billy's beer from the coffee table, and handed it to him. Billy nodded gratefully and took a long drink. He patted Ben on the knee, and, having become an artist of the smile, rewarded Ben with one, also. It was a smile that spread like a gentle wave across his round face.

"It's OK now," said Megan, and again took Billy's big hand in hers.

Billy nodded gravely. "It's OK." Lena came in from the kitchen, laughing, and found them so. She stopped and looked down at them. She leaned over and kissed Megan. She straightened up and giggled to herself. "Don't I have a beautiful husband?" she asked. "Yes," said Megan.

Ben pondered this business of Megan and Billy and thought he would never know the whole story of the missing remains of Henry Flanagan. Megan thought that Billy had tried to tell her that he had moved the body by giving her the diary from the cave. Maybe. But Megan, with good reason, had never seemed to be especially worried anyway about the body being found. It was hidden pretty well as it was. She had good reason to think that Tyler wouldn't talk. Maybe Iris worried that some spelunker would happen on it; maybe she worried about Tyler. What seemed certain was that lines radiated outward from Billy: certainly to Iris, probably to George, Buster when he was alive. Hector? Who knew? The family, Ben's prospective in-laws, rightly wasn't talking. So be it.

Ben found Laurie sitting in the recliner that had been her father's favorite chair. He sat on the floor beside her chair. She reached over and patted his head.

"Yo," Ben said.

"Yo?"

"What's up with you?"

"Ben, be serious."

"Why?"

Laurie giggled. "Yes, why?"

"Are you still happy to be home?"

"Yes. I'm staying. Mom and I are getting along. We get mad at each other sometimes. But we kiss and make up. She's not like Dad, but she likes having me here. I can tell. I go out in the morning and get the paper for her. She likes that."

"I know. I sometimes see you and Ollie going out when I'm having my morning coffee."

"I'm happy," Laurie said.

"I'm glad."

Iris and George came in from the kitchen, with Sarah trailing behind. Iris carried a pitcher of eggnog and made sure everyone's glass was full. Ben showed her his whiskey and waved her off. Iris raised her eyebrow as she eyed the whiskey glass.

"Where'd you get that?" she asked.

"Santa Claus," said Ben.

Iris grinned. "Ben, Ben, Ben. Here's what you can do for me for Christmas. Every time that glass gets low, I want you to go back to the hutch and spank it right up."

"Yes, ma'am."

Iris lowered her voice. "Do you want to hear the latest I got from Hector on Tyler?"

"More joy, less worry," Ben said.

Iris gave him a puzzled look. Ben said, "It means I'm not interested." Iris frowned but was distracted by George as he pushed a tray of finger food aside and climbed up on the battered coffee table. Iris's frown deepened, but she kept silent.

"A toast," George said. "To the season. To a good snow year. To powder so deep they close the highway and the tourists can't make it up here to steal the fresh tracks. To family. To friends so good they're the same as family."

Everyone cheered and drank. Iris motioned George to lean down and whispered in his ear.

"Yeah, yeah. To Sarah and Laurie, who are having special nights tonight."

Iris motioned him down again.

"You should just make the damn toast yourself," said George. "To Megan and Ben. I'm not sure why they get a special toast. Iris should just mind her own business because I think they can manage to do their thing without any help from her. To Iris, for being such a damn busybody. To me, for unappreciated genius."

Iris pulled George off the table to general cheers and took the floor. "Sarah is leaving tomorrow to spend Christmas with her mother. She got to come to the grownup party because she is leaving and, anyway, she is a lot more of a grownup than her father. We hope she has a wonderful time. She'll be warm in Texas while the rest of us are freezing. Since she is leaving, she gets to have an early Christmas."

Megan brought out two brightly wrapped presents. Sarah, the center of attention, sat on the floor and began to slowly, carefully unwrap them.

"I can't stand it," said Megan. She sat down beside Sarah and ripped off a piece of wrapping paper. Sarah, released from being proper, tore into the wrapping and pulled out the lavender ski jacket. She held it up and then held it to her face. She ran over and hugged her father.

"How did you know it was what I wanted?" she asked.

Ben rolled his eyes and told her to put it on. Sarah did so and twirled around to the applause of her fans. Ben pointed to the other present, and she raced to unwrap it. She pulled forth the snow boots and put them on. Ben pointed to Megan and Sarah sat in her lap, hugged her, and whispered in her ear.

"And one more present," said Iris, "from Laurie and me."

Laurie came in from the bedroom, beaming, and carrying a pair of skis—pink skis. Sarah cradled them in her arms and ran a finger across the smooth surface. She put them aside and nearly knocked Laurie over with a hug. The two of them laughed and danced around each other. Sarah went to Iris and held tightly to her neck.

"And now," said Iris, "an early Christmas for my Laurie."

Laurie clapped her hands.

"And do you know why you're getting an early Christmas? Because I said so. And I'm your mother. And don't you forget it."

Megan brought in the picture, wrapped in brown paper, and tied with a red ribbon. Laurie did not like being the center of attention, but she pulled the end of the ribbon and it dropped free. She tore awkwardly at the paper and put her hand to her mouth when she saw her father's face emerge from the tear. She stood and stared at it, and only Sarah had the wit to jump in. She carefully pulled off the rest of the paper and then stepped back and held Laurie's hand. The two of them stared at the picture.

"Your dad is beautiful," said Sarah.

The enormity of it confused Laurie, and she grabbed Sarah and hugged her and said, "Thank you, thank you," as though Sarah had given her the picture. Iris shrugged cheerfully in the background. Laurie sat on the floor in front of the picture and tried to put her arms around it.

Everyone in the room stood in front of the picture and admired it. In the picture, Buster, a big man, wore a flannel shirt and an absurd floppy hat and grinned as if he were about to swoop out of the frame and grab Iris's behind and tickle Laurie's feet until she screamed. George, the master of the toast, raised his glass and said, "To Buster. May he always be Buster."

Chapter Forty

Ben stumbled into the kitchen. "I smell coffee."

"Merry Christmas," said Megan.

"Can I wait to be merry until after I have my coffee?"

Megan tousled his unkempt hair and handed him a cup. Ben sat down at the table and put his feet up. He rubbed his face. "I think I got run over by a train last night."

"You did. And I loved every minute of it," Megan said.

"See, I told you there was a train of happiness the other day. All you could do is make fun."

"I'll never make fun of you again, Ben Wallace."

"You lie. You lie to a man who hasn't even finished his morning coffee."

Megan slid a small giftwrapped package across the table. Ben opened it. It was the small bird from the cave. Megan had woven a nest for it from pine needles.

"Thank you, love. It's beautiful."

Ben got up and reached to the top of the kitchen cabinet. His face was puzzled as he groped with his hand. He began pulling a chair over to stand on. Megan reached behind her and pulled out another giftwrapped package. "Looking for this?" she asked.

"You are a scamp. How'd you find it?"

"Not exactly an inspired hiding place."

"So, did you open it?"

"Of course not. But it's heavy. And it doesn't rattle."

"Open it," Ben said.

Megan opened her present. Inside were two leather-bound books: *Huckleberry Finn* and *To Kill a Mockingbird*.

"Oh, Ben. They're beautiful."

"Read the inscription."

She opened the flyleaf of the Twain and giggled.

"Now the other," said Ben.

She read and looked gravely at Ben. "Only you would propose in a book...in this book."

"Well?" asked Ben.

Megan closed the book and ran her fingers over the leather cover. "My mama, if I had had one, would have raised no fools."

"And?"

"Yes. Yes."

Ben pounded his chest. "Ha. Foolish woman. Putty in my hands."

Megan got up, pushed Ben's feet off the table, and sat in his lap. She held his face tightly against her neck. "Shut up, Ben."

"I didn't say anything."

"Shut up, Ben."

"I can barely breathe."

"Shut up, Ben."

"Yes, ma'am."

Megan got up and wiped her eyes. She began fixing breakfast. "Let me do that," said Ben. He got up and Megan pushed him back down.

"You can't cook, Ben."

"I can cook breakfast. Anybody can cook breakfast."

"Anybody but you. Besides, I'd rather you wash the dishes. I plan to cook a huge breakfast. You'd better eat a lot because you'll need your strength. Today, I'm going to kick your butt all over the mountain."

The sun was out, but it was cold and the snow was crisp under their skis. They stood at the top of Spaulding Bowl and looked over at the Ten Mile Range as the wind whipped their backs. Megan dropped off the cornice with a whoop and carved wide, lazy turns across the broad top of the bowl. Halfway down, rock outcroppings pinched the terrain, and her turns became tight and disciplined, with Megan rising out of one turn and falling seamlessly into the next. Ben watched her disappear through a chute and followed, with the sharp air on his face and the sound of the snow slicing away from his skis. Megan, leaning against her poles, was waiting for him well below the chute.

"Not bad for a flatlander," she said. "More commitment to the turns."

"Commitment. Is that all women can talk about?"

"Shut up, Ben. Gravity is your friend, especially in the steeps. Embrace it. Imagine that you are diving into my arms. I will save you. Or, if I forget, your skis will save you."

"Yes, ma'am. I will try."

They skied through Spaulding Glades, following the smooth tracks of other skiers through the trees. The tracks branched endlessly through the dense evergreens. Turning around a tree, there were always two or three alternate ways down, and they ducked tree limbs and made instant decisions about which path to follow. They became separated and Ben pulled up for a rest at a turn so tight he was not sure he could make it. A Steller's jay, deep blue and black feathers puffed, watched him critically from beneath narrow white eyebrows. Ben called out and Megan's voice came back to him through the trees from somewhere below. All roads through the trees led to the same place, and Megan was waiting for him where the orange boundary rope funneled tree skiers back onto the main trail.

The rest of the trail was groomed, and they loafed carelessly down, plumes of snow flying up to catch the light at each turn. The two of them coasted into the Resolution Lift, where there was no line. There was a smiling liftie with a Santa hat, who wished them Merry Christmas as he grabbed and braked the chair. They watched a good skier on a monoski snaking through the bumps on Highline.

"This run next?" asked Megan.

"Yes."

"Did you call Sarah?"

"Right after breakfast."

"Is she having a good Christmas?"

"She sounded good. They were about to open presents, so we only talked for a minute. I think she's happy to see her mom. Karen can be more fun even than Christmas when she puts her mind to it."

"Do you miss having Christmas with them?"

"No, don't…"

"Ben, that's a perfectly reasonable question. I think I might if I were you."

"You're right. I should give truth a chance. Part of that truth is that I don't let go easily of dreams. When I was a kid, I was visiting a friend and I grabbed a refrigerator door handle that had an electrical short in it. The current caused my fists to clench around the door handle, and I couldn't let go of it. Getting shocked was no fun, but what I remember most clearly was the mental shock of telling my fist to open, and it wouldn't obey. My friend's mother heard me yelling, came over and knocked my hand loose, and went back to shelling peas. She clearly had no time to waste on a kid who could not figure out how to get loose from an electrical appliance. I do remember she pointed to a towel tied around the handle, which I came to understand was what people in the know used to open the door."

"Great story," said Megan, as she pulled her poles from beneath her legs. "Try to see if you can find a moral in it by the next ride up."

They skied the bumps on Highline. Ben loved the bumps. He did not ski them as well as Megan, but he thought that one day he might. He loved the feeling of turns streaming towards him, no turn exactly like the last. Sometimes it felt like he was standing still, and the mountain was flowing up beneath him. Each turn took a little more of his wind, until he could sustain it no longer and pulled up. He looked for Megan, and she slid in behind him.

"Beautiful," Megan said. "I was skiing your track. You nailed them."

"Shucks, ma'am."

"Now you ski my line," she said, as she slipped past him. But he didn't. He simply stood and watched her float through the minefield of bumps. You could, he thought, put a plate of cookies on top of her head, and at the bottom you would not need to count to know they were all still there. Her arms moved rhythmically as though she were swaying to a slow samba. On the snow, at the bottom of all this stillness, her skis were a slashing blur. I have, he thought, much to learn, and no one better to learn from.

"Merry Christmas," said the liftie, as they got back on the chair.

"The moral to my story is that you ski like an angel," Ben said.

"That's the moral?"

"Maybe somehow I knew you would be able to ski like that."

"Huh?"

"I am a simple man. I require no greater moral. Once upon a time, I wandered into the library for a copy of *Huckleberry Finn*. I can close my eyes and still see you looking up at me. You were not the librarian I expected to see."

"Love at first sight?"

"Nope. Can't be that because it makes all the stuff in between trivial. None of those days in between were trivial. Mostly they were, to me, miraculous."

"Mostly?"

"If you will take the unusual step of being honest with yourself, I think you will admit that sometimes you were a pain in the ass."

"And you, a saint, put up with me?"

"Exactly. So, here's the best I can make of it: something happens, too wonderful for words, powerful enough to overcome even a short in a refrigerator door, and all we can think to call it is love. So that's what brought me here, to this chairlift, to this moment, sharing the secrets of my soul with you, Marjorie, the one true love of my life."

Megan leaned against Ben and patted his knee. "I'm so relieved."

"You are?"

"I was afraid for a minute that I was the only one who had no clue."

"Not as long as I'm around."

"I do have a real question for you."

"Go."

"Will you be as stubborn about holding on to the dream of me?"

"Who's stubborn?"

Megan ignored this and said, "I have to be some kind of help to Nathan."

"Agreed."

They ate lunch sitting outside in the sun at Solitude Station. Gray jays hovered for handouts, and Megan pitched pieces of French fries at them. She leaned back and looked at the sky. "Do you remember when we climbed San Luis and watched the falling stars?"

"You were frightened and I protected you," Ben said.

"Do you remember when we sat in the Roaster and took turns reading *Huckleberry Finn* to each other?"

"I helped you with the big words."

"Do you remember when we used to meet in the library after hours?"

"With the river outside, singing in the dark."

"Let's go skiing," Megan said.

They skied every run they could get to in the time remaining. Taking the Sierra Lift, they hiked on the packed trail to the top of Union Peak, skis over their shoulders. They rested briefly and looked across to the white peaks of the Gore Range, glinting in sunshine. Megan pointed across the valley to an invisible trail that wound into the mountains and over Uneva Pass. Ben rested his chin on her shoulder so that he could follow her finger as she traced the trail on the contours of the far land. They skied Union Bowl, and Ben reminded himself, on the steep turns, that he was falling into Megan's arms. They raced across the mountain and skied the long bump runs under the Alpine Lift. When the bumps set on fire their thighs and their lungs, they pulled up, panting, and leaned against each other. Always, a little before Ben was ready, Megan sent them down again into the streaming bumps. They caught their last lift ride five minutes before closing and had the mountain mostly to themselves. The shadows now were long across the snow and the winter sun was far in the west. Megan, no longer so driven, allowed them long rests on this last run.

At home, they put wood in the stove and propped their cold feet against it until Megan smelled their shoes burning. Too tired for cooking, they ate leftover stew for dinner. Ben put on a pot of coffee to keep himself awake. They lay on the couch, each at one end, stretching their aching muscles, and read Megan's Christmas presents. Megan had trouble keeping her eyes open. She asked Ben to read something from *Huckleberry*. Ben flipped to the back and read the ending where Huck lights out for the territory, and Megan smiled sleepily. She left to get a bath. After a long time, Ben went in and found her asleep in the tub. He gently woke her and helped her climb out of the cooling water. Without really waking up, she allowed herself to be dried off. Ben wrapped her in a bathrobe and guided her, stumbling, to bed. As he tucked her in, she looked up at him, grinned, and said, "Shut up, Ben." She snuggled in under the down comforter and was asleep.

Chapter Forty-One

Iris came over in the morning while they were having coffee. Iris noticed Ben hobbling as he fixed her a cup. "How was the skiing?"

"Wonderful," said Ben. "But for the second morning in a row I feel like I've been run over by a train."

Iris was perplexed and looked a question at Megan. Megan waved her off. "Private joke," she said. "I think my boy has potential," continued Megan. "Give him another ten years, and he might become a real mountain man."

Iris was dubious. "He's not that fast a learner. But I agree. I've told him that all he has to do to belong in these mountains is to hang around for another fifty years and pay his dues."

"Whatever happened," asked Ben, "to that whole idea of supportive women? Where did that get lost exactly?"

Iris hooted. "Poor baby. Doesn't have enough supportive women in his life. Megan, me, Sarah, Laurie—always there to serve your every need. And all you can do is whine."

"I'm a fragile flower," said Ben, "and I have complicated needs."

"How is Laurie?" asked Megan. "Buster's picture is a hit?"

"I think so. It hasn't made her too sad. I hung it in her room, and I can hear her in there having long conversations with her father. I think she is probably complaining to him about me, but what the hell."

They could hear the front door opening.

"Laurie," said Iris. "Come to check on me."

Ben, his feet propped on the table, turned to look over his shoulder at the kitchen door. He was preparing to ask Laurie to rub his sore neck, but it wasn't Laurie. Tyler was there, his eyes opened wide, holding in front of him a pistol. Ben swung his feet off the table and, doing so, bumped Iris off stride as she rushed toward Tyler. Megan got there first, to a place between Tyler's gun and the people she loved, and in that place, Tyler shot her. Ben got there next, the sound of the shot raging in his ears, and drove his shoulder into Tyler's chest. Ben's charge carried Tyler backward through the kitchen door, and they crashed against the wall of the living room. Tyler's head bounced against the wall and Ben could hear the breath rush out of him. Tyler dropped to the floor and lay still.

Ben looked at him and, groaning with fear, turned back to the kitchen. Iris kneeled over Megan, pressing a kitchen towel hard to her chest. Ben knelt on the other side. Megan stared at the ceiling, her eyes confused. Her breath was ragged. Ben held her face with his hands, and her eyes came to his and were no longer confused. Her face became for a moment serene and full of joy. Ben struggled to get words out, and Megan summoned a broken piece of smile and whispered, "Shut up, Ben." Her face went limp in his hands, and that was all.

Ben continued to hold Megan's face. Iris quit pressing on the towel and sat back on the floor. Iris pushed herself unsteadily to her feet and staggered into the living room. Megan heard nothing, but Ben heard four gunshots, carefully, methodically spaced, and then the dry click of the hammer on an empty chamber. Ben heard this, but the sound came to him from far away.

Chapter Forty-Two

Ben did not shut up. It was not in his nature. He even became for a while more energetic, but this was for Sarah, to make life more cheerful. Megan had parted with a joke, and Ben decided he could do the same, although his going out looked to be much more drawn out than Megan's. He sometimes wished to speed things up, but he looked at Sarah and understood the wish to be an idle one. He and Sarah put together a kind of memorial to Megan. Since the kitchen, with its warm woodstove, was their favorite room, they put some of her things in a corner of the counter: the two leather-bound books, the porcelain bird, a small photograph of Megan wearing the seaman's cap that Ben loved, the cap itself, some pencil drawings, one of an ermine, which Megan and Sarah had done together. They were small things, and they did not take up much space. A visitor would think they were part of the natural clutter of this home. Hector brought over Megan's collection of skis and other outdoor gear because he thought Sarah could use them one day; these they stored in the basement against future years. Hector also swiped for Sarah Megan's teapot, with its trellis of red roses, and this they kept on the stove.

Although it was a little hard for her, Sarah read *To Kill a Mockingbird*, taking care not to smudge or tear any of the pages. She had read the inscription from Ben in the flyleaf the first time, but afterwards she carefully skipped over this page when she opened the book. It was a book about a daughter's love for her father, for Megan, a book of revelation, for Sarah, a simple book of common prayer. Sarah suffered sharp episodes of grief for Megan, for the life that might have been, but she wasted no time in taking up again the care of her father, the mission she had always given herself, the same mission Ben had given himself when he was a child. Ben took the leaf out of the kitchen table and made room beside the stove for two small rockers. He and Sarah spent their evenings there, talking, doing homework, and reading. They rarely used the living room, and Sarah lost interest in TV. The two of them plotted opportunities to make each other laugh.

At unpredictable intervals, Sarah fell apart, and Ben understood that she was beginning at a tender age her own studies on the meaning of finality. It was a hard subject, like studying the sun with the naked eye. Knowledge of finality came in quick, scorching glimpses that left on the eye an afterimage, a fiery and incomprehensible slash, slow to wash away. Megan was not coming back. It was a hard subject, studied in glimpses.

Sarah had her new pink skis from Iris, and Ben made sure that they skied every weekend. Ben loved to watch Sarah ski. She was beautiful with her pink skis and lavender jacket and her streaming blond ponytail. They did not ski hard. They both loved to ski bumps, but they stopped often to rest and talk and feel the mountain air on their faces. Once, they spotted a porcupine lazily munching bark high in a tree beside the trail. Ben and Sarah took off their skis, stuck them in the snow, and lay on their backs, watching the porcupine. The porcupine did not mind being watched, nor did the trees or the mountains.

Sometimes they made Iris go skiing with them, but Iris often came only for the afternoon because she did not like being away too long from Laurie. Iris was a strong and stylish skier, and Sarah unconsciously began to absorb her style, something that only Ben noticed. Iris did not do well when they made their frequent stops to talk because, since Megan's death, she had trouble finding small things to talk about. Ben and Sarah often flopped down in the snow with their skis on, but Iris stood silent and ramrod straight, as though she were their personal guard, which she was. Iris continued to run six miles every morning but could not remember why. Although her small talk was lousy, Iris did better in the kitchen. She baked bread and meals in endless procession for Ben and Sarah; they learned to open their refrigerator carefully to keep the overflow from tumbling out.

Sometimes they went to Iris's house for dinner because it was good for Laurie. Laurie struggled with Megan's death; she cried and sometimes threw things and picked at her arms until they bled. One night, rocking beside their stove, Sarah put her book down and pointed out to Ben that Laurie needed someone to take care of. After this, Ben and Sarah each found a way to tell Laurie that the other needed cheering up, and Laurie, given a purpose, began to find ways to do this. She helped Sarah take Ollie for his afternoon walk; she stole Iris's paper every morning and brought it directly to Ben. Iris did not catch on to what Ben and Sarah were doing with Laurie until one morning when she was running in a steady snow. When she saw it, she stopped beside the road and put her hands on her knees and cried until her ribs ached. Then she ran the remaining three miles.

At work, Ben's students watched him nervously for signs of grief, but his lectures became funnier and more animated. He quit telling shaggy dog stories and told them more of the homespun yarns that Mr. Lincoln narrated to anyone who would listen, while the Civil War swirled about him like a red snow. One day, retelling one of these tales, Ben came to understand that lively was the only true opposite of dead. At his liveliest, Ben found a kind of lightness, lifting him, strangely enough, into the remoteness of his father, drifting over a world made serene by distance. Ben drifted over his world but never far from it because of the tether that Sarah so carefully held, the same tether Ben had held at her age. God had warned Ben against the dangers of a remote life, but it was, for now, comfort and refuge.

Like Iris with Laurie, Ben rarely went anywhere that he could not take Sarah. He no longer ran into George at the Moose Jaw. Sometimes he met George and Julie for breakfast at the Kokomo, and, as the winter wore on, George and Julie had Ben and Sarah to dinner. Sarah was growing increasingly fond of the island of gentle calm that surrounded Julie. Sarah became adept at drawing George into argument, and the two of them blustered at each other. George managed to plant in all of his arguments a fatal flaw and let it lie there for Sarah to find. It was his version of an Easter egg hunt.

Ben and Sarah rarely saw Billy because he was always out in the mountains on his snowshoes, searching the hidden places where solace used to be.

Karen came up for a couple of weekends to help out and to be sure that Ben could still take care of Sarah. Karen stayed in a hotel, and she tried hard to be kind and cheerful, but her visits created such bewildering emotions for everyone that she tactfully quit coming.

Ben and Sarah made it, thus, from winter into this next springtime of their lives. God left when Megan died, and Ben did not notice. God was always coming and going, anyway, and it took Ben some time to realize that he was not coming back, that he had only been there for the time of Megan. Perhaps God could stand no longer "to feel what wretches feel." It was too much for anyone, and Ben did not blame him for moving on. Even so, Ben still sat at the kitchen table late into the night, carrying on murmured conversations. Often he lost track of the difference between talking to himself and talking to God, lost track of whether he was alone or alone with God. Sarah, getting up in the night to go to the bathroom, listened at the door but could rarely make out distinct words. She paid attention more to tone, to cadence, and as long as these murmured lyrics were those of the Blue River, flowing from sky to ocean, she was reassured and went back to bed. She thought it odd, but if her father needed someone to talk to in the night, she could find no room in her heart for blame. After all, he carried on, determined to serve out the fifty years that Iris had always insisted were required to belong in these mountains. He carried on, mostly with wit and good cheer, and reveled, from afar, in Sarah's joyful moments.

End

About the Author

Mac Griffith lives in a small mountain town in Colorado. Mac skis from winter to spring. In summer and fall, he hikes and runs and casts flies in the rivers where trout live. In between, he reads and writes and sometimes works.

CPSIA information can be obtained at www.ICGtesting.com
Printed in the USA
LVOW12s0331180214

374121LV00003B/13/P